I0668211

GLIMMER IN THE SHADOW

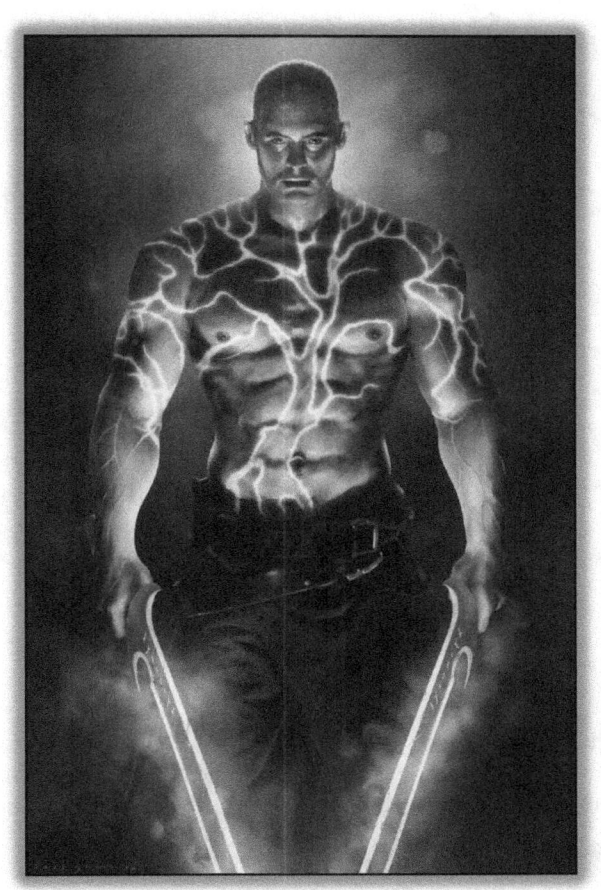

JASON L. MCWHIRTER

WWW.TWIINENTERTAINMENT.COM

A Twiin Entertainment Book

Books by Jason L. McWhirter

THE CAVALIER TRILOGY

Book 1: The Cavalier

Praise for THE CAVALIER, book one in this series
"The Cavalier (Book One of the Cavalier Trilogy) is a descriptively strong story, staying true to the style of similar fantasy novels. If you enjoy being drawn into a world laced with heroes, goblins, orcs and magic, then this is the story for you."
Fantasy Book Review (M.G. Russell)

Book 2: The Rise of Malbeck

Book 3: Glimmer in the Shadow
The last book in the Cavalier Trilogy

Published by Twiin Entertainment
www.twiinentertainment.com

Copyright © Jason L. McWhirter, 2013
Library of Congress
All rights reserved

Cover art by Luis Gama
Title page art by Luis Gama
Epilogue poem by Devin McWhirter
Maps by Jason McWhirter
Edited by Twiin Entertainment and Sarah Finley

Without limiting the rights under copyright reserved above, no part of this publication may be reproduced, stored electronically, or transmitted, in any form, or by any means, without the prior written permission of the copyright owner.

AUTHOR'S NOTE

This is a work of fiction. Names, characters, places, and incidents are the product of the author's imagination or are used fictitiously, and any resemblance to actual persons, living or dead, business establishments, events, or locales is entirely coincidental.

Dedication:

I would like to dedicate this book to all our men and women who serve, or have served, in our armed forces. You are all the true warriors, and because of you we live in a free country, where our life's choices are protected by your steel and courage. Without your vigilant stand, the world in which we live would be very different.

I would especially like to honor my wife's father-in-law. He passed away in July of 2013 at the age of ninety six. He served in World War II, the Korean War, and the Vietnam War. He was in the army and has three combat infantry badges and he always said he would still be in the military if they let him. Manuel Montesdeoca, thank you for your service. Thank you for your many sacrifices over the years. Thank you for enduring the pain of lost comrades and protecting our freedoms. You were a true warrior, and a real hero.

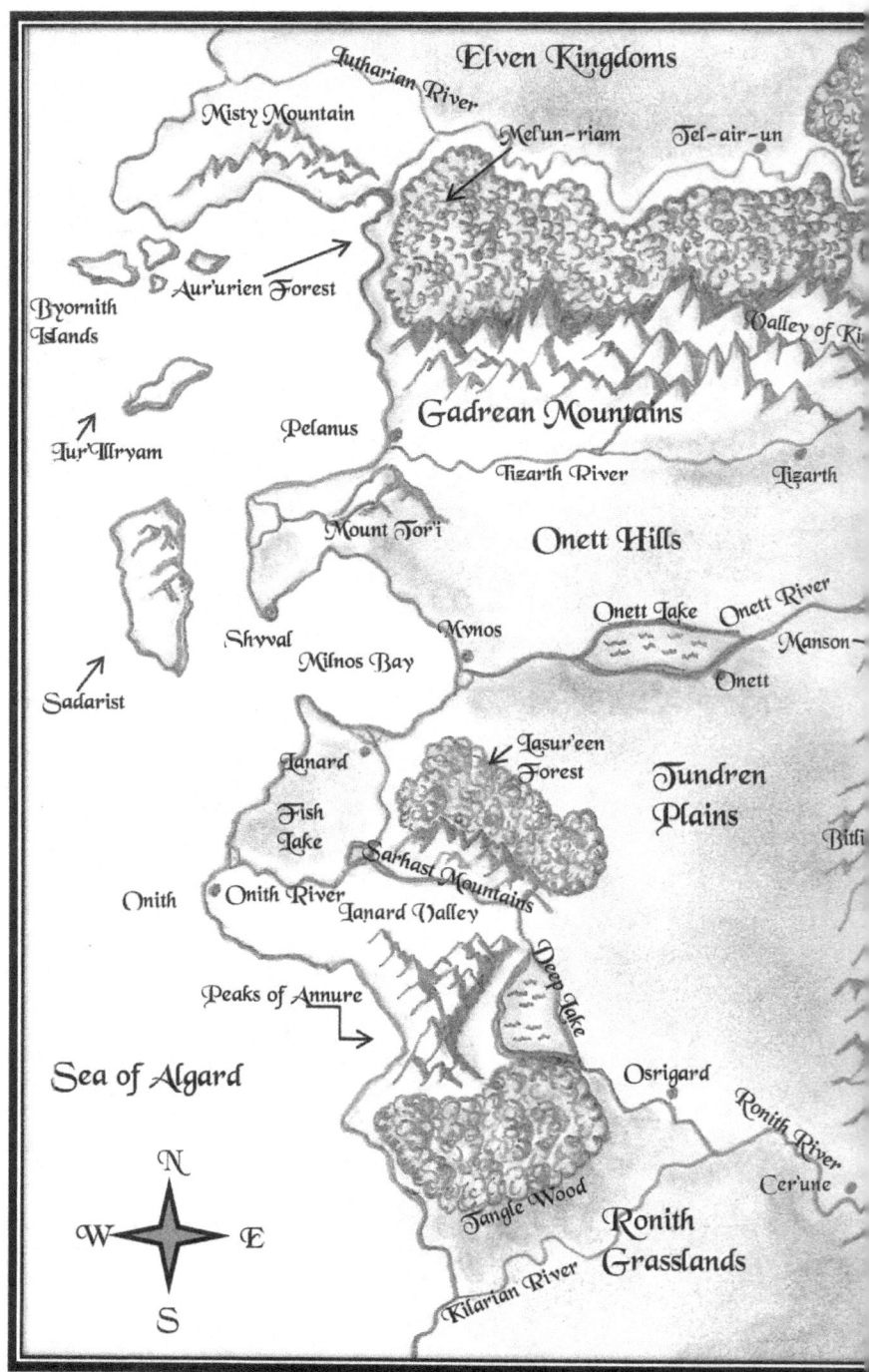

The Lands Of Kraawn

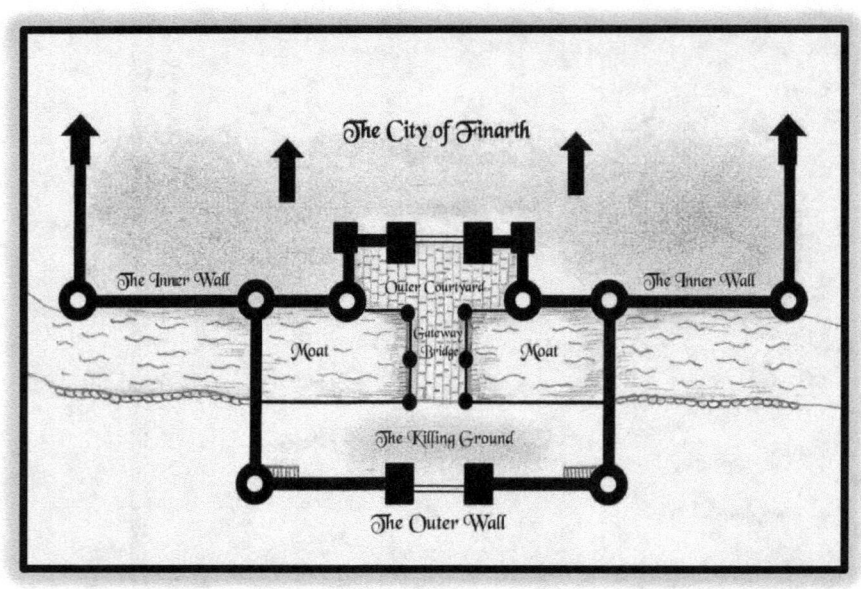

Fortifications for the City of Finarth

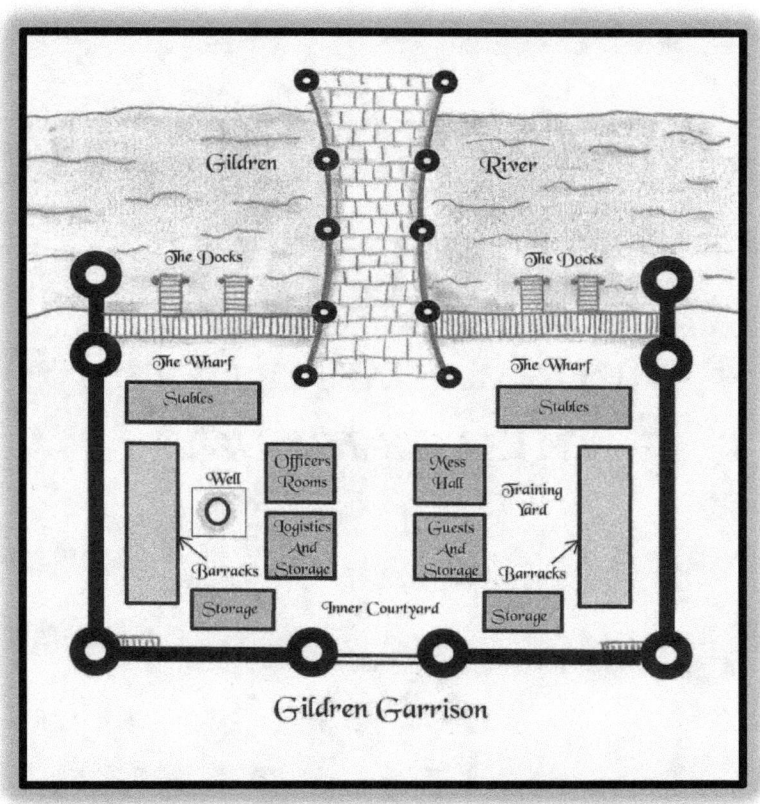

The Gildren Garrison

GLIMMER IN THE SHADOW

THE FINAL CHAPTER OF THE
CAVALIER TRILOGY

JASON L. MCWHIRTER

Prologue

Cuthaine was in ruins. The Cuthainians had put up a valiant fight, but in the end it was hopeless. Malbeck's army was too large, too ruthless, and too strong. Some had packed up their belongings and left, while others had stayed behind to help bolster the city's defenses. None who stayed behind survived the onslaught, and their bodies littered the streets.

Smoke and flames rose from burning buildings, fouling the night sky in violent billows on the evening breeze. Malbeck's warriors ran through the streets killing any survivors and looting anything of value. Their grunts and growls, interspersed by the screams of the wounded and dying added another layer of horror to the grisly scene.

Flocks of carrion crows, drawn by the scent of death, cast ominous shadows across the full moon, their sheer numbers blocking its bright glow. They had come to feed.

Malbeck stood in front of Cuthaine's graveyard, his milky white eyes scanning the vista of tombstones. But he was not interested in these stone markers. He was looking for something else, a prize that would be identified by freshly turned dirt and mud. His prize would have been buried in a mass grave with the rest of his warriors who had stormed the Oasis gaming house. They had hoped to kill King Kromm and his meddlesome band of warriors, but they had failed.

Behind him stood thirty Gould-Irin Orcs waiting for his command. Their charcoal gray armor and weaponry, along with the greenish gray hue of their thick skin, would have made them almost invisible in the darkness if it were not for the white eye of Gould clearly painted on their breastplates and shields, and their red eyes that shone in the night.

"There," Malbeck said, his voice heavy and powerful as he pointed the Spear of Gould towards a large mound fifty paces to his left.

Malbeck's thick chest was bare. He wore only black leggings and boots made from the skin of a black dragon. His blue gray skin was thick and tough like leather and his short hair was black as coal, absent of all light. He was a demonoid, part man, part demon, twisted by the magic of the Forsworn. Strapped to his broad muscled back was his mighty double bladed battle axe. He was easily eight feet tall and his shoulders were impossibly broad, contrasting sharply with his narrow waist.

In his left hand he carried the Shan Cemar, the ancient elven book that held the original words of magic, enabling the possessor to access vast amounts of power from the Ru'Ach, the energy of all things. It was believed that the book had been created by the first elves and had then been hidden, so the true power of the Ru'Ach could not be tapped, could not be taken and twisted by evil men.

But now Malbeck possessed the book. And he would use it to spread the disease of the Forsworn over Kraawn and blacken the very ground with their desire. The Forsworn, a trio of evil gods who wanted nothing more than to conquer the lands of Kraawn. Once that goal was accomplished then their dark stain could spread to all the lands and even the worlds beyond. Malbeck was their general on this plane of existence, and nothing, and no one, was going to stop him.

Five orcs from the back came forward and two of them were holding a man in blood splattered armor. The man was powerfully built with a head of thick unruly hair. But he did not look powerful now. Bruised and beaten, his thick hair was matted with sweat and blood. He could barely stand; in fact he would have fallen if the two Gould-Irin Orcs had not been holding his arms.

The man was General Kurarris, and despite his condition, he looked straight at Malbeck and spit a mixture of blood and saliva at the demonoid's feet.

Malbeck ignored him and addressed the orcs standing near the Free Legion general. "Stand him on the mound and slit his throat," he ordered casually, as if the command were nothing more than a daily chore.

The orcs dragged Kurarris to the mound of dirt and pulled his arms behind his back, yanking his head back and exposing his thick neck.

The general was too weak to struggle. He had been beaten so badly that his entire body was numb, which was good considering how many broken bones he had sustained. But he knew that death was coming. Through the daze of pain and fatigue he had heard the order. But strangely it did not matter. He had fought hard, and he had done his duty. Besides, his men had all died defending the city, and it was only fitting that he should join them in their fate.

With the last bit of his strength he smiled at Malbeck and laughed.

His laugh was cut short by the sharp blade slicing through his throat. As he fell limply to the ground he could vaguely smell the damp earth as it mixed with the coppery odor of his blood. Then his mind went black and he fell into nothingness.

"Back up," Malbeck ordered as he held up the Sham Cemar.

The orcs silently walked back behind their master as Malbeck began to recite the incantation, a powerful spell that required the blood of a battle hardened and accomplished warrior, a role that the departed general unknowingly played. The words of the spell rolled off his lips and after a few seconds the blood pooling around Kurarris began to sizzle and smoke. But the smoke didn't drift away into the night. It rose up and spun into a small vortex. As the blood slowly boiled away, the coalescing smoke picked up speed as Malbeck continued the spell. Then it spun up into the air and shot straight down to disappear into the earth just as Malbeck recited the last words of the spell.

At first nothing happened. But Malbeck did not move, nor did the orcs behind him. They stared at the mound of fresh dirt and waited.

It didn't take long.

The dirt heaved sluggishly back and forth like a slow wave. Then a hand shot up from the damp ground. The mud did little to mask the pale bloated skin that covered it.

"Ah...yessss...come forth, my servant," Malbeck whispered as he took several steps closer to the mound.

The hand began to dig at the dirt and after a few seconds another hand burst forth, followed shortly by a hooded head. Dirt and the smell of rotting flesh clung to the corpse as it slowly emerged from the ground.

The reanimated body wore a dirty gray robe, and it stood up slowly, as if it were acclimating itself to its surroundings. The hooded creature flexed its pale hands. Bits of its skin had been eaten away, exposing rotted flesh and bone. The thing reached up slowly and pulled its hood back, revealing its face.

It was Gullanin, the wizard, though a pale and hideous version. His face was bloated with decay, and bits of flesh hung loosely from his skull. Gullanin's eyes were narrow points of red light, and his decayed and torn lips exposed yellow rotting teeth. A gruesome red and black scar encircled his neck. Somehow the magic of the Shan Cemar had fused Gullanin's head back to his body and brought him back to life.

"My master, is that you?" Gullanin said uncertainly, his voice rough and raspy and carrying the weight of magic.

"It is I, my faithful servant. I have brought you back to serve me again," Malbeck said as he stood before the undead corpse.

"I feel different," Gullanin said as he gazed at his hands. His eye sockets were black pits of rotting flesh and his bulbous eyes could clearly be seen nestled within the bony pockets, the pupils now red and glowing with malice.

"Of course you do. You are a Lich, an undead wizard who stands halfway between the realm of the living and the realm of the dead. You have power, more power than before, as the links to the Ru'Ach are no longer invisible to you. Do you not feel the power around you?" Malbeck asked.

"I do, my Lord."

"I have given you this power to serve the Forsworn, to serve me once again. I need a general, and despite your previous failures, you are the best that I have."

Gullanin brought his hands forward, palms up, and crackling blue energy erupted from them, arcing back and forth.

The Lich's eerie laugh echoed throughout Cuthaine. "I will not fail you this time, my Lord".

One
New Friends

Jonas sat cross-legged in the darkness. His mind had drifted while he had sat, unmoving, floating above his inner shield, a small core of humanity he had created within his mind. It was the place he swore not to retreat to while the darkness of the Forsworn overran his body. He would rather die than let that happen, and he was prepared to do just that. But nothing came for him. There were no dark talons reaching out of the black for him, no tentacles snaking towards him trying to destroy the last speck of who he was. He did not know why but he was alone within his own consciousness. He did not quite understand where he was, or what was happening. He felt it more than anything. He had no idea how much time had passed while in this state. There was no sound, smell, nothing. It was disorientating. But he was alive; at least he felt that he was. He knew that what made him *him* was protected within that one sphere of light below. But here he was, alone. *I will not give up*, Jonas thought to himself as he positioned his arms on his knees, his silver swords still held firmly, crossing blade to blade. They burned with a white light and Jonas looked into them, concentrating on them as he waited for what was to come.

He had no idea how long it had been since he had been captured. Dykreel's clerics had tortured him, and in the process they had put something inside him, something filled with the dark magic of the Forsworn. This magic had forced him to fight in an underground arena where desperate warriors came to win glory or gold, and whatever it was that controlled his body had made him kill. Fortunately, Jonas could not remember the events clearly since his mind had retreated deep within himself, forming a barrier against the black magic that was seeping into his body, trying to capture his very essence. He felt hopeless. There was nothing left of him that he felt he controlled, nothing except the circle of light he now sat upon. He was a construct in his own mind, at least that was how it felt. His body had lost the fight, but he still fought to maintain his essence. If he lost that, then he would lose everything. That would not happen without a fight.

***

Tuvallis huddled quietly under the snow laden bows of a small fir tree. The limbs were near the forest floor and the weight of their white cargo forced them even lower, almost kissing the snow covered ground. Just in front of him the green fronds of a large bushy fern fought through the snow in a losing battle as they sagged towards the ground, pushed down by the weight of their snowy cargo. He was well hidden under his thick furs. They, and his heavily bearded face, camouflaged him from view. There was no way the small group of orcs would spot him as they trudged by his hiding spot. They probably wouldn't even smell him as his potent odor would likely be similar to their own animal-like scent. The large beasts wore mismatched pieces of armor and thick furs similar to his own garb. They carried short cutting swords at their sides and long crude spears in their thick calloused hands.

The burly mountain man gripped the leather handle of his long sword tightly as he watched the lumbering beasts march methodically by, oblivious to his presence.

Tuvallis had spent the last fifteen years roaming the mountains around Finarth and Tarsis, and his appearance reflected the mountain life he lived. He was thick and strong, built like a bull, with a barrel chest and wide shoulders tapering down to his muscular torso and supported by powerful legs accustomed to carrying his large frame over mountainous terrain. Nearly a head taller than most men, his sheer bulk belied his height until he stood next to someone. The furs he wore were a mixture of mountain bear and wolf, with leggings made from the long haired mountain elk. In contrast to his disheveled look was the bright shirt of chain mail that he wore under his furs, a gleaming counterpart to the polished silver crosspiece of the sword he held easily in his meaty hand. His ash wood bow and quiver lay next to him as he squatted in the shadows of the young tree. The re-curved bow was longer than most of its kind. He had it made special for him many years ago and it was worth every gold coin he had spent on it. The bow was shorter than a traditional long bow, making it easier to maneuver through the brush, but it had more power than one of its longer cousins, and very

14

few men were strong enough to draw it, let alone use it with the ease that Tuvallis could. It was his favorite weapon and it always glistened with the oil that Tuvallis meticulously rubbed into it to protect it from the elements. It was apparent that he cared more about his weapons and gear than his appearance, but that was learned over many years of trying to survive in the dangerous wilds. After all, it was his tools and weapons that carried him through each winter, and not his charms or good looks.

But it wasn't his tousled dirty orc-like build that was disconcerting. It was his face, if you could call it that. His entire head was covered with long scraggly black hair which seemed to continue growing down his face before melting into his unkempt bushy beard. Wiry, greasy, and streaked with gray, it looked as if it could house several rats. His skin, dark and weathered, was only visible around his eyes, and even his lips were concealed behind his snow encrusted mustache. He was alone, and he liked it that way, therefore his appearance was never a concern.

Tuvallis shifted slowly as he removed his gloved hand from the hilt of his sword and grabbed his bow. He remained still for a few more minutes until the orcs had marched well beyond his location.

He had seen several groups of the monsters over the last few weeks, and that concerned him. He had also recently been attacked by two boargs. They could have simply been hunting, or perhaps they were scouts for a band of orcs, it was hard to know. It was uncommon to see so many beasts in such a short period of time, especially in such close proximity to the mountain villages that dotted the valleys of the Tundrens. Something was amiss. But that was no surprise to Tuvallis, as he was no stranger to the increasing number of unsettling occurrences that had been happening around Tarsis and Finarth.

Four years ago, he had witnessed the destruction of the town of Manson, a quiet hunting village deep in the Tundrens. It was as close to a home as he had ever known, a useful place to trade his meats and furs for supplies that he needed to survive in the mountains. He was a tough man, hardened not only by his life in the mountains, but also by the combat he had faced while serving in the Tarsinian army many years ago. Even so, the scene he had witnessed after the town's destruction still fed his nightmares.

The boargs had ripped the town apart, killing everyone and feeding on their bloody corpses. He had entered the town several days after the fight, but the stench from the decaying and half eaten bodies reached him long before he saw the destruction.

He shivered momentarily as the terrible memory again flashed through his mind, like scenes from a horrible dream.

After the destruction of Manson he had moved his home base farther south and closer to the edge of the Tundrens. He could trade with smaller villages there, and the winter conditions were not as harsh as they were higher in the mountain passes. But he had not seen many orcs or other monsters since, until now.

Something was happening, and Tuvallis kept hearing a little voice in his head, as if his subconscious was whispering in his ear. The voice was subtle, but insistently saying the same thing; *leave the mountains and join the world of the living.*

He had been alone for most of the last fifteen years, except for the few trade excursions to various towns that he made each year. But being alone was what he wanted; at least that is what he continued to say over and over again as if to justify his chosen solitude.

But recently his subconscious seemed more persistent. It was as if he was missing something, or was needed for some task. He felt like he needed to find a village and see what was happening in the world that he had chosen to leave so many years ago. This pull became so strong that he eventually found himself hiking lower and lower, heading to a small village called Egrin, one that he had visited several years back.

Grabbing his bow, Tuvallis slung the quiver over his backpack and silently vacated his hiding spot. Though he was a big man, he could move like a ghost if he wanted. Not even the drooping bows he crouched under noticed his presence.

The town was a few days from his location and he was eager for a warm room, and a soft bed; hopefully both would be available.

It took him several hard days of hiking to reach Egrin. As he moved farther and farther down the Tundrens the snow began to diminish until it was no more than a foot deep. The small village was nestled beyond a frozen stream and was tucked safely in the shadows of a fifty foot rock face. It was a good spot to settle, thought Tuvallis, as he gazed down at the candlelit windows and smoking chimneys. The sun had just set and the timing was perfect as he did not want to stay another cold night huddled around a small fire tucked in some cave or shelter.

There was no wall around the town, but the design of the homes and buildings, combined with the fact that there was only one main road that entered the town, created a makeshift funnel to lead all newcomers into the village from one direction. The village watch could post guards at the entry point if need be. The town was just large enough to deter any roaming monsters from wanting to do anything rash. But you could never be too careful in the frontier lands where there was nothing to protect you except your own steel and that of your townsfolk. And the men here were men such as he; tough, accustomed to hard physical labor, and not afraid to bloody their knuckles or their swords. You had to be of that mindset to survive out here.

Tuvallis walked at a steady pace toward the lantern light just beyond the small bridge that spanned the frozen stream. His breath billowed out in puffs of steam in the cold air as his dark narrow eyes squinted toward the light ahead of him. There was a small building beside the road which probably housed the watchmen for the night.

Sure enough, as Tuvallis crossed the bridge and neared the little stout building built of logs, a man in a heavy dark wool cloak emerged from the entry holding a lantern up high. The man was medium height and build and Tuvallis noticed that his right hand rested on the pommel of his sword. Tuvallis held no doubt that he could use it if need be. There was a large bell hanging nearby that could be rung in alarm if anything attacked in the night.

Tuvallis stopped and let the lantern light bathe his features as he looked up at the guard. "Greetin's," he said, "Me name's Tuvallis and I be hopin' to get food and shelter fer de night."

The man didn't say anything for a second as he eyed Tuvallis. "Where ya comin' from, mountain man?" the guard finally said. It was obvious by Tuvallis's appearance that he had spent most of his time hunting the steep peaks of the Tundrens.

"Here and there," Tuvallis answered back.

"Where ya goin' then?" the guard asked.

"Not sure yet, but I be thinkin' of headin' out of de mountains in a few days, maybe towards Cuthaine or Finarth," Tuvallis replied.

The guard spit on the ground, but Tuvallis noticed that he no longer held the pommel of his blade, and he had slowly lowered the lantern so it was out of his eyes. Now Tuvallis could make out the man's features. His face was bearded with a thick mat of dirty blonde hair and his eyes sparkled turquoise blue. His features were nondescript, but his eyes gave him some character. They were unique, and there seemed to be a fire behind them, ready to burst out at any moment. He looked a bit younger than Tuvallis, who had seen nearly forty five winters.

"Not sure why you're wantin' to leave the mountains with all that's going on, but that's your choice I guess," the guard said.

"What do ya mean?" Tuvallis asked curiously.

"Ya don't know? Well I can see from your expression that ya don't. Tarsis was destroyed by the Dark One's army," the guard said somberly as he shook his head in disgust.

"What! The city is no more? What of the king?" Tuvallis added quickly.

"Not sure, stranger. But the tidings are dark, there is no question about that. Enough talk in the cold. Come on in. I know our local barkeep has a couple rooms and I don't think they are occupied."

"At the Dancing Elf?" Tuvallis asked.

"Yup, you been here before?"

"Been a while, but yes, some years back."

"Well, in case ya forgot, continue down the road and you'll be seein' the building on the right."

Tuvallis grunted his thanks and continued down the snow covered road. His thoughts were dark as he thought about Tarsis burning in the shadows of Malbeck's army. But his mindset couldn't ruin the beautiful winter night. The bright stars and moon cast an ambient glow off the sparkling snow and he easily found his path through the well laid out town.

Sure enough, the building he remembered was on his right, looking just like the picture in his mind. It was entirely built of logs giving the walls a solid look, and a huge thick oak door was dead center and covering most of it was a giant brown bear pelt. The pelt had been hammered onto the door with iron nails and burned into the fur were the initials D.E., the Dancing Elf. Through the tavern's several windows Tuvallis could see the glow of the room's flickering candles and could almost feel the warmth from the fire in the hearth. It looked welcoming, and Tuvallis entered with barely a pause.

The heavy oak door squeaked open and the cold winter air rushed in and dashed about the room for a second before the door shut behind him, cutting the brisk breeze off from its source. Tuvallis stamped his snow covered leather boots down hard several times on the

18

iron grate in front of the door as he looked around the room.

It was a simple structure, made from the local materials. There was a giant stone fireplace to the right filled with three foot flaming logs. Tuvallis smiled as he felt the heat from the fire wash over him. It had been a while since he sat in front of a large warm fire sheltered from the cold winter conditions. There were six wood tables and benches placed sporadically around the room, and one simple bar to the left. Flanking the bar were several doors that Tuvallis knew led to the kitchen and to the guest rooms; at least they had when he had visited several years ago. The walls were lined with antlers of various sizes, as well as several wolf and bear pelts.

The bar was empty except for two men sitting by the fire talking quietly and drinking from clay mugs. They looked up at Tuvallis and he didn't miss their surprised expressions. They didn't get many strangers coming into town during the winter, and they were not successful at hiding their curiosity. But after a few seconds they resumed their conversation, glancing at him occasionally when they didn't think he was looking.

Tuvallis set his heavy pack down by a table and lifted off his thick fur jacket. He leaned his bow against the table and walked toward the bar. Just as he neared the plain wooden structure, the door to the left swung open and a portly old woman stepped through it and behind the counter.

"I thought I heard the door open. What can I do for ya, stranger? Me name's Lydia, and I be the proprietor of this here establishment."

She was not an attractive woman, but not really ugly either, just plain. Her long gray hair was held back with a leather head band. Her skin was aged but not overly wrinkled, and when she smiled her whole face lit up. Her teeth were perfect; straight and white, and they made her face come alive. It was rare to see teeth like that on anyone, let alone on an old woman living in a remote mountain village. Tuvallis liked her immediately, as she had a friendly aura about her.

"I be lookin' fer warm food and a bed," Tuvallis grunted.

"Sure, stranger, but I won't do either 'til you give me a name," she replied with a smile.

"Sorry, ma'am, me name's Tuvallis." *Sorry*, what was he saying? Tuvallis never said sorry to anyone, let alone a bar maid. But there was something about this woman that seemed to bring out the best in him, and he smiled as he tried to think of the last time he had said *sorry*. But he had so much hair on his face that Lydia didn't even notice the expression.

"Where ya from?"

"All around, don't call one place home," Tuvallis answered.

"I'm sorry to hear that," Lydia said. "What would you like to drink? I'm sure you're hungry as well?"

It was a peculiar comment, but Tuvallis shrugged it off quickly as he thought about the food and drink. "I'll have a mug of mead and whatever you have warm to eat."

"I have some braised pork with potatoes and onions. Should still be warm. Will that do?" Lydia asked with a smile.

"Yes, thank you," Tuvallis said, then added hesitantly, "I passed by here some few years back; the bar keep was er… a man named Clark. Thought he be the owner."

"Clark was me husband," Lydia said, her smile all but disappearing. Tuvallis didn't miss her past tense reference and he immediately wished he had not brought it up. "He was killed last year by raiding orcs. If you will excuse me," she said as she turned to pour his mead and prepare his meal, the light from her face gone like the moon on a cloudy night.

Tuvallis shook his head and moved back to his table. Her statement didn't surprise him as he had seen more orcs over the last few years than he had throughout his entire life. Malbeck's rise had definitely stirred up the foulest of creatures and they were increasingly making their presence known.

The two men by the fire stopped talking and looked at Tuvallis as he sat down near them. One man was tall and thin, maybe fifty winters, with skin worn and weathered from the elements. The other was younger, probably around forty, bigger, more fat than muscle, with a plump rosy cheeked face flushed from the mead and the warm fire.

The tall man smiled and nodded his head in greeting, while the younger man looked at Tuvallis with an uncertain expression. "Welcome to Egrin, trail burner, my name's Jonstin and this is my friend, Smit," the older man said warmly as he indicated the heavier man sitting next to him. Smit just looked at Tuvallis and took a long drink from his mug.

"Tuvallis."

Tuvallis was usually a man of few words and he rarely mixed

pleasantries with dialog. If it didn't need to be spoken, he wouldn't say it. Besides, he was so used to solitude that talking did not come easy for him. His fragmented speech and poor grammar made these townsfolk sound like pompous royalty.

Lydia came back with a tray of steaming food and a large mug of mead. She set them down near Tuvallis along with a knife and fork.

"That will be two coppers for the food and one Tarsinian silver for the room," she said briskly, her warm smile returning.

Tuvallis dug in the leather pouch hanging at his side and paid the woman, all but ignoring her as the smell of the warm food assaulted his senses. It had been a while since he had eaten a hot home cooked meal, and the smell of the braised pork was making him salivate. He grabbed the fork and knife and attacked the food, only pausing to breathe and drink the cold mead.

"It's good isn't it?" The tall man chuckled. Tuvallis grunted in agreement as he all but inhaled his meal. "I'd eat here every night if I could afford it. But don't think my wife would approve."

Now it was the bigger man's turn to laugh. "What *does* your wife approve?"

"I'll drink to that," Jonstin replied as they clacked their mugs together and drained both their glasses. "You live in the mountains?" Jonstin asked. It was really more of a statement than a question. Tuvallis's appearance made it a foregone conclusion.

"Yup," Tuvallis replied as he finished off the last piece of gravy drenched pork.

"Guess you haven't heard then," Smit said somberly.

Tuvallis didn't' miss the tone or their expressions. "'Bout Tarsis?" he asked gruffly as he finished off his mug of mead.

"Yup...how did you...," Jonstin began to ask.

"Watchman, blue eyed fellow," Tuvallis said.

"Colvan's his name. Good man, pretty good with his sword too," Smit added.

"You hear that Malbeck is marching his army toward Finarth? He's razing everything to the ground along the way. Horrible destruction they say," Jonstin said bitterly.

Tuvallis set his mug down hard, surprised at his own anger. It shouldn't have been such a surprise to him. Of course the Dark One was going to continue his relentless advance, a path of murder, destruction, and utter conquest. That was what such men, or demons, whatever he was, did. They took and took, until there was nothing left to take. But it still caught him by surprise when he pictured Tarsis burning and his black army marching south, destroying everything in its path. It surprised him how much it upset him. His knuckles turned white as he unconsciously squeezed the edge of the table in both hands. Both of the villagers didn't say a thing as they looked at his still form, wondering how he was going to react. "How long ago they leave Tarsis?" Tuvallis asked sharply.

"We had a trader come in just before the snows fell. He said the Dark One's army would reach Cuthaine by the end of winter," Smit said.

"Dat puts 'em in Finarth by spring or summer," Tuvallis whispered to himself.

"We just hope we don't see any part of his vileness up here," Jonstin said. "We've already had some problems with marauding orcs. They seem to be getting bolder."

"Orcs be everywhere, but yer safe from his army, fer now anyway. You're not in its path," Tuvallis said.

"Yeah, well, we figured that," Smit said testily.

Tuvallis glared at him and Smit's confident expression melted away. Tuvallis sat there quietly for a moment, taking in all that he had been told. Malbeck was back and he was re-forming his army. The drums of war were sounding again. In that moment Tuvallis made up his mind.

"Where can I find supplies fer hard travel?" he asked the two men.

"I can help with that," Lydia said as she came up behind him with another mug of mead. "What will ya need?" she asked with a brilliant flash of her white teeth.

***

Not all the Free Legion warriors were dead. Captain Hadrick, despite his protests, had been asked to escort the thousands of refugees from the city. He was accompanied by fifty horsed and heavily armored Free Legion warriors. It was not a job that any of them wanted, but nonetheless they would see it through. It was no easy task to walk away from the city knowing that their comrades were defending their home without them. They should be next to their sword brothers, fighting and dying if need be.

There were over two thousand men, women, and children who had left Cuthaine in the face of Malbeck's army. Of that number, just over a hundred were men who were armed and could fight if forced to. They had left two days before Malbeck's army would arrive at the gates. Some refugees had left earlier to find new homes, foregoing the safety of traveling with larger numbers. Others stayed, unsure of their next move.

Captain Hadrick and the rest of his men did not want to babysit, they wanted to fight. But it was not that easy. They could not just leave the people of Cuthaine. Besides, what could fifty more warriors do in the face of Malbeck's army? They had some decisions to make.

"I say we continue on to Finarth," Groben, a gray haired veteran suggested to the small contingent of warriors sitting around a warm smoldering fire.

They were taking rest after a hard day of marching. The refugees were scattered around the grass field flanking the road. Fires were lit while men and women unpacked carts and saddlebags to prepare for supper and a night of well-earned rest. Orders were given and Free Legion warriors were either on perimeter guard or taking rest and food.

"It is a long way," Norith replied. "Some of these people may not want to go that far."

"Some might not be *able* to go that far," interjected Jons, a young brown haired soldier. His eyes were tiny, giving him the appearance of one who was always squinting. "There are over four hands of the elderly that I know of."

"That is not our concern. Finarth is in Malbeck's path. We will have our opportunity to avenge our comrades if we go there. You know this to be true!" Groben protested loudly.

"Calm, Groben. We all want to avenge our brethren. But the reason you just stated may be reason enough not to go to Finarth. We would be taking these people from one danger just to face it again. What is the sense in that?" Captain Hadrick asked, though his voice lacked conviction.

It was obvious to many that the captain wanted to go to Finarth as well, but he felt obligated to the refugees to take them to safety, wherever that may be.

"Captain, I agree with Groben, and not just for revenge," Silvy stated slowly, pausing briefly to sip his tea. Silvy was short for Silvanus, and he was broad and thickly built. The men knew him as one who did everything methodically. He spoke slowly, ate slowly, and made up his mind slowly. The only thing he didn't do slowly was fight. He was a skilled fighter, and the men all respected him for his quick blade and pondering wit. "The way I see it, we have few options, Captain," Silvy continued. "There is no place safe for these people. Malbeck is sure to have roaming scouting parties. We have nowhere to take them. Finarth will be where the final stand is made, and although it will be dangerous I don't see it any more so than leaving them out here and hoping that an orc scouting party doesn't find them. I say we take our chances at Finarth where we can at least fight for their protection." Silvy stopped talking and took another sip of tea.

The warriors pondered his words briefly before Captain Hadrick spoke again. "I think I will talk with our people in the morning. The choice will be theirs to make. I think you are right, Silvy. We will be departing for Finarth with as many refugees that wish to come. The Gildren Garrison should only be a week and a half away. We head there and then to Finarth. The others will have to find their new homes on their own. I hate to even speak those words, but I agree with you in that our choices are few, and none are appealing."

The Gildren Garrison, Finarth's most northern outpost, guarded the bridge over the Gildren River and provided the only accessible route across the massive river. From there it would be another week to Finarth.

"Gutting an orc at the gates of Finarth sounds appealing to me," Groben added with a smile. The rest of the evening passed quickly as stomachs filled with warm stew and the hard traveling began to rest heavily on their eyelids.

"Get some sleep," Captain Hadrick ordered after they finished their meal. "We have a long day tomorrow. Lieutenant Silvy, check the perimeter. At night I want five watches set, relieved every four hours. See to it."

"Aye, Captain," Silvy replied as he stood from the fire.

The attack came during the third watch. Captain Hadrick was awoken by screams and the sounds of battle. At first he thought it was a nightmare, but that thought was quickly dismissed when he heard the horn of alarm.

He leaped up from his wool blanket and grabbed his sword and shield. He had no time to don his plate armor as the chaos outside moved to a louder crescendo of screams and fighting. But he always slept wearing his chain mail, and he silently thanked his old sergeant who had instilled that habit in him.

He raced out of his tent and sprinted toward the sounds that came from his left. The refugees had also been roused from their slumber by the noise and they looked at the captain with frightened eyes. Some were holding young ones close, and a few of the men were holding weapons in shaking hands, unsure of what to do. Luckily his men had kept a perimeter of fires going, and the moon was out in full, painting the grassy landscape a glowing blue. So he could see well enough as he raced through the campsites of the terrified Cuthainians.

Captain Hadrick saw two of his warriors emerge from the darkness in front of him. *Thank Ulren* he thought as he saw that they too were wearing their chain mail. He had passed that lesson on to them as well, and luckily none had shirked that duty tonight.

"Groben, Sury, good…follow me!" Captain Hadrick ordered as he bounded past them. As they neared the western perimeter the sounds of fighting drew them directly to the source. Five other Free Legions warriors had joined them and they spread out into a flanking position as they neared the commotion.

Six dark clad orcs were locked in battle with two Free Legion fighters. Hadrick's trained eyes flicked across the scene as he and his men jumped to help their comrades. He saw a score of dead bodies littering the grassy ground, and only one was an orc.

The two men were fighting back to back, using the longer reach of their long swords to fend off the clumsy swings of the short orcish blades.

Hadrick and his men erupted from the darkness to help his frantic men. The orcs on the far side disengaged and ran into the black night, knowing that the element of surprise was gone. But three of them were stuck between the newly arrived men and the two fighting soldiers.

One orc frantically swung his sword toward Hadrick, simultaneously trying to backpedal and escape into the night. But Hadrick was having none of that. He took the sword directly on his shield and pivoted at the last minute, lessening the impact of the strike. He spun full circle and led with his sword. His blade struck the orc in the side with enough force to drive it to the ground. Hadrick lifted his sword and hit the beast right in the face just at it looked up. The heavy body fell silently to the ground.

Meanwhile, Hadrick's men easily dispatched the remaining orcs.

"Silvy, are you okay?" Hadrick asked as he ran towards the two warriors who were previously fighting for their lives. Silvy was wearing his plate mail and he looked unhurt, other than a slight cut on his hand.

"I'm fine, Captain," he replied as he wiped sweat from his forehead.

"And you, Torum, are you hurt?" The captain asked as he turned towards the other man who was leaning heavy on one leg.

"Just a cut on my leg, sir. I will be fine." Torum was wearing his chain mail shirt over cream colored leggings. His feet were bare and it was obvious by his appearance that the attack had come as a surprise. Fresh blood dripped freely from a long cut across his thigh.

"Get that wound cleaned and bound. Sury, get more fires lit and reset the perimeter. Tell the refugees to arm themselves and to make sure the men are alert. We need lots of light and eyes open to use it. Who knows how many are out there or if they will be returning," the captain added.

"Yes, sir," Sury replied as he ran into the night.

The rest of his men had already begun to assess the damage and form a perimeter. They were all seasoned veterans and they knew their job. The Free Legion did not get their reputation for nothing; they earned it through constant conflict with the marauding tribes and nomads that lived across the plains surrounding Cuthaine.

"Silvy, what happened?" the captain asked.

"Orc patrol, sir. They slipped out of the darkness and killed Morgan who was on watch. Then they snuck in and began to attack some of the refugees as they slept. It's a good thing orcs can't walk softly as they might have gotten to more. I was relieving myself over yonder in the grass when I heard them. It was my horn that you heard."

"Very good. Well done, Lieutenant."

"Thank you, sir," Silvy replied.

"Get a count of the dead and see me in my tent shortly," Hadrick ordered as he turned and walked briskly back to his tent.

Inside his tent, Hadrick buckled his breast plate on and went to the maps on the table. His tent was small, barely big enough for the one table and sleeping furs. But he had certainly slept in worse conditions. After several minutes the tent flap opened and Silvy strode in.

"What is the damage?" Hadrick asked as he buckled on his sword belt.

"Morgan, Cons, Ardis, and Teagen, dead, sir. Along with ten refugees."

"Good men," Hadrick muttered as he shook his head sadly. He had been fighting alongside Ardis for ten years and he considered him a good friend.

"But that is not all, sir," Silvy continued.

Hadrick narrowed his eyes. "Yes?"

"Seli is missing, sir."

"Missing, what do you mean?"

"She was on watch with Morgan. But we can't find her body anywhere. She is gone."

"Ulren's blade!" Hadrick swore. Seli was the only female in his command. It was not common for a women fighter to make it through the training, but it wasn't unheard of. Seli had proven herself year after year, and he hated to think what those scum would do to her.

"Captain, what are we to do? You know what they will do..."

"I know, Silvy, but what can we do?" the captain asked, his anger and frustration evident in his voice.

"But I think they didn't kill her because she was a woman. I heard her scream just after the fighting...and..."

"I know, Silvy. But we are blind. We cannot go marching around in the dark. They can see and we can't. Besides, if we took a small force out, then we would be leaving these people unprotected. We have to hope that Ulren will protect her."

Silvy ground his teeth in frustration, but he knew Hadrick was right. There was nothing they could do for her. At least not at night.

Captain Hadrick sighed. "Be vigilant, Lieutenant. We will send out scouts in the morning to look for her. Pass the word that we leave at first light. I will speak with the refugees in the morning." The captain then dismissed Silvy and gave another heavy sigh. He knew it was going to be a long night.

***

It was nearing sundown and Tuvallis had moved out of the thick forests of the Tundrens several days ago. He had pushed himself hard as he felt an urgency that he could not explain. He would need more supplies to get to Finarth. He thought to head more southeast towards some of the small towns that dotted the fields around Cuthaine, before turning south towards Finarth and the Gildren Garrison. He could re-supply himself there before moving on.

He knew that Malbeck's army could be close. Scouting and raiding parties could already be roaming the lands nearby, so he had to be careful, which was why he decided against a fire as he picked a comfortable spot near a lone oak tree to lay down his bedding. It was cold and patches of snow covered the ground, but he was well outfitted with a thick fur coat to keep him warm during the night.

He made a soft bed of dry grass and laid his wool sleeping roll over it. His breath puffed out in clouds, but at least it was dry and the clear sky showed no signs of rain or snow.

He rummaged around in his pack and pulled out a hunk of cheese and dried mutton to eat for supper. He ate it quickly, as he was hungry from the day's long, hard trek. He washed it down with water and noticed that his canteen was almost empty. So he stood up and walked over to a patch of nearby snow. He stuffed the snow into his water container knowing that it would melt throughout the night tucked under the warmth of his furs.

He turned to move back to his bed, but the beautiful sunset grabbed his attention. The last remains of the sunlight were dropping behind the horizon, causing a pinkish glow to streak the sky. And it was when he was looking at the dazzling skyline that he noticed, off in the distance, a flickering orange light. *What was that?* Tuvallis wondered.

It looked like a large campfire off in the distance, but that seemed unlikely this far from any homestead or town. Tuvallis looked back at his make-shift bed and wondered if he should go investigate the mysterious light. He'd have to pick up his bedding and repack it, as he would not be able to find it again in the dark. He certainly didn't like the idea of sleeping so near a fire that could be the nightly home of thieves, or worse yet, an orc scouting party from Malbeck's forces.

With that in mind, Tuvallis packed up his bedding and strung his bow. He kept his bow string tucked tightly in a dry warm pocket to protect it from the elements. It only took him a few seconds to string the bow, then he shouldered his pack and he was off.

The night was faintly illuminated by the soft glow of the stars which cast enough light to lead him slowly through the grass. The light from the mysterious fire acted like a beacon, and he had no trouble zoning in on it.

As the fire grew closer, his fears were realized. He could clearly hear the guttural grunts and growls of orcs. It looked as if they had built a raging fire on the outer edges of a lone patch of low growing oak trees that were sporadically splattered across the grassy landscape like paint on a canvas.

Tuvallis stopped forty or so paces from the scene and quietly took off his pack. He gently laid it down and crouched in the low grass to observe the scene. He was covered by the shadows of night, but he had to be careful as an orc's sense of smell could prove dangerous, and their eyesight at night was that of a hunting cat.

He counted ten orcs and what looked like a long haired human tied roughly to a wooden pole stuck into the ground.

Tuvallis slowly inched closer to get a better look. The flames of the fire danced around and cast flickering shadows over the captive. One of the orcs threw a stick at the poor soul, and hit him in the face, causing his head to jerk back. The captive was bleeding and dirty, and Tuvallis could not get a good look at him. Just then the same orc moved next to the captive and ripped off his dirty wool shirt.

Tuvallis was momentarily taken aback by what he saw. The captive was a woman, and as soon as her breasts were exposed the orcs started yelping and growling like a pack of excited wolves. They surrounded their captive and groped and prodded her, ripping off more clothes in the process. She was so beaten that she did not protest at all. She simply stood there as her head lolled up and down, fighting against unconsciousness.

Tuvallis swore under his breath as he slowly crept around the clearing toward the patch of trees, while his mind wondered if that was such a good decision. He was a tough and seasoned warrior, but taking on ten armed orcs alone would be no easy feat.

It was not uncommon for orcs to rape human women. The end result could be a half-orc child, but more often than not the woman would not survive such abuse. If she did survive the rape, and was unfortunate enough to conceive a child, the birth would more than likely kill her. The baby would be too big.

Tuvallis decided that he would not let that happen.

He made it safely to the dark cluster of trees and slowly inched his way to a large oak that offered a clear line of sight to the clearing that was now only twenty paces away.

The orcs all wore black hardened leather armor, mixed with pieces of plate mail that they had scavenged; they carried short swords, and there were some shields and crossbows nearby. Tuvallis didn't see any of the crossbows loaded, and that made him feel a bit better. The woman was muscled and lean, and Tuvallis could see several scars across her torso and arms. She was obviously a warrior, and by the looks of the dirty tunic and red sash, he thought she might be from the Free Legion. That puzzled him since Cuthaine was more than several days ride from his location.

Tuvallis began to form a plan in his mind. It would not be easy, but if things went well, then he might live to see another day. He drew two arrows from his quiver and stuck them into the ground at the base of the tree. Then he moved quietly to the left to another tree at the far end of the glade. He placed another two arrows there, before slowly moving back into the grass. The grass was about waist high, so he dropped down to his hands and knees and crept slowly forward another twenty paces. He then used his body to push the reeds of grass down into a soft clearing, like a deer or animal would do to bed down for the night. He stuck two more arrows there before moving again around the clearing to his last location.

It was getting darker as patches of thick clouds drifted around the sky, covering the moon and decreasing visibility beyond the firelight. And the orcs were so intent on their victim that they were paying little attention to their surroundings.

Tuvallis had one knee down as he slowly lifted his head and nocked an arrow. He was roughly twenty paces away, so he could clearly see the orcs tire of their play and cut the woman down. Now was the time to attack.

He took two deep breaths, pulled back on the string of his powerful bow, and put the biggest orc right in his sights. Tuvallis had spent the last fifteen years mastering his skill with the bow, and he knew he could place two arrows almost anywhere he wanted at that distance. He released his breath and let the shaft fly. He didn't even wait to see if his arrow hit its mark, before grabbing the second arrow that was stuck into the ground at his feet. He had that arrow whistling into the night in less than a heartbeat.

Then he was off, running hunched over in the darkness towards his next location. In the darkness he would have missed it if he hadn't spotted the clearing that he had previously patted down. Dropping to his knees he grabbed an arrow and let that shaft fly.

Most of the orcs were frozen in shock, or fear, as they saw two of their comrade's drop to the ground. It wasn't until Tuvallis's third arrow hit its mark that they began to move. Several orcs grabbed their crossbows and began loading them. Others drew their swords, grabbed their shields, and faced the darkness from which the arrows had come, growling and yelling at each other in orcish.

Tuvallis silently thanked the stupidity of orcs as he noticed that the remaining six orcs had remained near the campfire. All they had to do was charge into the darkness and then he would be in trouble. He would be hard pressed to take on six orcs, at night, with just his sword. They could see well in the dark and he could not. The bright fire would hinder their night vision, but provide Tuvallis with just enough light to see.

Tuvallis made it to the first tree when he heard a shout, followed by louder growls. He nocked one of the arrows and quickly leaned out from the tree trunk. He knew he had been spotted as three orcs were running towards him with sword and shield.

He released the shaft and it took the lead orc in the chest, launching it backwards to its death. Tuvallis then spun and grabbed the second arrow, quickly stepping to the other side of the tree and releasing that shaft into another orc who was not more than ten paces away. That beast took the shaft in the throat and went down quickly.

Tuvallis knew that the third orc would be on him in seconds, so he leaped into the brush toward the last tree. In the darkness, however, he did not see the downed log before him. He hit it squarely with his right foot causing him to pitch violently forward while he frantically spun his body to avoid landing on his bow. He spun to his back and tried to get his feet underneath him, but the third orc was already upon him. Tuvallis had a hard time seeing, and he could not pull his long sword from its scabbard from his prone position.

The orc swung its sword down just as Tuvallis kicked out violently with his right foot. He hit the orc solidly in the knee, hyperextending it and causing its swing to veer to the right. The orc's blade spun and glanced off his thigh, inflicting a shallow but painful cut. Luckily the blade had spun in its hand, and most of the contact came from the flat of the weapon and not its edge.

The orc howled in pain and dropped to its good knee where it met Tuvallis's second kick. This time its head snapped back and the beast toppled over while Tuvallis frantically scrambled to his feet and ran toward the last tree.

He got a quick look back and saw two more orcs running to meet him. He knew he would not reach the tree in time so he drew his blade and spun to meet the threat. His leg hurt and he could feel a little blood run down his thigh. But he could still stand. He knew he had better press the attack before his leg gave out on him.

One orc charged through the brush and launched forward with its sword, hoping to catch Tuvallis off guard as he spun to meet them. Tuvallis back stepped and barely got his blade up in time to deflect the orc's weapon.

Then the second orc joined the fray.

The fight was a flurry of shield and sword work. Tuvallis grunted with the effort as he fended off both swords. But the orc on the left was clumsy and lacked skill, so it was there where Tuvallis focused his attacks.

He blocked the orc's sword and moved in toward the beast. The orc thought to put its shield up in defense, but that was just what Tuvallis had hoped. He grabbed the edge of the shield and pivoted to the side, putting the orc between himself and the second beast. Then he yanked the shield sideways and down, causing the orc to stumble forward, completely off balance.

As he expected, the second orc was already in full swing, trying to cut him down while his focus was on his comrade. But Tuvallis's sword was already in motion and a few seconds ahead of the orc. The tip of his longer sword sliced through the surprised orc's throat as its swing was in its downward motion.

The dying orc spun away into the brush as Tuvallis continued his momentum, reversed his swing, and skewered the second orc in the back as it fell to the ground.

Then he felt a sharp pain in his left arm. The force of the blow spun him sideways but he did not fall.

He kept moving and took cover behind a nearby tree. He was panting heavily as he glanced down at his arm. A crossbow bolt had penetrated the fleshy part at the back of his arm, and the nasty black barb punched all the way through to its fletching.

Tuvallis growled away the pain and quickly peeked around the tree to find the last orc standing near the edge of the glade loading a second bolt. Tuvallis looked for one of the deceased orc's shields nearby, when he caught some movement behind the remaining beast.

It was the woman. She slowly stood up on wobbly legs holding an orc short sword in her hand. The beast with the crossbow was so intent on frantically loading its weapon, that it did not notice her behind him.

Tuvallis watched her raise the weapon, stumble forward, and swing the blade with all her might. The sword caught the orc in the neck, driving all the way to the beast's spine. It stumbled forward, trying to yank the weapon free from its mortal wound. But after a few moments the creature stumbled in the dark brush, never to get up again.

And then the woman fell to the ground just behind it.

Tuvallis cautiously stepped from around the tree and scanned the area around the fire. Then he heard some movement to his left and saw the orc that he had kicked in the face slowly regain consciousness. He stabbed the beast through the heart and made his way towards the fire.

The woman was unconscious and lying on the ground. Her tunic was in shreds and it did little to cover her body.

"Well done," he whispered to her, knowing full well that she did not hear him. He looked around to make sure there were no more orcs moving about. Then he gripped the end of the bolt in his arm, and snapped off the tip. He grunted in pain. But he had suffered worse before. He slid the bolt from the wound and dropped the bloody shaft to the ground.

The fire was still burning bright and the remains of a field deer still roasted on a spit flanking it. The smell of the cooked flesh made him salivate. *It could be worse* he thought, *at least I'm still alive with a warm fire and cooked meat.*

After Tuvallis had retrieved his pack he quickly checked on the woman. Once he knew that she didn't have any life threatening injuries, he went about dressing his wounds. His arm was painful, but it wasn't bleeding much. The bolt didn't hit any major veins or arteries. He used the red coals to heat up some water in a tin cup from his pack. Once the water cooled enough he used it to clean his wounds before he packed them both with an herbal healing salve that he had learned to make many years ago. The dark green concoction had an unpleasantly pungent odor, but it did the trick. The cut on his leg required stitching, so he quickly set about his task. In his pack he carried a hooked needle and thread for just such a purpose. It only took him only a few painful seconds to close the wound. It was rough, but it would stop the bleeding. Then he bound both his wounds with clean cotton that he had purchased in Egrin.

After his wounds were seen too, he put more wood on the fire and dragged the orc corpses into the grass so they were out of sight.

He then went to attend to the woman. He rolled her over to get a better look at her wounds. She looked to be about thirty winters, but it was hard to tell. Her body was thin, but well-toned and muscular, typical of a seasoned soldier. Her light brown hair was trimmed to shoulder length. Her features were plain, but not unattractive, rather average by all accounts, but Tuvallis had not seen a woman in some time, and he let his eyes linger for a brief moment on her scantily clad body.

She had suffered a few cuts but it looked as if most of the damage had resulted from fists and boots, as she was covered with dark purple bruises. He also found a large bloody knot on the back of her head that must have caused her unconsciousness. She had obviously been struck with some type of blunt object. Who knows what other wounds she had that Tuvallis could not see. He dressed her wounds with hot water and the stinky salve. Her bruised and battered face was covered with dirt and dried blood which he gently cleaned as best he could.

Tuvallis then fished around in his pack until he found his second shirt. It was not very clean and much too big, but it would have to do. He pulled it over her head and cinched it down with her belt. At least she would be covered up when she woke. He then made a soft bed of grass and put his wool blanket down before gently laying her by the warm flames, draping her body with his fur coat. He wouldn't need it if he kept the fire burning hot. Tuvallis knew it was a risk having a bright fire, but he also knew that the chances of having two orc patrols traveling close to each other were pretty minimal.

Then he cut off a large piece of venison with his knife and sat down on a log facing the fire, greedily tearing into the now very overcooked flesh. Fighting always left him famished.

He didn't want to sleep as it was risky with the fire, but his wounds and exhaustion had sapped his strength, weighing down his eyelids until they finally shut.

It was the cold that brought him back from his dreamful sleep. He woke to a dying fire of red embers, and the night chill embraced his body. He figured he had been asleep for a handful of hours based on the size of the dwindling fire.

He glanced at the woman who was still asleep. *Her color looks better*, thought Tuvallis. Her skin was now rosy and he sighed with relief after he touched her forehead and didn't feel any signs of a fever.

Tuvallis was no longer tired so he occupied his time inspecting the orc bodies that he had piled up around the perimeter. They had few good weapons or armor, with the exception of a nice set of chain mail and a short sword. *It must have been the woman's,* thought Tuvallis as they were definitely too small for any of the orcs. He found a few copper pieces that he pocketed, but other than that they carried nothing of value.

He brought the armor and sword back to the campsite and noticed that the woman was just stirring from her sleep. Tuvallis kneeled by her side as she slowly opened her eyes.

She knew something was different as she was still alive and no longer tied up. The comfort of the warm fur over her also made her feel less threatened. But nonetheless, she shuffled her body away from Tuvallis when she saw him, and reached for her sword that was no longer at her side.

"It be all right. I won't be hurtin' ya," Tuvallis said as gently as possible, which for Tuvallis was not easy, as accustomed as he was to speaking harshly and abruptly. And even an attempt at a soft smile would hardly be noticed as his hairy face masked most expressions.

"Who are you?" the woman asked defensively. She struggled to her feet and Tuvallis could tell that she was in pain. *Perhaps she had broken a rib or two*, he thought.

"Me name be Tuvallis, and I'm just a traveler. Those vermin won't be hurtin' ya no more."

"What happened to them?" she asked as she looked around the clearing.

"They died," he said, matter-of-factly.

She stood up a bit straighter, obviously struggling to control her pain, and then looked him over again as if she were reappraising him. "I remember a couple of orcs falling around me and then some commotion. They were getting ready to…," the woman shuddered as she thought about what had almost happened to her.

"I attacked from de darkness with me bow, the rest with sword," Tuvallis replied. "Yer armor and sword are there," Tuvallis indicated to her left. "There be some cooked meat there by de fire. I reckon ya should eat wit yer wounds an' all."

Tuvallis saw the woman look at her weapons, the food, and back at him. Her eyes rested on the bloody bandages on his leg and arm.

"You were hurt," she said.

"I'll be fine." Tuvallis noticed that she had a subtle accent.

"My name is Seli. I'm a Free Legion soldier and I thank you for coming to my aid. You saved me from a most horrible death, and I am in your debt."

Tuvallis just grunted acknowledgement and moved towards the meat to cut her off a piece. He noticed her look down at the tunic she was wearing.

"Yer tunic be torn up a bit. That be all I have," he said as he handed her a piece of meat.

"It will do, thank you," she replied.

"I cleaned yer cuts, but you were beat bad. Do ya feel any broken bones?"

"Hard to tell. My body aches everywhere. I could have a broken rib," she said as she moved her arm about and grimaced from the pain.

"They beat you good. You should rest longer." Tuvallis sat back down with another piece of meat.

"You may be right," Seli said as she dug into the meat, sitting down on Tuvallis's furs. "Do you have any water?"

"Aye," he replied, tossing her his water tin. "Where ya comin' from?"

"I was with a patrol escorting refugees from Cuthaine. We must still be nearby as I was captured last night, and I know we did not travel more than a quarter of the night."

"Has Malbeck attacked Cuthaine?" Tuvallis asked.

Seli looked up from her food and her eyes were moist with tears. "Yes," she said softly. It was obvious to Tuvallis that Seli was upset, but she reined it in quickly. He was a stranger to showing much emotion, and he did not know how to react to her. But he too was a warrior, and he thought he could empathize with her.

"The Free Legion stayed behind…but you wanted to be fightin' with 'em," he said.

Her expression changed to curiosity as she regarded him again. "Are you a soldier?"

"I was, but no more."

"You're right. None of us wanted to go, but we were given orders."

"Not all orders are meant to be followed," Tuvallis said bitterly.

"Strange words for a soldier."

"I told you, I am soldier no more." He left it at that and Seli stared at him for a moment, expecting him to elaborate. But he did not.

"Where ya from? I be hearin' an accent," Tuvallis asked, changing the subject and softening his tone.

"Really? Most do not. I am from Longset. Have you heard of it?"

"No, I can't say I have," Tuvallis replied through a mouthful of meat.

"It is far to the north, past the Mazgar Forest on the shore of Lake Eown."

"I know of de forest, but not beyond."

"Well most don't. What brings you out here?"

Tuvallis shrugged nonchalantly. "I'm headin' south, towards Finarth."

"We were heading south as well. May I travel with you until we reach our column? I could use your help, and I'm sure you could use supplies, which we have in plenty."

Tuvallis looked up from his food and gave Seli a nod. "Aye, I'll take ya to yer column." *After all*, he thought, *it wouldn't make sense to save her and then leave her alone, wounded, and barely able to defend herself.*

They sat in silence for a long while as they ate. The meat lacked salt and was overcooked, but the warm meal did them both wonders.

"You don't talk much do you?" Seli asked.

Tuvallis looked up from his meal. "Nah, haven't been round people much."

"Why not?"

Tuvallis was not used to talking with people, and it made him a bit uncomfortable. But there was something about the woman that made him want to talk. Who knows, maybe he had just spent one too many years in his own company, or maybe it was the sense of danger surrounding them. Or maybe it was just that he could see that this simple soldier was actually curious about the man in front of her. He smiled as he actually realized how good it felt to have someone ask about him.

"Been livin' on me own for over fifteen years now," he said softly. Seli didn't say anything as she waited for him to continue. So he did. "I was a soldier in de Tarsinian army many years ago." Tuvallis paused, not sure how to continue.

Seli, sensing his hesitation, probed him with a question. "Did you have a family, Tuvallis?"

Tuvallis paused as he turned to look into the fire, images of his wife and children flashing by in his head. "Aye," he said finally. "I had a wife and three little ones. But I have them no more."

"Will you tell me what happened?" she asked gently.

Again, Tuvallis wondered why he was talking to this complete stranger. She seemed sincere, but he thought maybe it was because he hadn't talked about what had happened to him for so many years, that he was afraid the memories of his family would disappear if he didn't. *Yeah, that was it*, Tuvallis thought. *I need to talk about it*. So he continued. "I was young, second year in the army, but well on me way to bein' a knight. I was very good with weapons and a skilled tracker already. In Tarsis you have to fight in the regular army for four years before dey even considers you to bein' a knight. I didn't see me family much, bein' a soldier and such. We had a small place built in de mountains, two days ride from Tarsis."

"Aren't those barbarian lands?" Seli asked. She had heard that various tribes roamed the mountains around Tarsis. It was rumored that King Kromm himself was a descendant of those massive warriors.

"It is, but they live much deeper in de mountains. So I figured at least." Tuvallis whispered the last few words as his mind drifted to old memories. "We had never had raids that close to Tarsis. I was away, hunting down orc bands that were raiding some of our remote garrisons, when a group of barbarians attacked the eastern settlements. They killed me youngens and I never saw me wife again."

Tuvallis paused and Seli didn't want to interrupt him. But he said nothing as his mind was obviously elsewhere. So she decided to break the silence. "I'm sorry, Tuvallis," she said. It sounded lame and inadequate, but she didn't know what else to say. After all, she was a warrior herself, not accustomed to fits of emotions. She worked with men, and men did not share their emotions often.

Finally Tuvallis looked up at her. His eyes were wet with moisture. "Me captain lost his family in de raid as well."

Seli sensed there was more to the story, so she gently nudged him to continue. "What happened?"

"He led us into de mountains until we came to de first barbarian settlement. Dey were not the ones that raided us. Most of de men were out fightin' de tribe that came from deeper in de mountains, the same one that raided our homes. But it mattered not. We attacked, the anger...was...uncontrollable," Tuvallis whispered as he thought back to that dark night. "I could not keep it in. We killed everyone, women, the old people...children," Tuvallis choked out the last word as he wiped away a tear. "King Kromm never ordered de attack, and when he found out about it, he was furious."

"But you were following orders," Seli said.

"Aye, but we all knew they were unjust. You see, we wanted to attack. We wanted to release that anger, to punish someone for our losses."

Seli could understand that kind of anger, any soldier could. But to slaughter women and children was something beyond her imagination. But then again, if she had children of her own and pictured them lying in the mountain dirt, cut down by heavy barbarian axes, she could begin to understand the big warrior's anger.

"What happened, Tuvallis?"

"The captain was tried and found guilty of murder, given fifty lashes, and banished from de kingdom. Normally it would be a death sentence, but de king understood the anger dat fueled the attack, so he stayed the executioner's axe. It mattered not, Captain Declan killed himself that day. The soldiers and me self received ten lashes and were kicked out of de army."

"But you followed orders," Seli said. It was drilled into all soldiers that orders are to be followed. It was not your place to question your officers. The chain of command was to be followed at all times. She couldn't understand why they would be punished for that.

"If you were ordered to slaughter a wife and her kids because the husband be a spy, would you?"

Seli thought about it and decided that she would not be able to do that. It would not be right. "No," she said softly. "I could not."

"Yet I did…because I wanted to."

"So you ran away into the forest?"

"Yes. I could not live with de guilt. It was wrong. I found me self retreatin' farther and farther away from de pain, the guilt, from people, from anything dat reminded me of me family and what I did. It was not long before I was deep in de mountains living a life of solitude."

"Until now," Seli said with a slight smile.

Tuvallis looked at her again and couldn't help but think that in her own way, she was beautiful. Her smile was genuine and lit up her plain features, making her look sincere and beautiful at the same time. He couldn't help but smile back.

"Aye," he grunted.

"I'm glad, Tuvallis. You saved my life. I know that doesn't bring back your family, and the people you killed, but for me it seems like it's one step closer to redemption."

Tuvallis thought about it. It did feel good to help Seli, and it felt very good to talk about it. Maybe she was right. Maybe that was why he was breaking down the wall of solitude that he had built for so many years. Maybe he needed to restore the balance. "I like that," was all he said as he looked back into the crackling flames.

They awoke the next morning and quickly prepared to depart. Seli could barely stand, and Tuvallis stared at her, momentarily wondering how she would make the trek to find her comrades.

She caught his stare. "I'll be fine. I just need to get my body warmed up," she said to him as she winced trying to lift her arms to stretch.

"You sure nothing is broken?"

"I think maybe some ribs are cracked. And my right arm is swollen and painful," she said as she gently touched her red and obviously swollen forearm.

"They beat ya up bad," Tuvallis said matter-of-factly.

"Yes, but the beating wasn't as bad as what would have happened next. Thank you again for coming to my aid. Not many would have risked it, being so outnumbered."

Tuvallis grunted as he turned and hefted his pack to his broad shoulders.

Seli was able to salvage her shoes, but all she had to wear were her torn leggings and Tuvallis's oversized shirt. The morning air was frigid and she had thought about trying to use one of the orc's cloaks, but it stunk so bad she gave up on that.

Tuvallis had strapped her armor and sword to the back of his pack as she was in no condition to wear it.

He looked at her as she hugged her naked arms to her body for warmth. "You gonna be okay?" he asked.

She smiled. "I'm just cold. Believe it or not I've dealt with worse."

"When was that?"

"Two summers ago. I took a Tulga javelin to the stomach." The Tulgas were a particularly violent tribe that lived in the eastern part of the Sithgarin Desert. "It ripped up my insides good and I was forced to sit in the back of a wagon for a week in temperature that could cook an egg on our armor. I would have died if our captain hadn't had a healing draught. As it was, I barely made the trip back to Cuthaine. And the pain was something that I hope to never experience again. Look at the scar," Seli said as she lifted up her shirt to expose her belly.

Tuvallis had seen the scar when he was cleaning her wounds. It was gruesome alright, not the normal scar one would expect from a javelin wound. The wound was round, puffed out and covered with thick white skin. It looked like a craggy mountain range just to the left of her belly button.

Seli noticed his expression. "I know what you're thinking. How could a javelin cause a scar like that? Well the wound got infected and my flesh began to eat away. By the time I got to a surgeon he could not fix it properly." Seli shuddered briefly. "In Bandris's name I can still smell the rot."

"Enough of this pleasant talk," Tuvallis said with the best smile he could muster. "Let us be on our way." He knew it looked lame, but it felt good to be smiling again.

Two

Allies

Kiln and Borum slowly circled each other. Sweat glistened on their bare torsos and their controlled breathing was the only thing that could be heard in the empty map room that doubled as Kiln's practice hall. It was spacious and void of anything except for a huge oak table near the north wall currently covered with a plethora of maps and other military documents that kept Kiln busy late into the evenings.

Borum was the master-at-arms, the best swordsman in the Finarthian army, the man who trained the elite swordsmen. He was the one who tested anyone worthy of the master mark and he was the only swordsman in Finarth who had the master mark himself since the death of Prince Nelstrom. For that reason he was the only warrior capable of training with Kiln, of raising steel to steel with arguably the finest blade wielder in all of Kraawn.

Borum was past his prime, but so was Kiln if age were the only criteria. Neither of them, however, let age diminish their confidence. The master-at-arms was thin, sinewy, and physically unassuming. His dark leathery skin had seen over fifty summers and the wrinkles around his eyes were testament not only to those many years of hard work under the sun, but also of many years under the visor of a metal helm scanning a battlefield. He had shaved his balding head many years ago and his scalp was smooth in contrast to the wrinkles that lined his face.

Kiln was an anomaly for his age. He moved with the quick step and bounce of a warrior half his age, and his jet black hair had only a few lonely strands of silver that stood out like diamonds in a coal mound. His angular face sported a thin layer of neatly trimmed black hair covering his sharp chin. Silver dusted the beard where it tapered into his side burns and thinly trimmed moustache. Kiln's intense gray blue eyes glowed like the eyes of a winter wolf reflecting the midnight moon. He was a killer, born to wield a sword, and everyone around him could sense it. The strength of his aura permeated his surroundings, leaving no question that he was not to be taken lightly.

They each wore loose cotton leggings and soft leather shoes that barely made a sound as they danced across the cold flat stones. The fight had started some time ago, which was about as long as the first act of a play performed by traveling entertainers. The point of the contest was not necessarily to win, but to work on precision, speed, and to maintain the muscle and lung fitness needed for long intense battles. Each blade master moved as if the weapon were an extension of themselves as they performed the many different positions and movements that had been ingrained in them since their youth when they had first wrapped their small hands around the cold grip of a sword.

But the session had to end at some point, and for as long as they had trained together, it had always been Kiln's blade that finished the contest.

Borum's eyes shone with intensity as he grunted with effort, flicking his blade smoothly and grazing it over Kiln's razor sharp edge as the commander lunged forward.

But it was a ruse, and Borum saw it at the last moment. Kiln was not trying to skewer the master-at-arms, Borum knew that. He was just trying to bait him into taking the seemingly appropriate path to counter the lunge, and Borum's body reacted on instinct just the way Kiln had hoped. As Kiln's blade was deflected down, Borum quickly reversed the direction of his sword by snapping it back towards Kiln, hoping that he was fast enough, but knowing that he was not. Kiln stepped forward so smoothly that Borum didn't even see his feet move. Then the master-at-arms felt an iron grip on the wrist that was holding his sword, ironically the same hand that bore the master mark, and an eye blink later he was flying through the air to land hard on his back. His sword clattered to the floor as Kiln twisted his wrist, pivoting his arm so that the tension felt like it would break at the elbow.

"I thought this was a sword fight," Borum said through gritted teeth.

Kiln flashed a smile and released the man's hand. "It's a fight that started out with swords. I never said it would end that way," Kiln said as he helped Borum to his feet.

"Where did you learn that?" Borum asked as he rubbed his elbow. He was clearly impressed with the throw.

"A Sharneen chief taught it to me many years ago," Kiln replied.

After Kiln had left the service of King Uthrayne Gavinsteal, his longtime friend, he wanted to get as far away from Finarth as he could. So he headed east, trying to distance himself from the pain of seeing the love of his life marry his best friend. He had been reviled by his people for breaking his oath to his land and king. But he did not care. His pain and anger destroyed all common sense. He had to leave. It was then that he found the Sharneen, a fierce people that lived many miles beyond the Sithgarin Desert. He spent a handful of years there, sharing his knowledge of war, and gaining much more in return.

Just then the large oak double doors flew open and a Finarthian knight briskly entered the room. "Sir, I'm sorry to interrupt but I have an urgent message," he said as he banged his fist to his armored chest in salute.

"It is fine, Darius, we were just finishing. What is it?" Kiln asked.

"Sir, dwarves from Dwarf Mount have just arrived."

Kiln looked at the knight with new interest. "Dwarves...how many?"

"A thousand, sir," Darius replied.

"An entire akron? That is good news," Kiln said smiling. It was the best news that he had heard in over a month.

"The king has requested your council immediately," Darius said.

"Very well. Master Borum, if you will excuse me," Kiln said as he reached out and shook the warrior's hand, forearm to hand, the traditional warriors' grip.

"Until next time, Commander," Borum said.

"Sir," Darius said as he turned towards Borum, "the king wishes your attendance as well."

Borum raised his eyebrows questioningly towards Kiln who merely shrugged in reply. "Thank you, Darius," Borum said as he slid a cotton shirt over his sweaty torso. "After you, Commander," he said as he gestured towards the door.

Three dwarves sat at the big oak table with King Baylin. Ballick had just slammed back a goblet of ale and banged it on the table when the door swung open as Kiln and Borum were escorted in.

Ballick's beard was an unruly tangle of amber, but it was his wide crooked nose that directed the eye's attention. It had been broken three times and looked as if it still was. The stout dwarf was wearing shining mithril mail dusted with dirt from the long road.

With him were two other dwarves, seemingly indistinguishable from the other. They were both built like a typical dwarf, but even wider at the shoulders, and their long beards looked just like Ballick's but much lighter, almost blonde. Their armor, too, was of the finest quality and Kiln could make out the glittering flash of an axe blade strapped to each of their broad backs. Strangely, they each wore a thick chain wrapped around their waist.

They stood as Kiln approached them and his eyes couldn't help but stare at their bald heads, atypical for a dwarf. A blue tattoo meandered around their heads like an undulating snake, and Kiln noticed that the snake, if that's what it actually was, was cut into many segments.

He had heard of dwarfs such as these belonging to the Dwarf Mount clan far to the north. They were called Dakeen, warriors tested by deed to be the dwarf king's personal guard. He did not know if the stories he had heard were true, as he had never met a Dakeen dwarf, nor many other dwarves for that matter since they seldom ventured far from their tunnels and precious metals. But Dakeen were even rarer as they never left their king's side. *Until now*, Kiln corrected himself. It was said that any dwarf desiring to be Dakeen, had to venture out on their own and defeat ten powerful opponents, fierce adversaries such as dragons, giants, and demons or other inhabitants from the lower planes. They must be opponents that few would have the courage to face, let alone be able to defeat. All Dakeen had their heads shaven clean and each kill would be marked by a segment of the tattoo. To guarantee the legitimacy of the marks, they were tested magically by the king's wizards, their minds probed for the truth…that was if they were lucky enough to return. The wizards could detect any lie or untruth. The king would then make the final decision whether they were worthy of the title based on their kills. It often took years for these warriors to accomplish such difficult feats, and even if they finally did, and managed to return home, there was no guarantee that all their kills would be considered worthy of Dakeen. Only the king decided this. And it was a rare occasion indeed for a Dakeen to leave his king's side. Yet here were two standing before him.

"Greetings, Togric Master Trader, I am Kiln, commander of the Finarthian forces. This is my master at arms, Captain Borum." Kiln shook hands with the red haired dwarf as did Borum. Togric was the dwarf term for second rank master trader, and Kiln knew that the red bearded dwarf claimed that title from the series of beads that interlaced his beard.

"I see ya be knowin' somethin' bout dwarven rank. That is good. Commander, me name's Ballick, and I bring with me a thousand dwarves eager to stain their steel. At me side is Dakeen Tolvar and Cade, but the name Dakeen gets them both listening as it's impossible to tell who is who, them bein' twins and all."

"Well met," the brothers said in unison.

They all sat down at the table.

"Commander Kiln, Master Ballick arrived just recently," King Baylin said as he sat down. "We need to find accommodations for the men and officers and figure out how they may best fit into our preparations. Captain Borum, I'd like you to help with this task."

"Yes, my King."

"It will be done," Kiln added. "Master Ballick, thank you for coming and we greatly appreciate your support, not to mention the honor of having your king send two of his Dakeen. Was it our scouts that informed you of our need?"

"Aye, they came, but we caught them on the road," Ballick grunted.

"How did you know…," Borum began before King Baylin cut him off with a gesture of his hand.

"Master Borum, Ballick was delivering trade goods to Tarsis when they saw the destruction. They were attacked shortly after by orcs. Everyone was slain except Ballick and the first rank trader…," the king faltered as the name would not come to him.

"Durgen be his name," Ballick said, "and his only son was killed in that raid. He bid me to Dwarf Mount to raise the king's standard while he went after his revenge. I do not know his whereabouts now."

"Your prompt arrival and help is much appreciated, Master Ballick," the king said sincerely.

"King Hammerstriker was eager to dust off his hammer and join in this fight, but his council bid against it. They did not want to leave Dwarf Mount unprotected and kingless. But he sent two of his Dakeen in his stead, and as you appropriately mentioned, that is a great honor," Ballick replied.

"Again, our thanks. We are stretched tight with sleeping quarters but we will do everything in our power to accommodate you," the king said.

"Bah, we are dwarves, we do not need much. A place to lay down for a start, and we have two weeks rations left, three if we stretch it," Ballick replied. "How much time do we have before the vermin arrive?"

"Our scouts have had difficulty getting information back to us," Kiln replied, "but we just received reports that Cuthaine was destroyed three moons ago and Malbeck's army is still there. That puts him three weeks out, but we don't know when he will leave Cuthaine."

"I see. King Baylin, we have marched hard and I'd like to rest my men. Also, we have brought with us engineers and sappers. After viewing your fortifications on the way in, I believe we may be of help," Ballick said with no hint of criticism.

"I know the worth of dwarven engineers and I welcome any help. Kiln, please see to their accommodations and show them around tomorrow," the king ordered.

"Very well. Master Borum here will find a suitable place for your men. I will send a messenger to your room at first light," Kiln said as he stood up. "See to it," he added as he pivoted towards the master at arms. Kiln patted the weapon's master on the arm as he caught the soldier's worried expression. Kiln knew that finding suitable quarters for a thousand dwarves would be no easy feat, but he had confidence in Borum and he winked at him before turning back to the dwarves. "Until the morning," Kiln said to the dwarves as he departed. Each one grunted a response as Kiln turned to the king. "Things are looking up, my King," he said with a slight smile.

"Indeed," the king replied, though no smile cracked his iron visage.

Sure enough, Master Borum was able to find quarters for the dwarves. If it were anyone else, the location he found would not have been suitable, but for the dwarves, it was home. Under the king's inner castle were layers of catacombs, small hallways, and chambers used as wine cellars and for other storage. The tunnels were dug with low ceilings, a head shorter than most men, but to the dwarves it felt spacious. The dwarves didn't know it but Borum had an ulterior motive for housing them there. The king's secret escape route was deep in the catacombs and who better to guard that rear exit than a thousand dwarves. Ballick and the other officers turned some dusty anterooms into sleeping quarters and they stayed in the damp darkness with their men. It was wet, dark, and dusty, but it bothered the sturdy warriors not at all.

The following morning Kiln met with Ballick, and Tooley, his head engineer, a cantankerous old warrior with more scars and age lines on his face than a battle king who had spent the last hundred years in the hot sun. Old scars crossed his cheeks and his skin was so wrinkled that it looked like he was perpetually squinting. Dirty, scraggly, and unruly hair covered most of his face except for his cheeks and eyes. Even his lips were invisible, buried deep in the hairy confines of his mustache and beard. He wore old ill-fitting armor, dented and battle worn, but nonetheless polished to a bright sheen. Hanging from his side was a heavy, and obviously well used, battle hammer.

Kiln, accompanied by his five personal bodyguards, escorted the duo to the front gate to look at the preparations. Everywhere one looked townspeople were busy preparing for the coming siege. Commanders directed soldiers and civilians alike in the endless tasks of making the city defensible. The tension in the air was palpable as the seriousness of their situation became increasingly apparent as the days progressed. The dwarves noticed none of this, however, as their critical eyes scanned the fortifications around them.

As the dwarves looked over the fortifications, they watched the training of the common people, those able to fight, in the empty fields beyond the city gate. It was slow going and not without frustration, but the capable officers led by Lathrin, Third Lance, were turning the thousands of commoners into a decent fighting force. They would never hold their own against a trained akron, but they could now maneuver well, and most could use a shield and sword almost as well as a first year untried recruit.

Scouts had returned the previous day with news that King Oleguard and his brother, Lord Dynure, were massing their armies together again, the second time in sixth months, and they would be leaving Annure in a fortnight. After the battle at the Lindsor Bridge the king had taken his army back to Annure. But they knew that they would be returning. They had taken that time to regroup and resupply their forces. Lord Dynure was the Prince of Ta-Ron, a vassal city to Annure and to the king. Annure was a rich and massive kingdom dominating the lands south of Finarth, and the city itself sprawled along the banks of Lake Lar'Nam. King Gavinsteal of Finarth had called on his neighbors in his time of need, and now, his son, King Baylin, who took the throne after his father's assassination, called on them again. The banner of Annure would soon be flying next to the fist and the rising sun, the symbol of Finarth. Everyone knew that if they did not stand together against this dark force, that they would surely fall individually.

Kiln and the dwarves passed through the inner gate to the bridge that crossed the moat when Tooley's voice halted them.

"Ah, by Moredin's hammer, this will not do," Tooley announced as he stood on the tips of his toes to peer over the bridge rail. The stone bridge was huge, over twenty paces wide and over twice that long.

"What is it?" Kiln asked as he stopped to see what had concerned the dwarf.

Tooley lifted his head up inquisitively. "Commander, have you any contingency plans to drop the bridge?"

"You mean if the enemy gets past the first gate?" Kiln asked.

"Aye, what if?" Tooley asked.

"Standard military procedure is to shut the gate and bombard the enemy with arrows and stones as they bottle neck here. The bridge was made long ago and strengthened by magic. I'm not sure if we could drop it even if we wanted too."

"Phffff," Tooley replied. "Any bridge built can be dropped."

"That would be devastating to the enemy, but we need a way across the moat. If we drop the bridge we will be trapped."

"Floating platforms linked together can be built…a temporary bridge after this one falls."

"How would we fall the bridge?" Kiln asked with interest. It would indeed create chaos and the idea of thousands of the enemy falling to their deaths into the deep moat piqued his interest further.

"We take out the two support columns underneath," Tooley said, his eyes crinkling from the smile hidden by the mass of hair covering his face.

"There are two columns on either side and each one three paces wide. How would we do that?" Kiln asked skeptically.

"That is dwarf work. Do we have yer permission?"

Both dwarfs looked at Kiln expectantly. Kiln hated to think of the magnificent bridge lying at the bottom of the moat, but if it came to that, it certainly beat the destruction of the inner wall and the enemy overrunning them.

"You do. Do we have time for that kind of work?"

"Hmmm, not sure," Tooley grumbled, "but life be nothin' but uncertainty. Let us look at the front gate," he said as he strode past Kiln across the large bridge.

The outer gate was open and beyond the walls were hundreds, if not thousands, of make shift homes and shelters for the refugees that were still pouring into the city. The road that led to the bridge was more or less clear and looked lonely in comparison to what flanked it. Tooley slowly walked around the gate inspecting everything from the woodwork, the giant steel hinges, and even the mechanisms in the gatehouse just inside. People nearby stared curiously at the trio and their armed escort, then returned methodically to their daily tasks. It was a testament to Kiln's reputation that he still elicited stares and a bit of awe from the people of Finarth.

"What of war machines?" Ballick asked as he used his eyes as an engineer to carefully inspect everything around him.

"We have travel catapults and larger rock throwers positioned just inside the inner wall," Kiln replied.

"How many?"

"Twenty two-man catapults and just fewer than ten larger four-man machines."

"What of the projectiles?"

"We have stone, oil jugs, and whistling chains," Kiln said. The whistling chains were two metal balls, each the size of a skull, connected by a length of spiked chain. The projectile had a devastating effect in close quarters as it spun and whistled through the air, shredding the enemy ranks.

"We need fire spears," Tooley announced as he scanned the large crank mechanism used to open and close the gate.

"What are fire spears?" Kiln asked.

"They be large balls, twice the size of me head, covered in thick canvas and soaked in oil. Inside are many metal balls 'bout as big as a boy's hand. The ball is lit and flung into the air by the catapult. As the canvas burns it falls apart, releasing all them balls that fly out and into the enemy ranks.

Kiln smiled. "I'll get my men on this right away. Jarvorium, come here," Kiln addressed the guard that followed him like a shadow.

"I need you to get Master Tooley here anything he needs. He has my permission to begin any work that he deems necessary. Am I understood?"

"Yes, sir," the knight said, slamming his fist into his cuirass in salute.

Just then three horn blasts sounded clearly through the morning air. It was the signal from an approaching pandar, a group of fifty knights, likely a patrol party returning from the north garrison. Pandars were constantly patrolling the northern and eastern borders, moving from garrison to garrison along the main roads, searching for any of Malbeck's scouts. Finarth was protected by two major rivers, the Sithgarin River and the Gildren River, its tributary. There was no way to get to Finarth from the east without crossing one of the two rivers, and the only way to get an army of any size over the rivers was to use the bridges. One was located on the Gildren River and guarded by the Gildren garrison. The other bridge was the Lindsor Bridge and to reach the Lindsor an army coming from the north would have to get past the Tuvell Garrison which guarded yet another bridge on the Tuvell River. Malbeck's army would have to go through one of the two garrisons so the Finarthian scouts were monitoring those locations constantly. Malbeck's scouts would be arriving soon in front of the demon lord's main army, and their presence would signal them all that war would soon be upon them.

"Master Tooley, if you will excuse me I need to see the patrol. If you need anything just ask Jarvorium here," Kiln said.

"Hmmmf," Tooley grunted as he deftly moved his small hands around the gears near the main crank handle that opened the gate, continuing to methodically inspect the machines.

Kiln and the rest of his guards moved towards the main road and the approaching knights. It was early and the sun's rays were low in the sky, enough to reflect off the bouncing lance tips of the approaching knights. As Kiln watched the knights' advance, he glimpsed a lone rider much nearer than the main group, galloping rapidly towards them.

"Commander, a rider," one of his guards said, seeing the rider at the same time.

"I see. He seems in a hurry."

A small crowd of people began to form as they saw Kiln move towards the fast approaching horseman. The rider was close enough now that Kiln could make him out. He wasn't a knight, that much was clear. He wore a long green cloak that flapped in the wind, and his horse was smaller than the typical Finarthian warhorse.

It was a scout, Kiln realized. All pandars were sent out with a trained scout, a tracker, someone who could move about quickly and collect reconnaissance for the pandar's leader. Something must be afoot if the patrol's commander sent the scout ahead.

The horseman road in quickly and pulled in expertly, pivoting the tired horse sideways. Kiln recognized the man. His name was Brogan, a stern looking veteran scout who was well known as being the best tracker in the king's service.

"Commander!" Brogan spat as he finally brought his prancing horse to a stop.

"Calm, Brogan. Take a breath, and then tell me the news," Kiln said.

"Sir, Jonas the cavalier is back. He is with the main column."

Kiln's face lit up with a smile that seemed uncharacteristic to the men around him. They looked at each other wondering if they were seeing the same thing, an actual smile on Kiln's face. But his smile did not disappear. "That is wonderful...have..."

"Sir, I'm sorry. But that is not all. He is sick, sir...unconscious. He has not moved since we found them four nights ago."

"Them? Are Taleen and Fil with them?"

"I did not see another cavalier. But yes, Fil is with him and so are others." Brogan hesitated as if he didn't know how to phrase his next words.

"Spit it out," Kiln snapped, more out of worry for his friend, who by all accounts was seriously hurt.

"Sir, Allindrian the Blade Singer is with him...and...King Kromm of Tarsis, along with the queen and prince and their court wizard," Brogan said. "A dwarf from Dwarf Mount is in their company as well."

Kiln had forgotten Jonas's mission in his excitement in hearing that he had returned. His mission had been to find the King of Tarsis, who, after his city was destroyed by Malbeck, was forced to retreat into the wilderness. Shyann had wanted him to bring the Tarsinian king to Finarth, although no one knew why. It looked like he had succeeded, though at what cost? Taleen was not with them, and that fact did not bode well with Kiln. And Jonas was hurt, unconscious, and for many days it seemed. This was indeed dire news.

"Keegan, alert the castle and tell the chamberlain to have rooms, food, and baths prepared for the Tarsinian royal family and the Blade Singer. Get the healers ready as well," Kiln ordered.

Keegan, a short blocky knight that was part of his personal guard, banged his fist into his metal chest plate and ran off through the open gate.

Kiln swung his eyes back to the tired scout. "Brogan, take leave and get some rest." Kiln looked down the road expectantly as more refugees, attracted by the tension in the air, moved closer to get a better look at the commotion.

***

"How is he?" Kiln asked as he moved to the bedside. Jonas had immediately been moved to a comfortable room in the king's inner castle, along with the Tarsinian royalty and the Blade Singer. The guests had been hastily escorted to their chambers and orders were given to the party that found them to keep their identities unknown. Kiln wanted to find out what had happened before any formal announcement was made. Durgen the dwarf stayed with his friends from Dwarf Mount, while Fil was allowed to stay with Jonas. It was he who Kiln found sitting by Jonas's side.

"No change, Commander," Fil said with a look of utter despair. "I talked with our priests and they do not know what to do. They are afraid that whatever they do may injure him more."

Fil shook his head and sighed deeply. He felt so helpless. He didn't understand what had happened to his friend, and if the high priests didn't know what to do, what could he do?

Kiln pulled up a chair to sit by Jonas's side, opposite Fil. "Tell me now what happened," Kiln said softly. It had been such a mad rush to get everyone inside the castle that Kiln had not yet had time to talk with Fil in any detail.

"Where do you want me to start?" Fil asked.

"For now, just tell me what happened to Jonas."

"As I told the priests, we were in the catacombs underneath the city of Cuthaine. We had used an escape route from the gaming house after the establishment had been attacked by Malbeck's warriors."

"What kind of warriors?" Kiln asked.

"They were mostly orcs, but they were huge, not like any orcs I had ever seen. And there were men as well, blackhearts, as the people of Cuthaine call them," Fil said.

"I'm familiar with the term. As far as the orcs, Lord Kromm said the same. He said they stood as tall as he and much broader. And smarter than their cousins as well," Kiln added as he tried to imagine what they might look like.

"We ended up getting away while Jonas stayed behind to cover our backs. The enemy had dark clerics, or warlocks or something. I am unsure, but magic was used for we were attacked by walking corpses. It was horrible, Commander. They kept coming, but luckily for us we were able to escape down a side tunnel," Fil continued.

"What happened to Jonas?"

"King Kromm was the last one and Jonas told him to leave him. He was supposed to be right behind him but he never came out of that tunnel."

"You just left him!?" Kiln asked, incredulously.

"No. Of course not," Fil replied vehemently. "We would never do that!"

Kiln shook his head wearily. "I know, Fil. I'm sorry, I did not mean that. So what happened when you went back for him?"

"Allindrian said that the opening had closed up completely. It was a stone wall."

"Magic," Kiln hissed angrily.

Fil continued for some time to tell Kiln everything he knew. Kiln had mulled cider brought in along with some smoked meats and cheeses. Finally, after the tale was told, Kiln leaned back in his chair and sighed with frustration.

"So, you found him standing on shattered legs, almost naked, fighting in some underground arena?"

"Yes, basically as you see him now." Jonas no longer had any armor or weapons and they had covered him with loose cotton leggings and a tunic after they found him. The white shroud of Ulren still draped his body and whenever the priests removed it Jonas writhed and moaned as if he were in great pain. Needless to say they did not keep Ulren's shroud off him for long. "We could barely recognize him. And he did not recognize us. He tried to kill us, Kiln," Fil said with astonishment.

"It was not him. Of that you can be sure," Kiln whispered softly. "Dykreel's symbol is magically embedded in his chest, and you can bet that the Forsworn have a tight grasp on him as we speak."

"Can't the priests get that evil thing out of him?"

Kiln shook his head sadly.

"Why hasn't Shyann helped him? What are we going to do?" Fil asked pleadingly.

Fil stared at Kiln, and for the first time he saw a look of uncertainty on the otherwise unwavering face of the warrior. "I don't know," was all he could say.

Everyone was in audience…that is, everyone except Jonas. They were all allowed a day of rest from their long ordeal and now they sat around the large table in King Baylin Gavinsteal's throne room. It was an impressive group.

The dwarves of Dwarf Mount were represented by Master Trader Durgen, Ballick, and both Dakeen warriors.

Kromm, the Tarsinian king, was sitting with his wife, Sorana, and their son, Prince Riker. Addalis, Kromm's court wizard, sat to his left. They had all been given comfortable clothes befitting of royalty, and they now looked nothing like the ragged group that had stumbled into Finarth just a day ago.

Allindrian sat next to Kromm. As a Blade Singer she represented the elves of Mel'un-riam. Word had been sent out many moons ago for help, but the elves from the north had not yet responded. No one was really surprised though. Elves were generally a reclusive race that rarely interacted with the other races of Kraawn. Still, everyone held out hope that some help would arrive from the fair skinned folk.

The Finarthian assembly consisted of King Baylin Gavinsteal, General Ruthalis, General Gandarin, General Kuarin, Commander Kiln, Fil, and Alerion, the Finarthian court wizard. Manlin, high priest to Shyann, was sitting near the king wearing a long simple gray robe. A necklace of bright silver hung from his neck and dangling from the end was a medallion embossed with a beautiful blue and silver oak tree.

"Thank you all for being here," King Gavinsteal began. "I know that many of you have suffered hardships beyond imagination. We are living in a precarious time and a very real threat to our lives is only weeks from our gates. I am asking each and every one to help defend my city with the hope that we can stop Malbeck here, and prevent the foul stain of the Forsworn from spreading death and destruction to the rest of Kraawn. I cannot do it alone, and I think that maybe we have all come together for this very purpose. We need to pool our resources, stand together, and end this here. Let us discuss the most recent events so that we may better plan our course of action. King Kromm, would you mind telling us what has befallen you and your family over the last few months?"

Kromm leaned his giant torso forward and rested his muscled forearms on the solid oak table. His long blonde hair fell loosely behind his shoulders and he wore a simple but elegant crème colored tunic lined with purple and gold. "King Baylin, first I'd like to thank you for your hospitality. As you know, I have no place to call home any longer. Tarsis was destroyed by Malbeck and my people are either dead or scattered with the winds throughout the lands. I, my family, Allindrian, and most of my elite guard escaped. We ran for weeks deeper into the Tundrens, fighting the enemy along the way. We finally broke through the picket lines and I thought that we had a clear path to Cuthaine."

"Lord Kromm, if I may ask," General Ruthalis interjected, "How did Malbeck's army defeat you? Legend of your battle prowess is well known, and, if I may be so bold, it is hard to understand how your city was overrun so quickly."

"It is a fair question, General. We did not even know that Malbeck was beyond our gates. He used some type of magic to send a poisonous mist over our walls. The mist killed every guard throughout the entire city. In one stroke, Malbeck had eliminated thousands of my warriors and defeated the defenses that manned the gate. He had a wizard with him who was able to get inside the castle and open the gates after the guards had been killed. The mist masked all noise, and before we knew it we were being attacked in our beds. It's a miracle that we made it out alive. In fact, we would not have if Allindrian had not warned us in time." Kromm finished with a brief nod of acknowledgment to the Blade Singer.

"I have not heard of such magic before. Are there spells with de power the king speaks of?" Durgen asked, addressing the court wizards.

"I have never heard of a spell with such power," Addalis said, shaking his head in disbelief.

"It is not a spell. It is the Shan Cemar," Alerion announced. Only a few in audience were privy to the fact that Malbeck now had possession of the Shan Cemar. So Alerion told the story of what he knew about the ancient book. That it had been found by one of Malbeck's followers and that it was the magic of the book that had brought Malbeck back from the swirling mists of the Ru'Ach.

"I cannot believe the book is actually real," Addalis whispered softly. As all wizards, he had heard tales of the book throughout his entire life. But he believed they were just that, tales told by those wizards who hoped to access the power of the Shan Cemar.

"Can we defeat such power?" Kromm asked.

Everyone was silent as they digested his words. Could they fight it? That was the question on everyone's minds. Would they simply be fighting a losing battle? What did they have in their arsenal that could withstand the power of the Shan Cemar?

"What about Jonas? Could the power of the cavalier counter the magic of the Shan Cemar?" King Kromm asked.

"Jonas is lost to us," Kiln said softly for the first time. All eyes swung to the commander and it was obvious that he had not gotten much sleep. Jonas's wounds had taken a toll on the commander. He was used to solving problems, to fixing things with his mind, or his sword. But he could do nothing for his friend, and that frustration weighed on Kiln's soul. "We have not found a way to counter Dykreel's poison. So, as of now, we will have to fight this magic without Jonas."

No one said anything, not even Manlin, as no one knew how to heal Jonas. The room was deathly silent for a few moments. Finally Alerion spoke up. "There may be a way to stand against Malbeck and the power of the book. As some of us know, the source that provided me with this knowledge also gave me a riddle, a clue as how to stop the magic of the book and Malbeck himself."

"Please inform our guests of this riddle, Alerion," King Gavinsteal ordered.

"I was told that Malbeck could be stopped by an Ishmian with the blood of Finarth in his veins."

No one said anything as they pondered his words.

"An Ishmian? We dwarves have no such gifts. Does anyone here know of an Ishmian with such power?" Ballick asked. Dwarves were well known for their tough heads and strong constitutions, which gave them certain defenses against charms, fear, and other mental spells. But despite that, there is no record of any dwarf ever being a cognivant, someone gifted with the powers of the mind. Cognivants were extremely rare in all races, but as far as anyone knew, nonexistent in dwarves.

There were a series of glances around the table as those that knew of Jonas's ability looked knowingly at one another.

"Jonas has such gifts," Kiln said. "He is an Ishmian, but I do not see how he could be the cognivant from the riddle. He has no Finarthian blood in him."

King Gavinsteal glanced unnoticed at Alerion. Alerion had information and the King was silently telling him that now was the time to divulge what he knew.

"Commander, Jonas is an Ishmian, but he is not the one spoken of in the riddle," Alerion announced.

"What have you found?" Allindrian asked, speaking up for the first time.

"I have spent the last two weeks researching this riddle. I found hidden away in ancient scrolls some early writings from King Ullis Gavinsteal, the very same man who defeated Malbeck during the great wars." Many eyes glanced up to the huge painting behind the royal dais and the Finarthian throne. The painting covered the entire wall, depicting in detail the scene of King Ullis Gavinsteal slaying Malbeck on the Shadow Plains over a thousand winters ago. "In his youth he had an intimate relationship with the daughter of an ambassador from Mynos."

"How old was he?" asked General Gandarin.

"He was seventeen…before he was crowned king. They had a child together that was kept secret. In fact, the king himself never even knew that she bore his child," Alerion continued.

"So there was a royal bloodline that no one knew about," King Kromm said thoughtfully.

"It would seem so," King Gavinsteal replied.

"Do we know this definitely?" Addalis asked.

"We do. I called the spirit of Larrea, the young woman in question, back from the Ru'Ach. She confirmed her child's birth," Alerion said.

Addalis was impressed. Conjuring people back from the dead took very subtle and precise magic. It was not a simple task. "What else did you find out about her?" he asked.

"The child was sent far away from Mynos to keep her existence secret," Alerion continued as everyone hung on his every word.

"Where to?" Allindrian asked.

"She was sent to Tarsis."

Everyone was silent as they took in his last words. All eyes drifted back to King Kromm, the queen, and the young prince. King Kromm slowly sat back in his chair.

"Are you telling me, Alerion, that there is Finarthian royal blood mixed within the Tarsinian royal family?" Kromm asked incredulously.

"Not exactly," Alerion continued, "The young child, Tamralyn was her name, was sent to the ambassador's cousin who was married to one of the Tarsinian princes. I was told that when she was old enough that she married a commoner. "

"It is my family that you speak of…right Addalis?" Queen Sorana spoke softly, her eyes staring at nothing as she thought back to her family lineage. When Kromm had married Sorana many people were upset. She was a simple commoner, and it was believed that it would weaken the Tarsinian royal bloodline. But Kromm did not care, he fell in love the moment he met her. The queen turned to look at the wizard. "It is my family that carried this blood, and it was I who transferred it to my son."

Everyone looked shocked, including King Kromm.

"That is my assessment, Queen Sorana," Addalis replied with a nod of his head.

"That cannot be!" Kromm roared. His outburst was not out of anger, but fright for his son. His son…his son could not be the person to whom the riddle referred, because that would mean that he would have to battle Malbeck. Then he saw hope and he grabbed at is desperately. "But he is not an Ishmian, it could not be him. Are you sure that the lost Finarthian blood line did not get mixed with my family line?"

"Lord Kromm, I thought at first that it must be so…that it must be you. You are a battle king, and rightly it would be you who fought Malbeck. But you are not an Ishmian, isn't that so?" Addalis asked.

"I am not," King Kromm replied slowly. "But neither is my son."

"Lord Kromm, may I speak?" Fil asked tentatively, unsure of the protocol for a common soldier like himself. Fil realized that the only reason he was at the meeting was because of his personal relationship with Jonas and the fact that he had accompanied them on the mission to get the king.

"Of course, Fil," Kromm replied.

"Jonas mentioned something to me once that may be of importance," Fil began, addressing the entire group. "He told me that when he healed King Kromm after the battle with Gould's hounds, that he felt something deep inside the king, like a presence waiting to explode. He couldn't describe it well, but he made it sound like it was a powerful force hidden within him." Fil hesitated as he saw recognition on the king's face. "Is it possible that you are an Ishmian, that you have some power that you are not aware of?" Fil asked the king. The silence in the room was brief, but it seemed to last forever.

"Is this possible, Addalis?" King Baylin asked.

"It is possible, but unlikely. By all accounts, Ishmians manifest their powers at adolescence, and I have never heard of an account where an Ishmian is not even aware of their power once it has surfaced," Addalis said, addressing the group.

"I am not an Ishmian," Kromm said frankly. "The presence that Jonas felt was my sword, Cormathiam. Magic was imbued within the blade when it was created hundreds of years ago. It was given to my great great grandfather by his court wizard, Sakaris, to protect the royal family."

"I did not know that Sakaris created your blade," Addalis said. Sakaris was an uncle to Addalis's great great grandfather. The royal wizards pass on their knowledge to their sons, who carry on the oath to protect the royal family. Sakaris was the greatest wizard in Addalis's family, and many people in Tarsis still hear his name mentioned in poems and sung in ballads. If he indeed created a sentient sword for King Kromm's family, then the weapon would be mighty indeed.

"If you are not an Ishmian, my Lord, then it must be…"

"My son," the queen interrupted. Queen Sorana looked at Riker with tears in her eyes.

"But I am not an Ishmian," Riker said unconvincingly.

Alerion leaned forward in his chair. "Are you sure, Prince Riker?"

Everyone looked at the prince.

"Is there anything that has happened to you recently that might make you think otherwise?" Alerion pressed.

"The lightning bolt," Allindrian interjected softly, thinking back to the attack at Cuthaine. Alerion quickly turned his attention to the Blade Singer as she continued. "He was hit from ten paces by a lightning bolt and suffered no burns."

"You are sure? Who performed the spell?" Alerion asked, leaning forward in excitement.

"Malbeck's wizard. We elves know him as Elthereen, but I believe you call him Gullanin," Allindrian said.

Alerion sat back in his chair and looked at Riker in wonder. "Were you wearing armor, young prince?"

"Yes," Riker answered. "I remember the power of the bolt hitting me hard enough to crush in my armor and fling me backwards to crash into a wall. I was unconscious at that point, and I don't remember much."

"Besides the elven Ekahals, Gullanin is perhaps the most powerful wizard in all of Kraawn. A bolt from him would literally melt a normal man. And your armor should have acted like an oven. You should not be alive," Alerion stated matter-of-factly.

"I too was hit by Gullanin's bolt and lived. What does that prove?" Kromm asked testily.

"You were burned badly, my love," the queen said. "In fact Ulren's priest said that the only damage that Riker suffered was caused by the impact of the bolt, not the bolt itself. He could not understand it either."

"Besides, you are no normal man. Many of your enemies would attest to that," Alerion added. "Not to mention that your sword, if it was made by Sakaris, probably imbues healing properties to its wielder. Is that not so?"

Kromm sighed. "It is."

"What does it mean?" Kiln asked. "Do you think Prince Riker is an Ishmian? Does he have the power to somehow negate magic?" he asked Alerion. Everyone turned their eyes to the wizard.

Alerion did not want to look at King Kromm and Queen Sorana. He knew he would see the sorrow there, the pleading that it not be their son who was placed in this dire situation. But he had no control over fate. Things were falling into place and he was just a pawn in the game. Besides, what *he* thought did not make it so. Riker was, or was not, the Ishmian to destroy Malbeck. What he thought would not change that. So he simply told them what he believed. "Yes, although we cannot be totally sure, I believe that he has that power. We must assume that there is a real probability that Prince Riker is the warrior to face Malbeck."

Kromm dropped his head into his hands and his wife made a barely audible cry. No one said anything for a few moments, and it was Prince Riker who spoke first.

"I do not know if I am the man you speak of, Master Alerion. I am not a tried warrior, and I am not afraid to admit that the thought of facing the Dark One frightens me."

"You will not fight him!" Kromm yelled as he stood up from the table. "I will take your place! You cannot…"

"Father! Please, let me finish," Riker said. No one said a word as Kromm slowly sat back down. "Father, you were fighting battles when you were my age. Jonas fights for his life as we speak and he is no more than four years older than I. Master Durgen has already lost his son in this fight. Taleen perished protecting us from the Malbeck's hounds. Myrell, Kilius, and many others have already died in the fight. We have all suffered, and we must all do our part. I do not know how I can defeat Malbeck. But with all your help, I will try. I will do my part, and if it means that I forfeit my life in the process, then who am I to argue against that same sacrifice that so many others have already made? You taught me, Father, that royalty must earn their right to rule. If I turn my back on this now, then I am not fit to call myself prince."

There was a pall of silence as everyone looked at Prince Riker, stirred by his words and proud to hear them.

"Well said, Prince. You will not be alone. Me son's axe will be by your side," Durgen said as he stood from the table and crossed his thick arms across his barrel chest.

"Elven arrows will also protect you," Allindrian added as she too stood.

Both Dakeen warriors stood in unison and raised their hands, touching the tips of their fingers to their foreheads and bowing slightly. "It would honor us to serve you in this fight," the twins said in unison.

"Finarth will bleed next to you if that is our fate," King Baylin said as he rose.

"Agreed," Kiln replied quickly, standing in one smooth motion.

It was not long before everyone was standing and swearing support and loyalty to the courageous young prince. Everyone except for Kromm, who still had his head buried in his hands, and his wife who held onto him, crying softly.

Three
Unlikely Friends

H agar had been walking for almost two weeks. He didn't really know where he was going, but there was a sense of something guiding him, like a beacon in his mind that was aiming him in the right direction. He knew that he was leaving the mountains, something that he had never done before. The thick forests of the Tundrens had always been his shield, protecting him from the outside world. But not anymore.

Hagar was an ogrillion, half-orc and half-ogre. Ogrillions were very rare; in fact Hagar had never met another like him. He had been cast out to die by his ogre mother and had lived a life of solitude ever since. He was an anomaly for an ogrillion, since he was not inherently evil, as were other ogres and orcs. In fact he didn't like to kill anything, even when he had to eat. He lived a life of loneliness, surviving day to day in the shadows of the Tundren's peaks. But everything had recently changed for the gentle beast. He had been captured by slavers who were scouring the desolate mountain villages that were far away from the protection of King Kromm of Tarsis. The slavers had been taking him and their human cargo to Stonestep to work the diamond mines of Mount Ule, when two cavaliers had saved him as well as the human slaves that accompanied him. Hagar did not know what a cavalier was, but the man's intent was clear, and he could feel that the human meant him no harm. He was a rare beast of compassion, and even though he was not by nature intelligent, he could recognize the good intentions of the young warrior that had freed him from his chains. That same sense of compassion was also apparent in the man's companions and the young human woman who had been freed with him. Hagar was intrigued by her. She did not seem to be afraid of him. He was stirred by how she touched him with apparent trust and affection. She saw him as something other than a blood thirsty beast.

And that was why he had continued to follow them farther into the Tundrens. It had been his instinctive desire to protect his benefactors that had carried him deeper into the mountains, using his keen sense of smell to follow the small group. When he had found them, he did not hesitate to fling himself into danger to protect them, and when he had done so, the giant demon hound had nearly killed him.

That was the last that he had seen of them. He remembered losing consciousness, but after that he could recall nothing. He had awakened to find himself lying in a grassy meadow. He hurt everywhere, and pink scars lined his entire body. The sharp claws of the beast had even found their way through his thick hard skin that covered his body like natural leather armor.

But he was alone in the field, so he did the only thing he could. He walked. He knew that he was venturing into lands where he'd never been because everything looked different. There were no longer any cliffs or huge spires of rock covered in snow. The ground was flat and covered with large glades of trees. It had been a while since he'd last had food, and the scrawny fox he was forced to kill did nothing to curb his appetite. He needed to hunt.

He walked slowly through the dense forest as the rays of the early morning sun burst through the gaps in the branches, creating patches of light within the shadowy forest. A low mist surrounded him, slowly dissipating with the sun's advance. In both hands he carried rocks that were the size of a human head, but in his giant hands they looked like little stones a child might skip across a calm lake. Hagar's need to hunt on his own at a young age spurred him to develop his rock throwing skills. He could hit a running deer at a hundred paces with devastating results. And that was the animal he was now looking for.

An hour later his patience paid off. He had just climbed a gentle rise and stepped over a fallen tree when he spotted a huge deer about fifty paces in front of him. The ground was covered with low lying shrubs, but the large buck easily stood above the foliage. It was the largest deer that Hagar had ever seen. The rack on the animal spanned his considerable arm's width, and its shoulders stood as tall as his own.

It was staring right at him, which made him pause in mid-stride. He didn't want to startle the animal, but he was easily within range and there were no trees or obstructions to avert his throw. Hagar slowly moved his arm backwards, keeping his eye on the animal. It still hadn't moved, so with one quick motion he snapped his powerful arm forward, releasing the deadly missile.

The throw was true, and Hagar was already moving towards the doomed deer. But at the last minute the deer did something impossible. It didn't flee or startle, it simply, and subtly, leaped aside at the last minute, and the stone crashed into a tree behind it.

Hagar skidded to a stop just twenty paces from the animal, who, miraculously, was still staring directly at him. The deer moved slowly to Hagar's right and pawed the ground with its front hooves. Hagar eased his left arm back, knowing that he could not miss at this distance.

Just as he was ready to throw the second stone, the deer pawed the ground again. The simple movement directed Hagar's eyes to the ground at the animal's feet. Metal glinted there, and he momentarily forgot about the deer as he stepped closer to get a better look. Behind a fallen log was a large silver breast plate with shoulder guards and what looked like a huge club. He had seen a similar breast plate on the cavalier, but he had never seen a weapon like this. The handle was long and polished, and the round metal head was covered in deadly spikes. He stepped closer and noticed the objects glittering in the morning sun's rays. He could not tear his eyes away from these magnificent items. As he stood admiring the incredible weapon and breast plate, he noticed that the deer was no longer there.

Hagar reached down and lifted the breast plate from the ground. His body was immediately flooded with warmth, and his hunger disappeared, replaced by a wave of contentment. Somehow he knew how to put it on, and that it would fit him perfectly.

He slid it over his head and cinched the leather straps tight on the sides. The armor fit his massively muscled body perfectly. Embossed in the center of the breast plate was the head of a deer sporting a set of majestic antlers. Above the head was a four pointed star shining rays down upon the stag. Hagar did not know the significance of the symbols, but he somehow knew that it had been placed in the clearing for him to take.

He reached down and wrapped his large knobby hand around the handle of the weapon. It felt warm to the touch, and even though the head of the weapon was twice the size as the stones he threw, he could lift it easily with one hand. The weapon was as tall as a man, its handle polished steel, light as wood, with a two handed grip made of silver wire. Hagar swung the weapon from side to side with one hand, creating a whooshing sound as the huge spiked head displaced the air around it.

Hagar smiled, amazed by the knowledge that he somehow knew that the weapon had been made for him. They were miraculous gifts, but he did not yet understand their significance. As he thought about their purpose his mind was flooded with images. He saw a huge city…he saw men fighting beasts….and most importantly he saw himself, wearing the armor, fighting with the men, scattering orcs with great swings of his mighty weapon.

Then the images disappeared just as quickly as they had come. But now he understood, and with a purpose that he had never before felt, he turned and hurriedly leaped through the trees. He did not know how he knew where he was going, nor did he question it. But he had a purpose, and the purpose felt good. He would get to this city, and he would fight alongside these men, of that he had no doubt.

***

Fil was sitting alone, eating his morning meal in the mess hall. He was tired. He had had been continually checking on Jonas, and the stress of not being able to help his friend was taking its toll. Dark circles surrounded his eyes and he was short of temper. His anxiety for Jonas, combined with the tension that hung in the air, was suffocating the young warrior. Everyone was preparing for the coming attack, and so should he be, but he couldn't. He couldn't think of anything else other than what Jonas was going through. What if his friend never came back from wherever he had lost himself? It was a thought that darkened Fil's already sour mood. Then a familiar voice snapped him out of his dark trance.

"My friend, I'm glad I found you."

Fil looked up and smiled widely, which felt good as he realized that it had been a while since a smile had graced his visage. The last few weeks had been filled with so many trials and tribulations, combined with Jonas's recent fate an aura of melancholy had been following Fil for some time now. Standing next to him was Calden, his friend from the knight apprentices. Calden had been their team leader when he and Jonas had joined the knight apprenticeship. He was a good leader, and a good friend, and Fil was very happy to see him.

"Calden, it is good to see you," Fil said as he set his spoon down and stood up to greet his friend.

"And you," Calden replied as they shook hands. "I was told I could find you here. Do you mind?" Calden asked, indicating the seat next to him.

"Please, join me."

Calden sat down. "I'm glad you are well. We have heard lots of rumors and I'm not sure what is true and what is not. Is it true that Jonas is here?"

"Yes," Fil said, his expression returning to its former grim look. "But he is not well. He was captured by Dykreel clerics…they did something to him, something that we cannot yet heal."

"Will he live?"

"I do not know."

They were silent for a few moments. "Is it true that you were successful in your mission? I have heard whispers that King Kromm is here."

"It is true…he is here. But what of you? How have you been?" Fil asked, changing the subject.

"Well, since you left not much is new. I'm still with Tanus's infantry. Most of our time is spent preparing the city for the Dark One's arrival. When I joined the military I had no idea that I'd spend more time holding a saw and hammer than a sword."

"You have definitely been busy. I couldn't believe how different the city looked when we came in the other day."

A young page quickly came through the door and made his way to Fil. The boy was maybe thirteen and had a mop of unruly brown hair. "I'm sorry to interrupt, sir, but your presence is required in the cavalier's room. Some new arrivals came in today, elves from Mel'un-riam, and they have requested to see you. The king asked me to inform you to go there immediately."

"Thank you," Fil responded as he stood up quickly, eager to find out the reason for the summons. His interest was piqued as he had no idea why elves would want to see him. Besides, he had never met an elf before, except for Allindrian, and she was only half-elf.

The young page nodded his head and moved off to other tasks.

"I'm sorry, Calden, but I have to go. It was great to see you," Fil said.

"You as well. I hope that Jonas will be okay."

"Me too," Fil said, gripping Calden's shoulder as he quickly moved past him, eager to get to Jonas's room.

Jonas had been given a quiet, comfortable room that normally would be reserved for visiting dignitaries. Fil quickly made his way through the castle halls. He passed several stationed guards who recognized him, letting him through the maze of halls with a curt nod.

Jonas's door was ajar and he quickly entered to find the room full of people. Allindrian and Kiln were both there, as well as King Baylin. But it was the three tall fair skinned elves that gave Fil pause. They weren't really tall, maybe Kiln's height, but their long thin limbs and graceful fingers gave them the appearance of someone much taller. Long blond hair hung well past their shoulders, and their large almond shaped eyes darted towards Fil as he entered.

Instantly Fil's senses were flooded with the smell of the forest, as if damp moss had been rubbed across his nose. It was a pleasant smell, almost intoxicating, with an earthiness reminiscent of a warm spring morning.

The elves wore soft flowing tunics and breeches of brown and green. Long green cloaks draped their shoulders and even the slightest movement sent them fluttering like leaves dancing in the wind. Each wore a hunting knife and a long slightly curved sword at their hip, all gilded with gold and silver.

As they turned to face Fil he saw that they had a similar design on their tunics. A beautiful pattern of interlocking leaves and vines formed a circle around a shining sun. The design was simple, but elegant, with gold and silver embroidery that made it look almost regal.

"Fil, good, we've been waiting for you," King Baylin said as he left Jonas's bedside to greet him. "We have three emissaries here from Mel'un-riam, Ekahals sent by King Ell-Rulnore. They are here to help us defend Finarth...and they said they can help Jonas."

Fil's heart surged with hope as he stepped toward the three elves. There were actually elves here to help, and Ekahals at that, said to be the most powerful wizards in Kraawn. If anyone could help Jonas it would be them. Fil eagerly greeted the elven wizards, "My name is Fil Tanrey and we are most grateful for your help. Jonas deserves it. I don't know what has happened to him, but he is alone somewhere, and more than likely suffering, neither of which he deserves."

The tallest of the three spoke first.

"Greetings, young soldier of Finarth. I am Lor-telliam and my two companions are Sar-gathos and Tel-andorsis. It will not be easy, but we think we can help this young cavalier, and we would be privileged to do so by all accounts."

"What is wrong with him, sir...Lor..."

"*Lor* is my title," the elf said with a subtle smile. It is my Ekahal rank and formal enough for this setting and circumstance."

"I see...thank you, Lor-telliam," Fil said, slightly embarrassed. He had never spoken with full blooded elves, let alone a high ranking Ekahal of the elven court.

"He is lost to our world, Fil Tanrey. The device has corrupted him beyond our repair. If we remove Dykreel's symbol then Jonas will die. If we leave it, and do nothing, then its dark power will eventually find him, and kill him."

Lor-telliam moved closer to Jonas and the other two Ekahals followed. Fil stepped near Kiln, Allindrian, and King Baylin, all of whom were standing on the opposite side of Jonas.

"What do you mean he is lost?" Fil asked. It became apparent to Fil that no one else was asking questions. They were just staring at Fil intently. "Why are you looking at me? What have you done?" Fil asked, concern and frustration edging his voice.

"Fil, friend of Jonas, listen very carefully," Lor-telliam whispered softly, "Jonas does not have much time. He is fighting against the blackness that is trying to overwhelm him, trying to take over his body. He cannot last much longer. We are extremely impressed that he has lasted this long, for it seems a most impossible feat. We cannot remove the device from his body, but we believe that we can permanently contain the magic within it so that it does Jonas no more harm. But we cannot do it while Jonas is lost within himself."

As if on cue, Kiln quickly added, "Fil, someone has to go and find him. And it must be someone that Jonas trusts, someone that he connects with the outside world."

"Will you do this, Fil Tanrey?" Sar-gathos asked, speaking for the first time.

"I will do anything to help Jonas. But what are you asking? How do we do it? How do I find him? It is a journey along a road I do not know," Fil said, his voice revealing the eagerness, doubt, and confusion that all seemed to overwhelm him at once.

"We will guide you, young warrior," Lor-telliam said. "But it will be very dangerous. It is difficult to explain. But try to imagine a long road that connects everyone's energy to the Ru'Ach. When you die, you travel that path, normally a quick journey. But not for Jonas, he is stuck on this road. He cannot fully return to his body, nor can he join his energy with the Ru'Ach, that is unless he gives up and dies. But from what I've learned of this young man, that possibility may be rather remote. You must find Jonas on this road, and bring him back. Your spirit self will be entering a very dark and evil place. You will have to fight through unknown horrors to reach Jonas. If you find him, you must bring him back to the living so that we can contain the darkness and give him *himself* back. But he may be lost already. His mind could be fractured, requiring someone very close to him to pull him out of this dark void."

"I will do anything for him," Fil said emphatically.

"If your spirit dies there, your body will also die, *you* will die, do you understand?" asked Tel-andorsis.

"He would do no less for me. When do I start?" Fil asked.

"Not *I*, Fil, but *we*. I will be going with you," Kiln said.

"And so will I," Allindrian added quickly.

"They agreed as readily as you. It seems that Jonas's actions have garnered him respect beyond his years, for he brings forth devotion that is rarely seen," Sar-gathos said.

"You will understand when you meet him. When shall we begin?" Fil asked eagerly.

Lor-telliam looked at his companions and nodded, "Now. We should wait no longer."

Fil looked at Kiln and Allindrian with a mix of fear and anticipation. They returned his gaze with a look of pure confidence and steadfast will. They gave Fil hope.

"What will I need for this journey?" Fil asked the three elves.

"Nothing," Lor-telliam said. "You are entering a place of nothingness and everything. A place where you can make it what you will. You will not need to sleep, eat, or do anything that you would normally do here, for only your spirit will be making this journey. Your physical body will remain here. If you want armor, all you must do is imagine it. If you have need of a sword, wish it. The possibilities are endless. But remember, you can feel pain, and you can die. So you must be vigilant.

"How do we find him?" Kiln asked.

"Just follow the light," Tel-andorsis replied, "The place you will enter will be dark and it will have begun to take on the appearance of that which Dykreel wishes.

"What can we expect in this place?" Fil asked, still confused and trying to grasp the enormity of what they were about to do.

"We all have a path to the Ru'Ach, each a creation of our own minds," Tel-andorsis continued as he struggled for the words. "Normally this road would be filled with the thoughts and images of the cavalier. But his mind is fragmented and corrupted and what you will see is not of his creation. You will see the images of Dykreel's evil power as its black stain slowly takes over Jonas's mind. The light that you will see is all that is left of Jonas. It needs to be restored, and the stain needs to be stopped. We can do this, but not while Jonas is still lost."

"So what do we do when we find him?" Allindrian asked.

"You must convince Jonas that you are who you say you are, and that you are there to bring him back," Lor-telliam said.

"Convince him? Why would we have to do that? Wouldn't he know us, and know that we came to help him?" Fil asked.

"He may not. You do not know what his condition will be. His mind may not be as you remember it. He may not recognize you. Dykreel will do all that he can to mask your true identity, to make the situation appear different to Jonas than it actually is. It will be very confusing for everyone. This is why we need his trusted friends for this task, or it will not work. When you find him, he must place his hand over this amulet. His touch will link him, and you, to us, and we will bring him back while simultaneously shielding him from the power of the device in his chest. If you are not touching each other while Jonas grips the amulet, then you will be left behind to be swallowed up by the darkness. Your soul will be lost." Lor-telliam paused for a moment to let that sink it. "Do you all understand?"

Fil glanced at Allindrian and Kiln, and without hesitation they nodded their affirmation.

"Let's get on with it," Kiln said, directing his gaze to several servants standing by the door. They left the room and returned promptly, each carrying a cushioned chair. Kiln directed them to place the seats near Jonas's bed.

"Now, please have a seat and we will begin," Lor-telliam directed them.

They did as the elf suggested while Tel-andorsis moved to Jonas's side. His body was still covered by the light blanket of Ulren. Jonas's body was clearly visible through the clear shimmering fabric. Shyann's mark still covered his entire torso, but the pink scars from the horrific wound on his chest marred the otherwise beautiful design. The God Mark on Jonas's forehead was gone and had been replaced by a small metal barbed halo. The barbs of Dykreel's symbol had burrowed into Jonas's skin, holding it in place. Shyann's God Mark underneath had melted away into a messy wound covered in dried blood and scar tissue.

Lor-telliam moved to a side table where there was a jug and several glasses. He reached into his tunic and produced a small pouch. "I am going to give you some bitter tasting tea. It will make you fall asleep quickly," he said as he poured the contents into three glasses and filled them with hot water. "Sar-gathos will place a small necklace around your necks. The stones placed in the necklaces will link the three of you together and will allow us to send you into Jonas's void. You will be disoriented at first but will soon become accustomed to it." The fair skinned elf turned and handed each person a ceramic cup. "Remember, trust only yourselves. And don't forget your hands need to be in contact with each other when Jonas grasps the amulet."

Fil was sitting next to Kiln while Allindrian was opposite of Jonas. Fil glanced nervously at the stoic warrior. Kiln smiled reassuringly. "Don't worry, we will bring him back."

Fil smiled back but he could not subdue the fear he was feeling. The thought of entering some dark hole inside Jonas's mind unnerved him more than he wanted to admit. He took a deep breath and steadied his nerves. His friend was waiting for him and he would not let him down. "I'm ready."

"Good. Here is the amulet, Fil. Don't lose it as it is your key to return," Sar-gathos said as he handed Fil the necklace. It was a simple leather strap with a beautiful turquoise stone set in what looked like a silver dragon's claw. It was very similar to the necklace that they each now wore around their necks.

Tel-andorsis lifted the light cloth off of Jonas and instantly his body began to thrash back and forth, but his arms and legs were lashed to the bed and they held firmly. Jonas's anguished moans pierced Fil's heart, giving him the strength and determination to help his friend.

"Now drink the tea," Lor-telliam said.

Without another word all three drank the bitter brew in one long pull.

An instant warmth flooded Fil's body and immediately his eyes felt heavy and his mind began to drift. The last thing he heard before everything went black was, "Good luck."

***

Suddenly piercing howls and screeches snapped Jonas from his meditation. He was sitting on grass with his legs crossed before him. But it was no ordinary grass. It was black and it had a decaying scent to it. He looked around at his dark and ominous surroundings. Black rock jutted up from the ground all around him and the strange dark grass covered the ground in patches all around the stone. In the distance he could see bigger walls of rock with dark caves that looked like the open maws of fanged dragons. A dull red light lit the horizon casting shadows all around him.

He had no reference of time and space. The last thing he remembered was being in a dark void, sitting casually above a sphere of white light, his inner self. Now he was sitting on black grass in a dark realm not of his making.

The howls sounded closer.

Jonas stood and noticed that he still wore his silver armor and carried his twin blades. Each one glowed with a white light and they hummed in his hands, eager to do what they were made for. He looked behind him and noticed in the distance the mouth of a cave. But this cave was different than the rest. A white light shone brightly inside the mouth, like a beacon of hope, drawing Jonas to it. Maybe that was his inner self. Some part of him knew that he should go there.

So that is where he went.

As Fil's eyes opened he immediately stumbled forward as he tried to gain his bearings. An iron grip grabbed his arm and kept him from falling.

"Your balance will come in a second," Kiln said.

Fil's eyes adjusted to the darkness and saw Kiln in front of him wearing bronze armor made of interlocking bands that glowed as if they were heated from the inside. He carried a long sword in his right hand and the razor sharp edge was lined with a subtle gold light.

Allindrian was there too. Light armor had replaced her ranger's cloak, and it was like no armor he had ever seen. It was made of small leaf-like scales which glowed softly green. She had an arrow nocked and her searching eyes scanned the new terrain.

Fil righted himself quickly and looked around their surroundings. It felt strange, and sounded strange as well, almost like they were under water. Sounds were muffled and the atmosphere had a heavy oppressive feeling. The ground was covered in patches of black grass and most of the land that he could see was scattered with black craggy rocks with large walls of the same material in the distance. It was very dark and the only light came from a distant horizon of soft muted reds.

"Where do we go?" Fil asked.

"We need to find that light," Allindrian replied without looking at them, her vigilant gaze searching their new surroundings for any threats.

Howls erupted in the near distance causing Fil to reach for his sword. But there was no weapon at his hip. He was wearing the same clothes that he had on when the elves sent him to this dark place.

"Arm yourself, we need to move," Kiln said as he turned away from Fil to look for any approaching enemy.

"How do…"

"Just think it," Kiln interrupted.

So he closed his eyes and mentally pictured himself in silver plate armor. He wanted a shield and a short sword as well as a long heavy spear with an eighteen inch silver tip. When he opened his eyes, they were there, and they felt as real as anything else. The armor was light, not nearly as heavy as plate armor should be. Its mirror-like finish should not have been as bright as it was since there was no light to reflect off of it. But it sparkled like fish scales in the summer sun. The long spear he was holding had a wicked razor sharp point. But he held it with ease and the familiar feel of the long weapon gave him more confidence.

"It suits you," Kiln said.

"I hear something," Allindrian said, her tone alerting both warriors to possible danger.

Then they heard a series of screeches followed by strange flapping sounds. Kiln and Fil stood alert with weapons in hand as they looked around them. But it was Allindrian who saw them first.

Her bow came up so fast that neither warrior saw the movement. But they did see the green flash of light as the glowing arrow zipped into the night. They followed the flight and that is when they saw the dark shapes zoom down on them from above. Allindrian's arrow took one in the chest, somersaulting it backwards into the night. She had three more arrows in flight before she yelled, "run!"

Kiln ran for a stand of rocks that would offer them some cover, a series of tall stone structures that might provide some protection from attacks from above. Without thinking, Fil followed on Kiln's heels.

Kiln, hearing flapping just above him, dove forward at the last second. He felt a gust of wind pass over him and in a blink he had rolled and come to his feet.

A beast the size of a man was standing ten paces in front of him blocking the entrance into the stone shelter. It had the body of a man with long arms ending in sharp clawed talons. Its legs bent backwards and it stood on horse-like hooves. Its entire body was the color of dried blood and its deep set eyes bore into Kiln like red embers. Bat-like leather wings were spread wide as the demon growled, exposing yellow fangs as sharp as a hunting cat's. Its head was shaped like that of a dog and its neck was covered in a greasy black mane.

Suddenly a long silver spear slammed into the beast's chest, flinging the monster backwards. Fil then sprinted up to Kiln as the body of the beast evaporated into a mist.

"Nice throw," Kiln said with a smile.

Fil lifted up his hand and his spear appeared there, called back by his will. He returned Kiln's smile as they both ran into the narrow opening created by two tall rock spires.

Allindrian sprinted towards them, firing her bow at the same time, arms and legs synchronized in an incredible blur of speed. Scores of bat demons had fallen to her arrows by the time she made it to the cover of the stones.

"What now?" Fil asked.

"Follow me," she said as she moved past them into the maze created by the many tall rock structures. Black shapes flew above them and their frustrated screeches continued as Allindrian guided them at a slow jog. They continued to scan the top of the rock structures expecting at any moment for a winged beast to come at them. But none did. The openings between the rocks above them were too narrow for their wide wing span. They were safe from the threat above, at least for the time being.

A few moments later they turned a corner and saw a small opening ahead of them. They all stopped abruptly, shocked by what they saw. Standing before them was Jonas, chained against a rock wall, his naked torso covered with slashes of red as if he had been whipped. Ripped and torn breeches covered his legs and his feet were bare and covered with bloody scabs. His face was a mask of sorrow and pain, but it lit up momentarily as he saw them enter the clearing.

"Are you real? Am I dreaming again?" Jonas asked softly, his voice a hoarse whisper.

"Jonas!" Fil said as he ran toward his friend. "What happened?"

"They won, my friend. I could not do it on my own," he said as tears spilled from his eyes. "They beat me. Shyann left me. Everyone left me." Tears were now pouring freely down his cheeks.

Fil grabbed the iron bands wrapped around Jonas's bloody wrists and looked for a way to free him. The solid chain was attached to iron pegs driven into the stone and Fil could find no weakness anywhere.

"I don't like this," Allindrian whispered to Kiln as she nocked another arrow. "It doesn't feel right."

"I agree," Kiln replied. "Fil, back away from Jonas."

Fil turned towards them. "What!" His tone was angry. "Come and help me."

"Yeah, Kiln, come and help me," Jonas whispered. This time his voice had changed. It was menacing and a low rumble, well beyond what a human could make.

Fil slowly turned around just as Jonas's body blurred into the shape of Malbeck himself. None of them knew of course what Malbeck looked like. To them they were gazing upon a hideous demon. His muscled torso was still bare and he looked like he was chiseled out of the very stone around him. But his skin tone was light blue and his hair was short and jet black. The chains were gone as well and that was the last thing that Fil noticed before the form of Malbeck lunged forward and grasped his neck with a clawed hand, his muscular arm lifting him easily off the ground. His spear dropped to the ground as he struggled for air, black talons sinking into his skin on the back of his neck.

Glimmer in the Shadow

It all happened in a blur and even the Blade Singer, who could fire an arrow with lightning speed, held her shot as she did not know the thing's power and speed, afraid that it could successfully use Fil's body as a shield. The clearing was small, but large enough for Allindrian and Kiln to fan out as they flanked the demon.

"Welcome to my new home," it spat as it lifted Fil higher, turning him towards the dangerous ranger, always keeping the struggling warrior between them.

"I don't think so," Kiln said.

"You cannot stop me from taking this young cavalier's mind and body. It is too late," the demon said, his baritone voice reverberating in the close confines of the stone walls.

Fil was struggling so hard to breathe that he momentarily forgot he still had his shield fastened to his arm. He lifted it and slammed the edge of the hardened steel into the demon's neck. The demon roared and stumbled into the rock wall near them.

Allindrian saw her opening and she took it. A glowing green arrow hammered into the demon's right shoulder, forcing it to drop Fil to the ground. The demon roared a second time, simultaneously lifting its left hand and sending crackling blue energy towards Allindrian.

It was close range and even Allindrian was not fast enough to avoid the attack. But she was quick enough to dodge the main bolt and was just grazed by the tracing energy of the shock wave. Rock erupted from the small explosion behind her and she came up rolling and instantly running, trying to shake off the pain from the burns she received on her left arm.

Fil, sitting below the demon, willed his short sword into his hand. In the same instant that the demon released the blue energy, he was jabbing upward with all his might, stabbing the demon in its stomach. The beast's torso was just like a man's and he was wearing black tight breeches made of some unknown animal skin.

The demon saw the attack at the last moment and pivoted slightly, causing the blade to sink into its muscled thigh. With a screech of pain it kicked out and connected solidly with Fil's chest, sending him flying into the air to land in a heap five paces away.

In a blink Kiln had closed the distance, his gold sword flashing left and right so fast that the glowing blade left arcing traces of gold light. Devastating cuts appeared on the demon's right thigh and left bicep forcing it back up against the wall.

Luckily for Allindrian, the demon was a good two heads taller than Kiln, and that height advantage gave the ranger a perfect shot. Her bowstring 'twanged' three times, three flashes of green light closing the short distance almost instantly. One arrow slammed into the demon's right eye, burying itself to the fletching. The second arrow took the beast in its open mouth as it roared in pain. The third arrow slammed solidly into its forehead, and the force of the attack hammered the demon's head into the stone wall, where it slumped to the ground and lay there unmoving. A few seconds later it evaporated into a thinning mist just as the bat-like creatures had.

Fil was struggling to gain his feet when Allindrian came to him and helped him up.

"Are you okay?" she asked with concern.

"Bruised ribs I think. I'm glad I had this armor on or they would be broken for sure," Fil replied as he winced from the movement. "I'll be fine. What was that?"

"I don't know, but it certainly was not Jonas. Remember, everything here is manifested from Dykreel, therefore we can probably expect more surprises like that."

"Let's get moving. I don't like sitting in one spot for too long," Kiln said as he looked up into the dark sky. As if on cue a black shape flapped overhead and screeched a hungry warning.

"Follow me," Allindrian said as she took a path to their right. They continued through the maze of rocks for half an hour before they came to what looked like an opening. From the shelter of the rocks they gazed down at a gradual descent of rolling hills covered with the same black grass. It went on for several miles at least before the rocks jutted up from the ground again.

"What now?" Fil asked.

"Look," Allindrian said as she pointed to the right. Everyone followed her gaze and saw what had caught her eye. It was subtle and barely visible, but off in the distance, deep in the rocks beyond the grassy field, was a soft glowing white light.

"We go there," Kiln said with determination.

It was a significant distance away and the shortest path there was across the open hills. Demons flew overhead circling their prey. But they had no choice. Jonas needed them and that was enough. Without a second thought Kiln ran ahead with Allindrian and Fil close behind him.

***

Jonas leaped back, barely avoiding the pincer-like appendage of the monster attacking him. Simultaneously he whipped his right blade down on the exposed arm, pivoted forward and skewered his left sword into the beast's side. The pincer arm was severed at the elbow, and the howling monster disappeared in a puff of black mist.

He had only ventured several thousand paces before the demons had emerged from the darkness and attacked him without hesitation. He had been frantically fighting them ever since, gaining very little ground towards the white light.

But Jonas didn't care. He had given up the idea that he would be freed from this prison inside himself. But he wouldn't succumb without a fight. He would not bow down to Dykreel and the Forsworn. If they wanted his body then they would have to fight for it. And a fight he was giving them.

Fortunately for him, he did not seem to tire in this place. He could fight on forever unless he was killed. He sensed that if he died here, that his life force would be extinguished forever.

Jonas ran ten more paces before a vicious looking beast erupted from the ground in front of him. Black stone and dirt showered over Jonas, forcing him to cover his eyes and shuffle backward. He heard flapping behind him and knew that something was attacking from the air. Without thinking, he quickly ran towards the beast in front of him and dove between its powerful legs. As he dove, he held both swords out and angled back. The razor sharp blades sliced into the demon's inner thighs as Jonas executed a perfect roll and came up running.

But he didn't get very far before two flying demons landed on the ground before him. Their wings were spread wide and their long arms, ending in deadly talons, blocked all forward movement. Without stopping, Jonas pivoted around and launched a series of attacks on the already injured beast behind him.

The demon was the exact color of the stone that surrounded them...black. It had long powerful legs ending in short feet with thick black talons. Four arms protruded from a squat powerful torso, and its thick neck held up a cone shaped head, two curved horns jutting forward on either side. It looked like the thing had no neck as its giant head just melted into its muscled torso. The thing's mouth was wide and filled with rows of needle-like teeth. Red sunken eyes bore into him and yellow spittle sprinkled the air as the beast hissed at Jonas. Jonas could see two long deep cuts across its legs, but the creature did not seem hampered by them.

Both swords flashed as Jonas again attacked. His first offensive moves were thwarted as the demon moved more quickly than expected for such a bulky creature. It blocked his swords with what looked like thick bony shields that covered two of his forearms, a hard exoskeleton that easily deflected Jonas's attacks.

The strength of the creature's unexpected blocks reverberated through Jonas's swords and into his arms, momentarily stunning him and giving the demon just enough time to swing another arm in a vicious blow that took Jonas on the shoulder. The tremendous strength of the blow flung Jonas sideways, and he cartwheeled through the air, hitting the ground hard about five paces away.

"It doesn't have to be this way," a voice materialized nearby as Jonas struggled to regain his footing. Standing in front of him was a man. He was of average height, with a strong athletic build, his long hair framing a chiseled angular face covered with fresh stubble. He wore simple hunter's clothes, breeches, tunic, and a long cloak. He looked familiar to Jonas. Jonas glanced around him and noticed that the demons were still there, but holding back. "Do you know who I am?" the man asked.

Jonas shook his head as if the answer to the man's question was there, and he was just trying to jostle it loose. He should know, he thought. For some reason he knew that he should know who the man was. Then it came to him in a flood of memories. "You're my father," he said as he lowered his sword tips toward the ground.

"Very good," he said. "I'm glad you have not completely forgotten me."

"I never knew you enough to forget you. What are you doing here?"

"Here?" the man asked as he used his arms to encompass the surroundings. "This is you. Of course I would be a part of you, after all, I am your father."

"But why show yourself now?"

"I don't want you to fight anymore. It is not that bad, Jonas. Look at me. I am whole. I am strong. You do not have to keep fighting. Give in and everything will find a way to work itself out. You have nothing to fear."

"But you are just a memory," Jonas said, hesitantly.

"I am more than that, Jonas. When you were born, they took me. I became something much more, something powerful. Don't you want that? It is better than the alternative."

"Which is what?" Jonas asked as he glanced again at the demons around him. Several more flying beasts had now landed and they had formed a perimeter around him.

"To die...to disappear forever. Surely you would take power over death," the man said as he stepped closer to Jonas. "You and I could be together. We could make up for all the time that we have lost. Doesn't that sound better than eternal death?"

"Yes," Jonas whispered. "It does." Jonas looked into his father's eyes and saw himself reflected there. This was his father, he thought. He had longed to meet him and he was now standing in front of him, offering him something that he had wanted his entire life. His sword tips lowered even further as Jonas looked at his father. He took in every aspect of his face. It was indeed him. He could see his own resemblance looking back at him. Before he didn't care if he died, but now, he felt different. The thought of living a life with his father filled his mind, replacing his resignation with hope.

His mind began to drift as he thought about what his life could have been like if his father had not been taken away. He would have been protected. He and his mother would not have had to struggle to survive on their own, as his father was a great hunter. They would have had plenty of food. His mother would have been loved and taken care of. The townsfolk would not have scorned them because his father would have been there to protect them from the insults and pain. Everything would have been different.

"Just grab my hand, son. I will take you away from all this," the man said as he lifted his hand towards Jonas.

Jonas, in a daze, dropped one of his swords and slowly raised his hand. Their fingertips were almost touching when there was a flash of green light as an arrow slammed into the man's hand, knocking him off balance and sending him spinning away from Jonas.

Jonas snapped out of his trance just in time to see a huge hand capped with wicked black talons snake out of the darkness and strike him hard in the chest. His armor deflected most of the attack, but the impact alone cracked ribs and sent him sprawling to his back.

Jonas reacted quickly, jabbing upward with his one remaining blade just as a huge clawed foot was descending to crush him. The demon howled as Jonas's sword skewered it dead center, causing the demon to jump backwards off of the sharp blade. Jonas scrambled for his dropped sword just as a shining spearhead exploded from the demon's chest, spraying black blood into the air before the beast vanished in a puff.

Jonas didn't have time to savor his luck as more black winged monsters were on him in seconds. But he did get a glimpse of two warriors running to join him, and he wondered if they, too, were figments of his imagination.

Allindrian had decided to take out the man in front of Jonas first. At least she hoped it was Jonas. The scene below them was very strange. A man resembling Jonas was ringed in by a two hand count of those same winged demons. Another monster near Jonas looked eager to tear him apart. The part that didn't seem to fit was the man standing next to Jonas. They were conversing, but it was too far away to hear their words. Something the man said had caused Jonas to drop a blade, which seemed odd to Allindrian. Also, as soon as he did, the demons surrounding him stepped a bit closer. It was subtle, but it appeared to Allindrian that they were getting ready to attack him.

But just to make sure, Allindrian put the first arrow into the man's hand. Instantly she knew he was foe, not friend. The man's head whipped around and red glowing eyes found her instantly.

"Save him!" Allindrian screamed as she followed her shot with two more arrows in quick succession.

But Fil and Kiln did not need her urging for they were already storming down the gentle hill to the flat open field below.

Jonas felt an icy pain slash across his arm as sharp talons raked him. But he managed to spin violently, ripping open the monster's throat with one sword, while deflecting another series of attacks from a second beast. Then he felt a solid strike to his back that knocked the wind from him and launched him straight into a demon in front him. Luckily, Jonas had enough sense to angle his blades point first as he crashed into the creature, piercing its chest and bursting through its back as they both tumbled to the ground in a heap.

Jonas felt severe pain in his chest, and his breathing was becoming difficult. He hastily worked to untangle himself from the dead demon, but sharp pain lanced through his body, making the task difficult. As he struggled to free himself, the demon disintegrated, melting away and leaving Jonas alone and in pain. He had broken a rib or two and he felt a stabbing pain everytime he took a breath.

Suddenly two legs covered in glowing armor stood above him. But they were not there long as the man pivoted and spun, his blade of gold light keeping the hoarding monsters at bay. Jonas recognized the movements. He shook his head and tried to stand, but the best he could do was get up on one knee.

Then a second warrior joined them, but this one wore armor of silver and carried a short sword and shield. A demon was about to pounce on Jonas when the warrior slammed the beast in the side with his shield. The power of the blow sent the beast stumbling and the man hamstringed it quickly with two quick cuts to its legs. The demon fell to the ground and the warrior rammed his blade into the back of the monster's neck.

This man, too, looked familiar to Jonas. Why were they helping him? He searched deep for the memories as he stood on wobbly feet, one hand holding his ribs, as if that would cause the pain to go away.

Meanwhile, the two warriors fought on, protecting Jonas as they moved around him, forming an impregnable wall of will and sharp steel.

Both of Allindrian's arrows had struck the man, or whatever he was, in the chest. He stumbled backwards, screaming in anger, but his scream ended abruptly as he vanished into the same strange mist before he could hit the ground. In the blink of an eye she was racing down the hillock towards her fighting friends.

Once Allindrian had joined them, she put her deadly whistling blade into play, destroying the remaining demons within moments.

Jonas was on one knee, struggling to breath, as the trio turned and approached him. "Who are you?" he said through gritted teeth.

Fil looked at Kiln and Allindrian with concern. Kiln stepped a bit closer. "You don't remember us?" he asked.

Jonas looked confused. "I know I should...I mean you all seem so familiar," he said through struggling breaths.

"Jonas, are you hurt?" Allindrian asked.

"My chest hurts. I can't breathe very well. I think I broke some ribs."

"Jonas, I am your friend. Do you remember me? I knew your mother. We grew up in Manson. You lived in a small stone cottage about a mile out of town," Fil said, trying to get Jonas to remember.

Then howls shattered their conversation and everyone tensed.

"Jonas," Kiln said quickly, "I am Kiln. I trained you. And this is Allindrian, a Blade Singer from the elven forest of Aur-urien. We have come to bring you back, to free you from this prison."

"You can do that?" Jonas asked. There was hope there, and Fil capitalized on it.

"Jonas, you were a cripple when our town was destroyed by boargs. You and I survived together in the mountains. You are my best friend," he said, his voice trembling with emotion.

"We have to hurry!" Allindrian interrupted, "More are coming," she said as she nocked an arrow.

"I think I remember. I was healed, right?"

"Yes, you were. Jonas, we must leave this place. More demons will be upon us," Fil said frantically. His words were followed by more screeches in the night.

"How can we leave?" Jonas asked.

Fil produced the amulet and held it out to Jonas. "All you need to do is touch this."

"That is it?"

Kiln and Allindrian moved closer to Fil, placing their hands on his shoulder. Then they heard it. The flapping of wings and the high pitched screeches and howls were nearly upon them.

"Jonas, hurry, touch the amulet!" Fil yelled.

Jonas reached out and hesitated, his eyes moving back and forth between the three, struggling to remember.

"Jonas! You were hiding in the fireplace when your mother was killed trying to protect you! I found you! We survived together! Now grab the amulet!"

Fil's words had triggered something in Jonas's memory. He reached up and touched the amulet, and the last thing they saw was a bright flash.

Four
Back from the Dead

Light slowly filtered through a dark haze as Jonas opened his eyes for the first time in several weeks. He was momentarily blinded by the brightness, but gentle hands on his arm comforted him. He began to see shapes around him as his eyes adjusted to his new surroundings.

"Jonas, are you okay?" a concerned voice fought through the fog.

It was Fil.

Finally he was able to see more clearly, his bed surrounded by many faces, most he recognized, but a few he did not.

Fil, Kiln, Allindrian, and King Baylin Gavinsteal were standing around him looking anxious, and on the other side of his bed were three elves that Jonas had never met before. He felt strangely numb and his mind was a jumble of images as he struggled to remember what had happened.

"How do you feel?" Allindrian asked.

"Hungry, but good I guess. I feel like I've been in a long nightmare."

"You were," Kiln said, smiling.

The group was momentarily silent as they solemnly realized the length of time Jonas had remained lost to them, as well as to himself, and was thus unaware of all that had transpired after his friends had left Cuthaine

"Bring in some food," the king ordered to several servants standing by the door. "Jonas, I would like you to meet three Ekahals from Mel'un-Riam. They are emissaries from the elven kingdom who have come to help us combat Malbeck. It is they who have saved you. They have brought you back from Dykreel's prison. This is Lor-telliam, Sar-gathos, and Tel-andorsis." King Baylin introduced them from left to right.

Glimmer in the Shadow

He looked at the Ekahals. He had never imagined that he would ever meet elven wizards, for it was rare for them to leave their forest kingdoms far to the northwest. Jonas addressed his fair skinned benefactors, nodding his thanks. "I cannot tell you how grateful I am, not only for your help in saving me, but also for your pledge to aid in the defense of Finarth. But I must be honest, I do not know exactly what has happened. My memories are so elusive and fragmented. Just when I think I have found one, it dissolves into shadow and mist. What has happened?" Jonas asked, directing the question to everyone.

Fil noticed that everyone in the room seemed to be looking at him expectantly, sending a silent message to tell the story. So he took a deep breath and began to tell the tale, beginning with Jonas's capture.

As Fil began his story, food was brought in and Jonas was helped into a sitting position. The aroma of the rich stew and fresh bread and butter caused Jonas to salivate as he suddenly realized how famished he was. He began to eat heartily as Fil continued.

"Jonas, the Dykreel clerics broke your legs at the knees, and your arms at the elbows. It was horrible."

"I remember now," Jonas said between bites, "Did they make me fight?" Jonas vaguely remembered something like an arena as he chewed thoughtfully on a piece of stew soaked bread.

Suddenly Jonas froze as a rush of memories came back to him. Fil glanced nervously at Allindrian, who also looked worried. She was the only one in the room who had been present that terrible night, and the memories of it made her shudder. She knew it would be devastating for Jonas if he recalled those events.

"Jonas, it was not your fault. No one could have withstood their power," Allindrian said as she touched Jonas's shaking arm.

Jonas swallowed his food and looked at her, his eyes filled with anguish. "I killed those men. I remember. I killed anyone they put into the arena...I tried to kill....you," he moaned as visions of that terrible night assaulted him. "Is that why Shyann has deserted me?" Jonas asked, the intense despair in his voice permeating the room and those within it.

"Jonas," Lor-telliam spoke for the first time. "Embedded within your chest is Dykreel's barbed halo, a symbol of evil permeating your very being. It was that symbol which controlled you. It was Dykreel's power that compelled you to fight, that enabled you to stand on broken legs, that forced you to subdue the very essence of who you were. You

86

could not have fought it. No one could have. The fact that it did not immediately consume you is beyond me. The power of your 'self' is what kept you alive long enough for us to save you. Do not blame yourself for actions that were not your own.

"Besides," Allindrian offered, "the men that fought you did so by their own choice. No one made them fight. It was an underground arena where men fought for sport, for money. You were the main attraction and those clerics probably offered a lot of gold to anyone brave enough to fight you. You did not kill those men. Dykreel and their greed did."

Jonas relaxed only a little at their words, recalling the pain and horror of Dykreel's symbol being implanted in his chest. He could not shake the ominous feeling as his mind found the faces of the men he had killed. He sighed and pushed the last of the soup away, no longer hungry, and looked at Fil again. "Go ahead, Fil," he said with resignation, "Tell me the rest."

So Fil continued with the story until he got to the part where they arrived at Finarth. He wasn't sure how to start that part as he himself was still processing what had happened to them. How could he explain where they had gone to find Jonas? It seemed so real that Fil swore he could still smell the place.

"How are King Kromm and his family?" Jonas asked.

"They are well," King Baylin answered. "I'm sure the king will want to see you once you have rested." No one ventured to tell Jonas what they had learned regarding the riddle, and that the 'Ishmian with Finarthian blood' was none other than Prince Riker. They figured that could wait.

"How is Myrell, can I see her soon?" Jonas asked. There was a brief, uncomfortable silence as his friends averted their eyes. Jonas suddenly did not want the answer to his question. "Tell me, Fil. What happened?" Jonas saw the expressions on his friend's faces and he felt a lump rise in his throat.

"Jonas, she did not make it. Neither did Kilius. They both died during the fight in the streets of Cuthaine. I'm sorry," Fil said lamely as his friend hung his head and stared at his hands.

After a few minutes Jonas finally spoke, his voice beginning to break, "I was not there to protect her. Everyone dies around me. I don't know if I can continue this fight," he said through his sobs as he looked up at his friends, his voice barely a whisper. His tear streaked face looked young and vulnerable.

Kiln placed his calloused hand on Jonas's shoulder. "I'm sorry, my friend. No matter what you think and how you feel, your mission was a success. You got the king and his family here despite the terrible forces that fought against you. By all accounts you should not be alive."

"Jonas," Fil said earnestly, "If it hadn't been for you, Myrell and Killius, along with their entire village, would either be dead or forced into slavery. You gave them a choice; I remember, I was there. They chose to come with you. And it was their choice to stand up and fight. You didn't kill them, Malbeck did, and soon his army will be here. We need you, my friend."

Jonas sighed as he fought to control his despair.

Lor-telliam then spoke up, "Young warrior, your sorrow for your friends is understandable, and reveals your noble character and strength of heart. This is a good sign as it confirms that Dykreel's black stain has retreated fully into the talisman in your chest."

"You mean it is still inside me? Why can't you take it out?" Jonas asked, the hint of panic creeping into his voice.

"I'm sorry, but we cannot. It would kill you," Sar-gathos said. "In fact, we believe this to be the reason that your goddess, Shyann, was not able to heal you herself. Jonas, the healing we performed on you was not just magical, it was physical as well. Look at your chest."

Jonas looked down and noticed for the first time a light cream colored cloth draped over his chest like a bandage. It was secured with several strips of cotton wrapped around his body. With Fil's help they easily removed the strips and Jonas slid the cloth off his chest.

He stared with wide eyes at a silver circle, about the size of a child's fist, embedded in his chest, right in the trunk of the oak tree that made up his God Mark. In the center of the circle was a blue stone that swirled with blue and white patterns. Jonas's flesh had fused with the silver, drawing it into his skin as if it welcomed it. The edges of his skin where it had been cut were slightly raised and swollen, dusted with remnants of dried blood. They had indeed performed surgery on him while he was unconscious.

"What is that?" Jonas asked, clearly concerned.

"That is an Al'dun-mera, or a stone of power," Lor-telliam answered. "They are very rare stones, believed to have dropped from the sky, and few can be found in the realms. They have the ability to hold a tremendous amount of power. We embedded this talisman into the barbed halo. Once we magically sealed the Forsworn's power into Dykreel's symbol, we sealed it shut with this talisman. It was very difficult, as it took two of us to contain the power, while Sar-gathos embedded the device in you. The spells imbued into the stone are containment spells, and they will forever keep Dykreel's magic at bay. We also removed Dykreel's symbol from your forehead, and you no longer have a scar there."

"I do not feel her anymore," Jonas whispered softly as he ran his fingers over the edges of the pink scar. When he touched the stone he noticed it felt warm to the touch.

"Jonas," Lor-telliam continued, "we were able to contain the black magic of Dykreel, but there may be unknown side effects. It is possible that the link you shared with Shyann is forever broken because of the symbol that rests in your chest. The containment magic acts as a shield, and as it shields you from Dykreel's magic, it may also shield you from Shyann's. We do not know for sure, but it is a logical assumption."

"Thank you all for your help. I apologize for not appearing more grateful. I feel a bit overwhelmed by everything and weighed down emotionally by our losses. But I am truly grateful nonetheless," Jonas addressed the three Ekahals. He looked down again and traced the edges of the Al'dun-mera. "You have given me a great gift. I will not squander it."

"We know, young warrior. That is why we gave it freely," Lor-telliam replied.

"Thank you," Jonas said once more before turning his gaze to Fil. "Fil, please tell me the rest. How did you free me from my own prison?"

The story went on for some time as Fil told the story of how he, Allindrian, and Kiln went in after him. He told Jonas every detail that he could remember. The oppressive memories of the place had burned themselves into Fil's consciousness, and he retold them quickly, as if to rid them from his mind.

Jonas did not look up once as Fil regurgitated the tale. Finally, after Fil had finished, Jonas looked up, his eyes wet with tears. "Thank you for rescuing me, all of you," Jonas said as he looked at each of his friends. "And thank you again," Jonas said to the three elves, "for giving my friends the chance to save me. I am forever in your debt."

"You were worth saving, friend Jonas," Lor-telliam said, bowing slightly.

Jonas looked back at his friends. "It was my father," Jonas said softly.

They all three looked at each other in confusion. "What do you mean," Kiln asked.

"The man that was talking to me, the man that you shot," Jonas said, nodding to Allindrian, "with your green arrow. It was my father."

"Are you sure?" Allindrian asked.

"Yes, I remember now. He was trying to get me to give up, to surrender my body to the Forsworn. They have him. They have my father's soul."

"I'm so sorry, Jonas," Fil said softly.

There was a long moment of silence before the king finally spoke up. "Jonas, I think that we should let you get some rest. When you have rested and regained your strength, I will send for Manlin to come and see you."

"I think that is a good idea," Jonas said wearily, his voice barely a whisper as the weight of everything he had experienced began to subdue his consciousness. He was so tired, all he could verbalize as his mind began to wander was, "Thank you all...for...saving....me. I would...be....dead." Finally succumbing to exhaustion, Jonas's head drooped to his chest as he fell into a deep sleep.

***

Uthgil sat at a heavy oak table far in the back of the tavern, away from the light of the few oil lamps that had been placed on the tables nearest the crackling fire. The shadows of the dimly lit corner where he sat reached out at him, offering him the darkness he craved. There were only a few patrons in the bar at the time, but Uthgil liked it that way.

It had been two weeks since his attempt to assassinate the warrior general, two weeks since he had felt the intoxicating rush of adrenaline he had experienced while battling an opponent that seemed to be his mirror image, an adversary with skills equal to his own. Finally he had found what he had been looking for, the ultimate challenge. The wait had been difficult. He longed to face the warrior again, to see who would triumph. For Uthgil, defeat was not an option and his desire to defeat this man was a thirst that could not be quenched.

90

He had moved from one small village to another, biding his time, waiting for them all to relax, to let down their guard, to forget about him. He had scouted the castle every night, studying the fortifications, and analyzing the guard configurations. He would be ready soon to make another attempt. Killing someone was easy. But providing a situation where two warriors could face each other in combat without anyone intervening was almost impossible. He had worked out several plans, but they all seemed to end with the possibility of his capture. It seemed impossible to orchestrate the situation that he needed to face the general alone, sword to sword.

As Uthgil sat pondering his predicament, his sixth sense suddenly jolted him alert. His hand quickly found the familiar grip of the crossbow tucked under the folds of his black cloak.

At the same instant the tavern door was flung open and the cold winter wind burst in, causing the small fire to flicker. In the doorway, silhouetted by the moon, stood a dark hooded form. A foul odor of rot and decay accompanied the sudden appearance of this apparition, causing Uthgil to unconsciously pull the cowl of his hood lower over his face. Along with the stench, a wave of oppressive fear inundated the room, and the six patrons in the tavern rose shakily from their seats and retreated in terror back toward the bar.

Uthgil had one hand on the crossbow and another on one of the twin knives sheathed at his hip. He was tense and ready to move, but there was something about this threat that warned him to stay still.

The hooded form limped toward him slowly, intensifying the odor of death and decay. Worse than the nauseating smell, however, was the fog of fear emanating from the creature, for surely it was not human. It was an almost palpable terror that quickly filled the room. The men at the bar were frozen with it. Several near the door worked up the courage to flee into the night, but the others ducked behind the counter or under tables that were as far from the intruder as possible. Even Uthgil felt the intensity of the fear, and his hands began to shake. It took all of his mental strength, which was considerable, to keep still and not bolt over the table and run from the approaching figure.

A soft orange light now draped the phantom revealing the filthy tattered gray robe that covered its body. Its face was heavily hooded and shadowed so the assassin could not determine the creature's identity. But it was not the face that he was staring at; it was the creature's staff. He had seen if before, a staff made of a black wood and polished until it resembled obsidian.

"Why are you bothering me, old man? I will perform the duty for which you paid me, do not fear. I never fail," Uthgil said in the common tongue. The old wizard had frightened him when they first met, a new experience for Uthgil who had never before been frightened of anyone. This was the same wizard who had materialized in his room several months ago, offering a king's ransom to kill Kiln, the warrior general. The wizard had unnerved the assassin, and he now felt that same ominous feeling, but this time it was worse. There was something very different about the wizard and it took all of Uthgil's courage to speak to him as he did.

A slow scratchy cackle came from the man as he slowly lifted his head. Two points of demonic red pulsed in the shadows under the hood. "Old man? I think not, my Sharneen assassin," Gullanin said as he slowly raised a decaying hand and removed his hood.

Uthgil tensed, but managed to control himself and remain still as he stared, frozen with fear and surprise, at the gruesome vision before him. The menacing old wizard he remembered had somehow been transformed into a vile and rotting demonic corpse. The wizard's head was now just a skull with pieces of decaying skin and flesh hanging from it like burnt parchment. Thin patches of greasy hair hung from his scalp and his eye sockets were caves of darkness from which two glowing red orbs stared back at Uthgil, draining him of all courage. Trembling uncontrollably, he had to release his grip on the crossbow as he was afraid he might accidentally pull the trigger.

"What...... hap-p-pened?" Uthgil stammered. He cursed himself for the lack of control that he seemed to have over his body. The wizard emanated a blanket of fear that was suffocating his courage.

"I was given a second chance," the wizard hissed, "immortality, and power. What you see is Gould's gift, Gould's power. I am no longer Gullanin the wizard, I am Gullanin the Lich." The Lich's jaw jerked as it spoke, causing the torn and rotting flesh to break, oozing black and decaying blood. "You have failed me, Uthgil."

Uthgil knew what a Lich was...an undead spell caster who sought to delay death through magical means. They are thought to exist half way between the realms of the living and the dead, enabling them to access the power of the Ru'Ach more easily. And Uthgil had also heard of Gould. He was a western god that was not known in his lands, but when you worked in the shadows like he did one came to know many of the dark deities. "I...did not want to kill him," Uthgil said. "Not yet anyway," he finished hastily as Gullanin's red eyes glowed bright with anger.

"What you want is irrelevant. Kill him, or die a slow death. You have no idea what I'm capable of. I would kill him myself but I would be detected by the king's priests within moments of setting foot on the castle grounds."

Uthgil knew that the Lich would not understand his desire to face the warrior on even terms, so he simply said what he wanted to hear. "It will be done."

"I'm giving you a gift, assassin," the Lich said as he produced a small canvas bag from inside his robe. He tossed it on the table and it landed with a thud next to Uthgil. "In the bag you will find a simple dark mask and a long black stiletto; both are magical tools that will help you in your task. Place the mask on your face and use the dagger to kill your victim. The dagger will then drink your victim's blood, changing your appearance to match that of the person who you have slain. It will disguise your face, body type, and even your clothing. If you succeed you can keep the gift, but if you fail, you will wish for death. Your soul will serve me forever in darkness."

Uthgil said nothing as he stared at the bag. If its contents could do what the Lich said then it would indeed be a valuable weapon.

Gullanin said nothing else as he slowly turned around, dragging his hunched body towards the door. The sound of his feet slowly scraping over the floor was unnerving in the silence.

"We have witnesses," Uthgil said, indicating the patrons that still cowered in the shadows.

"Not anymore," Gullanin said, waving his staff nonchalantly.

As he did so, the men frantically grabbed their throats, suddenly coughing and choking as they fought for the air that had suddenly disappeared. Eyes wide with terror and surprise, their frantic movements grew weaker as they stumbled to their knees, still gagging, before falling to the floor, their struggles silenced by death.

The Lich's gravelly laugh pierced the eerie silence and clawed at the nerves along Uthgil's spine as it stepped into the snowy night. And though Gullanin was shrouded in darkness, Uthgil could still clearly see his red eyes boring into him as he turned to face him one last time before the door slammed shut from some invisible force.

***

Fil and Jonas had been talking for hours, catching up and discussing the recent events. Jonas also had a lot of questions about Malbeck's whereabouts and the city's defenses and Fil did his best to update him. Jonas was regaining his strength quickly, but he was having a difficult time shaking his somber mood.

"Fil, can I tell you something?" Jonas asked.

"Of course, you can tell me anything."

"Well, the night that we were attacked at Cuthaine, Myrell and I...well...we sort of...you know," Jonas stammered, trying to get it out, but not sure exactly how.

"She came to your room didn't she?" Fil asked, knowing that on that night Myrell had been wearing Jonas's night shirt.

"Well, yes."

"That's great, Jonas. You deserve some fun. You can't be 'cavalierish' all the time," Fil laughed. But then he stopped, realizing that his reaction was not very appropriate considering what had happened to Myrell. "I'm sorry, Jonas. I did not mean to make light of your affections for her, nor of Myrell's fate. I was just trying to make you feel better."

"I know, Fil. Do not fret," Jonas added. "Cavalierish? Did you make that up?"

"I did, and I'm quite fond of the term. When you start to get too serious about life that is the word I will use," Fil grinned.

"Perhaps you're right. But I just can't get her out of mind. I can't believe she is dead."

"Jonas, I can't believe that any of us made it out of Cuthaine alive. It was so crazy, for all of us. You know, it was Myrell that actually saved you. Did you know that?" Fil asked, forgetting that Jonas had not yet heard that part of the story.

"What do you mean?" Jonas asked, obviously intrigued.

"When you were taken, everyone was at a loss as to how to find you. We had no idea what had happened to you, or where you might be. So Addalis performed a search spell, but he couldn't do it without something that had belonged to you, an article of clothing or something that you had possessed."

"My shirt…Myrell was wearing my shirt," Jonas said, recalling the memories of that night.

"Exactly. Allindrian had to get your shirt from her body. If that night hadn't happened, we might never have found you," Fil said gravely, suddenly realizing the importance of their liaison. "Your last act together saved your life."

"How was she buried?"

"In honor, with all the other Cuthainian soldiers that died that night," Fil replied.

They both sat for a moment, lost in their own thoughts before Jonas finally broke the silence.

"Fil, do you think I will ever be a cavalier again?"

"What kind of question is that? Of course you will. You are a cavalier," Fil said.

"Fil, I cannot feel her. I cannot call her magic, I have tried. If I can't do that, then I am no longer a cavalier. What will become of me?" Jonas asked.

Fil sighed. "I don't know. Shyann picked you, and there is no reason why she would purposefully abandon you. You want to know what I think?"

"Yes, I do."

"Jonas, no matter what happens, you will always fight for the right side. You will always use your skills to combat evil. If you no longer have Shyann's magic to do that, then so be it. It matters not, it does not change who you are. You are more skilled with the blade than anyone I know except for Kiln and Allindrian. You have your cognivant abilities. You have more talent than most to fight that which opposes us. You still have her mark on your chest. That must mean something."

"I thought of that too," Jonas said as he looked at the beautiful symbol. "But I have no idea how God Marks work. Are they permanent? Can they be taken away if you do something to anger your god?"

"You don't really think you did anything to anger Shyann do you," Fil said incredulously.

"Fil, I killed those men," Jonas said despondently.

"Jonas, I know you feel that way because you can picture them in your mind. But you were free from your body when those acts occurred. It was those Dykreel clerics who orchestrated those acts, not you. By all accounts you fought against their control with more courage and strength than those elven Ekahals thought possible. You could do no more to stop them than a baby could overcome an ogre. Besides, those men were not completely innocent. They were fighting in an underground arena, using blood and death to earn coin. They made the choice to be there, and it was their choice that caused their deaths. Think of it another way. It was Shyann who was not there to help you. If it's anyone's fault, it's hers," Fil dared to say.

Jonas sighed. Just two months ago he would have reacted defensively at Fil for those words. But when it came to the gods, maybe things were not as black and white as Jonas had originally thought. "I don't think she could find me in that temple, Fil. I think it blocked her. I vaguely remember the clerics saying something to that effect."

"That could be what is happening now, with your chest," Fil said. But just as he said this, he wished he hadn't. The expression on Jonas's downfallen face was too hard to bear.

"That means that she will never be able to find me again. I cannot remove the symbol inside me. I will be forever lost to her," Jonas said dejectedly.

"I'm sorry, Jonas. That is a real possibility. Don't forget though, ordinary people fight against the darkness every day. Herders combat thieves who try to take their cattle. Merchants fight against brigands who try to steal their goods. Somewhere a woman is fighting off a rapist even as we speak. The list goes on. And none of them have the power or skills that you have. With or without Shyann, you are a formidable opponent against evil."

Jonas thought about Fil's words and felt ashamed. Fil was right, of course. Good people fought every day with none of his skills. They faced terror with courage as their only weapon and he lay in a king's bed complaining about not having magic from a god. He was a master swordsman, skilled with many weapons, and a cognivant. He should not feel pity for himself and he would not skulk while others faced darkness with nothing. "Thank you, Fil. You are right. When did you get so wise?" Jonas smiled.

"You're skilled with the sword, I am skilled up here," Fil said, as he tapped his head with a smile.

"Thank you, Fil, for everything. I know I would not be here now if it were not for you. There are times when I think that I don't deserve your friendship," Jonas said seriously.

Fil just smiled. "Yes you do, my friend, yes you do."

That same day Jonas was able to talk with Manlin, high priest to Shyann. He had come later in the afternoon upon the king's request. Jonas was still tired but his strength was returning and he was beginning to feel more like his old self.

Manlin pulled up a chair and sat next to Jonas. He was wearing his traditional robes and Shyann's silver oak tree symbol hung from his neck. Jonas noticed the priest looked older. His dark hair was grayer now, and his eyes were red and puffy with fatigue. But the priest smiled warmly and put his hand on Jonas's arm.

"Jonas, it is so good to see you again. We feared that you would not make it this time," Manlin said seriously.

"You and me both, sir."

"I want you to know, Jonas, that I did everything within my power to help you. I feel ashamed that I could not use Shyann's power to heal one of her cavaliers. And to think that three godless elves could make you well. But I cannot deny my joy that they were able to do it. It's a paradox I guess," Manlin said, forcing a smile.

"Sir, I do not fault you. I know you tried and I thank you for your efforts. Did you see what the Ekahals did to me?" Jonas asked.

"Yes, I was here in the room. I have never seen anything like it, and I foresee that I never will. Their magic is beyond me, Jonas. When they were sealing Dykreel's symbol you should have heard it. It was as if the Forsworn were in this very room. The room went black, as dark as night, and there were piercing howls and shrieks of the demons inside you fighting against them. You were thrashing and yelling, and just when I thought that Dykreel himself was going to burst out of you, there was a large clap of sound, almost like thunder, followed by a flash of blue light. That was when Sar-gathos embedded that talisman into you. I have no idea how he did it with all your frantic movements and those horrible sounds assaulting us. But he did, and you are here now. I will admit, Jonas, that I was very frightened and I prayed to Shyann for courage."

"Sir, why do you think I can no longer feel her? Have I offended her?"

"Son, I doubt that is a possibility. I can only guess, as my knowledge of how a cavalier's power is derived is actually quite minimal. As Shyann's priest I have the power to heal mostly, therefore we are limited in our knowledge of how it all works. But my guess is that the symbols in your chest, both Dykreel's and the one that is imprisoning the Forsworn's power, are both acting as shields. If I recall from one of our last conversations, you have actually spoken with Shyann. Is that not so?" Manlin asked.

"Yes sir, on several occasions Shyann has come to me in my dreams."

"You should be proud of that Jonas. I know of no high priest that has actually spoken directly to her. I will admit my envy, young man. I have to admit, it would be a dream of mine to meet the goddess to whom I've devoted my life."

"Sir, I didn't ask for any of it…I…"

Jonas was cut short by a gentle wave of Manlin's arm. "I know, Jonas. Perhaps that is why it is even more vexing. But my petty jealousy is not what is at stake. You are asking me why you cannot feel her anymore. I only brought that up to say this. She would never have come to you as she did and given you her power if you were not worthy. Therefore she would never have purposefully abandoned you after all that has happened. Something is keeping her from you, and it is not her lack of trust in you."

"So I will no longer be her cavalier," Jonas said, posing it as a statement rather than a question.

"I'm not sure. But I know this. You will always be her warrior. You do believe that, don't you?"

"I know I will always fight against the Forsworn."

"Ulren's will, my boy. You are fighting her fight, there is no doubt," Manlin said with a smile. "Jonas, with your permission I would like to try a healing on you while you are now awake and free from Dykreel's influence. I may be able to sense something that I could not before."

"Of course, I would welcome it."

"Very good," Manlin said as he put one hand on Jonas's arm while the other grasped the silver symbol on his neck. Manlin closed his eyes and began to pray.

For most priests, the link to their gods, and thus their power, was through their holy symbols. Their symbols connected them to the source of magic provided to them by their god. Manlin was a high priest capable of healing, detecting evil, and in some cases expelling evil. When he prayed, it felt as if there was a channel open to him where he could load the magic and guide it to a location of his choosing.

But this time it felt different.

Instantly there was a flash of light inside Manlin's mind and he was momentarily blinded. It was painless, but he was startled. He then felt soft warmth and a peacefulness come over him as his mind's eye slowly cleared. He was standing on a grassy hill looking down onto a city nestled amongst smaller hills. It was winter and the tall grass poked up through the snow in patches. But interestingly it was not cold. And standing beside him was Jonas, smiling and looking right at him. They said nothing as a soft voice directed their attention in front and below them.

"Please, sit next to me." They both looked on the down side of the hill and saw a woman, about ten paces away, sitting on the snow and gazing at the city below. Her glossy black hair cascaded down her back and she wore a simple white blouse, gray leather breeches, and black knee high leather boots. The snow might as well have been warm sand as Manlin could feel nothing of its coldness, and apparently neither did Jonas or the woman. Jonas could smell the familiar fragrance of cherry blossoms and smiled warmly.

"Come, Manlin, I think your wish has been granted," Jonas said as he moved down beside the woman. Manlin followed slowly and when he got to the woman's side he looked at her face for the first time. He was stunned by her beauty, but she smiled at him reassuringly.

"My priest, surely you recognize your own goddess?" Shyann said with a smile.

Manlin unconsciously grabbed the symbol around his neck. "Is it really you?" he asked dumbfounded.

"In a sense, it is me, but not my real body. I am far away on another plane of existence. Please, sit with me for a moment. We have some things to discuss."

"I cannot just sit next to you as if you were a common woman," Manlin stammered, unable to fully comprehend that he was actually communicating with the goddess that he had spent his life serving.

Jonas had already sat next to her and he looked at Manlin with a sympathetic smile. He had felt the same way when he first met Shyann, and even now she took his breath away. It was hard to be in her presence and act 'normal'.

"But I am a common woman, surely you know my history," Shyann replied.

"Of course, I do, but...I just don't...how..."

"Would it help if I ordered you to sit?" Shyann interjected with a smile.

"Well, it might...I just..."

"Sit down, Manlin."

And he did. Shyann smiled and turned to look at Jonas, her smile all but disappearing. "Jonas, it does my heart well to see you healed. I have been very worried about you. I'm sorry I could not aid you at Cuthaine. My power was blocked. I'm so sorry I could not stop them from hurting you. I hope you can forgive me?" Shyann's voice was so sincere that tears welled up in Jonas's eyes.

"Of course, my god..."

"Shyann, remember?"

Jonas recalled that she preferred it when he called her by her name. He smiled at the memory, remembering how awkward he had first felt in her presence. "I feel ashamed. I had lost heart. I felt so alone and I felt...well...I felt..."

"Betrayed?" She asked.

Jonas looked down at the ground as the truth of her words stung him. "Yes."

Shyann reached out and touched his chin softly, lifting his face towards her. "Jonas, do not feel ashamed. I can only imagine the pain and suffering that you endured from those clerics. If anyone should feel ashamed it is I. I have sworn to protect you, as you have sworn to serve me. I failed. I could not find you. And," Shyann looked down at the city below, "I cannot feel you now. The only way I could bring you here was through Manlin." She looked back at Jonas and tears streaked her face.

"I have been wondering about that," Jonas said softly.

"Is there anything I can do, my goddess?" Manlin asked.

Shyann turned to face him. "Manlin, you have served me honorably. I am proud to call you a servant of my light. But there is nothing you can do. The web of magic around the symbol in Jonas's chest is so strong that even I can't break it. You have to understand that the power of the Forsworn created those symbols. All three of the dark gods cast their dark power into those talismans, infusing them with webs of magic that are impossible to break without killing Jonas."

"So, I am a cavalier no more," Jonas said softly.

"Yes, Jonas, you can never be a cavalier, and the pain those words cause me just add to the heaviness of my heart for failing you to begin with."

"Perhaps if I would have been stronger, I could have..."

"Jonas, do not speak like that. No one could have withstood what you went through. No one could have fought the Forsworn for that long without help. The Banthras were created in just that way. Six powerful cavaliers were turned into dark monsters, the essence of all they had been crushed from them by the same talisman that now sits in your chest. You didn't succumb to it, Jonas. What you did was no less than a miracle. Your courage and strength of spirit have no equal. I am so proud of who you are and what you've become. You saved King Kromm and brought him and his son to Finarth. It is Prince Riker that is the key to Malbeck's death. He is the Ishmian that is needed to defeat Malbeck." Shyann could see the surprise on Jonas's face. "Don't worry, Jonas. It will all make sense soon. Jonas, what do you see below?"

For the first time Jonas focused intently on the city below. "It is Cuthaine, and it has been sacked." Jonas noticed that much of the city's gate had been destroyed and sections of wall lay in rubble. Inside, the buildings smoldered and Malbeck's entire army had set up camp in and around the city. "Malbeck has taken the city?"

"Yes. He will be marching to Finarth within the month," Shyann said.

"Why wait so long?" Manlin asked.

"I believe he is creating something, something of great power. I can feel it," Shyann replied.

"What can I do against that kind of power? I cannot wield your magic anymore. What am I to do?" Jonas asked, worry and frustration evident in his voice.

"Jonas. You are no longer my cavalier. But I will not leave you powerless. You have served me well and I will not abandon you. You are going to be something else; you are going to be able to do things that no cavalier could. You are going to be a different weapon for me. Do you remember those men that attacked you at Annure?"

"I do. Neither Taleen nor I could detect them."

"Do you remember what Taleen had said about that?"

"She said that there are different shades of evil. That the men that attacked us were not pure evil yet, but normal men who were forced into evil acts due to situations not of their choosing."

"That's right," Shyann said. "It begins slowly...a young homeless child steals bread to feed himself. With no family or support he continues to survive the best he can, stealing, cheating, whatever it takes to survive. Eventually, as years go by and he experiences nothing but hunger and pain, he becomes more callous and bitter. Then one day he resorts to violence to obtain food or money. Those he attacks become the 'others', the 'outsiders' who do not know his pain. The next time he may use a weapon. Then he becomes a murderer who cannot see beyond the suffering that the world has dealt him. Eventually his heart turns gray and that is when the Forsworn swoop in and turn it black. By that time it is too late. We have lost him in the battle."

"I understand," Jonas said.

"Manlin, how many vagrants and homeless people come in to see you?" Shyann asked.

"Many, my goddess. Most of my work is trying to help them in your name."

"How many familiar faces do you see from year to year?" She asked again.

Manlin thought about it. "Hardly any."

"That is because they do not last that long. The strong ones die of starvation. The weak ones go into prostitution, become thieves and bandits, and eventually become the very evil that we fight. Jonas, you are going to be my shadow warrior, my night stalker. You are going to infiltrate the dark corners of Kraawn. You will hunt down these men and women and try to turn them, try to persuade them in a better direction. You are going to attack the part of the Forsworn's network where they are most vulnerable."

"A place that he could not travel as a cavalier. It is brilliant," Manlin said excitedly.

"That's correct. Jonas, don't you see? You may be of more value to the fight in this role than you were as a cavalier. Before your injury, your armor, your weapons, everything about you resonated power and lifted the spirits of the people and gave them the strength to combat evil. Your very presence was needed to fight evil. But now your job is to prevent this evil from happening, from taking root. As a cavalier you could not infiltrate these dark corners. But you can now. You will learn to fight in the shadows so darkness cannot live there. You will now be a warrior who does his work in the shadows of every city, town, and village. You will seek out men and women when they are weak and guide them. You will be one of them. They will see in you a reflection of what they could become.

Jonas thought about all Shyann had said. It made sense, and it was so simple. The irony was that it was the Forsworn who forced Shyann's hand. Their very attack on him may have made him even more dangerous to their cause. He was not yet convinced, but the idea had merit.

"I am, and will always be, your warrior. If you wish this of me, I will do it," Jonas said.

"Jonas, I do not ask for blind obedience. If this does not suit you, then I will release you from your oath to me, and I would know that you would continue to fight against the Forsworn in whatever role you found to your liking. For this to work, you need to believe in it, as I do."

"Jonas, think on it," Manlin said, "As a cavalier you could not go anywhere unnoticed. Your very presence was a target for the Forsworn and their minions. But that would not be the case now. You can move into situations and places and go unnoticed. You will not have to show your hand until you choose to do so."

"You will be my shadow knight, Jonas. What say you?" Shyann asked.

Jonas thought about everything they had both said. The idea was sound, and quite frankly he didn't think he would miss the attention that a cavalier attracted everywhere he went. He had never felt comfortable with it, and now he would not have to worry about it.

"What of my weapons and armor?" Jonas asked, "They were lost when I was captured."

"You will have new ones, befitting a shadow knight of Shyann."

"And Tulari, will I ever see my cavalier steed again?"

"You will indeed, but in a different form. Tulari would attract too much attention. Do not worry, Jonas, Tulari will be yours again," Shyann reassured him.

"I would be honored to serve you in this fashion," Jonas said.

"I am glad to hear it."

"May I ask another question?" Jonas asked.

"Of course."

"The last time we spoke, you said that Ulren and the Forsworn have been known across many worlds, and by many names, for longer than I can imagine, and that at times the darkness had defeated the light." Jonas paused as he thought about his words. "I asked why Ulren would allow that to happen, and you said that he did not have the power. I don't understand that. Can you help me understand that?"

Shyann sighed. "Jonas, you ask a lot."

Jonas smiled. "I've been told that before."

"It is very hard to understand, Jonas, and many of the answers that you seek I cannot give. But I will try to explain what I can. I think you deserve that." Shyann paused to gather her thoughts. "As I said before, there are many worlds, many places, some like our own, and some very different. But they all have one commonality."

"The Ru'Ach?" Jonas questioned.

"Yes. I try to think of it as tendrils of energy that connect everything and everyone across the universe. This energy is invisible to most, but some can see it, can access it."

"Like Ulren and the other gods, and now you?"

"That is so. As a farm girl I was ignorant of the world. Now, because of Ulren, I am connected to this power in a way that I never could have imagined. Jonas, when your body was taken by the Forsworn, the energy within you that makes you *you*, was leaving your body to join the Ru'Ach. You were within these shadow layers when Fil, Kiln, and Allindrian had found you and brought you back. They could only do so because you were still connected to your body. If you had died, the connection between your *self*, and your body, would have been broken, and your energy would have joined the Ru'Ach."

"Everything is so much larger than I thought. I am having a hard time understanding the vastness of which you speak," Manlin muttered to himself, clearly deep in thought.

"Manlin, I have only scratched the surface. But let us go back to your question, Jonas. How could Ulren allow the Forsworn to ever win the fight? To answer this question, you must first know that Ulren is not who you think he is, although I do not yet fully understand his identity myself. Ulren and the other gods are products of something else, not creators in the sense that many view them. Keep in mind that my time as Shyann, the goddess, is but one grain of sand on an endless beach. Ulren's existence may be a hundred grains, or a thousand, I know not, but either way, even his own existence is nothing compared to the vastness of our worlds."

"It is so hard to wrap my mind around," Jonas said.

"It is, and the more I talk, the more confusing it becomes, because there are gaps that I cannot fill. But know this; the Ru'Ach has always been here. I know not how, or by whom, but the power within this vast network fluctuates between worlds, and whoever can control it, can control everything."

"Are you saying that there have been times where evil controlled more of its power?" Manlin interjected.

"Just that, Manlin. Jonas, thoughts are power, literally. Your cognivant power is a reflection of this. You of all people can see this connection, can view, in your mind's eye, the links between all things. The thoughts of every being can bring power to be, and in large enough quantities that can change the world." Shyann paused and looked at Jonas. "Jonas, don't you see it? The gods don't give their powers to others; their power comes from those who believe in them."

"Are you saying that Ulren's power, or the Forsworn's power, or any god's power, fluctuates with, and depends upon the belief of their followers?" Manlin asked in disbelief.

"I am. I cannot tell you how everything came to be. I cannot tell you how the Ru'Ach came to be. But I can tell you that it is the belief of thousands, of millions potentially, that harnesses our powers. The common streams of consciousness create individual rivers of power that only the recipients can harness."

"If that is true, then if people stop believing, the gods will disappear," Jonas added as he began to make some connections.

"And that has happened. Like I said, there are many worlds and there have been many ancient people with their own gods that are no longer, gone from the fabric of the world as beliefs have changed with time," Shyann said.

"So gods can die," Manlin muttered to himself.

"Yes, that is true. But that also means that…"

"…the Forsworn can die," Jonas interjected.

Shyann smiled. "Yes, that is correct. But we can speak of this no longer. I'm afraid that the more I try to answer your questions, the more questions you will have. But do not worry, I am not going anywhere soon." Shyann smiled again and gently touched his hand. "It is time for you to leave. You have both made me proud." Shyann reached out with her other hand and touched Manlin's arm as well.

Light flashed and faded to complete white. Neither could see anything for a few moments until the normal shade of darkness converged on their vision. Manlin realized that his eyes were closed and so he opened them. He was sitting next to Jonas, with his hand resting on Jonas's arm while his other was grasping his silver symbol. Jonas was looking at him with a big smile on his face. It was contagious, and Manlin returned his smile. Within moments they were laughing giddily.

"Jonas, I cannot believe that just happened. Please tell me it was real," Manlin said excitedly.

"Well if it wasn't, I have no idea how that got there," Jonas said, pointing to the middle of the room. Manlin turned around and his eyes grew wide. On a table in the center of the room were an assortment of clothes, weapons, and armor. At first glance Jonas could tell they were nothing like anything he had ever seen.

"She did say you would have new weapons befitting a shadow knight," Manlin said as he stood beside Jonas.

Jonas moved to the table to inspect his new gear. His eyes first caught two familiar looking blades. Their pommels were somewhat like his old blades, but quite different as well. The shape and length was identical to his old deer bone handles, but they were gray and non-descript, lacking the flair of his old swords. He grasped one of the handles and felt the familiar warmth as the magic within it hummed to his touch. He slowly slid the blade from the black scabbard and his eyes grew wide at the stark difference. The blade was completely black, except for the razor sharp edge, which was a dull gray, the same color as the handles. He held the blade out in front of him to test the weight, and they felt exactly the same. He wondered why they lacked the luster of his previous weapons, and just as that thought came to him, the edge of the blade lit up with a glowing blue light that exploded with such brightness that Jonas almost dropped it. He also noticed, engraved on the blade in the same blue light, some writing that appeared to be elvish. Jonas had to take a moment to decipher it.

"Retribution," Manlin said over his shoulder. Instantly the light disappeared, retreating into the black blade. "A fitting blade for a warrior who is supposed to blend into the shadows."

Jonas silently agreed as he looked at the rest of the treasures. There was a long charcoal gray hooded cloak stacked neatly next to black leather boots and gray breeches. None of the clothing had any symbols, markings, or anything that would make them stand out. They simply looked plain, for a lack of a better word.

"Those are not normal clothes, Jonas," Manlin said as he noticed Jonas's look. "They are made to look that way, but I can detect magic flowing from them like a vast river."

"I had a feeling that would be the case," Jonas said as he went to examine some armor and more weapons. There was a breast plate of a design that he had never seen before. He picked it up and examined it more closely. Suddenly the armor flared like the swords had, but this time it didn't last as long. The light came from the center plate, which was made of hardened black leather and reinforced gray steel. Shyann's oak tree symbol flared for a few moments, then it quickly disappeared again, giving it the appearance of just another piece of armor. Jonas smiled; Shyann was full of surprises. The armor was very unique. Though it was made of hardened leather and reinforced metal, there were seams all over it that were clearly chainmail. The armor moved and buckled in his hands and then he understood the design. It would move freely with his body and hamper his movement much less than traditional plate armor. The hardened leather with reinforced steel protected the chest and other vital areas while the chainmail connected everything together, allowing for more movement as the entire cuirass was not one solid piece. He marveled at its construction and noticed that the chainmail sections were also black, like the metal in his sword. The shoulder guards were a dark gray metal, nondescript, just like the metal chest plate that protected his heart and lungs. There were leather wrist guards lined with black steel and black leather gloves that had small plates of the same metal protecting the hand and fingers. Jonas noticed a long hunting knife with a slightly curved blade, and a bandolier that contained four throwing knives with handles wrapped in black leather. A gray leather belt with an iron clasp held two short knives strapped horizontally to the front and back. The one on the front could be drawn with his right hand and the one on the back with his left. The handles were wrapped in black leather and the razor sharp blades were also black. Leaning against the table was an unstrung bow. It was shorter than his previous bow, but the recurve on in made it look just as powerful. A leather quiver of black feathered arrows lay on the table next to the bow. Jonas smiled as he thought about Shyann's words. These were the tools that he would need to fight a new battle, a battle that would take place in the backwoods of rural towns, in the dark streets of cities, and in the shadows of places where a cavalier could not go unnoticed.

Jonas drew the other blade from its scabbard and willed it to light. Instantly blue light flared along the edge and more elven writing materialized along the blade. It read 'redemption', and Jonas smiled as his new purpose became clearer.

***

Tuvallis and Seli were found at midday, two days after her rescue. Traveling had been difficult, as Seli's wounds were deep and any movement caused her pain. And since most of her clothes had been destroyed the night the orcs had captured her, the cold winter air was not making her movement any easier. But she gritted away the discomfort and moved doggedly on toward the Gildren Garrison that guarded the Gildren River Bridge. They had no idea if they would find her patrol before they arrived at the garrison, but they really had no other options. Luckily for them, Captain Hadrick of the Cuthainian Free Legion had been sending out scouts to the front and to the rear of their column. He was worried about more orc patrols, and he was also hoping to find some clues as to Seli's whereabouts. A lone scout had found them and brought them back to the main group.

They had set up camp early that day so that Seli's wounds could be seen to. Most of the refugees were still with them. Only a handful, maybe twenty, had left on their own when Captain Hadrick offered them the opportunity to go to Finarth. Most had chosen the relative comfort and safety of traveling with the soldiers over the uncertainty of venturing into the wilds on their own, with no means of protection. They were not soldiers. They were mostly just farmers, tradesmen, and herders.

Tuvallis was given food and a warm spicy drink as he rested by a blazing fire with Captain Hadrick. He was hungry and the hot concoction did wonders to warm his insides.

"What is dis?" Tuvallis asked.

"We call it Tissani. It's a tea made from the Tissani root and combined with other spices. It's a little bitter, but brings back some life to a tired body," Captain Hadrick replied.

Tuvallis agreed. He could feel a subtle, but definitely rejuvenating energy begin to spread through his body. "So Cuthaine is no more?" Tuvallis asked bluntly.

Hadrick looked up from his Tissani. "It is gone." He paused a few moments before speaking again. "Tuvallis, thank you for rescuing Seli. She is a good soldier."

Tuvallis grunted acknowledgement as he sipped his tea.

"She said you killed all the orcs single handedly, and that you were once a soldier. What you did was impressive for anyone, even the most skilled and highly trained soldier."

"I be better den most," Tuvallis said unabashedly.

"You don't look like a soldier," Hadrick said as his eyes swept over Tuvallis's tattered dirty clothing and his unkempt grimy hair.

"I'm a soldier no longer," Tuvallis said with a tone that told Hadrick not to push the subject.

"Fair enough. What is your plan now?"

"I be goin' to Finarth."

"We too. We would be honored to have you travel with us if you wish it."

Tuvallis drank the last of his Tissani. "Aye, I would."

Hadrick smiled as he caught Tuvallis's eyes dart quickly to the tent where Seli was sleeping. "If you're interested, there is a small creek just north of camp. It's freezing, but refreshing. You can borrow my razor and soap," Hadrick said as he stood and walked towards his tent.

Tuvallis reached up, stroking his long beard. Perhaps it was time to get clean he thought…in more ways than one.

Five
Doppelganger

The war leaders met almost nightly, but this was only the second time when a group this distinguished was present. King Baylin's council table was as full as it had ever been. There was much to discuss, and many people who wanted to be, and should be, involved in the discussions. Every party who would be involved in Finarth's defense was represented at the table. King Olegaurd had arrived with his army from Annure along with his brother, Lord Dynure, the prince of Ta-Ron, vassal city to Annure. The army from Ta-Ron was small in comparison to the Annurian army, but the three thousand warriors were fully equipped and well trained, and they would be a valuable asset.

The three Ekahals sat together, representing the elves from Mel'un-Riam, and the dwarves from Dwarf Mount were represented by Durgen, Ballick, and the two Dakeen warriors. Allindrian sat next to the Ekahals since she was a ranger from their kingdom. All of the demi-humans sat silently, waiting for the meeting to begin.

King Kromm was present along with his son, Prince Riker and his court wizard, Addalis. Sitting next to them were Jonas, Fil, Kiln, King Baylin, and Alerion, his court wizard, along with General Gandarin, Kuarin, and Ruthalis.

"Thank you all for being here," King Baylin Gavinsteal began. "Many of you have traveled long distances, facing many perils to do so. And you will surely face many more in the months to come. Finarth recognizes your sacrifices and we thank you for your swords. Now, let us discuss what we know and what we will be facing. Kiln, if you will." Baylin turned to his commander.

"Our scouts have finally been able to bring some information back to us," Kiln began. "Cuthaine was sacked a week ago and the entire Free Legion was wiped out."

"Any survivors?" Jonas asked.

"We do not know yet," Kiln replied. "But we know that Malbeck's army has not yet left Cuthaine."

Jonas of course already knew this as Shyann had told him as much. But there was no reason for him to speak of his recent dream, at least not yet. Nor was he wearing any of the armor or clothing given to him by Shyann.

"Do we have any idea of their numbers?" King Kromm asked.

"We cannot get exact reports but my scouts think their army is near sixty thousand strong, and that is a conservative estimate," Kiln replied.

Everyone shifted uncomfortably at the weight of Kiln's words.

"And our numbers?" Durgen asked.

"The Finarthian forces have been depleted to twelve thousand. We went from twenty akrons down to twelve. Lord Moredin's attack last year had a devastating impact on our numbers," Kiln said.

"The Dark One's intent I reckon," Ballick said.

"King Olegaurd, how many men did you bring?" Allindrian asked.

"My lady, we too lost men at the Battle of the Lindsor Bridge. My brother has three thousand and I have brought eight thousand. Of those numbers we have three thousand cavalry and five hundred of them are Annurien Knights."

"And we have just over a thousand Finarthian Knights left as well," King Baylin interjected.

"That gives us twenty four thousand trained warriors. How many refugees can fight?" Kromm asked.

"We have been training them as they come, but progress has been slow. We can put another four thousand in the field now, and maybe a thousand more by next month," Kiln replied.

"What are their capabilities?" Kromm asked.

"They will recognize signals. They can march, barely, and they know the basics of formation fighting," Kiln replied.

Everyone was silent as they pictured the refugee fighters facing off against an army of orcs, goblins, and who knew what else. It was not a pleasant thought. Most of the men were too young or too old, and they had very little, if any, military experience.

"Added to those numbers are the thousand fighters from Dwarf Mount. At our very best we can put thirty thousand on the field," King Baylin said.

"What of the female refugees?" Allindrian asked.

Baylin looked at Kiln who shrugged. They barely had the time and resources to train the men, let alone the women. "Blade Singer, we do not have the time to train the women, our resources are too limited."

"How many archers do you have?" Allindrian asked.

"Maybe two thousand," Kiln said.

"Women bleed just as men," Allindrian chastised. "I imagine you have several thousand women who could train to use a bow within three weeks. Give me a hundred female volunteers and I will train them in two weeks. Each one will then train another hundred, and so on. We do not need them to be skilled. With sixty thousand coming at our gates, we just need them to be able to pull the bow back, respond to orders, and aim in the right direction."

"Most will not be able to pull back a longbow, and we do not have the time to help them build up their strength. I suggest we put our energy elsewhere," Kiln countered.

"What about training bows?" Allindrian asked. Typically, young men first learned to use a bow by training with a smaller version of the longbow, one with an easier draw.

"I hadn't thought of that," Kiln admitted.

"How many do we have?" asked King Baylin.

"Several thousand I should think. I will get someone on it right away." She was right of course. When Malbeck's army arrived, the vermin would kill everyone indiscriminately. They had just as much right to fight and defend their homes and families. "It will be done," Kiln added.

"Let us discuss our defenses. When Malbeck leaves Cuthaine we have around three weeks before he arrives here. We can assume that he would head for the Gildren Garrison and try to cross the river there," Kiln said.

"How many men do ye have at de Garrison?" Durgen asked.

"Around two hundred," Kiln replied.

"Not enough to hold it for long. I hope you plan on bringing the bridge down," King Olegaurd said.

"We do. I've already sent engineers," Kiln said.

"If the bridge is so important then don't you think Malbeck will have planned for that?" Fil said, speaking up for the first time. "I mean he must know that the only way to get an army into Finarth is to cross the Gildren River, or pass through the Tuvell Garrison and cross the

Lindsor Bridge on the Sithgarin River. He must have a plan to take one or the other bridge."

"Taking out both bridges traps us as well. Trade will come to a standstill," King Baylin said, "preventing us from obtaining needed supplies."

"It has already, my King," General Ruthalis said.

Everyone thought about the dilemma. Destroying the two bridges would stop Malbeck from getting to Finarth, at least for a while, but it would also trap his armies within the Finarthian lands. And not only would trade halt, but it would also cut off any possible retreat if the tide of battle turned against Finarth. The only other option would be Gandar Pass to the west. But it wouldn't be passable for another month or so. And even then, the refugees would be hard pressed to make that difficult journey through the Tundren Mountains.

"Keep in mind," Allindrian said. "The western passes will be open in less than a month. We can retreat in that direction if we have to."

"That is true. It would be a difficult journey, but it is a viable option if Malbeck forces us to make that call," Kiln said.

"We will not leave Finarth to the Dark One," King Baylin announced, his voice firm with iron resolve.

Kiln nodded his head in acquiescence. "Of course not, Sire."

"How long does it take to march from the Gildren Garrison to the Tuvell Garrison?" Lord Dynure asked.

"It would take about a week and a half for an army of Malbeck's size to reach the southeast garrison," King Baylin said.

"May I offer a suggestion," Lor-telliam interjected.

"Of course," King Baylin responded.

"We are outnumbered by more than two to one. It is a rare tactical advantage to know exactly where an enemy army will be. We know with pretty good certainty that the Dark One will march his army towards the Gildren Garrison. Or he may send an early scouting party to try and take the bridge. Either way, we know where he will be. I suggest we take a few thousand men and march double time to the garrison," Lor-telliam said.

"For what purpose?" Prince Riker asked.

"Toforial lathraine duwana," Lor-telliam said in elven.

"Hide, attack, divert," Allindrian translated.

"I suggest that we do our best to reduce their numbers before they come to these gates. Let us take the attack to them, where we can control the ground and the tactics," Lor-telliam said.

Everyone was silent for a few moments as they digested the Ekahal's words.

"Your reasoning is sound, Lor-telliam," Kiln said. "The garrison is easily defensible and we can still destroy the bridge when we retreat. What do you think, my King?"

"I agree," King Baylin said.

"We will need to travel hard, so I recommend that we take a ludis of Finarthian Knights," Kiln suggested.

"You can count on a thousand of my men as well," Lord Dynure added, as eager as most young men to bloody his sword.

"Sar-gathos will also accompany the war party," Lor-telliam added.

"And meself as well, along with a hundred dwarven fighters," Durgen said.

"I will send Graggis with another ludis of infantry," Kiln stated. "My King, if you will, I would join this fight as I know the garrison better than anyone."

"Very well, Commander," King Baylin agreed. "We will continue to prepare the city. Do not take any unnecessary risks. We will need you all for Finarth's defense. Now, let us look to the immediate problem of destroying Malbeck," King Baylin said as he looked at the young prince. "Many of you were not present when the reason for Jonas's last mission was unraveled. Alerion, if you will please explain it again," the king ordered.

So Alerion explained to everyone the answer to the riddle. It took him several minutes as he explained his research and where it had led him, by necessity a rather abridged version

"So all along Jonas was led to believe that it was King Kromm who was needed, when it was really his son?" King Olegaurd asked.

"Yes, that seems to be the truth of it," Alerion said.

Kromm sat silently, his face a mirror of frustration. It was obvious to all that he was impotently angry about the situation, but what could he do? If his son was this man, then it was his destiny to fight Malbeck.

"I mean no disrespect, Prince," King Olegaurd added, "but I do not see how an untried warrior who just learned he was an Ishmian could defeat Malbeck. It seems an impossible task."

"Untried does not mean unskilled. And he will not be alone," King Kromm said, almost growling out the words.

"I meant no offense," King Olegaurd continued, "but you know as well as I that being taught to fight is much different than actually being a warrior. It is experience that wins battles, and you just hope that you have enough talent to survive enough fights to gain that experience."

"Perhaps I can help," Lor-telliam said. Everyone looked at the elven wizard. "Do you know how King Ullis Gavinsteal was able to defeat Malbeck many centuries ago?"

"He faced him on the battlefield and killed him," King Baylin said, indicating the huge painting behind them. The massive canvas took up most of the wall and it was at least six paces high and ten paces wide. The painting, overall, appeared dark and ominous, with the only light, and thus the focal point, coming from a bright glow emanating from the weapons of the two main combatants. The smaller figure wore shining white and silver armor, and he wielded a long two handed sword, which he was using to strike a massive axe held by the Dark One. Malbeck's form was covered in black plate mail and he stood at least a head taller than the king. At the point where their blades had met there appeared a flash of blue and white light that looked like a star. The expert rendition of it gave one the feeling that that light was about to consume the entire room.

"Yes," Lor-telliam continued, "but he was able to do so because of the sword and armor that he wore. Do you know the history of that armor and sword, which, by the way, is the same sword that you have replicated at your hip?"

"I do not. Some say they were given to my ancestors by the dwarves at Dwarf Mount as a gift. I've heard other stories about them being made by his court wizard, but we do not know the truth of it," Baylin said.

"They were not made by us," Durgen added.

"No, they were not. I made them," Lor-telliam said. "Well, they were forged by Tsillerian Cho Andorin, the same weaponsmith who forged Allindrian's blade. But it was I who imbued them with the power to fight Malbeck."

Everyone stared at the elf, slack jawed.

Jonas's head was swirling with the implications. That meant that the elf was over a thousand years old and that he very well could have been at the battle at the Shadow Plains when Malbeck was originally defeated. Jonas knew that elves lived unusually long lives, but the sheer idea of living a thousand years still shocked him. By the looks on everyone's faces, except for the dwarves, everyone else felt the same way.

"I made those weapons for King Ullis Gavinsteal for the purpose of slaying Malbeck," Lor-telliam continued, " Did you know that Ullis was an Ishmian, Sire?"

"No, there is no record of it," Baylin said with astonishment.

"I imagine not. Most Ishmian's kept their talent hidden, since so little was known about their ability. Ignorant people thought they were warlocks or witches, and many were burned at the stake for having such gifts. Mage magic frightened many people, but inherent magic could not be explained, and caused even more fear. Ullis had the ability to absorb magic, and so did the blade he wielded. That is how he defeated the Dark One," Lor-telliam addressed everyone.

"And it cost him his life," Baylin said softly.

"A small price to pay fer savin' his people," Ballick said bluntly.

"By using the sword, he absorbed Malbeck's magic, and it was too much, even for him. He could not contain the power. The explosion killed hundreds, including himself and Malbeck."

"And you all want my son to face him, a boy without King Ullis's experience, and Malbeck now possessing the Shan Cemar, which by all accounts has made him even more powerful?" Kromm said, his voice trembling with anger, fear, and frustration.

"We do not *want* him to face Malbeck, Sire. But it is his destiny," Alerion said.

"How do you know?" Kromm almost yelled as he stood and pounded his massive fist on the table. "You are betting my son's life on a riddle given to you by a pit-fiend!"

Everyone was silent for a moment as they let the king's anger subside a little.

"Shyann said he was the key to Malbeck's defeat," Jonas said softly as he thought back to his last conversation with her.

"What?" Kromm asked, turning his angry eyes on Jonas.

"You have spoken with her?" Kiln asked, surprised. Kiln of course knew of Jonas's disconnect with Shyann and how much that had affected the young warrior. He was eager for Jonas to be healed completely, both physically and mentally. It pained him to see him so depressed.

"I have, last night in a dream," Jonas replied.

"So you are a cavalier again?" Kiln asked hopefully.

"I am not, and I shall never be."

Everyone seemed to visibly deflate at Jonas's words. They all knew that it was a possibility that Jonas would never be able to wield her magic again. They were privy to the fact that Dykreel's taint, even though it was now blocked, could cut off Jonas's connection to Shyann. And apparently it had. They felt for the young man. But that was not all. As far as they knew, Jonas was the only cavalier left to combat the Forsworn's evil. It would be a great disadvantage to not have access to Shyann's magic when Malbeck's army arrived at the gates of Finarth.

"I am truly sorry, Jonas," Allindrian said.

Jonas looked at her and everyone else. He knew that they did not know what to say, and he also knew that this was not the time for their pity. King Kromm was upset, and they were facing a dire threat much more serious than Jonas's problems.

"Thank you, Allindrian. But not all is lost. I am her warrior still, and she has given me new weapons to face the Forsworn. But I cannot brandish the power of a cavalier, as my conduit for such power has been broken. Be that as it may, Shyann informed me that Prince Riker is the key. He was the reason I was sent to get you, Sire, although I did not know that at the time."

Kromm's eyes, still intense with anger, gradually relaxed, reflecting only sad resignation. He sat down again without another word.

"Prince, if you will permit me? I'd like to test you," Lor-telliam said.

Prince Riker shifted uncomfortably. Like most warriors, he did not understand magic, and he was uneasy at the prospect of being subjected to it. "What will this test entail?"

"You will feel a slight tingle only. It will be brief, and I can do it now."

"Very well. You may proceed."

Lor-telliam stood up and moved toward the prince. "I must touch you if you don't mind."

Prince Riker slid his chair back and stood up to face the Ekahal. The young man was tall, like his father, and he looked down at the slender elf. Lor-telliam reached out with both hands and grasped the young prince's wrists. He closed his eyes and began to chant quietly. No one could really make out the words as he was speaking in a soft whisper. It sounded like he was mumbling, but they would not have recognized the words even if they had heard them clearly. The ancient elven language that he spoke was the source of the Ekahals' true power, allowing them to access the river of the universe, the source of all energy, unhindered and without restraint.

Prince Riker felt a slight tingling all over his body. It felt like goose bumps from being cold, but it was deeper, not just on the surface of his skin. But as the tingling moved into his center, he felt something stir within him. It was like a shield, a wall of consciousness. No one else felt it but Lor-telliam. There was an immediate, but subtle shock wave, and Lor-telliam was taken aback at how quickly he was repelled. Prince Riker's body was reacting to the intrusion. It was pushing the Ekahal's magic away from him. Lot-telliam had gently probed the prince, and his body had gently pushed him away, but with a firmness that warned the elf to push no further. The Ekahal had no doubt that if he probed harder that the prince's body would respond more violently.

Lor-telliam stopped chanting and opened his eyes. The prince was staring at him with wide eyes. "Your gift is strong, young prince," Lor-telliam said. "I felt a powerful presence, much more powerful than that of your ancestor, King Ullis Gavinsteal."

"I felt *it* push you away," the prince said excitedly.

"That *it*, is you. When magic gets close to you, your body reacts. My magic was subtle and harmless, but if something attacked you magically, your body would shield you in a much stronger way. Perhaps a bright flash or a shock wave, which is what I felt just now," Lor-telliam said as he moved back to his seat.

Prince Riker sat down, his eyes now bright and alert, somehow energized by that which had stirred within him. It felt as if a sleeping part of him had finally awoken, and it felt good.

"There is no doubt. He is indeed an Ishmian," Lor-telliam announced.

"And you feel that he has the power to defeat Malbeck?" Kromm asked, his voice a mixture of skepticism and hope.

"I do not know, Sire. But, if we combine his power with the weapons of King Ullis Gavinsteal, then he may have a chance," Lor-telliam said.

"It must be a possibility, Sire, if Shyann said it was so," Jonas said hopefully.

"Shyann could not even protect you from the Forsworn, what makes you think she is correct about my son?" Kromm snapped.

No one said anything at the king's words. Even Jonas did not respond as he knew King Kromm was speaking from emotions that no father should have to face. After several moments, the king sighed heavily and looked at Jonas.

"I'm sorry, Jonas. You of all people don't deserve my anger. If it had not been for you, I don't think I, or my family, would be here right now. Nor does Shyann deserve my scorn. It was her power, given to you, that brought us from the clutches of the Dark One. I'm sorry for my rash words," the king said softly.

"Ekahal Telliam, you just said that if we combine the prince's power with the weapons," Allindrian paused as she looked around the room. "Are you saying that you know the whereabouts of the sword and armor that defeated Malbeck at the Shadow Plains?"

Lor-telliam glanced at Allindrian before returning his attention to everyone. "I do."

"Why have you not told us?" King Baylin asked. "That sword is a family heirloom. Finarth has a right to it."

"King Gavinsteal," Lor-telliam replied, "the sword and armor have been in safe keeping until they are needed again. We have not brought it to your attention over the years because whoever had those weapons in their possession would be a target for the Forsworn. They were both elven forged and imbued with the Light of Ela. Then I and several other Ekahals spent an entire year weaving magic into them. They are unsurpassed in power, and despised by all who live in darkness. Every foul creature on Kraawn would be drawn to it. You have not needed it, so we thought it best to keep it hidden."

"So where are these artifacts now?" Kromm asked.

Lor-telliam sighed and brought his hands together in front of him. "They are at Ullis Hill."

"What! They have been at the Shadow Plains the entire time?" King Baylin said incredulously.

Jonas had been to the hill before, during his early training to be a Finarthian Knight. All new recruits were taken to the barren battle field where Ullis Gavinsteal defeated Malbeck many years ago. Many thousands of warriors had been buried there in mass graves, and a monument had been built on a hill overlooking the battlefield and the bones of the fallen. It was simple, but impressive, consisting of eight massive stone pillars rising ten paces into the air and set in a large circle. In the center of the circle was a statue of King Ullis Gavinsteal in full battle armor with a shield on his left arm and the famous sword held high in his right hand.

"The statue was a gift from my queen," Allindrian said as she recalled the history.

"That is correct. I was sent to erect it and build the monument. There is a secret chamber built under the statue that has been the home of the armor and *Tihr-alliam,* the sword's true name. The weapons will only work for someone with Finarthian royal blood. Nothing evil can even touch it without being destroyed."

"And you think it will work for my son?" Kromm asked.

"Yes."

Everyone sat in silence as they took in the scope of the Ekahal's words. Jonas looked at Lor-telliam again as if it were for the first time. He had some lines around his eyes but other than that he looked maybe only ten years older than Allindrian. Yet he was over a thousand years old. No matter how hard he tried, he just couldn't comprehend it.

"Then we need to go to Ullis Hill tomorrow," Kiln reasoned.

"It will not be that easy. The Dark One has already found the location of the artifacts," Lor-telliam said. Startled curses and questions erupted at this announcement, and Lor-telliam waited patiently for everyone to be silent. After a few moments he was able to continue. "We believe that the Shan Cemar gave him some insight, or maybe a means to locate them, but we do not know for sure."

"Does he have them in his possession?" Jonas asked.

"No, he cannot remove the artifacts without destroying himself. In fact, no follower of the Forsworn can enter the chamber that guards the sword. The Light of Ela protects it, and even they cannot overpower it."

120

Jonas had only heard of this *Light of Ela* one other time in a class that he had taken while he was going through knight training. The elves believe it to be the power of the stars, a power that only they can access. There is a theory that the elves themselves came from this same magic. Jonas did not know much more about it, but it was obvious that there was some truth to what he had been taught.

"So they are safe?" Prince Riker asked.

"No, young prince, they are not. On our way here we went to Ullis Hill to check on Tihr-alliam. We were within five miles of the monument when we detected a disturbance in the Ru'Ach," Lor-telliam said.

"What do you mean?" Addalis asked, intrigued by the Ekahal's words.

"The land around the monument is different. A completely different landscape now surrounds the sword. Black swampy water boils from the ground and a low mist covers it like a guardian. The Forsworn's stain oozes from the land in a five mile radius around the monument, and we could sense their dark magic everywhere. We believe that Malbeck has used the Shan Cemar to form a protective area there. We do not know of their defenses, but there can be no doubt that they will be impressive," Lor-telliam explained.

"What does it mean?" Kromm asked.

Lor-telliam looked at the other two Ekahals. Their faces were devoid of emotion but everyone else around the table was leaning in, eager to hear his words.

"Malbeck could not take the sword or destroy it, so he did the next best thing," Sar-gathos said.

"He is protecting it...from us," Alerion said as the reality of the situation came to him.

Jonas thought about it. It made sense. The only way Malbeck could keep the weapon from being used against him was to keep it out of his enemies' hands. If the weapon was that important then he could only imagine what evil beasts would be guarding it.

"We believe that to be true," Lor-telliam said.

"We still have to get it," King Baylin said adamantly.

"Yes, we do. The prince will have no chance without that sword," Lor-telliam said.

"And de Dark One be knowin' it," Durgen reasoned.

"We need to form another party to get those weapons back," King Baylin said.

"Why not send in an army?" Fil asked.

"I think a small powerful force may be able to sneak in and out easier than hundreds of troops," Lor-telliam reasoned.

"I would like to be part of this party," Jonas said quickly.

"Very good, Jonas," King Baylin agreed. It didn't escape Jonas that the king referred to him as Jonas, and not Cavalier. It stung more than he would have thought. To be a cavalier was to be placed above even kings. Everyone looked up to the cavalier and what he represented. Now he was just Jonas. But he had been far worse off before, and part of him looked forward to being *just Jonas* again.

Fil could read Jonas better than anyone and he must have seen the expression of pain, or sorrow, or self-pity, whatever it was that flashed briefly across his face. Jonas felt Fil's hand gently pat his leg under the table. He looked at his friend who gave him a subtle but reassuring smile. Jonas remembered Fil's words earlier. He still had formidable weapons, more than most, and there was no reason for self-pity in his situation. Besides, Shyann didn't see it that way, so why should he.

"With your leave, my King, I'd like to accompany Jonas in this quest," Fil said.

"Of course, you've earned it," the king said.

"I am the only one who can get us in, so I will go," Lor-telliam said. "The prince must go as well, as he is the only one who can retrieve the artifacts."

"Can't anyone with Finarthian blood draw the weapon?" King Baylin asked.

"That is so," Lor-telliam said.

"Then we should not risk his life in retrieving it," King Baylin said bluntly. "If he is the only one who can defeat Malbeck, then he should be protected at all costs. Sending him into unknown evils to find the sword is an unnecessary risk. I will go and retrieve the blade so that Prince Riker may wield it," the king said matter-of-factly.

Everyone looked at King Baylin and back to Lor-telliam, not sure how the Ekahal would react to the change in his plan. But the logic made sense and everyone knew it.

"Sire, I believe your judgment is sound, but who will run the kingdom while you are gone if Commander Kiln is at the Gildren Garrison?" Lor-telliam asked.

"He will stay here as my regent. I'm sorry, Commander, but you are needed here. General Ruthalis will take your place at the Garrison," King Baylin said.

"Yes, Sire," Kiln said with a slight nod.

Cade, the dwarven warrior then spoke up, "Me brother and I would be joinin' dis group as well. Our weapons be collectin' dust and I think our skills will be needed at dis hill. It sounds like a mission fit for Dakeen."

"If this weapon is truly my son's only chance, then I would never forgive myself if the mission failed and I was not part of it. My steel will be joining yours as well," King Kromm said.

"I will also go," Allindrian announced.

"Very well," King Baylin said, "We are all tired; I have orders to write, and we have much to prepare for. If there is nothing else anyone wishes to discuss, I suggest we end this meeting."

There was a chorus of agreement as everyone stood up from the table and departed, quietly continuing to comment on the day's events.

Kiln said goodbye to everyone and stayed behind. "Gibon," Kiln said to one of the guards by the door. "Send for Master Borum. I am in need of some exercise."

Gibon smiled, as he always enjoyed watching the two master sword fighters practice. It was a sight that not many would ever see, and Gibon was not afraid to rub that in to the other soldiers who were not one of the private guards of the commander.

"Yes sir," he said as he left through the double doors.

Kiln stripped down to his leggings and drew his sword from its scabbard. The stress of the impending battle against Malbeck sat on his shoulders like the weight of a black dragon, its claws gripping his head in an iron grasp, giving him a headache that only a good workout and a large amount of sweat could remedy.

He loosened up his muscles by slowly going through several basic sword forms. It would be at least a half hour before the weapons master would arrive so he had plenty of time to warm up. He slowly picked up the speed of his movements and it wasn't long before beads of sweat glistened on his body even in the cold castle air. He had entered Ty'erm, a mental state of consciousness that allowed him to slow down movement and concentrate on everything around him to a level beyond most human cognition. He could hear and see every nuance of sound and sight around him. His sword became an extension of his body and everything within him became one with the moment. His heart beat was a rhythmic drum that united his sword with his body.

He was in this mental state when he heard the main door to the huge throne room open. Kiln spun through his last movement and stopped instantly in the end position, sword arm straight up and body tall and rigid. Kiln closed his eyes, took a deep breath, and lowered his body into a relaxed state.

"Thank you for coming, my friend," Kiln said as the weapons master moved toward him from the door. Gibon had entered with master Borum and had shut the door behind him.

"It is my pleasure," Borum mumbled under his breath as he moved closer.

Kiln walked over to the table and took a drink of water as he wiped his sweat covered face with his tunic. "Sword forms first?" Kiln asked, knowing that Borum would not yet be warm. It was standard procedure to cross blades slowly and move through the basic forms until both opponents felt the warmth of their blood flowing through their bodies. Borum did not respond and then Kiln heard a sound that was out of place. It was a "fffrump" sound followed by a slight gargle.

Kiln quickly spun around and saw Borum standing ten paces away in a fighting stance. Something was obviously not right. Kiln glanced behind Borum and saw the body of Gibon sprawled on his back with a small black feathered shaft protruding from his neck. Then the man in front of him reached up with one hand and pulled something off his face. It looked very strange to Kiln, as the hand moved upward across the face, a new face emerged. Instantly the shape of the man in front of him shimmered and changed to a familiar sight. Standing in front of Kiln was the Sharneen assassin he faced a month ago. He wore the same black clothes, but this time wore no mask. He held no weapons, but in his right hand he grasped a simple black mask.

Kiln's eyes narrowed as he readied his body for the attack.

"I will not need a warm up, Commander, but thank you for offering," Uthgil said. His use of the vernacular was choppy and his Sharneen accent was strong, but Kiln could easily understand him.

Kiln replied in Sharneen. "You will pay for the man you murdered a month ago, and for the man that lies behind you."

Uthgil's expression registered momentary surprise as he heard his own language spoken. Not many this far west would even recognize the language, let alone be able to speak it. "Do not forget your fellow swordsman, whose body now lies in a pool of his own blood as we speak."

Kiln hadn't thought of that. Whatever magic the assassin used to take on Borum's guise somehow required his death. Kiln ground his jaw as anger threatened to take over. Borum was a great man, and a great swordsman, and he deserved a better death. "How did you kill him, assassin?"

"Does it matter?"

"It does to me."

"I stabbed him in his back while he made himself some tea."

Kiln said nothing as he fought back the anger that was so close to the surface. "And now you have come for me."

"Yes, you are my target. But don't worry, your death will be honorable," Uthgil said as he whipped his left hand across his body so fast that Kiln could barely register the movement.

Kiln reacted on instinct and spun his blade back and forth in front of him. He could barely see the projectiles but he heard a 'ting' as his blade made contact with something metal. Then he felt a slight sting on his leg and looked down to see a small metal dart sticking out of his thigh. The assassin must have thrown two or three knowing that Kiln would block at least one. He yanked it out and threw it on the ground. "How is poison honorable?"

"The poison now in your blood is called Blackcoil. It is made from a desert plant far to the east. It is a slow acting poison that will take hours to kill you. In fact you will not even feel the effect on your body for some time. In a black vial located here," Uthgil said, tapping his side under his tunic, "is the antidote. Without it you will die."

"Why are you telling me this?" Kiln asked, although he thought he already knew the answer.

"It's simple. I wish to fight you. If you win, which you won't, you deserve the antidote. You should also know that the person who hired me to kill you is a wizard named Gullanin."

"Impossible. The wizard, Gullanin, was killed by King Kromm of Tarsis," Kiln said.

"How long ago?"

"A week."

"That explains his recent condition. He is an undead monster now. I fear nothing, Commander, but this thing frightened me. He radiated a power beyond my comprehension. He has asked for your death, and I will deliver it."

"My death will not be so easy."

"I know, that is why we will fight."

"Nothing would please me more," Kiln smiled coldly as he fought back his anger and focused on his center. In seconds his body relaxed and he found Ty'erm again.

Uthgil dropped the mask to the ground and drew both blades at his hip. They began to circle each other. They had fought briefly before, but the meeting had been short, and neither had found a weakness in the other.

Kiln did not hesitate and attacked immediately. His sword was longer, but he fought a man with two blades and it was his reach alone that kept those wicked swords at bay. They spun, danced, and pivoted as steel clashed against steel. Sparks flew as the magical blades fought for openings. They floated across the stone pavers and any who watched would have been mesmerized by their grace and skill. The blur of the blades, the speed of the dance, and the fluidity of the movement would have entranced anyone lucky enough to witness it. A person could live ten lifetimes and never have the opportunity to view a contest of sword skills such as this.

Kiln had no idea how long they had been fighting. It seemed like a flash in time, but he knew that it had been much longer. Sweat dripped from his forehead and his lungs ached with exertion. But his movements showed no signs of fatigue, nor did the movements of Uthgils.

Uthgil's heart pounded as adrenaline coursed through his body. He relished every flex of muscle, every lightning quick riposte from himself and his opponent. He smiled outwardly as his opponent deflected his attacks and matched his speed and agility. No one had ever come close to matching his skill with a blade. And now he faced an opponent that could possibly be his equal. No, not his equal, Uthgil thought, but close to it. The man was very skilled, but Uthgil was at least ten years younger, and soon the commander's sword arm would slow with fatigue. That would be when his blades would taste his blood.

That moment came only seconds after he contemplated it. Kiln deflected a forward movement from Uthgil's left blade and turned his sword over the attack, snapping his razor sharp point towards Uthgil's exposed lead arm. Uthgil, faster than Kiln though possible, snaked his right sword across his body blocking Kiln's attack, while simultaneously spinning with his other blade.

Kiln saw it coming and reacted as fast as his body could. But it wasn't fast enough. He leaped back and felt a sting as Uthgil's blade cut him across his exposed belly. Luckily Kiln had sucked his stomach in and the blade just broke the surface of his skin. If he hadn't done so his entrails would now be piled on the floor at his feet.

"First blood," Uthgil hissed with exultation.

"It's last blood that matters," Kiln said as he glanced at his wound. Blood welled from the cut and dripped down his torso. But it didn't hamper his movement as it was relatively shallow.

Uthgil just smiled and attacked again. They fought on and on, both sweating profusely. Kiln had been pushed back to the long conference table. At least that is what he wanted Uthgil to believe. In one smooth motion he jumped up and back and landed on the table. Uthgil came at him, blocking a downward stroke and swinging his other sword at Kiln's ankles. Kiln leaped up over the blade shuffling backwards further.

"You can't run from me, Commander," Uthgil said.

"Run?" Kiln laughed as he snapped his foot down. Uthgil caught a quick glimpse of his movement and saw a loaf of bread with a long carving knife resting on the edge of the plate. Kiln's quick maneuver spun the blade up into the air where Kiln snatched it like a striking adder. Kiln smiled and ran at Uthgil, his long sword held before him like a lance.

Uthgil stepped backwards, blocking Kiln's blade as he launched off the table, then following up the move with more attacks. The pace had now accelerated as Kiln expertly matched the speed of Uthgil's twin blades.

Kiln, however, was beginning to struggle. The bread knife was not built for combat, nor capable of facing magical blades such as these. Also, it had no guard, so any block with it was a serious risk. So he was leading with his sword and using the knife sparingly. Uthgil, on the other hand, did not have to hold anything back, and that was beginning to make the difference.

Kiln was forced into a block with the bread knife, and for the first time the Sharneen used the other end of the knife. The blade was a unique design as it continued over the hand like a guard and stuck out past the pommel a good six inches. This blade enabled him to deal death on both ends. And Uthgil was a master with this weapon. As his short sword came into contact with the knife, Uthgil spun the blade around his fingers and whipped the other end of the sword across Kiln's wrist. It was so fast that Kiln could not avoid it. The razor sharp steel bit deeply into Kiln's wrist and the long bread knife clattered to the stone pavers.

Uthgil smiled as Kiln shuffled away, his blood splattering on the floor. Kiln glanced quickly at his wrist, concerned about what he saw. His blood was not squirting out rhythmically, which reassured him that the assassin had not hit an artery, but he was bleeding heavily, in thick waves of crimson, indicating that the wound was indeed deep. It would not be long before Kiln would begin to feel the fatigue from the loss of blood.

"It seems you have lost," Uthgil said as he slowly advanced towards Kiln.

"A fight is never over until your opponent is dead," Kiln replied as he fought to regain control of his nerves. It was only a flash, but he felt it clearly, it was fear. Not fear of dying, but fear of being beaten. Or maybe it was the fear of leaving Finarth before the battle, or the fear of leaving Jonas and his friends. He wasn't sure, but he tucked the fear neatly away and used it to fuel his tiring body. Uthgil was perhaps a better swordsman, although the contest was very close. The difference might be age, or it could be a result of the fact that Uthgil fought with two weapons. But Kiln also knew that sometimes better swordsmen succumbed to lesser warriors. A fight was not always determined by skill alone. The components of a great warrior were a combination of skill, endurance, courage, luck, and most importantly, a complete lack of concern about who won. That was the hardest skill to master, entering a fight without thinking about whether or not you were going to win or lose. Most warriors, no matter how skilled, could not help but think about the consequences of victory and defeat. Duels, by definition, required a winner and a loser. And someone like Uthgil, no matter how skilled he was, could not stop thinking about his victory. He lived to be the best, and that would be his downfall. Not to mention Kiln was not just a master swordsman, he was an expert at tactics. No one could read an opponent better than Kiln, or read a situation and manipulate it to his advantage. And that was just what Kiln was doing now.

Kiln forced himself to maintain his center, as he renewed his focus on Uthgil's movements. But the assassin did not make any mistakes. He fought with a precision and speed that was unmatched, and Kiln was gambling on the assassin's skills. He snapped his bloody hand forward splattering his blood across Uthgil's face. The warrior hesitated for a second, and Kiln capitalized on that by lunging forward with his long sword.

Uthgil did exactly what he thought he would. He deflected the blade and jabbed forward with his other knife. This time Kiln reacted differently than he should have. Instead of spinning or pivoting sideways away from the blade, he jumped forward towards it. Uthgil's eyes widened in surprise as his short sword sunk deeply into Kiln's side. Kiln had hoped that he had judged the assassin's strike correctly and that he had angled his body just enough so that it wouldn't cut into his lungs or vital organs. But he had no time to ponder whether or not his maneuver was successful.

Kiln bit back the pain, dropped his sword and grabbed Uthgil's tunic so he could not withdraw the blade and retreat backwards. Simultaneously, using his bloody and damaged hand, he quickly grabbed a knife from the bandolier on Uthgil's chest and rammed it hilt deep into Uthgil's neck, yanking the razor sharp edge up and to the left, slicing through the artery in his neck.

Everything about Kiln's move showed desperation. He did not know where Uthgil would stab him, nor did he know if he could even grasp the knife with his damaged hand. Any mistake would be Kiln's death. But the alternative was still death, as he knew he could not defeat the warrior with a damaged hand and one weapon.

The entire move was almost instantaneous. If you blinked you would have missed it. As blood sprayed over Kiln, he staggered backwards to his knees as Uthgil landed with a thud on the floor.

Kiln looked down panting, cringing at the sight of his wound. The assassin's blade had buried itself nearly hilt deep into his side. The blade had not hit his lungs, but it had sunk in deep a hand span left of his belly button. He had seen enough wounds to know that this one was fatal if not healed quickly.

Before he passed out he had to get to the vial that held the antidote. If he could do that, and maybe raise an alarm, he might survive. So Kiln crawled forward on his hands and knees. The movement caused severe pain as the assassin's sword still dangled from his belly. But he reached Uthgil, found the vial, and consumed it quickly.

Kiln stood up on wobbly legs and slowly ambled towards the main door. The pain was intense and he left a path of blood across the stone floor. He fought back the pain in each grueling step and finally made it to the door. Using his good hand he opened it, stumbling through the doorway and landing hard on one knee. The jolt sent a new wave of pain through his stomach. But he found the resolve to stand and he continued down the hallway towards the guard's anteroom. Kiln knew that there should be two more guards stationed there. Even if the fight could have been heard by someone, which Kiln doubted, they would likely have just assumed that it was the sparring bout between Borum and himself. It would not have raised an alarm.

Finally Kiln reached the door to the guard's anteroom that served as a hub to the other hallways that housed the royal chambers. There were several rooms such as these, through which any intruders would have to pass through. Kiln was in a daze when he finally reached the door, lifted the latch, and swung the door open. He had lost a lot of blood and his vision was hazy. He stumbled through the doorway, again landing on his knee. This time he could not get up, and he fell to the cold pavers. He had just enough sense to turn his body so he would land on his side and not embed the short sword any deeper into his abdomen. The last sounds he heard were the frantic voices of the guards shouting in alarm just before he passed out.

Six
First Blood

Tuvallis continued to absently stroke his newly shaven face as the two thousand men and women marched toward the Gildren Garrison. This garrison, with its massive bridge, was the gateway to the Finarthian Kingdom, and the only place within hundreds of miles where an army could cross the turbulent river into Finarthian lands. It had been four days since he had shaved his long unruly beard, and his smooth skin still felt strange to his touch and unaccustomed to the embrace of the cold winter air. It had been many years since that skin had felt the elements without the protection of his long black beard. One thing he hadn't considered was the cold. The other was how odd he would look. Years of wilderness living had tanned and weathered the skin around his eyes and cheeks, while the skin that was buried under the protection of his beard was as pale and smooth as a baby's. He looked like a raccoon, and he caught more than a few smiles and fingers pointing his way.

Seli was smiling at him as he rubbed his velvety skin. "Regretting that shave?" she asked.

"Maybe," Tuvallis grunted. "It be feelin' strange. Been a long time."

"Well I like it. You look almost human now," she said smiling. Seli was healing well. She had several cracked ribs but luckily they had caused little damage. She had also suffered a concussion, as well as heavy bruising still visible around her eyes and on her arms. But most of her wounds were superficial and would in time heal completely.

They had spent the last few days travelling hard and talking a lot. At least it seemed like a lot to Tuvallis, who was still getting used to the idea of communication. He was surprised at how good it felt to actually talk to someone. They talked about their time as soldiers and what it was like growing up in Tarsis and Cuthaine. They talked a little about their childhoods and Seli even got Tuvallis to talk a bit more about his family and his children. She was slowly breaking down the walls that he had built up for so many years. Tuvallis was aware of this, but he didn't stop her. It felt good to bring his family into the light again, to let their memories flow freely, to acknowledge their existence.

Tuvallis had also become something of a hero. Word had spread quickly about how he single handedly killed ten orcs and rescued Seli. The Free Legion soldiers respected his courage and greeted him wherever he went. The refugees, especially the children, looked at him with wonder as the story spread throughout the camp. He was not accustomed to so much attention, but he had to admit that it felt good at some level.

"So you're pretty good with that sword," she said, tapping the long sword at his hip.

"Aye, a natural they say," he said unabashedly.

"Who says?"

"Kernan, the weapon's master at Tarsis. A few more years and I coulda got me mark."

"Really? Well we'll have to see about that," she said as she tapped the pommel of her infantry sword. Tuvallis just smiled back at her. Then he shook his head and chuckled slightly under his breath.

"What? You don't think I can beat you?"

"Nah, wasn't laughin' 'bout that. Was laughin' 'bout how much I been laughin'. Seems odd, eh?"

"A little. But it suits you, especially now that everyone can see your face."

They laughed together and continued on silently for a few minutes, taking in the beautiful morning. The sky was clear and the sun was shining brightly, but its warm rays could not penetrate the cold brisk air. Patches of snow still covered most of the ground. Winter still held its tenuous grip on the land, and it would be another full cycle of the moon before the coming of spring would melt all the snow.

"Is he really as good as they say?" Seli asked Tuvallis.

"Who?"

"King Kromm. I saw him once when I was younger. He was a giant, a good head taller than you, with arms as big as my thighs. Is he really the fighter they say he is?"

"Aye, and more. He was a battle king in all rights. He marched with us, fought with us, and bled with us. I had the privilege of fighting beside him on one occasion," Tuvallis said, recalling the memory.

"Tell me about it."

"Well, we was havin' some difficulties with some giants."

"Giants? Really!?"

"Yup...they were comin' down from de Vanguard Mountains and raiding some villages. It was a bad winter and food was scarce for dem."

"I have never seen a giant before," Seli admitted.

"And ya wouldn't. Day tend to live in de mountains far from people. Dese giants were mountain giants that were rarely seen. Anyway, de king was restless and he led a group of men to dere villages to hunt 'em down."

"And you were part of this group?"

"Yes, and we found 'em. It was a large group, much larger den we expected. We lost fifteen men in dat fight. I saw de king kill two giants on his own," Tuvallis continued. "Let's just say that it was impressive."

"You said earlier that he *was* a battle king. You do know, don't you, that he is still alive?" Seli asked.

Tuvallis looked at her with surprise. "He is? I assumed that he died when his city was destroyed. How do you know this?"

"He came to Cuthaine several weeks after Tarsis was destroyed, with a cavalier by the name of Jonas. I never saw him myself but many of the soldiers were talking about it. There was fighting in the streets with Blackhearts, and an entire gaming house was destroyed by orcs. I was away with a scouting party so I missed it. But Captain Hadrick was there, and he fought alongside the king. You can talk to him if you want to learn more," Seli suggested.

Tuvallis had stopped in the road, forcing Seli to turn around and look back at him. "What is it?"

"The cavalier's name was Jonas? Are you sure?"

"Yes, I never saw him but the men talked about him a lot when I returned. Very young, they said, for one with such power. They said he had been captured and tortured by Dykreel agents." Seli tapped her chest four times in the pattern of Ulren's star. "But they found him and he somehow survived."

Tuvallis shook his head in wonder and continued walking with Seli. "I met a young man over four years ago by dat name. He was one of two survivors from de town of Manson that was destroyed by boargs. It be a long story but he had been a cripple, and den he was miraculously healed. I don't know much more, but I always wondered what happened to him. Could it be de same person?"

"How could it be? I thought a cavalier's training took at least five years."

"I thought that as well. But I guess it shouldn't surprise me da king is alive, de man is hard to kill," Tuvallis said. "Where did they go?"

"To Finarth."

Tuvallis looked at her, shaking his head. "Looks like me past will catch up wid me after all."

"It will be a good place to face it," Seli reassured him.

"Aye, I think you're right there," was all Tuvallis said as his mind drifted back, recalling old memories.

***

Hagar's sensitive nose had brought him to the deer carcass easily enough, though the smell of the dead orcs laying nearby nearly overpowered the scent of the venison. He could smell the familiar smell of humans in the clearing as well. It looked to Hagar that there had been some sort of fight. Luckily for him the wolves and other scavengers had not yet found the carcasses. Though the deer meat was old he ravenously tore into its cold flesh, consuming it all with relish. He had certainly had worse fare before. He had only slept a few hours that night, driven by a relentless urge to keep traveling south.

Hagar's appearance would have stunned anyone who saw him. Huge and heavily muscled, he was a combination of his orc and ogre ancestry. His facial features were relatively human-like, but much more prominent, with deep set yellowish eyes, a large flat nose with nostrils like caves, and a large mouth filled with long sharp teeth. His course black hair ran down his neck like a horse's mane. And his thick ogrillion skin, greenish-gray in color, was as tough as hardened leather armor, providing significant protection against most weapons.

But if an observer could have seen Hagar as he sat on a large rock eating the venison, there would have been even more surprises regarding his appearance. His entire chest, back, and shoulders were covered with a stunning cuirass, as bright as polished chrome, brilliantly reflecting the sun's light. The incongruous beauty of the cuirass contrasted sharply with the dirty furs that the beast wore around his waist. But that was not all. Leaning on the rock next to him was a weapon that had obviously been created just for him. As large as a small tree, it had a mace-like head covered in spikes as long as daggers. The silver metal shaft was as thick as a human arm and the handle was wrapped in brilliant silver wire. The deadly looking weapon appeared unmarred, perfect in appearance, the type of weapon worthy of a knight, not something an ogrillion would possess. But nonetheless they were his, and his new purpose was somehow linked to these weapons, although he knew not how.

Hagar consumed the last of the meat, grabbed the long mace at his side, and moved south towards his destiny.

***

Captain Hadrick was riding at the front of his column when one of his scouts, Orin, returned in a flurry of hoof beats. The scout was dressed in dark clothing and he carried a short sword and long hunting bow sheathed alongside his saddle. He was sweating and his eyes were wide with excitement.

"Sir, I spotted a small army paralleling us!" he reported.

"What! How many?" Hadrick asked, pulling back on the reins on his own horse and slowing the column to a halt.

"Around five thousand. I don't think they know we are here."

"How far away?"

"Quarter of a day on foot at the most. They are mostly orcs but I spotted some goblins and a handful of ogres. They are hauling siege machines, Captain," Orin added.

"How many machines?"

"I saw four catapults and three towers," Orin said quickly.

"Damn! They must be going to the Gildren Garrison," Hadrick muttered, "hoping to capture the Garrison in preparation for Malbeck's main army. You sure they didn't see you?"

"Yes, sir."

"Good work, Orin. Did you spot any of their own scouts?"

"No, sir."

Hadrick knew that orcs didn't generally use scouts. And an army that size would feel pretty safe. If they used any scouts at all they would probably not roam too far. But he had no idea who was leading this group. They had to get to the Gildren Garrison first and warn them. And those siege engines were a problem.

"You say they were paralleling us?" Hadrick asked.

"Yes, sir. They might even be a bit behind us since they are not traveling the roads. I could get to the Garrison a full day ahead of them if I leave now," Orin suggested, coming to the same conclusion as Hadrick.

"Do it," Hadrick ordered. "Take Anthony with you and another horse. Make haste, my friend."

"Will do, Captain," Orin replied as he pivoted his horse and rode to the back of the column for provisions and to find Anthony, another of their scouts.

"Stephy, order a quick break, water only. I want you, Bositch, Groban, and Sury. And find that new guy, Tuvallis, then meet me back here as soon as you can," Hadrick ordered.

"Yes, Captain," Stephy answered as he spun his horse around and rode down the column to carry out the orders.

It didn't take long for everyone to convene, while the refugees relaxed briefly under the vigilant supervision of the Free Legion soldiers. They were standing together at the front of the column as Captain Hadrick briefed them.

"My concern is the siege engines. A force that size with siege engines will easily be able to take control of the garrison," the captain explained.

"What do you suggest?" Bositch asked. Bositch was a Free Legion scout, short and thin, but quick as lightning. With his dark tanned skin and short black hair he could almost pass for a Sithgarin desert nomad.

"We need to take those engines out," Hadrick said vehemently.

"How?" Sury asked, "They are five thousand strong and we have only fifty."

"Ya be wantin' to sneak in and burn em down," Tuvallis suggested, though he felt a bit out of place with these men who knew each other, had fought together, and trusted one another implicitly. It was the type of bond that could only be forged through years of shared

136

combat and camaraderie. Tuvallis guessed that this might be the captain's idea as well, since nothing else seemed plausible, though he thought even that seemed far-fetched.

Everyone looked at Tuvallis, and when Captain Hadrick didn't say anything, they looked back at him questioningly.

"Is that your plan?" Stephy asked the captain, unsure if he really wanted to know the answer.

"It is," the captain confirmed. "I'm asking each one of you to go with me, but I won't order it. Tuvallis, I have no rank over you, but by all accounts you have the skills that may help us. I'm asking you all for help, but I won't hold any grudge if you refuse. It will obviously be dangerous, but I feel that the results will be worth it. If we can burn the machines, even some of them, it will greatly improve the chance of the garrison holding out. If not, the garrison will fall in a night."

"No doubt de garrison will fall anyway," Tuvallis added, "At de most they have several hundred soldiers there. Even if dis lead group don't take it, Malbeck's army will walk over de garrison like it wasn't even there. What be da point in riskin' our lives for the inevitable?"

"Ya scared, mountain man?" Groban chided with a playful smile.

Tuvallis almost reached out and grabbed Groban by the throat, but he subdued the urge. "Watch it, boy. I know I look passive, but my bite hurts." The other soldiers laughed at the jest, as it was obvious that Tuvallis looked anything but passive.

"Don't be stupid, Grobin, the question is valid," Stephy said.

"I agree," Hadrick interjected. "But, if we can give the garrison more time, then that means that Finarth will have more time to prepare and plan for a siege, more time to collect food and water, bring soldiers in from the fields, assemble allies, produce more weapons, reinforce fortifications, and train the many refugees that I'm sure are pouring into Finarth even as we speak. The list of tasks is endless, and the more time Finarth has to prepare, the better chance we'll all have in defeating the Dark One. Besides, Finarth must know that they will eventually have to destroy the bridge and that will take some time to prepare for and accomplish. Dropping a bridge of that size is no easy feat. But destroying those engines will give them the time they need," Hadrick concluded.

Tuvallis just grunted, and everyone looked at him wondering what that meant. He smiled back. "I'm in. Ya got a plan on how to destroy dem engines?" The others shook their heads but smiled back. They were beginning to like this mountain man.

"A hasty one, but yes, I have a plan."

***

Jonas had risen early the morning the small group was to depart. He was restless, and despite his tiring ordeal he could not sleep well. The attack on Kiln had left him nervous and he had spent several waking hours with the swordsman as he rested from his wounds. In addition to his worries about his friend, nightmares plagued him and anxiety from the upcoming mission had his nerves strung tight. He was no longer a cavalier, and although Shyann had given him some new powerful weapons, he knew that he would be venturing into a dangerous mission without her direct guidance.

It was very early and it was still dark outside. He slipped out of bed, donned his new clothes and armor, buckled on his sword belt and strapped his quiver and bow onto his back. The clothes and armor felt good, almost warm, as if they were welcoming him. The clothing was so soft that it literally made no noise as he moved. And the armor was equally light and it didn't hamper his movement. His garments, including his boots and gloves, felt warm and almost alive when he first put them on. It was as if some sort of living force stirred within them. Everything felt warm and alive, and he had never worn anything so comfortable and welcoming. He decided that a good workout was in order to calm his mind.

He made his way through the quiet halls until he found himself standing on the flat stone pavers of the inner courtyard. The outdoor space was large, capable of holding a pandar of cavalry if need be. Jonas could see several guards standing at the two main entrances, as well as a few others standing guard at the single door entrances that led to various parts of the inner castle. There was a guard flanking the entrance from which he came, holding a spear and standing alert. Many torches stuck into sconces lit the entrances and several large braziers filled with burning wood cast an orange light around the large space.

The guard clearly recognized him. "Good evening, Cavalier," the man said in a deep baritone voice.

Jonas did not correct him as the explanation would take too long. He simply nodded his head in acknowledgement. "And to you.

Do you mind if I practice some sword maneuvers? I am having trouble sleeping."

"Of course. As you can see, you have the space to yourself."

"Thank you." Jonas moved to the center of the courtyard and drew both of his blades. He wanted to get a feel for his new weapons and armor, eager to test the gifts that Shyann had bestowed upon him. He took a deep breath and dropped into the state of Ty'erm. Once there, he began the positions slowly, gracefully moving across the pavers as his body and swords worked in unison. The swords felt exactly the same, and Jonas smiled as he relished in their weight and balance. But something didn't exactly feel right, and Jonas could not place his finger on it. As he picked up the speed, the problem presented itself quickly.

He actually tripped, stumbling and nearly falling to the ground. He had never tripped before, and he stopped to check the ground for any abruptions or raised stone edges that he might have hit with his foot. But there wasn't any.

"It's the boots." Jonas looked up to see Allindrian glide towards him, her movement as smooth and graceful as always. "Couldn't sleep either?"

"Not really. What do you mean it's the boots?"

"My guess is they are enchanted for speed. You didn't notice it but you were moving rather quickly, for a human that is," Allindrian added with a smile. "Where did you get them?"

"From Shyann," Jonas said, not sure exactly what to say.

"But you are not wearing the clothes and armor of a cavalier," Allindrian questioned. "Does she have a different role for you now?"

"She does. When the Ekahal's healed me, they sealed the Forsworn's magic into the talisman, but their magic also blocked me from Shyann, forever. I can no longer be a cavalier."

Allindrian reached out to touch his hand, gently holding his gloved hand in hers. "I'm sorry, Jonas. I really am."

"Me too. But I am not helpless. She gave me these clothes, this armor, and my new swords, although they are the same blades as before."

"They don't look like it. I can't even see the blades in these shadows. And I could barely see you. It was like you were part of the darkness, blending in completely," Allindrian added.

Jonas smiled. "I think that is the point. She asked me to be her new shadow knight…her warrior that will fight in her name in the places where a cavalier could not venture. She wants me to try and help people before they get corrupted, before they find themselves slaves to the Forsworn."

"And you could not do this as a cavalier as you would stand out. You would be incapable of infiltrating their networks, of working in the shadows. It is a sound idea."

"Well, if I am to be her shadow knight, I better get used to these new gifts," Jonas added as he looked at his feet.

"I think your body is not accustomed to the boots and it caused you to trip. Perhaps we should spar so you can get the feel of them."

"I would like that. But I am painfully remembering the last training tips you gave me. I can still hear the smack of wood on flesh," Jonas added with a smile.

"You were just a boy then."

"And now?" Jonas asked as he held his arms out wide, as if he were presenting himself for inspection.

Allindrian smiled. "Now you are a man," she paused, "and as a man, surely it will not be so easy to disarm you."

This time it was Jonas's turn to smile. "Let us see, shall we?"

Allindrian didn't say anything, but her answer came in the form of her sword being withdrawn from the sheath on her hip. She only had one blade to Jonas's two, but she did not seem worried. "Let us start slow, so you can get a feel for your new speed."

"Very well."

They began their movements slowly. Allindrian allowed Jonas to take the lead as he eased into the dance. He picked up his speed rather quickly and Allindrian had no trouble keeping up with him, blocking his blades with her silver sword. Then her sword begun to sing, and the tempo of the music matched their speed as Jonas pushed even further, moving in a blur as he sought an opening in her defenses.

Jonas felt a bit strange at first, like his mind was dragging behind his body, fouling up his movements. The stumbles were very subtle. In fact most observers would not have noticed them, but to Jonas they seemed glaring. Allindrian saw them as well, but didn't push him as he acclimated himself to his newfound speed. But as he picked up speed, and confidence, she too narrowed her focus until both warriors moved with a speed and grace never before witnessed by the guards in the courtyard.

Both combatants were sweating, and Jonas felt alive as his body moved more fluidly than it ever had. Smiling with glee, Jonas lunged forward with his right blade. His smiled disappeared quickly as he realized he had been lulled into a false state of confidence. Allindrian moved faster than anyone he had ever seen, side stepping to Jonas's right, simultaneously deflecting Jonas's blade, reversing the direction of her weapon and smacking Jonas on his side, leaping away before he could launch a counterstrike.

It was a brilliant move. She had moved to the side of his body that he could not reach quickly enough with his other blade. Normally, he could have easily pivoted his body and brought his other blade to bear, blocking the attack. But Allindrian was too fast. Even with his enhanced speed he could not move his body fast enough to position his opposite sword for the block. His magical armor probably would have protected him from most attacks, but it would have done little good against Allindrian's sword if she had used the bladed edge.

As soon as she halted her movement, the singing disappeared, and Jonas was left staring at her with a shocked expression. "How did you move that fast?"

"What do you mean," she countered as she lowered her blade. "I *am* that fast."

Jonas smiled and shook his head. "I've seen you move quickly before. But that was different."

"I move as fast as the situation requires. You are very good Jonas, and now, very fast. The speed was needed to defeat you."

Jonas sheathed his blades as well. "Do you think I will ever be that fast?"

"I do not know. It is unlikely, as you do not have elf blood. The boots and gloves you wear both enhance your speed, and with time, you will master their enchantments. As you progress with your swordsmanship, that too will add to your speed. Do they feel *strange* to you?"

"A bit. I feel as if my mind and movement are not synced," Jonas answered.

"I think that will fade as you become more comfortable with them. You are very good. Kiln has taught you well," she added.

"Thank you."

"Keep in mind, you are very young, and have only been using the sword for a blink compared to the time that my hands have been wrapped around the handle of this blade. Your skills will progress."

"Do you think you could beat him?"

"*Him?*" she asked, knowing full well who he was speaking of.

"Kiln."

"Kiln is the deadliest human I have ever met. It is not just his skill with the blade, it is his tenacity, his drive, his utter lack of fear that makes him dangerous. Even so, I do not think that Kiln could best me with a blade...but could I beat him?" Allindrian paused. "I do not know. Fights are not duels. Fights are won with skill, courage, fearlessness...the ability to take risks, to be daring, and Kiln is a master of all these things. With someone like Kiln, you never know what might happen."

Jonas looked up and noticed that the darkness was starting to take on a different hue, a shade of dark red.

"The sun is waking from its slumber," Allindrian said, following his gaze. "Let us head to the main gate. I'm sure everyone will be gathering soon."

It was not yet dawn but the small group was already waiting in the dark at the inner gate, prepared for the short journey and outfitted for war. They packed light since the trip to the Shadow Plains and the Ullis Hill would take less than a day. They were all mounted on sturdy horses and the atmosphere around them resonated with the seriousness of the mission. They had to claim the ancient weapons of Finarth if they hoped to defeat the Dark One and the Shan Cemar. But they were each apprehensive in their own way as they had no idea what threats they might face when they reached the monument. One thing was certain. Whatever guarded those weapons would be formidable and terrifying.

Kiln was not there to see them off as he was still healing from his attack. Luckily Kiln had made it to the guards before he bled out. If he had not had the strength to stumble to the guard's anteroom, than in all likelihood he would have died from the ghastly wound. Jonas had visited Kiln for most of the night, which mattered little as he was having difficulty sleeping anyway. The castle was on heightened alert and the soldiers were tense and furious at the same time. Their weapons master had been killed dishonorably, stabbed in the back by an assassin, the same one who had killed their beloved Dagrinal.

When Jonas and Allindrian arrived from the courtyard there were horses already waiting, both complete with saddle bags filled with provisions for several days. They both mounted their horses and silently joined the group.

Last to arrive was King Baylin, accompanied by several assistants carrying supplies and a huge shield. Jonas looked at the shield more carefully and noticed that the front of it was embossed with the Tarsinian royal insignia, a decorative T. It was beautifully done with intricate lines and details, and the shield itself shone with a silver brilliance.

"King Kromm," Baylin announced as he approached the Tarsinian king. "I have a small gift for you. I knew you were in need of a shield and I had this crafted for you. I hope you can put it to good use." A servant hefted the giant shield up to Kromm who was sitting astride a large chestnut mare. Kromm grabbed the shield with one hand and tested its weight while inspecting the insignia on the front.

"It is beautiful, King Baylin. I thank you, and the insignia is perfect. Give my respects to your armorer," Kromm said as he used the strap on the shield to flip it around and secure it on his back.

The Finarthian king nodded and mounted his own horse. "Is everyone ready?" The king addressed the formidable looking group. There was a chorus of grunts and affirmations as the king spurred his horse forward.

***

Tuvallis and the rest of the small group lay hidden in the tall grass looking down upon the large orc army. Their breath was visible in the cold air and patches of snow still dominated the surroundings. The night was darker than usual as thick swollen clouds had meandered in covering the flickering stars. The enemy campfires danced in the night shedding a soft light around them. They had ridden hard and had left their horses to get closer on foot. So far they had not run into any scouts. They all wore dark clothing and had spread cold black mud over their faces and hands. They wore no armor or anything else that would weigh them down or make noise, and the only weapons they carried were short swords and knives. This was going to be a mission of stealth, not brawn. And besides, if it actually came to a fight, they were completely out numbered. Armor or long swords would make little difference.

"Orin was right, I see only three siege towers," Captain Hadrick whispered. The towers were positioned at the rear of the army, and luckily they were all located in the same area.

"Aye, but it looks like they be battering rams too," Tuvallis said. Hadrick squinted and looked closer. Tuvallis was right. Closer inspection revealed that each of the massive towers had a huge steel capped log projecting from its front. The towers could be rolled up to a wall or gate and the ram would be used to attempt to break through the structure. If that didn't work then the tall tower, which housed a series of stairs, would bring the attackers to the top of the wall. Each machine was a fortified set of stairs with access points every five paces allowing the towers to work on different size walls.

The catapults were located on the far side of the enemy army and they could barely be seen in the distance. They were counterpoise catapults that used a fulcrum point and heavy weight to hurl an object.

"Okay, so remember the plan," Hadrick said. "Tuvallis, Stephy, and Bositch are responsible for the towers, while I, Sury, and Groban will make our way to the catapults. You need to give us some time to get to our marks before you set them ablaze. While your fires create havoc and distract them, we should be able to ignite the catapults."

It was a risky plan and everyone knew it. Any number of things could go wrong. Orcs could see well at night, while they could not. If any of them were detected, it would be over.

"Remember," Hadrick said. "If any of you are spotted, don't be a hero. We can't fight them. Run and evade pursuit until you can get to the horses. Then make haste back to camp, but make sure you are not being pursued."

These men were seasoned warriors and none of them said a word. They all knew the risks. The two groups nodded to each other before parting ways, disappearing like shadows into the night.

It didn't take long for Tuvallis's group to get near the engines. There was plenty of tall grass and sporadic trees to hide their movements, and all were adept at moving silently and remaining concealed. This was just one of the reasons why Captain Hadrick had picked them to begin with. Stephy was a bit out of practice, but he had done a lot of hunting as a child, and as he followed Bositch's movements he found that his skills came back to him quickly.

Tuvallis was like a ghost, and several times both men had to look around for him as he blended into the shadows. Years of hunting and solitude had honed his skills, and when he didn't want to be seen, he wasn't.

The three men were huddled around a stout oak tree well beyond the light of the campfires. The engines were clearly in sight now and their size was impressive. Each machine was over forty paces high, and even though Tuvallis had never seen the Gildren Garrison, he was pretty sure that the walls would be no match for these engines. The square walls of the towers were built of solid oak, thick as an orc wrist, and the front of each tower was encased in sheets of steel for more protection. Each machine rested on four huge wheels and Tuvallis figured it would take a team of at least six oxen to move them. As he looked around he noticed a small pen east of the towers and saw flickering shadows of large oxen moving about in the darkness.

"I see only a few guards," Bositch whispered as they carefully scanned the area. True enough, each siege engine had only one guard stationed near it. The rest of the orcs sat around a series of fires scattered throughout the area. Luckily, the fires were far enough away from the siege engines that they were covered mostly in shadow.

"I'll take the machine on the left," Stepy announced. "Bositch, you take the middle one and Tuvallis, you take the one on the right. If an alarm is raised before we light the fires, remember what the captain said, no hero stuff."

Bositch just smiled and Tuvallis grunted. Then each one began the slow and silent approach to their targets.

Tuvallis crawled fifteen paces forward before he stopped to survey the scene. He glanced to his right to see if he could see his comrades moving in the tall grass. He could not, and that was good. But an orc's vision was much better than his at night, and he tried not to think about that as he continued his slow advance. He had been told by a wizard long ago that orcs could see better at night because they could actually *see* body heat. He didn't know if that was true but that thought alone made him feel naked, and it was another reason why he had suggested they rub cold mud all over their faces and hands.

As the two towers loomed in the darkness before him, he could now clearly hear the grunts and growls of the orcs. Crouching on his hands and knees, he slowly raised his head to the tops of the grass where he could get a better look. There was no avoiding it. He had to see the position of the orc guard near the engine. He cursed silently as he saw two orcs in front of him, about ten paces, crouched down by the base of one of the engines. They appeared to be playing some sort of game and were rolling something along the ground. One was clearly angry as the other continued to win. Each orc wore crude pieces of plate mail and they carried thick heavy short swords at their hips.

Tuvallis quickly took his pack off so he would have quicker access to the jars of oil and the tinderbox inside. Glancing to his left, he saw only one guard near the middle machine, but he could not see the far machine as it was positioned behind it.

How was he going to silently take out two orcs? He tossed the problem around in his head for a few seconds and none of his ideas seemed to be a plausible solution. But one had more merit than the others, and he knew he had to act fast. Stephy and Bositch would be acting quickly, and he at least wanted to be in position when they started their fires. Tuvallis drew two daggers from their sheaths and stood up from the tall grass. He was already a big man, and the wide hood and dark furs he wore made him seem even larger. Perhaps big enough for the ruse that the situation forced him to attempt.

Tuvallis walked confidently forward toward the two orcs whose backs were facing him. Long ago he had learned some orcish words, but it had been so long ago that he was not sure if he recalled them correctly. They were not the choicest of words, but they may give him the time he needed.

"Short tooth's," Tuvallis grunted. He was told that it was a slang term that really made orcs mad. I guess he would find out. "More food for ya at the fire," he continued in choppy orcish.

Both the orcs got up from the ground and stood up tall. They were equally his height and wider. But their stance was not offensive, so Tuvallis guessed that his orcish was at least passable.

One of the brutes stepped closer as if trying to get a better look at Tuvallis. "Who are you?" it said in orcish as his hand moved closer to his blade. "You don't..."

Tuvallis didn't give him time to finish his sentence. He rammed one knife straight up under the chin of the nearest orc while stepping closer and slashing his other knife across the throat of the second astonished beast. He struck so quickly that the second orc didn't even have time to bring his hand to the hilt of his sword. The first orc died instantly while his comrade fell to the ground grasping his throat as blood pulsed through his fingers. He coughed and gurgled loudly, so Tuvallis quickly followed up the strike by pouncing on his chest and ramming the bloody knife into his brain.

He got up quickly, reclaimed his backpack, and glanced to his left towards the nearby machine. He thought he could hear a scuffle of some sort, but he didn't have time to worry about it. He took out the jugs of oil and silently went to work soaking the lower wood boards and planks. He couldn't completely cover the machine, but he thought it would be enough to ignite the engine and he could only hope that it would become fully engulfed in flame before they could put out the fires.

Tuvallis looked one more time to his left and just caught the flicker of a spark. Bositch must be using his tinderbox to light the engine. It worried him how bright that spark was. If he could see it so easily, then so could someone else. He too used his tinderbox and on the third attempt was able to get some tinder lit, quickly placing it on one of the soaked boards which immediately burst into flame.

Within seconds he was running through the grass, hunched over, toward the dark shadows of the surrounding trees. He could see that Bositch had ignited his engine as well, but he still had no visual of Stephy's. It wasn't until he got to the trees that he could see, with relief, that Stephy had also been successful.

A loud and furious commotion erupted in the orc camp as leaping flames completely covered the base of the engines, reaching upward as they began to consume the upper structures. Two shadows joined Tuvallis and even in the darkness he could clearly see their white teeth behind their broad grins.

"Let's go," Stephy said hurriedly as he took off towards their horses. Despite the darkness they were able to make their way in the correct direction. They had paid close attention to their surroundings on their approach, and had used various markers to guide them. They had gone maybe a hundred paces when they heard several deep growls ahead of them. Stephy stopped instantly, and Tuvallis and Bositch joined him.

"That were no orc growl," Tuvallis whispered.

Just as he said this, two large gray wolves appeared at the top of the hill directly in front of them. Standing next to them were two orc handlers. The wolves' eyes, bright red, bored into their own. Tuvallis guessed that they must have been a scouting party that had picked up their scent.

"Dire Wolves," he said. "Don't run." Just as he said it both wolves attacked, leaping at them without warning. Incredibly large beasts, their shoulders were as high as a man's, with jaws capable of ripping off one's head with a quick flick of their powerful necks. "Spread out!" Tuvallis yelled. "Go for their necks!"

They were upon them instantly. One jumped for Stephy's throat while the other went for Bositch, who had done just what Tuvallis had told him not to do. He ran. But he wasn't running away, he was running to the side to try and flank them. Tuvallis hadn't moved an inch. He drew his sword and crouched, waiting for his opportunity. And it came quickly.

Stephy drew his short sword and had just enough time to take a defensive stance as the first wolf flew through the air with its deadly fangs leading the way. The seasoned warrior lifted his left hand up to protect his face and neck, which he knew the wolf would go for, and positioned his sword for a strike. Unfortunately Stephy didn't have a shield, so the only thing he could do was sacrifice his arm in the hopes that he could get in a mortal wound with his sword. The wolf's jaws clamped onto his forearm as it slammed into him like a battering ram. Stephy felt his arm snap as they flew backward in a tangle of limbs. Despite the force of the attack Stephy was able to angle his short sword upward, cutting a nasty wound along the wolf's flank before they landed in the grass and snow.

But he was no match for the strength and speed of a Dire Wolf, and as soon as they landed the massive animal jumped on top of Stephy, using its powerful neck to violently shake his already broken arm. Stephy screamed in agony as its jaws ripped through his flesh, breaking more bones in the process. Just when he thought his arm would be ripped off, he heard a squeal and then a release of pressure on his arm.

Tuvallis withdrew his sword from the wolf's side and shoved the huge animal off of Stephy. As Tuvallis stood above him, Stephy thought he saw him wink before he disappeared into the darkness.

Stephy got up slowly, cradling his mangled arm. He felt a sharp pain shooting through his shoulder. His shoulder could be dislocated, but he couldn't tell for sure, distracted by the intense pain from his crushed and bleeding arm. The smallest movement caused severe pain. But he had to move. His screams would have drawn the attention of other orcs, and his friends might need him. With his good arm he gripped his short sword again. But as soon as he stood up to survey the scene he heard fighting to his right, and at the same time he saw two orcs bounding down the hill in front of him. The first one was almost upon him, short sword raised for attack, while the second orc veered to the right toward the other commotion.

Bositch's attempt to flank the wolf had not gone unnoticed. One wolf had caught his movement and turned to go after him. Bositch caught a glimpse of the flying wolf out of the corner of his eye and reacted on instinct. Luckily he was amazingly quick. He was a relatively slight man, but his small frame was covered with sinewy well defined muscles, enabling him to move with lightning speed. He could run incredibly fast for his size. Though his legs were short, he could move them so quickly that he could outrun most seasoned sprinters.

He dropped low just under the flying wolf, spinning his body with the animal as it leaped over the top of him. As the wolf flew over him he thrust his knife upward, its razor sharp blade slicing across its belly. The animal growled in pain, landed, and immediately leaped at him again.

But Bositch was ready. Crouching low, he threw his bloody knife at the wolf, simultaneously diving to the side as he drew a second knife from his hip. The first knife had embedded itself into the wolf's shoulder, causing the animal to hesitate just enough to give Bositch time to draw his short sword.

But now the wolf's handler had joined the fight and both crouched before Bositch, growling and ready to attack. Bositch grimaced, realizing that his odds of survival had just gotten worse. But his grimace turned into a smile as a large shadow emerged behind the orc, and in a flash of glittering metal its head was flying in the air.

The wolf then turned on Tuvallis, which gave Bositch the opening he needed. He lunged forward and skewered the beast in the side, just as Tuvallis swatted its deadly claws away with his sword. The wolf howled and spun towards Bositch, ripping the sword out of his hands. But it mattered not as Tuvallis quickly buried his sword in the wolf's throat, its howl becoming a gurgle as it fell, its warm blood steaming as it spread over the cold ground.

"Thanks," Bositch said as he quickly withdrew his blade from the wolf's side. Tuvallis gave him his usual grunt, and they both ran back towards Stephy.

Stephy bit back the pain as he let his damaged arm dangle, doing the best he could to ready his body for the attack. The orc growled as he brought his heavy cutting blade down towards Stephy's head. Stephy moved back and brought his short sword up to block the strike. But the orc was strong and he was attacking from an elevated position. The strike shook Stephy's entire body, causing excruciating pain to shoot through his arm. He hastily back peddled as the orc came at him again. Stephy was on the defensive, blocking strike after strike, but was unable to react quickly enough to bring the attack to the orc. The pain was so severe that it was all he could do to keep the beast's blade away.

Suddenly the orc stumbled and he saw the beast reach up and grab at its throat. He heard the orc gasp and cough, then watched in a daze as it fell dead to the ground. Then Bositch and Tuvallis were at his side.

"Can you walk?" Bositch asked as he withdrew his dagger from the orc's throat.

"Aye, hurts like hell though," Stephy said through clenched teeth.

"We have to move," Tuvallis growled as they both followed his gaze down the hill towards the enemy army. The engines were now fully enflamed and in the distance they could also see the large fires of the catapults. Chaos had erupted around the conflagration, with bodies scurrying frantically about trying to extinguish the flames. But some orcs had heard the commotion of their battle with the wolves, and Tuvallis could see several small groups fan out into the grass towards them. They could not risk another fight, especially with Stephy's injury.

Bositch led them into the night and Tuvallis brought up the rear. Tuvallis grimaced every time Stephy groaned in pain. He felt for the man, but he also knew that if the enemy had more wolves, they would not get far before they were upon them. And that fight would not go so well. They had no choice but to run as fast as they could and hope that Captain Hadrick and his group were also in full retreat. They had left their horses about two miles from the enemy camp. It would be a long two miles, especially for Stephy, as they tried to elude their enemies in the night.

They had covered about half the distance when Stephy stumbled and fell. Tuvallis reached down and quickly righted him, concerned at how pale he was.

"I'll be okay, just a bit lightheaded," he mumbled. Tuvallis looked down at the wound and saw for the first time how bad it was. His entire forearm was shredded and Tuvallis could see his broken bones through the torn flesh.

Tuvallis swore under his breath. "Bositch, hold on, need to make a quick tourniquet." He used his knife and cut off a strip of cloth from Stephy's cloak. He cinched it tightly around his bicep and tied it quickly. The bleeding slowed but Stephy had already lost too much blood, and his eyes fluttered between consciousness and sleep. It was then that Tuvallis heard the howls.

"In Ulren's name we have to go!" Bositch whispered fiercely.

"I'll carry him," Tuvallis replied firmly.

"You'll never make it. He's too heavy."

Tuvallis said nothing and with a grunt he reached down and hefted Stephy up and over his shoulder. Bositch shook his head in amazement and raced into the night. Bositch was right. Stephy was heavier than one would expect for someone with such a slight frame. But he was a compact warrior, densely muscled from years of hard travel and fighting. Tuvallis felt like he was carrying a load of rocks. Tuvallis grunted with the effort as he ran after Bostich. Soon his legs began to tire and his lungs heaved with exertion. But he continued on sheer will alone.

He got a quick reprieve when he stumbled on a snow patch and went down, dropping Stephy to his side. Stephy groaned and momentarily awakened. "Just leave me," he said in a hoarse whisper.

The howls began again, this time sounding much closer. Tuvallis and Bositch looked down the gentle hill on which they stood. Racing up the hill, maybe two hundred paces below them, were three Dire Wolves, this time ridden by their orc handlers. Tuvallis reached instinctively for his arrows but realized they were not there.

"Damn the Forsworn!"

"What do we do?" Bositch asked frantically.

"We can't run," he said as he drew his short sword and a dagger. "Good luck," was all he said as he smiled at Bositch and readied himself for battle.

Bositch was amazed at the man's brazenness. Or maybe it was his recklessness, or his calm demeanor. He couldn't tell. But the smile surprisingly relaxed him, and he too drew his sword and unsheathed his dagger. If this was his day to die, he couldn't think of a better companion with which to share the experience.

As the orcs and their wolves bounded quickly up the hill, Tuvallis and Bositch crouched side by side and waited for the inevitable. But suddenly, from their left, they were amazed to see a giant apparition burst from the darkness and barrel into one of the wolves. It hit the wolf and rider so hard that they were lifted from the ground and flung fifteen paces into the night.

The wolf and rider at the rear of the group pivoted quickly, instantly turning their attack to this new assailant. Tuvallis could just make out the fight in the distance, and he couldn't believe what he saw. Their savior was perhaps twice as tall as a man, massively built, and resembled a giant, or an ogre. But what was really amazing was the giant's attire, in particular the brilliant and beautifully crafted cuirass that covered his torso and shoulders. Tuvallis watched, mesmerized, as the creature swung a giant silver mace as large as a small tree. The weapon glowed in the darkness and Tuvallis heard it swoosh through the air as it connected solidly with the unfortunate wolf, crushing it instantly, the sheer force of the blow sending both rider and beast flying through the air.

Tuvallis's stunned expression disappeared instantly as he realized the remaining wolf and its rider were almost upon them. "Take de rider, I'll get de wolf," Tuvallis said just before the wolf leaped toward them. Bositch quickly flicked his wrist, aiming his dagger at the orc while Tuvallis jumped to the side, bringing his blade down hard and slashing a deep gash across the wolf's flank.

Bositch's knife struck the orc's shoulder, but bounced harmlessly off its armor. However, the force of the blow threw the creature off balance enough so that, as the wolf pivoted, the orc was unable to hang on and fell from its back. The orc scrambled to get up, but not quickly enough. Bositch lunged forward and brought his short blade down into its skull, slicing through bone and brain.

Tuvallis quickly danced backwards as he spun his blade left and right, fending off the wolf's deadly jaws and claws. Suddenly, something hit the wolf with enough force to spin it in a complete circle. Tuvallis could hear bones break as it shrieked in pain. A rock had been thrown from the darkness, completely crushing the wolf's hind legs. As it laid thrashing on the ground, growling and howling in pain, Tuvallis ran his sword through the heart, ending its agony.

Bositch joined Tuvallis as their newfound savior slowly emerged from the darkness nearby. The beast, for surely it was no human, seemed to hesitate the closer it got. It stopped five paces away and just stood there with its teeth exposed in a wide grimace. At first Tuvallis didn't know what to make of it, but then he began to smile.

"What?" Bositch asked, nervously gripping his bloodied short sword.

"I think its tryin' to smile," Tuvallis replied.

The creature looked like a cross between an orc and an ogre. Its body was ogre-like, thick and covered with course hair, while its face and skin color looked more like an orc's, gray green in color, with deep set eyes and heavily pronounced brows protruding over a squat wide nose and large mouth filled with sharp teeth yellowed with decay. He wore dirty furs around his waist and his huge feet were bare. But the strangest part of his appearance was his armor and weapon. They shone brightly even in the darkness of the cloudy night. Both were brilliantly polished and immaculately clean. Embossed in the center of the cuirass was a stag head with a rack of horns that fanned out over the beast's massive chest. Its weapon was as thick as a man's arm and nearly as long as the creature's body. The head of the mace was polished silver, as big around as an orc's head, and covered with spikes each the length of a short sword. Blood still dripped from the weapon as Tuvallis gazed at it, amazed at how easily the giant held it in his hand.

"Isn't that one of Shyann's symbols?" Bositch asked.

"It is," Tuvallis said. He had seen the symbol many times in the years that he had visited the mountain town of Manson. Shyann was an important goddess there, and the stag was a symbol of luck and wealth.

"Hagar," the ogrillian said as he tapped his chest with his empty hand.

Tuvallis couldn't believe it. Standing before him was a beast whose ancestry obviously included the most hated evil creatures in the realms, wearing Shyann's armor and carrying her weapon, who had saved them from certain death, and was now introducing himself to them with a toothy grin. He had seen everything now.

"I be Tuvallis, and dis is Bositch," Tuvallis said, indicating the small scout. "My wounded friend be Stephy."

Bositch went to Stephy and helped him stand. "Tuvallis, we have to keep moving."

"Leeft," Hagar said to Tuvallis as he moved his empty hand up and down.

"What is he saying?" Bositch snapped, his anxiety increasing as more howls and commotion erupted in the distance.

"I think he be saying dat he wants to lift him," Tuvallis said. "What say you, Stephy?" But Stephy had lost consciousness again. "Well, we have no choice. Go ahead Hagar, carry him and follow us."

Bositch hesitated, not fully trusting the massive creature before him. But what other choice did they have? Bositch moved aside as Hagar slowly stepped toward them. Hagar seemed to recognize that slow movements would help them relax in his presence. He reached down with one hand and hoisted Stephy up as if he weighed no more than an infant. Slowly and gently he lifted him up, placing him over his shoulder; then he turned toward them and gravely announced, "I follow."

And with that they raced into the night.

With Hagar's help they reached their horses quickly. Captain Hadrick, Groban, and Sury were already there and mounted. They looked anxious as they watched their remaining comrades emerge from the darkness. The horses whinnied and stomped about in fear as Hagar approached slowly behind Tuvallis. He was so big that there was no hiding him. Captain Hadrick and his men had to hold their horses' reins tightly to prevent them from bolting into the night.

"What in Ulren's name!" Sury exclaimed softly, instinctively drawing his sword as Hagar came into view.

"It's okay," Tuvallis said quickly. "He saved us."

"Bandris's blade! That's an ogrillian," Hadrick said. Then he noticed Stephy draped casually over Hagar's shoulder, and he too brought his blade to bear. "Is he dead?" Hadrick demanded, pivoting his horse toward Hagar and causing the huge beast to step away from him, lowering his head submissively.

"I told ya, he's not our enemy. Put yer blades away," Tuvallis ordered. "He killed two Dire Wolves and their riders. He could have killed us easy, and he's been carryin' Stephy fer de last mile. We're alive because of him."

"He's right," Bositch said. "And his armor has Shyann's mark on it."

Hadrick looked at the armor for the first time and his eyes grew wide with astonishment. "I've never heard of such a thing," he said. "But we don't have time to analyze it further! We need to get out of here! Mount up, and secure Stephy on his horse!"

And that is exactly what they did. Tuvallis quickly took Stephy, who was still unconscious, and gently tied his limp body to the saddle. Hagar kept as close to Tuvallis as he could, without getting so close that he'd spook the horses.

"Hagar, you follow?" Tuvallis asked.

Hagar turned his head sideways as if he were trying to sort out his words. Then he opened his mouth, revealing that awful tooth filled smile, and grunted, "Hagar follow."

Seven

Ullis Hill

Jonas and the rest of the group rode hard all morning. They stopped once to rest the horses and refresh themselves with some water, dried beef, and cheese. During the few times when they slowed to a trot to rest the horses, the group talked softly but sporadically, since everyone was so tense about their mission, where there were so many unknowns. Not knowing what to expect hampered the smooth flow of casual dialogue over their anxious tongues. Fil and Jonas, riding in the rear, managed to converse fairly regularly.

"So Jonas, how are you feeling?" Fil asked nonchalantly.

"What do you mean?"

"Well, about this new role of yours. I imagine you're a bit apprehensive and all going into this fight with the meager weapons that we all possess," Fil said jokingly, "or am I guessing correctly that Shyann has given you some blessings in disguise?" Fil asked as he eyed the plain looking swords hanging from Jonas's waist.

Jonas had to look at Fil to make sure he was joking. "Meager weapons? Oh no, my friend, they just look that way," he said, tapping the hilt of one of his swords. The black pommel did look plain, and it certainly lacked the cavalier luster of his previous weapons and armor.

Fil raised his eyebrows in interest, urging Jonas to continue.

"The weapons are magical," Jonas continued. "Everything is actually, even my boots. I'm just not sure how it all works yet."

"Figures," Fil said. "Don't you ever wonder why the gods just don't explain things? I mean, why make everything so secretive? I don't get it, reason number nineteen for my lack of allegiance."

"What are the other eighteen?" Jonas asked.

"You really want to know?"

Jonas laughed. "No, not really."

Allindrian had slowed her horse and moved next to the two young men. She smiled at Jonas as she positioned her horse near his. They had only talked briefly since Jonas had been rescued from the grips of the Forsworn. Everyone had been so occupied, and Jonas had needed a lot of rest from his ordeal. Early that morning they did have an opportunity to spar and afterward to talk briefly about what Shyann had asked of him, and of his new role in her name. But they had not had a chance to delve into much detail.

"So shadow warrior, what *do you know* of these weapons, besides the enhanced speed of the boots and gloves?"

"I can make the edge of the blades light up at will, and I think Shyann's symbol on the breast plate will shed light when I wish, or maybe when evil is near, but I have not yet tested that theory," Jonas said.

"Enhanced speed? What symbol?" Fil asked, staring at the plain charcoal gray metal plate that covered Jonas's chest and most of his stomach. The rest of the cuirass was black hardened leather and dark chainmail, all lacking fancy symbols or intricate designs that you might see on expensive armor.

"I think that is the point," Allindrian said. "To blend in and look normal. But when the time comes he can show his true power."

"I see. I guess that makes sense," Fil said thoughtfully.

"Jonas," Allindrian continued, "I think the magical properties of your clothes are similar to my ranger cloak."

"How so?" Jonas asked.

"I think they may help you blend into the shadows or surroundings. And your boots and gloves, along with their enhanced speed, may help with silent movement, or maybe even climbing."

"How do you know this?" Jonas asked.

"I don't. But that is what I would create for you if I were Shyann," she said smiling.

Jonas looked at his clothes and held his plain gloved hand to his face. "Makes sense," he said. "I guess I will find out. And I hope you're right."

They rode silently for a while before Jonas spoke again. "What do you plan to do after all this?" he asked Allindrian. "I mean, if we survive."

Allindrian looked at the young warrior. He was getting older she thought. He looked older for sure; no doubt the trials and ordeals he had been through had definitely matured him. He was certainly no longer the same young man that she had met five years ago. The five years of training, combat, and numerous trials, had molded him into a man, someone who had seen and experienced more in the last few years than most do in a lifetime, someone who had gained not only incredible physical skills, but also an immense emotional strength. She liked that about Jonas. He was so strong, so powerful, and yet so humble, and...what was the word...insecure. That wasn't really the word she was looking for, but it fit in a way. He questioned everything, always wondering if he could have done something better, or different, to create a better outcome.

"I will go back to my home. I will visit my king and queen. It has been a long time," she said as she thought about returning to her homeland.

"What's it like there?" Jonas asked.

Allindrian smiled broadly. "Very different. It's beautiful, the most amazing place you have ever seen. The forests are lush and green with trees much bigger than here. Everything we build is a part of our surroundings, unlike here where you destroy the land so that you may live. Things are much...slower...my people talk much less."

"I don't understand."

"Elves live a long time, Jonas. There is no hurry. Silence is preferable to the random chatter often associated with humans. We do not feel the need to rush anything, whether it be the crafting of a sword or the dialogue between lovers. In a lifespan longer than multiple human lifetimes, there is no need for haste and things are worth doing well. You might find my home rather quiet and boring," she said.

"It actually sounds nice." Jonas turned and looked directly at Allindrian. "How long will you live, Allindrian?" he asked bluntly.

She locked eyes briefly with him before looking away. "My human blood speeds up the aging process somewhat, but I could live as long as five or six human lifetimes. But the life of a Blade Singer is dangerous, and I can die by an arrow or sword just as easy as you."

They heard a commotion ahead as King Baylin prodded his horse into a run, signaling for the group to move out. The rest of the group followed, urging their horses to a gallop as they fell in behind the king.

"Guess our break is over," Jonas said with a smile. Allindrian smiled back, and they raced after the rapidly departing group.

It became obvious when they neared their destination. Dark clouds had moved in and their surroundings took on an ominous look.

Up ahead a low lying fog covered most of the ground, and everything about it seemed to say *do not enter.*

Lor-telliam pulled his horse to a stop and motioned for everyone to dismount. There were a number of stubby oak trees in the vicinity and they would make good spots to tether their animals. "I think we should walk from here. We are close. I can feel the magic, and that mist up ahead is the border," Lor-telliam announced as he dismounted.

Suddenly the horses whinnied, dancing and stomping on the ground nervously as they pulled on their reins. Kromm, who had already tethered his horse, drew his blade. Lor-telliam stood next to him gripping his wooden staff in both hands. The tip of the staff was carved into three leaves surrounding an oblong stone which began to emanate a bluish glow. He wore a slender sword at his side paired with a hunting dagger.

Then they all heard it, a deep rumbling growl coming from some shrubs ahead of them. The group froze, quickly unsheathing their weapons, their eyes intently searching the shrubbery ahead. They gripped their weapons tight as they looked tensely into the mist shrouded shrubs. Then they heard it again, this time much closer.

That's when Jonas felt something probing his consciousness, and the word *friend* echoed in his mind. The connection was subtle but familiar. He couldn't explain it, but he had felt this mental touch before. Then it came to him. It was Tulari. "Wait!" Jonas yelled as he sheathed his blade, "Put your weapons away!"

They looked at him with surprise. "Why do you say this, Jonas?" Lor-telliam asked.

"Whatever is out there is here for me. I can hear its mind, a familiar voice that I've heard before," Jonas said trying to explain the connection.

"Tulari?" Fil asked.

"Yes."

"She, or he, whatever it is sounds much different," Fil said with his eyes raised. "A bit more aggressive if you know what I mean." But he slowly sheathed his blade and the others followed suit, though not without some apprehension.

Just then a giant wolf-like creature emerged from the mist ten paces ahead. A thick coat of mottled gray and black fur covered its massive frame. Its shoulders were as high as their own, and the eyes in its large canine head glowed blue in the shadows. It opened its mouth, revealing teeth as long as daggers, as a low rumble escaped from its powerful lungs. Then its piercing eyes swept over the group before landing on Jonas.

"What is that? Jonas, you sure about this?" Fil asked, his hand still resting on the hilt of his blade.

"It be a night wolf," Cade said, "a distant cousin of the dire wolf. They are rare, almost extinct, and they don't hunt in packs like their cousins," the Dakeen warrior explained. He had already re-slung his battle axe on his back and he casually stood before the beast with his arms crossed over his muscled chest. "We have seen a few in de mountains back home. If he meant us harm, then he would've attacked us silently, from the shadows. We are safe."

"*She* would have," Jonas corrected. "Tulari is now female." Jonas wasn't sure how he knew it, but somehow he could sense that the wolf before him was indeed female.

"Who be this, Tulari?" Cade asked.

"It is, or was, my cavalier steed."

At the mention of her name, the night wolf casually trotted over to Jonas and sat down on her haunches in front of him. Jonas could not believe how big she was. As large as a horse, her head alone was the size of his torso, with paws as wide as two human hands. Jonas could see the sharp tips of long black claws emerge from the thick pads. Tulari opened her mouth panting, letting her long pink tongue hang out. She could have easily clamped those jaws around his entire torso as if he were no more than a bone to chew on. Instead, she leaned forward to nuzzle his body, almost knocking him over with her powerful strength. He felt the wolf nudge his mind again, *yes, Tulari*, she said, affirming what Jonas had said.

Jonas reached around and rubbed the thick fur around her neck. He could feel powerful muscle underneath and a deep low rumble reverberated through his hand. She was purring like a kitten. Jonas smiled and scratched behind her ears. "I've missed you, my friend."

"It is said they can hear and smell prey miles away, and that they are called night wolves because they are like shadows. You will not hear or see them, until it's too late," Tolvar said.

"There is magic around her," Lor-telliam added.

Tolvar grunted agreement. "There be mystery around these beasts. Some say they can shift form. Others say they have power in their eyes, that if you look into them too long you will be lost. Their pelts are worth a fortune."

Tulari swung her head toward the Dakeen warrior and barred her teeth, with a look so menacing that even Jonas stepped back from her.

Tolvar just laughed with is arms still crossed before him. "Do not fret, night beast. I'm allergic to fur."

Cade, Tolvar's brother, chuckled under his breath and nudged Tolvar with his elbow. That was the first time that Jonas realized that dwarves had a sense of humor. Even Tulari recognized it for she stopped growling and stood passively next to Jonas as if she were waiting for orders.

"Welcome back, Tulari," Allindrian said as she slowly stepped toward the night wolf and put her hand out. Tulari leaned forward and sniffed her hand. Then she licked it, allowing Allindrian to come close and pet her huge head. "A fitting companion for a shadow knight," Allindrian noted.

"Let us go while we still have light," Lor-telliam suggested. Everyone prepared themselves, tethering their horses and securing their weapons. They stayed close to each other as they moved up the gentle hill towards the mist that lay ominously across the grassy terrain. Tulari flanked Jonas, drifting in and out of the shadows. As they came to the top of the hill they looked down upon a completely different landscape, a dark foreboding place with thick fog swirling on the ground and dark clouds hovering above. Black swampy water bubbled up through the patchy grass, permeating the air with the smell of rotting vegetation. "Ullis Hill is two miles through this," Lor-telliam said. "Stay close and be vigilant."

"In Ulren's name what has the power to do this?" Fil asked.

"The Shan Cemar," was all the Ekahal said before he led them forward.

They moved slowly after Lor-telliam, hands grasping pommels, their eyes intensely scanning the area. Occasionally Jonas would see a shape looming in the mist that seemed to resemble some sinister creature only to have it turn out to be the silhouette of a tree. Everyone was nervous and jumpy, and Jonas felt his palms and forehead begin to sweat. They had advanced maybe several hundred yards when Jonas heard Tulari growl nearby, though he couldn't see her. In the same instant he noticed that the center plate of his armor began to glow brightly with an intense blue light, illuminating Shyann's tree. The fiery blue beacon alerted the rest of the party and the sound of blades being drawn from scabbards filled the air.

"A warning" Allindrian said as she nocked an arrow to her bow.

"I think so," Jonas responded. But he didn't like the light glowing in the darkness, silhouetting his body in blue, making him and the group a target for any nearby enemies. So he wished it away, and it disappeared in a flash.

Just then Tulari whispered in his mind...*trolls*!

"Trolls!" Jonas yelled.

"Run! Follow me! If we keep moving then they can't surround us!" Lor-telliam shouted as he led the group farther into the darkness. "Protect the king; if he dies we can't retrieve the sword!"

The trolls were upon them almost immediately. Out of the darkness they came, bringing with them an overwhelming odor of decay that surrounded them like a hoard of buzzing flies. Taller than Kromm they were, with long arms and legs. The fingers and toes of their claw-like hands and feet extended into nasty black talons, hooked and razor sharp. Sparse tufts of matted hair covered their monstrous heads. Broad bulging noses and large thick lipped mouths filled with rotting teeth dominated their facial features. Their thick skin resembled that of a diseased toad, bile green and covered with sores and warty growths. Jonas thought they were the ugliest, most disgusting things he had ever seen. And they were fast.

One leaped from the darkness at Jonas and he was so surprised by its speed that he barely avoided it. If it hadn't been for Cade he may not have. As Jonas ducked and tried to spin away from the creature, Cade swung his massive double bladed axe in a vicious arc, slicing deeply into its thigh, causing it to stumble and just miss Jonas.

Both of Jonas's blades erupted in blue flame as he launched himself toward the distracted troll, ramming both swords through its back, their flames flaring even brighter as the troll screamed in pain and fear, yanking itself off the vicious blades and stumbling into the mist.

More trolls came at them from the shadowing mist, forcing them to stop and form up. "They will regenerate if not cut by magical means!" Tolvar yelled as he sliced off the leg of an attacking troll. Cade was there to cleave its skull in half.

Jonas noticed that both of the dwarves' weapons glowed with an iridescent light. *Fil*, he thought, suddenly worried. His sword was not magical. He looked ahead for him and was almost blinded by fiery red flames shooting from the hands of Lor-telliam, flames that quickly and completely consumed four attacking trolls. Several others howled in fear and jumped back into the protection of the mist. They were afraid of fire.

Fil, meanwhile, brought his shield up to block the wicked punch of an attacking troll. Nearly as strong as an ogre, the force of its strike sent Fil stumbling backwards, his arm throbbing in pain. But he had no time to recover as the beast's long arms shot out with lightning speed, grabbing both edges of the shield, and yanking hard to the side. Fil flew into the air and landed several paces away in a puddle of black water. He was frantically trying to get up when he felt an immense pressure on the back of his neck, then suddenly he felt weightless. The troll had lifted him into the air and spun him around to face him, its grip on his neck like an iron vise. He knew with certainty that in a split second the beast could snap his neck like a twig. He had dropped his sword, but had instinctively drawn his knife, slicing the blade across the troll's wrist. The beast paused momentarily, but Fil was horrified to see that the wound had miraculously closed and the troll responded with a wicked grin. Time seemed to slow as Fil saw his death before him. In a surreal daze he stared into the beast's open jaws. He knew he could do nothing to prevent those deadly teeth from tearing into him. Even in his stupor he could smell the creature's fetid breath and he gagged and screamed in revulsion, bringing his hand up to his face in a futile attempt to protect himself.

Just then he heard a loud roar and found himself flying through the air again. This time he landed on his back and quickly righted himself, relieved beyond measure to see Tulari on top of the beast, the long black talons of her powerful hind legs raking into its abdomen, completely disemboweling it. Tulari then clamped her powerful jaws on the troll's head, and with a mighty jerk of her neck, tore off its head as if it were a plum being plucked from a tree.

Meanwhile, Kromm and Allindrian were fighting side by side as they had done deep in the catacombs of Cuthaine. As he blocked their powerful fists with his shield, he swung his giant blade left and right, cutting down troll after troll. The sound of their fists striking Kromm's shield resembled the cadence of a war drum, with each beat marking another casualty of his blade. Allindrian had dropped her bow and the reassuring song of her sword sang death to any who came near. Her silver blade whistled through the dense mist, weaving and slicing into arms and legs. They came at her with foot and claw, but it was like trying to snatch a fly from the air as she eluded every attack.

Lor-telliam was standing near King Baylin, one hand alight with fire that was reflected in his eyes. No trolls were willing to risk attacking them, fearing the fiery destruction from the diminutive elf. Lor-telliam was watching the fight, waiting for an opening to unleash his fire. King Baylin moved to help his comrades. "No, stay behind me!" Lor-telliam yelled over the din of the battle.

"I will not stand here idly while everyone else fights!" the king yelled back, his eyes blazing.

"You will! This mission depends on your survival!"

"I am king!" Baylin shot back.

"I know! Now act like it and stay behind me!" Lor-telliam ordered.

The king looked as if he were about to strike the Ekahal. No one had ever spoken to him like that and certainly had not dared to order him around. But this was an Ekahal, and deep inside he knew the elf was right. "For now I will do as you say," King Baylin growled. He remained next to the elf but he kept his sword drawn, clenching it angrily as he glared in frustration at the continuing battle.

Cade and Tolvar fought side by side. In fact it looked as if they were glued to each other's hips. And in a way they were. Each warrior had a three foot chain looped around his belt. One of the chains now spanned the gap between them and connected each other solidly together. One or the other chain could be quickly connected to the other's belt by custom built clasps. Tolvar carried his two handed battle axe easily with his right hand while Cade used his left. Tied together as they were they became a fighting juggernaut. Under most circumstances, and with most warriors, this technique would not be successful. The chain would get in the way and their movement would be hampered, fouling blocks and attacks. But with the brothers, who had mastered the technique over a hundred years of fighting together, it worked perfectly. Their blades worked harmoniously together, blocking each other's flanks like they too were twin brothers. Their silver axe blades cut and spun as they moved together in unison. They had obviously perfected this tactic and no troll could come near them without being cut down by either axe. The duo's short stature enabled them to slice into the trolls' long legs, bringing them down like timber.

When the beasts tried to use their long arms to grab the stout warriors, they ended up with bleeding stumps. Soon the ground was littered with slithering arms and legs, while what remained of the trolls stumbled about or even crawled across the ground, panicked and confused as to why their limbs were not regenerating. Normally a wound would heal or a severed limb would grow back in minutes, but these injuries were being inflicted by dwarven made axes imbued with the magic of their best priests. Dakeen only fought with the best.

There was a quick reprieve from the fighting since all the nearby trolls were dead. "Let's go, we have to move!" Lor-telliam yelled as he raced ahead. The others quickly gathered themselves and ran after the nimble elf. Jonas helped Fil find his sword and Jonas brought up the rear, with Tulari loping easily behind him, drifting in and out of the greyness.

The next several hours were spent running and battling trolls, as the beasts followed and attacked them from the shadowy fog. They fought their way onward, but for every troll they dispatched, it seemed another appeared to take its place. They had only managed to progress maybe a mile into the misty realm and they still had a ways to go.

Everyone, including Jonas, was beginning to tire. He could no longer pray to Shyann and feel her energy flow through him. He was on his own now, and he had to rely only on his physical strength, just like everyone else.

And yet, though he was beginning to tire, he was a bit surprised at his improved speed and how easily he was able to keep up with Allindrian and Lor-telliam. It had not been difficult for the Blade Singer to outpace Jonas in the past, but now he was leaping across logs and dodging holes filled with black stinking water almost as quickly and nimbly as she. He caught her glance at him briefly a few times, and noticed her smile as her eyes moved to his magical boots. Jonas had to admit that his newfound speed and agility were exhilarating. Shyann had not left him without some powerful tools.

And it was a good thing too, for a huge uprooted tree suddenly flew at them. He and Allindrian spun and jumped at seemingly impossible angles, narrowly avoiding the somersaulting missile. But King Baylin was not so lucky and the tree clipped his shoulder sending him spinning into the mist.

"To the king!" Kromm yelled as the giant warrior ran over to King Baylin.

Jonas then quickly turned to face a huge troll who was bounding at them from up ahead. Jonas guessed that it must have thrown the tree, and now its long strides were bringing it closer to Jonas and Allindrian faster than he thought possible. Jonas readied himself, but the attack never came as flames suddenly engulfed the creature, burning it to ash.

Lor-telliam was next to him instantly, one hand holding a silver sword and the other grasping his long staff, its tip glowing with blue light. "We must find the king," he said as he followed Kromm into the mist.

Kromm had found him ten paces away lying in a pool of black water about a foot length deep. He was struggling to rise from the muddy ground, but Kromm didn't have time to help him, as three more trolls came at him like ghosts from the fog.

Kromm roared as Cormathiam, Kromm's sentient sword, infused him with new energy. His shield came up, blocking a strike from the troll on his left just as he crouched under a clawed hand, swinging his glittering sword in a dangerous arc, disemboweling the troll in front of him while severing the leg of the troll to his right. Fueled by battle lust he spun toward the opponent to his left. He took two more powerful blows with his shield, which dented it badly and forced Kromm back away from the king.

But King Baylin was up now and his blade sliced into the troll's thigh, giving Kromm the second he needed to push forward and ram Cormathian up and through the beast's chest. The troll howled in pain and in its last dying moment it brought both fists down towards Kromm's head. Kromm quickly released his grip on his sword, side stepping to avoid the blow, then thrusting his heavy boot into the troll's knee, the power of the kick crushing its kneecap and causing its legs to buckle. The troll, already dead from its chest wound, fell face down in the muddy ground. Kromm gathered his sword as the others joined them.

"Are you hurt?" Lor-telliam asked King Baylin. The king was holding his arm at an awkward angle. His face was pale and it was obvious to all that he was biting back pain.

"I think my shoulder is broken. I cannot move it."

"I will heal it. Form a perimeter," the elf said. But no one needed to be told. They had already made a circle around them.

Lor-telliam placed both of his hands on King Baylin's arm as the others quickly drank from their canteens and watched the perimeter. It wasn't long before the elf's hands glowed, and as he continued to chant healing energy found the king's broken bones and fused them back together, mending the surrounding tissue in the process.

Jonas again felt Tulari's presence in his subconscious. *New danger*, she said as she silently came to him from the shadows. He wondered what words she was able to communicate and comprehend. So far her messages had been brief and simple, but it had been enough.

"Something else is coming!" Jonas warned the others. The razor sharp edge of his blades were glowing a translucent blue. It seemed that his weapons and armor had the capability of warning him of imminent danger, or evil, he was not sure which yet. Or maybe they could do both.

"I need a few more moments," Lor-telliam said.

"And you shall have it," Kromm growled. Jonas looked at the king, seeing only iron resolve. He had never fought next to anyone like him. Kromm had just dispatched three trolls as if they had been new recruits. He feared nothing, and every inch of his body resonated with devastating power. He stood tall, covered in sweat, mud, and the blood of his enemies, his shield dented so badly that it was nearly unusable. And yet he might as well have been riding a white horse and wearing the armor of a cavalier, for he had the same effect on those around him. He was a leader, born to show men what kind of iron they had inside them. Jonas found himself calming standing next to the man, eager to fight, and not afraid to die if need be. If he were to die, he would be proud to die in his company.

Tulari growled and lowered her massive body to the ground, ready to spring at any moment.

"They are near," Jonas whispered as the others surrounded Lor-telliam and readied themselves. As Jonas's heart began to pound, he sought the state of Ty'erm, hungrily searching for the calming effects and heightened senses of that meditative state of consciousness. He focused his mind, breathing deeply, finally connecting with it, as an iron wall surrounded his emotions, calming his mind and focusing his energy on the task before him.

The grayness of the thick mist permeated their surroundings, making it seem as if it were perpetually dusk. Everyone knew it was not yet night, and they could catch glimpses of the sun futilely trying to push its way through the dark clouds, but even that could not mask the oppressive and ominous darkness that filled the air.

Dark gray forms began to emerge from the murky surroundings. They looked human in shape, but their movements were slow and jerky, bird-like and awkward at the same time.

"What are they?" Fil asked, nervously gripping his sword and holding his shield before him.

"How long, Elf?" Kromm asked tensely, his eyes scanning the new threat.

Whatever they were, they were in no hurry. Slowly they moved to surround them, closing the noose as they drifted closer, finally coming into view through the shifting mist. They did, in fact, resemble humans, but their skin was gray and their faces were distorted with grim demonic features. Yellow eyes peered at them through the darkness and they caught glimpses of long fang like teeth reflecting against their ashen faces in the dim light. Their hands had abnormally long fingers ending in curved black talons. Some wore the remnants of tattered leggings and tunics, while others were covered in rusty armor or decaying robes. Some were completely naked, oblivious of the cold and their surroundings. And though none carried weapons, their appearance was terrifying. But what was worse was the stench of death that surrounded them, a suffocating smell of rot and decay even worse than the trolls. Jonas felt his stomach rise in his throat.

"What are they?" Jonas gagged.

"I'm not sure," Allindrian replied, her face twisted in a grimace of disgust.

"They are ghasts," Lor-telliam said as he joined them with King Baylin, whose arm was now healed. The king's shield was again strapped to it as if it had never been broken. "Evil creatures that were cannibals in life and are worse in death. Their touch causes brief paralysis so be wary," Lor-telliam warned. He then whispered a few words, and from the tip of his staff shot a metal blade as long as a man's forearm. The blade glowed with an intense blue light, and crackled with magical energy.

"Lead the way," Kromm said to Lor-telliam. "Jonas, bring up the rear. We will have to fight our way through, so be vigilant. If someone becomes paralyzed we must stop and protect them, so keep an eye out for each other."

Everyone nodded in agreement and ran after the Ekahal. The nearest ghasts were only twenty paces away by now so the elf had to punch his way through them. But no one had anticipated how fast they were. As soon as they had moved it was as if the creatures had become animated with unnatural speed. Some ran hunched over while others flew across the ground on all fours, but all moved with lightning speed, and they were upon them before they had moved fifteen paces. Their blood chilling screams filled the air, a deafening cacophony of shrill screeches and piercing howls so awful that the very sound sent shivers down Jonas's spine and he almost dropped his swords to cover his ears.

The stench hit Jonas first. And then they were on him. The group was forced to slow their pace as they engaged the ghasts. The creatures were fearless, and two came at him with no apparent concern for his glowing blue blades. Deadly claws shot for his throat while out of the corner of his eye he caught the shape of another one flying through the air at him. His right sword cut the attacking hands off at the elbow, but the thing still came at him with snapping teeth and yellow eyes burning with hunger.

The leaping ghast never reached Jonas, but instead found itself flying through the air in the opposite direction dangling from the jaws of the night wolf. Tulari dropped the beast, then pounced on it, ripping into its belly. Undaunted, the undead creature struggled to get up and continue its attack. But its damaged torso could no longer keep it erect, and it collapsed, landing again in the mud where it continued to crawl on its hands and knees towards its enemy, its hungry mouth searching for warm flesh.

Jonas kicked the handless ghast in the chest, launching it away from him while dancing left and right, deflecting more attacks while slashing at two other ghasts who had come at him. The group was forced to a standstill, engaged in a whirlwind of fighting as they frantically battled the hordes of creatures that pressed in on them from all sides.

Tolvar roared loudly as three ghasts jumped for his brother. Cade rammed the spike on the end of his axe directly into the chin of one, spearing it through the brain and clear through its skull. But then Cade found himself launching backwards as Tolvar yanked hard on the chain, while simultaneously jumping forward toward the other two attacking creatures. His axe flashed as it cut the closest one in half, but the third ghast struck Tolvar in the side, raking its deadly claws across any skin it could find. Tolvar wore no helm, but his shoulder and torso were protected by armor. But the beast managed to find flesh on the side of his head, neck, and exposed arm. Rivulets of red poured from the gashes and he grunted in pain. He felt a sudden jolt hit his body, and his dwarven constitution kicked in, trying to fend of the deadly paralysis. But for a few seconds he couldn't move, and he tumbled to the ground with the howling ghast on top of him.

Cade roared as he copied his brother's technique. Tolvar had used the chain to pull him from the immediate danger, and now Cade did the same, yanking on the chain, hoping to pull his brother from the monster's grasp. The ghast would not let go but the action saved Tolvar's life. The ghast's hungry mouth was just diving towards the Dakeen's exposed throat when he was yanked violently through the air, jerking the beast's head back and exposing its gray sinewy neck for Cade's axe. The ghast's head flew from its shoulders and Tolvar, landing at Cade's feet, slowly regained his movement. "Do ya always have to copy me moves?" the dwarf asked as his brother helped him up. With a quick chuckle, they both rejoined the fight.

Lor-telliam and King Baylin fought side by side. The elf was a blur of seemingly effortless movements, while the powerful king swung his long sword in great arcs, blocking with his shield and cutting into the advancing beasts. Lor-telliam's staff spun in wide circles, easily slicing through their flesh, the magical blade relentlessly and precisely dismembering beast after beast. He flowed like water around rocks with no black claws breaking through his defenses.

But though they fought with the skill of heroes, they were being overwhelmed by the sheer numbers of the undead beasts. Even Allindrian could not totally avoid the array of black claws flying from the mist. One ghast managed to rip a nasty cut across her thigh, causing her to spin, foiling her parry of another's attack. She tried to regain her balance but her body wouldn't react as it should, the pain from her thigh accompanied by a bolt of paralysis. Dwarves and elves were naturally more immune to such attacks, but even though the paralysis was brief, the seconds lost to it could be life threatening in combat.

Luckily, Kromm was near and he slammed the edge of his shield down on the head of the attacking ghast, crushing its skull as if it were a rotting pumpkin. But no one was there to stop another beast from leaping on top of the Blade Singer's frozen body.

Allindrian felt the thing's claws dig into her shoulders and knew that its vicious teeth would find her throat in seconds. Her shaking body was still immobile but she thought she could still use her mouth, at least enough to cast a simple spell, as it would be her only chance. "Ul anthar

Luminos!" she screamed. A bright light instantly flared from her hand shooting into the side of the ghast and exploding in a brilliant white. She had hoped to hit the thing in the face but she could not move her hand well enough to aim properly. But the light flared bright enough that it startled the creature just as its nasty teeth were descending toward her throat. The creature screeched and jumped off of her, away from the light. The light did the ghast little harm, but it was enough to give Allindrian a few more seconds, which luckily was all she needed. As she regained the ability to control her limbs, she scooted quickly away from the beast, giving herself a few more moments to recover completely.

But once the ghast had recovered, it readied itself for another attack to finish off its elven prey. But before it could attack, a fiery blue blade erupted from its chest, while a second blade flashed through the air relieving the howling creature of its head.

"Are you okay?" Jonas asked frantically as he pulled her to her feet. She reached down and picked up her sword, fully feeling her senses come back to her. But that was a two edged blade since the deep wounds in her shoulders now rocked her with pain.

"I am now," she returned with a forced smile.

Jonas saw the blood and immediately felt useless again. New frustration overwhelmed him as he realized that he could not heal his friend.

Allindrian saw his pained expression. "I will be fine, Jonas. You saved me. Besides, I can heal myself when I have time. They are just scratches."

There was a small break as the first wave of ghasts had been destroyed, but no sooner had they caught their breath when several dozen more of the creatures began emerging from the surrounding darkness, their fetid stench preceding their arrival.

"We cannot keep this up," Fil said, sweat still pouring from his face. Everyone was tired and splattered with mud and blood, thankfully not much of their own.

"If we stay here and wait for them to come to us then we will die here. We have to move," Kromm said.

"Agreed," Lor-telliam added. "Everyone! Quickly, come near me!"

They hurried to obey, surrounding the Ekahal as he began to chant. The ghasts marched slowly and relentlessly closer. They seemed to sense there was no hurry, that they had them trapped, almost as if they enjoyed the added suspense of delaying the kill.

But they had never before battled an Ekahal. Suddenly Lor-telliam shot his staff into the air as he completed the words of his spell. Everyone looked up to see dazzling blue arcs of lightning flash across the black sky, then almost immediately they bolted straight back down towards them. Everyone instinctively dove for cover, expecting the lightning to burn them to ash. But instead, the blue bolts converged on Lor-telliam's staff, shooting back out from its glowing tip in dozens of bright tendrils of lightning that pierced the darkness, bouncing from one ghast to another, incinerating them into dust. In seconds they were all destroyed, and the lightning had disappeared as quickly as it had materialized.

Lor-telliam, panting heavily, slumped to one knee, propping himself up with his staff.

Kromm was up first and helped the elf to his feet. "Are you okay?"

"Give me a moment. That spell is very wearing on the body."

"It looked it," Cade rumbled, clearly impressed.

Tulari trotted from the darkness and nuzzled her massive head against Jonas's chest. She was so large and strong that her gentle touch almost knocked him over. No one said anything as they regained their breath and waited for the Ekahal to find his. After a few moments he stood tall and breathed deeply.

"I am ready, let us go," he said.

"Lead on, wizard," Tolvar said, gripping his axe and unhooking himself from his brother. The wounds on Tolvar's arm and neck looked bad, but they bled very little and he appeared oblivious to them.

"Allindrian, how are your wounds?" Jonas asked.

"I will survive," she said with a reassuring smile. "My armor did its job and kept most of the claws from my flesh."

"Most?"

"As I said, several scratches only. Let us be on our way," she said, averting his worried gaze. She was going to heal herself but changed her mind, opting to save her strength for the possibility of more serious wounds.

They were off again and running at a fast jog, hoping to eat up the distance and get to the monument without further pursuit. Though they knew that would be highly unlikely. Still, one could hope.

They had run a decent distance without further attacks. Finally Lor-telliam stopped at the base of a gentle hill. Jonas recognized the spot. It was Ullis Hill, and before them were the stone steps that meandered up the slope to the monument at the top. On a bright sunny day you could easily see the structure erected above. But today the hill was covered in mist and darkness. And the stairs led into it.

"Do we need to take the stairs?" Fil asked. "They will surely be guarded."

Everyone was wondering the same thing and no one knew the land better than King Baylin, or perhaps Lor-telliam, but it had been a long time since his return.

"The other side of the hill is a cliff face over thirty paces high. We can climb the rise on this side without using the stairs, but there are small cliffs and boulders scattered across it that would make traversing it difficult," the king said.

"I think whatever is here knows we be here," Cade said, "I'd rather face me enemies on stable feet than guess what obstacle I will be facin' while I fight." His brother nodded agreement. Everyone looked at each other and assessed the situation.

"Let us take the stairs," Lor-telliam agreed, breaking the silence.

The stairway was wide, maybe four paces, allowing two or three people room to fight on them. Jonas recalled that they meandered up through a series of switch backs, periodically leading to a landing that opened out onto lookouts where visitors could rest on benches and take in the beautiful scenery. But it wasn't beautiful on this day and there was no rest to be had.

They had made it to the first landing when Jonas noticed that his chest had again begun to glow blue. At the same time Lor-telliam halted them and Tulari growled, each of them sensing danger. They fanned out defensively at the base of the next set of stairs, their eyes peering into the shadows, searching for signs of the next attack.

Fil's hands were sweating and his heart was pounding. He had never felt this kind of tension before. Here they were, facing creatures that would make even a seasoned soldier run in terror, and yet this group was standing firm and resolute, eyes focused intensely, facing whatever would come. If he were with any other group he was convinced that he would have run long ago. But the strength of their will was contagious and helped Fil find his own courage. He glanced at Jonas and saw that same calm focus and wondered if Jonas felt as nervous as he did. Maybe he wasn't giving himself enough credit. He wiped the sweat from his hand and re-gripped his sword. His shield felt heavy and he took two deep breaths to calm his nerves.

Jonas glanced at Fil and met his eyes. He worried for his friend. Fil was a strong fighter, there was no doubt. But he did not have the experience that the others had in fighting foes such as these. He could face a man, or even a boarg or an orc, but had never faced an enemy that could not be harmed by normal weapons. They were fighting creatures that only cavaliers, heroes, and wizards should fight, not young infantry soldiers. Nor did he have the weapons and armor needed to combat some of Malbeck's minions. But he did not lack courage, and despite his meager experience, Jonas felt much better with him near. He nudged Fil with his hand and smiled. "We will make it, my friend."

"And if we don't?" he said with a wry grin.

"Then we die a hero's death, boy," Tolvar said matter-of-factly.

It was then that they heard a slow rhythmic *clanking* coming from above, descending towards them on the landing. The sound grew louder, but the pace stayed the same. It sounded like iron shod boots walking on stone. And sure enough, that's what it was.

From the stairs above a dark form materialized from the shadows, moving toward them with slow deliberate steps, the black metal of its boots clanking ominously on the stone stairway. It wore black armor covered in serrated spikes and a long tattered red cloak swept the ground behind him. In one hand he carried an oval shield with Gould's white eye embossed in the middle and long wicked spikes sticking out around the perimeter. His other hand held a long sword that glowed an intense red, matching the eyes that were glaring down at them through the black slits of its helm. The helm encased his entire head and it too was covered with black spikes.

"A Banthra," Jonas whispered nervously. He had faced one before and had come out of that fight victorious. But that had been when he was a cavalier, with all the powers of one. Now as he looked at this creature waves of fear washed over him. He felt himself unconsciously slowly stepping away from the demon warrior.

Then, from behind him, a devilish laugh nearly shattered his nerves and he almost dropped his sword. Next to him, Fil did drop his sword, and the clanging of metal on stone reverberated loudly in the stillness.

Another Banthra rose from the mist behind them. The demon knight looked the same, but its cloak was a deep purple, almost black, and it was lined with some sort of dark fur. He carried no shield, only two maces capped with spiked heads. They were large, about as big as Kromm's fist, and the spikes were each as long as a dagger. The weapons looked cumbersome and yet the Banthra carried them with apparent ease.

"Now these two be worthy of a Dakeen," Cade grumbled behind Jonas. Jonas looked at the dwarf and noticed he was smiling. How could that be? He himself was struggling against the desire to flee into the darkness, and yet this dwarf faced two Banthras with a smile on his face. Jonas knew that these undead warriors projected a magical fear few men could withstand. As a cavalier he could combat that fear, but now, he had a difficult time subduing his desire to run.

"Stay close to me!" Lor-telliam ordered as he chanted a few quick words. Again, light flashed from his staff and washed over the group. Suddenly Jonas felt himself again. The elf had dispelled the Banthras' magic spell, repelling the fear that emanated from them. It was as if there had been a fist squeezing his heart, and then it just disappeared. His nerves calmed and his focus returned. He saw Fil quickly reach down and grab his sword from the ground. Obviously the effect was universal as everyone readied themselves for battle.

"Your spells just prolong your inevitable deaths," the Banthra behind them hissed. Its demonic voice grated on Jonas's spine and he shivered with the vileness of it. "I will relish spilling your blood, especially yours," the Banthra said, easily lifting his mace and pointing it at Jonas.

"One of your own said that to me before, and yet I survive, and he did not," Jonas retorted.

"You were protected then, now you are not."

Somewhere from deep inside, Fil found the courage to speak. "We protect each other." It sounded lame, but it resonated well with everyone, and they gripped their weapons with new courage bolstered by the proximity of comrades.

Just then Tulari turned and growled into the mist that covered the sloping hill. Silent shapes had emerged from the darkness and were advancing toward the landing. Jonas's breath caught in his throat as he recognized their forms and movement.

Fil did as well. "Boargs," he said through gritted teeth.

175

The landing was twenty paces square and the back side had been dug into the hill to keep it level. The hillside had a stone retaining wall, three paces high, and the downward side was wrapped in a smaller wall lined with various benches on which to rest and enjoy the view. The terrain beyond the landing was sloped and rocky, but the boargs traversed it easily. They were surrounded on all sides.

"Time to die," the Banthra on the stairs growled.

"Exactly!" Kromm roared and charged the Banthra with the sword.

Everyone reacted instinctively as they readied themselves for battle.

But the boargs were quicker, and their powerful leaps carried them up and over the wall to land in their midst. Bodies tumbled and screams erupted as the landing became a chaotic whirlwind of steel and blood.

As Jonas attacked the second Banthra he noticed that Shyann's symbol on his chest was glowing with a blue light, which grew brighter as he got closer to the demon. Jonas felt alive again, rejuvenated, and he easily parried and spun, avoiding the descending mace. His other sword led the spin but it was intercepted by the Banthra's second mace, and they exchanged attacks and parries as they moved across the far end of the landing.

Kromm came in low at the Banthra. He had no choice as the demon was standing at an elevated position. His sword missed as the black knight jumped back, bringing his sword down on top of Kromm's shield. The red glowing blade cut into Kromm's shield and struck his forearm guard underneath, like a hammer, forcing him backwards. His shield was not magical, but his armor was and that was what saved him. The force of the blow would leave a nasty bruise, but other than that his arm was intact. And he didn't have time to remove his shield; besides, it was still usable.

The Banthra leveled his sword at Kromm, red flames shooting from the tip. Kromm could do nothing but crouch low, and lift the damaged shield in front of him, hoping that it would save him, but instantly feeling intense heat as his shield turned red and his skin began to blister. Just as he thought he couldn't bear the pain, he heard a *swoosh* and the flames vanished. He frantically unstrapped the red hot shield and dropped it to the ground. He glanced up and saw that the Banthra had been forced up the stairs by Lor-telliam. The elf's staff was alight with the blue blade and they fought in a shower of sparks as their weapons made contact. Kromm had no doubt that the Ekahal had just saved him from a fiery death.

But Kromm had no time to revel in his salvation as two boargs immediately came at him. One came in low, going for his powerful legs, while the other was preparing to leap off the edge of the wall towards him. Kromm snapped his leg out and his metal shod boots took the boarg in the face, stopping it instantly and crushing the beast's jaw. A kick from any other man would have been thwarted by the aggressive power of the boarg attack. But from Kromm it ended the fight.

He spun, pivoted, and swung his blade in a deadly arc that took the flying boarg in the side. Cormathian sliced through ribs and organs and by the time the boarg landed it was already dead. But he had no time to rest, as more boargs came for him.

Kromm, Allindrian, Fil, King Baylin, and the Dakeen brothers had their hands full with boargs, while Jonas and Lor-telliam battled the Banthras. Boarg bodies littered the landing and it didn't take long before the stones were slick with their blood.

The space was too tight for the brothers to chain up, but they still fought next to each other with deadly efficiency. They knew each other's moves and they had honed their fighting styles over many years of combat together. They were experts in axe fighting where every part of the weapon was used. The flat of the blade blocked deadly claws while the spikes at either end punctured more than one boarg hide. But it was the deadly razor sharp blades that were the most efficient, cutting through boarg flesh like a butcher preparing his wares for sale. And they relished the fight. Dwarven battle cries bellowed as blood splattered their faces.

Allindrian was trying to get to Jonas's side but boargs were coming at her from all directions. She used all her skill to keep them away and was forced to use her magic yet again. She had skewered a boarg through the chest but in its dying spasms it ripped the sword from her grasp. "Fihr Anthos Seathay," she said, calling forth six glowing bolts that appeared in the air next to her. She sent three into an attacking boarg and three more into another that was attacking her flank. They both fell to the ground while she catapulted on top of the dead boarg behind her, yanking her sword clear.

"Look out!"

Allindrian turned on a coin just in time to glimpse a boarg before it struck her solidly in her torso, forcing the air from her lungs as she landed hard on her back with the boarg on top of her. Claws dug at her chest but once again her armor saved her, though it felt as if her ribs would break from the weight of the beast. The force of the strike had caused her to drop her sword again, and she struggled to grasp the hunting knife at her hip. Then suddenly she was drenched in blood as the boarg convulsed. She heard the solid thump of steel hitting flesh as more crimson splashes splattered her. She scrambled out from under the dead boarg to see Fil standing before her, panting heavily, his eyes filled with rage, and grasping his shield and sword. Allindrian retrieved her sword but had no time for gratitude as more enemies attacked.

The banthra's mace had struck Jonas in the shoulder, the force of the blow causing him to stumble backwards. Though the pain was severe, his shoulder guards had kept the spikes from biting into his flesh. The Banthra just laughed and swung its other mace in a downward strike at Jonas's head.

Jonas quickly summoned his cognivant powers, forming an invisible mental shield in front of the demon's arm. In the cognivant spectrum he saw the world for what it was; millions of tiny particles that made up everything, all of them connected. Jonas could not explain it to anyone, nor would they believe him, but what he saw in his mind looked as if everything was made up of the same stuff, although he had no idea what it was. But he could control the particles to a significant degree, and that was what mattered. He could have controlled the particles around the demon's arm and willed them to hold it still, but that would have taken too long and the mace would have already crushed him. But forming a small invisible shield could be done in seconds. The flying mace struck the shield and was repelled backwards...and Jonas took advantage of it. He lunged forward and rammed his right blade into the exposed stomach of the black knight. Blue sparks erupted from the wound as his sword broke through its magical armor. The Banthra dropped the extended mace and shuffled backwards away from the deadly sword. But as Jonas pressed the attack, the Banthra lifted its empty hand which instantly erupted in red flame. Jonas was only a few steps from the demon when the searing flames shot towards him. But just before they could reach him, something struck Jonas, pushing him away from the fire's path. He heard a wrenching howl pierce the din of battle and as he landed and scrambled to his hands and knees he saw Tulari, her fur erupting in fire, but before it could consume her, she took a powerful leap and flew over the stone wall, escaping the continued onslaught of deadly flames.

Jonas's eyes narrowed in fury and he again called on his cognivant powers, this time forming a swirling translucent shield in front of him, just as the Banthra again aimed its flames towards him. He felt the heat, but the flames roared around him causing him only discomfort. He strained against the mental fatigue as the power of the Banthra's attack pounded against the shield. Finally the flames subsided and Jonas, fueled by anger, bolted forward, jumping off the body of a dead boarg, with both swords coming down to strike the Banthra who had raised his mace to block the attack. Sparks flew as the swords struck the mace. But the Banthra, who had been a skilled warrior in life, angled the mace downward, side stepping at the same time, and forcing Jonas's blades down and away. The demon knight followed up with a punch to Jonas's side. Its gauntlets, covered with deadly spikes, slammed into Jonas with enough force to lift him off the ground. The air left his lungs and pain lanced through his kidney, and though he was fortunate that his god-made armor had kept the spikes from puncturing his flesh, it could do nothing to stop the damage of the blow. Jonas tasted blood in his mouth and he fell to the side in tremendous pain, the Banthra looming over him like a deadly shadow.

Meanwhile Lor-telliam, still battling the other Banthra, had whispered a protective spell as he held his staff up with both hands, catching the powerful strike of the demon's blade. The power rocked his shoulders and he thought they would break. His spell would protect him from other spells, but not physical attacks. But he thrust his staff up with surprising strength for one so lithe, and then snapped his leg up at a seemingly impossible angle, his foot connecting solidly with the Banthra's chest, forcing it off balance. His staff, in a blur of movement, sliced left and right with its blue blade across the demon's chest. Sparks flew as the blade cut a deep X pattern on the demon's cuirass. The Banthra lifted its shield as Lor-telliam's staff reversed direction seeking an opening at its neck. But the Banthra met it cleanly, lunging forward while attempting to smash the agile elf with its sword. Lor-telliam jumped down six steps away from the Banthra and called on his magic again. With a few quick words crackling energy erupted from his hand and crashed into the Banthra's shield. Sparks and smoke erupted into the air and the Banthra stumbled backwards farther up the steps. But the demon righted itself and returned magic with magic, aiming its sword at the elf for the second time as it shot forth a searing barrage of flames. The roar of the fire assaulted the Ekahal's senses, but it harmed him not at all, his protective spell doing its job.

King Baylin yanked his blade clear of the dead boarg and briefly met Kromm's gaze as he too dispatched another enemy. Their blood spattered chests heaved with exertion as they fought to regain their breath. They quickly glanced around trying to discern how many boargs were left, but with the fog and shadows it was hard to see more than twenty paces away. But their respite was brief, as the handful of remaining boargs came at them.

Growling ferociously they attacked with reckless abandon. King Baylin lifted his blade and intercepted two flashing claws, cutting deep slashes across the beast's arms in the process. Then, reaching within himself for more strength, his powerful arms responded, bringing his magical blade down and across the boarg's arm, cutting through to the bone. Then, reversing direction, he brought the keen blade up and through the boarg's throat, splattering more blood on the rough stone.

Jonas had nearly collapsed from the pain, but he knew he had only a few moments before the Banthra attacked again. He turned to intercept the attack that he knew must be coming, futilely lifting a blade to block the deadly spiked ball descending toward him. He knew it was a useless gesture, and in a flash he could picture his head caved in by the mace. But the end never came, and instead he heard the grunt of a dwarf and the crash of weapons coming together.

Jonas stumbled away and saw that Tolvar had intercepted the Banthra's attack and the two combatants were now in a deadly fight. Jonas gritted his teeth from the pain and stood up, hoping to join the dwarf. A new bolt of pain shot through him, and he keeled over. The demon must have shattered a rib, or damaged an organ, for the pain was excruciating.

The mace struck the dwarf in the shoulder as he spun away, trying to deflect some of the power. He continued the momentum of his spin back toward the demon, and stepped in low, bringing his deadly axe blade across the demon's thighs. Sparks flew as the magical dwarven blade sliced through its armor and into its flesh. The Banthra stumbled back, lifting its empty hand and bringing forth a bolt of crackling blue energy. The bolt struck Tolvar in the chest, but two heart beats later it vanished and Jonas saw the Banthra pitch sideways, a hand axe buried in its chest.

"Moredin!" Cade had roared as he had charged the Banthra, swinging his giant axe down and into the chest of the stunned demon. The dark knight howled as the axe bit deep, bringing the demon to its knees. Cade then ripped the axe from its chest and went for the demon's head. The powerful dwarf was thwarted, however, thrown back by a powerful red wave of energy that pulsed from the demon's chest, blasting outward in a ten pace diameter.

The wave hit Jonas, knocking him to the rough stones. Tolvar, who was squirming on the ground from the electrical attack, was pushed hard against the landing wall behind him. Cade, who was the closest, was launched off his feet, landing fifteen paces away on his back. He grunted from the impact and struggled to get up.

And so did the Banthra. The demon's legs were wobbly but it managed to grab its mace and regain its footing.

Jonas was holding his side growling in frustration. He had no chance of fighting the beast one on one now, not with his injuries. Still, he instinctively reached for his sword, but as he glanced at the blade, a determined smile spread across his face. Fiercely concentrating, he summoned his cognivant energy one last time. Grimacing with pain he struggled slowly to his feet and aimed his sword at the Banthra. "Shyann!" he screamed as he used his cognivant energy to shoot the sword straight into the demon's helm. Soaring like an arrow, the blade found its mark, sliding right between the black slits in its helm. The Banthra dropped its mace again, emitting an eerie scream. The sound made Jonas cringe, and everyone nearby turned their faces away, holding their ears, trying to shut out the auditory onslaught.

The sound suddenly ceased when the Banthra fell on its back, literally imploding into a destroyed heap of bent metal.

The flames were still roaring around the Ekahal when he heard the awful screeching. Suddenly the flames subsided and Lor-telliam looked at his enemy, who was now looking over him to the fighting beyond. Wasting no time he quickly activated the power of his staff causing the blue blade to extend to the length of a sword. With lightning speed, the agile elf hurled the staff like a javelin at the distracted Banthra. It flew true and struck the demon in the chest, skewering it with devastating effect, the power of the throw forcing the Banthra backwards where it stumbled to its knees.

Lor-telliam then brought both of his hands together and chanted the words of yet another spell, this one bringing forth the power of the Ru' Ach to quickly form a small ball of energy. By the time the demon had ripped the spear from its chest and slowly regained its feet, the energy ball had grown to the size of the Ekahal's head. "Fihr Sirthose!" Lor-telliam yelled, pushing his hands out and shooting the blue orb into the Banthra's chest. The elf jumped backwards as the ball hit the demon and exploded. In a brilliant flash of blue, a wave of energy struck everyone on the landing, causing them to stumble, but otherwise doing no damage.

But the Banthra was not so lucky. When the light receded the only thing remaining of the demon was a pile of charcoal gray ash.

"Lor-telliam, quickly!" Allindrian said.

The elf regained his footing and stood on wobbly legs. The spell had taken a lot out of him, but a few deep breaths soon infused him with new energy. The landing had been cleared of enemies and his exhausted companions stood about looking dazed and nearly unrecognizable, covered as they were in so much blood, sweat, and the grime of battle. They were panting heavily, exhausted from the intense fighting, and some held and nursed wounds.

The elf found Allindrian kneeling next to Tolvar. Cade was there supporting his brother's head. Lor-telliam masked his obvious shock and concern when he saw the Dakeen warrior. He had been severely burned by the demon's lightning. Nearly all of his face had been charred and his beard was burned to stubble and ash. His entire body was smoking, and the elf was sure that he had suffered even more wounds internally.

"What happened?" Lor-telliam asked, although he was pretty sure he knew the answer.

"The Banthra's lightning," Allindrian replied.

"And he lives?" It was obviously a rhetorical question. Lor-telliam was just voicing his shock that anyone could survive a direct hit from a Banthra's spell.

"He is Dakeen," Cade said, his voice strained. "Can you help him?"

Tolvar, barely conscious, whispered hoarsely to his brother, "Did ya get em'?" His voice was so weak they could hardly hear him.

"Aye, we did."

"Half my kill," Tolvar sputtered.

"He saved my life," Jonas said, standing awkwardly from the pain.

"I have a healing draught and I can risk some magical healing. But I am weak too, and I fear our fighting is not yet done," Lor-telliam said.

"What are you saying?" Cade growled.

"I can ease his pain and he will live, but I do not know if I can restore his face or get him ready to fight. Is anyone else hurt?"

Almost everyone had cuts, bruises, and nasty wounds, but the only other person with a debilitating injury was Jonas. "I took a severe blow to the side from the Banthra's gauntlet. I don't know the extent of my injuries, but I taste blood and I can barely move. I am bloated and my insides burn with a constant pain."

"Show me where you were struck," Lor-telliam said. Jonas, holding his side, lifted his hand and showed the elf the black and swollen area where he had been hit. Lor-telliam looked worried. "Jonas, the Banthra probably damaged your internal organs. You are tasting blood because you are bleeding from the inside. You will die if it is not treated."

"Heal him, wizard," Cade said, "Tolvar needs nothing more than the potion. He is already ugly and scars are of no concern to him. He will wear them with honor."

Tolvar chuckled weakly and everyone looked at him with amazement. Tolvar had just battled a Banthra and seemed to be near death, and yet the brothers joked, making light of Tolvar's grievous wounds. It was strange to see, but it seemed to lighten the intensity of everyone's mood and they welcomed the change.

"Very well, then," Lor-telliam said, "We must keep moving. The sword is within our reach."

Eight
The Garrison

The two thousand men had traveled hard and fast, pushing the pace to the point where several refugees had collapsed from exhaustion and had to be placed either in one of the spare wagons or on one of the horses of a Free Legion soldier. Once Hadrick and the rest of his small group had evaded capture and had found the main force, they immediately broke camp and moved double speed towards the Gildren Garrison. Stephy, who had been severely wounded, would likely have died if one of the Free Legion warriors had not brought forth a healing draught. The warrior, a friend of Stephy's, had been saving the potion for an emergency, and Stephy's wounds definitely necessitated its use. Healing potions were rare, and hence very expensive, since most towns did not have an alchemist or wizard with the skills to produce the concoction. But it was not uncommon for career warriors to save up their hard earned coin to purchase a potion if they could find one. Even with the elixir, Stephy's arm would be badly scarred, and it would take some time before he could fight again, and even then his arm would never be the same. But at least he could travel, which was good considering the pace they had set. They had to arrive at the garrison before the orc army or all would be lost. If the orcs arrived first, they would be blocked from crossing the bridge, with no way to get their army and the refugees across the expansive river without traveling hundreds of miles more to the Tuvell Garrison on the eastern regions of Finarthian land. Once there they would have to reach the Lindsor Bridge on the Sithgarin River and finally head west to Finarth. It would add weeks to their trip. Besides, they had to make sure that the garrison was warned and if they could help bolster its defense, they would do so.

Hagar was a problem though. Even Tuvallis and Stephy, who by all accounts were saved by him, were unnerved by the huge beast's presence. There was no way he could travel with the main group. The soldiers and the refugees would not understand who or what he was. Even so, Tuvallis had no doubt that Hagar had saved them all. Their chance of survival would have been slim, and getting Stephy out of harm's reach with his injuries would have been near impossible. Hagar had not only killed two dire wolves and their riders, but he had carried Stephy the last several miles.

It had taken Tuvallis many frustrating minutes to try and explain the situation to Hagar. Finally Tuvallis had to draw the ogrillion a picture showing himself with the main group of soldiers and refugees and Hagar traveling alone beside them. He thought the beast understood, but he wasn't sure.

Tuvallis walked briskly with Seli all through the night. The Free Legion soldiers could travel faster, but many of the refugees were older, while others, lacking horse or cart, were forced to travel by foot. Torches had been lit along the line and everyone was tense. Tuvallis kept scanning the darkness for Hagar or enemies, knowing he would most likely see neither. The torches, a beacon for Hagar, meant that the enemy could see them just as well.

"The torches make me nervous too, but we have no choice," Seli said, "we must travel and we must see." They had been traveling half the night and Tuvallis had filled Seli in on what had happened in their encounter with the dire wolves. "What will we do about this 'Hagar' when we get to the garrison?" Seli asked.

Tuvallis shook his head uncertainly. "I know not. The beast seems to have a purpose. He wears Shyann's armor, at least that be what it looks like, and he saved us, of this I'm certain. It must count for something."

"Of course it does. But having a monster walk with men seems impossible," Seli added. "They may not even allow him in the garrison."

"We will just have to convince them otherwise," Tuvallis said. Then he chuckled. "I'm not so sure we could stop him anyway."

When they finally arrived at the garrison the following morning they were met by armed guards and a closed gate. Hadrick's scout had managed to warn them, and the garrison was now on full alert. The gate opened as they approached, and several armed men came forward.

Tuvallis was at the rear of the column, but as they neared the compound he and Seli made their way to the front. He looked about them and saw no sign of the ogrillion. Perhaps he was hiding out nearby in some stand of trees watching the scene from a safe distance.

Hadrick and several other Free Legion soldiers dismounted, while Tuvallis stayed a short distance back with Seli, but he was close enough to hear the exchange.

"I assume you're Captain Hadrick," a tall barrel chested man said as he extended his hand. "I'm Captain Malazene, commander of this garrison." The captain appeared to be in his forties, with a long prominent nose dominating his stern face. His dark leathery skin looked as if it had soaked up the sun for years.

"Well met, and yes, I bear that name. My scout arrived safely I take it?"

"Indeed, and thank you. We are in your debt."

"What is your plan of defense?"

"My plan? I think maybe first you had best come in and refresh yourselves. If what your scout said is correct, then we have maybe a day before the orc scum arrive, if that," the captain replied.

"Exactly, so how can we aid in your preparations?"

"You misunderstand. I am not in charge at the moment. We have been reinforced by General Ruthalis and a thousand of his men. They are going to take down the bridge. They have asked me to bring you to them when you arrive. They want a full report. The captain turned on his heels. "Follow me please."

The garrison was a simple structure but impressive nonetheless. Its walls, constructed of white granite, were twenty paces high. Two towers thirty paces high were built into the river banks on each end of the garrison. The massive walls spanned the towers, forming a partial rectangle with two more towers built at each corner. The front wall of the garrison was at least a thousand paces long with a sturdy gate built directly in the center. Two more towers that housed the gate mechanisms flanked the thick oak gate. The gate was beautifully crafted, bound by huge bands of intricate iron and protected in the middle by a steel plate that bore the Finarthian symbol, a fist above the rising sun. Inside was an expansive courtyard that funneled down to the river and the equally impressive bridge. The two thousand refugees fit easily inside the courtyard, which was walled in by various structures such as warehouses, stables, and housing for the men who guarded Finarth's northern border. The garrison was built for defense and its appearance gave no doubt that it did its job.

"Have your men and the refugees set up camp on the other side of the river. They will be safer there. We can accommodate you here if you'd like," Captain Malazene added as they moved further into the courtyard.

"I will stay with my men," Hadrick said.

The captain eyed him with respect and simply nodded. "I'm sorry, Captain. I know you must be tired. But I have strict orders to take you to the general as soon as you arrive. Will you please follow me?"

"Of course. But let me give the orders to my men first."

"Very well. See that building there?" Captain Malazene pointed to the largest building in the garrison. It was at least three stories and built from solid stone. "Go there and my men will escort you to the general." The captain reached out and shook Hadrick's hand one more time. "Thank you again for warning us and coming here; your reputation is well known and fifty Free Legion warriors bring us new hope."

Hadrick nodded and gripped the man's arm in return. "Let us hope it will be enough."

The captain left quickly and Hadrick issued orders to his men.

Tuvallis, who was standing nearby, intercepted Hadrick. "Captain, what's de plan?"

"They want us to camp on the other side of the river. That's all I know, but I'm going directly to see a General Ruthalis and I will learn more," Hadrick said.

"What of the ogrillion?"

"I know not. Do you think he is still out there?" Hadrick asked.

"I do. We must help him," Tuvallis said as he gripped Hadrick's arm.

Captain Hadrick sighed. "Tuvallis, I was there too, remember. But I have no answers for you. They will never let the beast in here."

"Then get me a boat big enough to move him and permission to exit dis garrison. I will see him across this accursed river meself, if that be his goal!"

Hadrick looked into Tuvallis's determined eyes and knew he would not be dissuaded. "I will see what I can do."

Tuvallis nodded and Hadrick turned on his heal, striding briskly through the throng of people who were already heading for the bridge.

He found the building easily enough, and a young garrison guard who was expecting him led him inside and up a flight of stone stairs. As Hadrick came to the top of the stairway he heard loud conversation. They entered through an open archway into a large, sparsely furnished room. A large round oak table, devoid of ornamentation, sat in the center, surrounded by a small group of men. On closer inspection he saw that one was a dwarf and another was a fair haired elf. One man was huge and looked like he was carved from stone. Another was of average stature but obviously commanded the room as he talked and gestured over the table. This must be General Ruthalis. He wore expertly made armor with the Finarthian symbol embossed on the chest plate. He had weathered skin and short dark hair with streaks of silver. He was a handsome man with a hard look. His gold cloak was splattered with dirt and dust and he obviously had recently traveled hard. Hadrick wondered if the man felt like he did, tired, dirty, and starving for a bath and some sleep. The warrior next to him was tall and wore the armor of an Annurian knight. Captain Malazene was there and he smiled when he saw Hadrick.

"Good, you're here," Captain Malazene said as Hadrick approached the group. "General, this is Captain Hadrick of the Free Legion."

The general smiled warmly extending his hand in greeting. They shook in the warrior's handgrip and Hadrick felt the strength in the man. He was built like a swordsman, slender waist, broad shoulders and an iron grip. "Well met, Captain. I'm sorry to hear about your home, and I thank you for your scout's warning. This is Captain Graggis, Third Lance of the Finarthian Knights, Master Trader Durgen from Dwarf Mount, Prince Dynure from Annure, and Sar-gathos, Ekahal from the elven lands of Mel' un-riam." Hadrick shook each of their hands.

Hadrick was momentarily shocked. He was in audience with a very powerful group. For Bandris's axe he had just shaken hands with an Ekahal. He had heard of the reclusive wizards but knew no one who had met one. They seldom left their forests as far as he knew.

After making his introductions the general continued. "I'm sorry to cut the pleasantries short but we have some very urgent business to discuss and we could use your help," General Ruthalis said as he directed their attention back to the map at the table. "Can you confirm what your scout told us?"

"Yes, sir, and more," Hadrick replied. "Myself and several other men infiltrated their camp last night. I would say my scout's estimate of five thousand is accurate," Hadrick said.

"And the siege engines?" Lord Dynure asked.

"What siege engines?" Hadrick smiled.

"I don't understand. Your scout said they had siege engines."

"That was the reason for the mission. We burned the machines, every last one of them." Hadrick was now grinning.

"Hah, I be likin' this one!" Durgen roared as he slapped Hadrick on the back.

"You're serious?" Dynure asked.

"Indeed."

Dynure smiled and shook his head. "Well done, Captain. You may have just given us the time that we need. Without those engines we should be able to hold off that many for weeks."

"Time? What is the plan, sir?" Hadrick asked.

"We are bringing down the bridge," the general said.

"You hope to buy more time for Finarth," Hadrick stated, quickly surmising the plan.

"We do. With this bridge destroyed Malbeck cannot bring his army across," the general continued, indicting the bridge on the map. "He will have to swing his forces around in order to get to the Tuvell Garrison and then the Lindsor Bridge. That will give us another month at least."

"What of those bridges?" Hadrick asked, pointing to both of them on the map.

"We have engineers there now. Those bridges should be at the bottom of the river within the week," General Ruthalis replied.

"Which will gain you even more time as he will have to find a way to get his massive army across," Hadrick reasoned.

"That is the plan," Lord Dynure said.

"How long before you can fall this bridge?" Hadrick asked.

General Ruthalis nodded towards Durgen.

"Four or five days. 'Tis no easy task to bring down support structures that have been enhanced by magic," Durgen said.

"So we need to hold off the army until the bridge can be dropped," Hadrick concluded.

They simply nodded.

"We? So you're staying with us?" Lord Dynure asked.

"Oh yes, we have a score to settle, and my men are ready to settle it with steel," Hadrick said.

"That is good news. We can use your experience, as well as your metal," the general replied.

"There is one more thing, General," Hadrick began a bit apprehensively, "Last night we barely made it out of the camp alive, in fact we wouldn't have made it at all if we had not been rescued by something."

"Some*thing*?" Sar-gathos said, speaking up for the first time.

Hadrick looked at the elf and was struck by how beautiful he was. He knew beautiful was not the right word, but handsome didn't fit either. It was the type of beauty one would see on a warm summer night when the sun is setting behind white capped mountain peaks, or the glistening glow of the moon reflected on the waters of a calm lake. His fair skin was smooth and his features were graceful, and even his voice calmed the spirit.

"Two of my men and a wanderer we picked up on the road were being attacked by dire wolves and their riders. One of my men was badly hurt and then out of the darkness emerged a form, a huge creature that not only killed both wolves and their riders but carried my injured man two miles back to our camp." Everyone was leaning in now, clearly interested in Hadrick's strange story. "Sir, it was an ogrillion."

"What!? You must be mistaken. An ogrillion *helped* you, by killing orcs?" the general said incredulously.

"It did, sir, and that's not all. Hagar, that is the name the beast goes by, was also wearing armor embossed with Shyann's mark and carrying a beautifully crafted mace the size of a small tree. They were polished like mirrors and the armor fit the creature perfectly, as if it had been made especially for him. I have never seen the likes of it. I can't explain it, sir, but I didn't feel a mean bone in him," Hadrick said.

"I don't mean to sound ignorant, but what is an ogrillion?" Graggis asked.

Sar-gathos, his eyes narrowed in thought, replied, "They are rare beasts, half-orc and half-ogre."

"Not a good combination," Graggis growled.

No one said anything for a few moments. The story seemed unbelievable, but none of them had any reason to think that Hadrick would make it up. What would be the point? It was too outlandish not to be the truth.

"You are sure the armor had Shyann's symbol on it?" Sar-gathos asked.

"Very much so."

"I mean no disrespect, Captain, but I find that very hard to believe," General Ruthalis said.

"Sir, if I hadn't seen it myself, I would not believe it either. But it's true. The wanderer I told you about, Tuvallis, wants to go outside the gate and lead him across the river," Hadrick continued.

"He is outside the gate now?" Sar-gathos asked.

"We believe so."

"I cannot let an ogrillion inside the garrison. It would create pandemonium," General Ruthalis said.

"Tuvallis figured you'd say that and asked me to commandeer him a boat to get the beast across."

"I would like to meet this Hagar. If he is as you say, I will get him across the river," Sar-gathos offered.

Captain Hadrick and Sar-gathos found Tuvallis easily enough. His Free Legion soldiers and the refugees were already lighting cook fires and preparing their tents and bedding. The ground was flat and relatively dry, making it a good spot to rest. Hadrick knew that everyone was running short on food, a situation that would have to be remedied shortly.

As Hadrick crossed the bridge he saw handfuls of dwarves scurrying about accompanied by the constant noise of hammering and sawing on stone that sounded throughout the night. The massive bridge was impressive, constructed of giant stone blocks, its four support structures plunging deep into the water, and spanning a river a thousand paces wide. He could not fathom how a bridge of that size could be brought down. He thought perhaps they could just drop one of the spans but then realized that would not be enough. The Dark One could possibly use magic to rebuild a span, but to rebuild the entire bridge would not be possible within a workable time frame.

He didn't speak much with Sar-gathos as they walked across the bridge. Hadrick didn't know what to say to the elf. The Ekahal's presence unnerved him for some reason. The elf wore light flowing hunter's clothes in shades of brown and green and his long hooded cloak fluttered around him like silk. His tunic was lined with gold and intricate leaf designs flowed gracefully across it. He carried a long wood staff that was capped with a green stone and at his waist was a delicate looking long sword. Hadrick knew that most human wizards did not wear swords as the study of magic took too much time and effort. They did not have the time or luxury to learn weapon craft. But he understood that elves lived much longer lives, giving them the time to study both crafts. He had no doubt that Sar-gathos knew how to use that blade at his side.

Tuvallis and Seli were with three other soldiers who were all busy setting up tents and lighting fires. Hadrick led the elf over to the group and approached Tuvallis as he was throwing wood on a fire. "Tuvallis, I would like you to meet Sar-gathos, an Ekahal from Mel' un-riam." Tuvallis seemed momentarily taken aback by the new guest, but he quickly composed himself. "Well met, sir," he said as he shook the elf's hand. Seli was next to Tuvallis in an instant and so he introduced her as well.

Hadrick then turned to Tuvallis again, "I have permission to take you to Hagar right now. Sar-gathos wishes to meet the ogrillion and help where he may. Are you ready?"

"I am."

"Sir, do you mind if I go? I would very much like to meet this ogrillion," Seli asked.

"How are your injuries?"

"I am feeling much better. Just some deep aches and occasional pain at times."

"Injuries? How were you hurt?" Sar-gathos asked.

"Umm," Seli stumbled over her words as she spoke to the Ekahal. "Umm, sir, I was captured by an orc raiding party. They beat me, and, umm..."

"Tuvallis here came to her rescue," Hadrick interrupted. "He was traveling out of the Tundren Mountains and heading to Finarth when he came across the orc party."

"And you stole her away in the night?" the Ekahal asked.

"No, sir, it was not possible. They were near ready to...kill her. I had to intervene quickly," Tuvallis said.

"You killed them," Sar-gathos reasoned. "How many?"

"Ten."

"Well done, Tuvallis, it comforts my soul to know there are still those capable of great acts of courage. If you don't mind, Seli, I would like to see to your wounds," Sar-gathos offered.

Seli looked at Tuvallis apprehensively. He nodded and she turned back to the elf.

"Do not worry, warrior of Cuthaine, I will not harm you," Sar-gathos said as he stepped closer.

"I meant no disrespect, sir. Magic makes me nervous, and I must be honest, you do as well."

Sar-gathos laughed, the sound of his laughter melodious and free, like the laughter of children playing before supper. "Honesty is a virtue, and one that I appreciate."

"It's just that I've never met an Ekahal. I have heard of your power, and stories of elven Ekahals were told to me as a child. And now one stands before me offering me healing. You can see how that would make my stomach flutter."

"Indeed, but worry not. I am just an elf with more power than most. But I bleed, just like you," he said as he reached out and gripped both of her hands. "You will feel a little warmth and tingling, and that will be all."

Sar-gathos closed his eyes and began to chant, whispering elven words that they could not understand. The memory of their sound disappeared as quickly as they were spoken. Seli felt a slight tingle and then a wave of warm energy flooded through her. After a few seconds it was gone, and so was her pain. She opened her eyes and looked at the elf who was returning her smile.

"You see, there is nothing to be afraid of. You had some very deep bruising that was causing a lot of pain. Several ribs were cracked but healing well, and your skull took quite a blow. But the pain should just be a memory now."

"Thank you. I feel…perfect," Seli said gratefully.

"I appreciate your healing of one of my soldiers," Hadrick said.

"It was my honor. Courage should always be rewarded. Now let us see to this Hagar."

It didn't take them long to find Hagar. They had moved outside the gate and Tuvallis looked around, unsure of where the beast would be. There were several stands of trees off in the distance where Hagar would most likely be hidden, and luckily they found him at the first, a collection of large oaks with thick branches that twisted only as oaks do. There was little underbrush to obstruct visibility, and they quickly found Hagar behind the largest tree, whose massive trunk barely hid his incredible bulk. But the ogrillion heard them easily enough when Tuvallis called his name. He emerged from behind the tree and stepped towards the group, hesitating when he saw the others. He seemed to know that his size and ancestry would scare them, so he held back with his gaze low, non-threatening.

"Interesting," Sar-gathos said as he stepped closer. He moved slowly so he wouldn't frighten the beast.

"Hagar, this is Sar-gathos, and my friend, Seli. We have come to help you," Tuvallis said. The ogrillion looked up at the sound of Tuvallis's voice. Well he actually looked down at Tuvallis, but his eyes moved upwards from the ground. His lips peeled back exposing vicious yellow teeth. Seli's hand instinctively went to her sword, but Tuvallis gently touched her arm to restrain her. "Don't worry, I believe that be his smile," he said with a chuckle.

"Hagar," the ogrillion said, thumping his chest and dropping to one knee. Now his eyes were just above their own.

"The armor shines like that worn by a cavalier. And that mace is magnificent, and clearly made for him. How can this be?" Seli asked.

"I know not," was all Tuvallis could say.

Sar-gathos began a soft chant and instantly Hagar's eyes swung to look at the elf. Then his eyes grew wide and his smile broadened. They stood there looking at each other for a few minutes before Sar-gathos turned back to Tuvallis and Seli. He was smiling.

"There is no evil in him, and he has quite a tale to tell," the Ekahal said.

"You spoke with him?" Tuvallis asked incredulously.

"Yes, in a sense. He does not know a formal language, not even ogre or orcish as he was cast out of his ogre clan when he was very young. The spell allowed us to converse with images."

"What does he want?" Hadrick asked.

"The same as all of us. He is heading to Finarth to fight, to fight alongside us, to fight against Malbeck."

"And the armor?" Hadrick continued.

"He said he received guidance in his head. I could not totally understand the images, but it sounded like he was led here, and to his armor. He was led to the armor by a giant stag." Sar-gathos didn't even finish his sentence as he saw the expression on Tuvallis's face. "What is it?"

"I have also seen a giant stag, bigger than a horse. The biggest I have ever seen. And I have felt something, something inside me leading me here. I cannot explain it, but de feeling is very strong, like I was needed here."

"When did you see this stag?" Seli asked.

"A handful of years ago, maybe four. The stag led me to two village boys who were attacked by boargs. I came to their aid and saved them. It was the same boy I told you about, Seli, the boy named Jonas that as you told me accompanied King Kromm of Tarsis to Cuthaine a month ago."

"And by all accounts he was a cavalier," Seli said.

"Which would not have been the case had you not saved him years ago," Sar-gathos reasoned.

"That has to be more than a coincidence," Seli said, amazed.

"I think, Tuvallis that you are being guided by Shyann herself, and it seems that Hagar is as well. She wants you both at Finarth," Sar-gathos said.

"I thought you elves did not believe in gods," Seli asked boldly. She now felt more at ease with the Ekahal, and her words were not checked by nerves.

"You are correct. But we believe in beings that humans and others *think* are gods. The power of the Ru'Ach is vast and all encompassing. It is everything that you see around you, including these figures that you call gods. But gods did not create the worlds, nor did they create you, or me. But this is not the time for a theological discussion; let us deal with the situation at hand. Hagar is clearly our ally, I will vouch for him. The armor he wears is blessed by Shyann herself, which proves his heart is free of evil intent. With that said, I still see no way to bring him into the garrison. The soldiers will not know how to react to him. Let us stick with your original plan and get him across the river where you and Captain Hadrick can deal with him. Captain Hadrick, do your men know of the ogrillion?"

"Only the few that were with us when he came to our aid. I ordered my men silent in regards to the beast's presence. For now anyway," Hadrick replied.

"I suggest you introduce him to your men. Start slow and maybe his acceptance will grow like wild-fire," Sar-gathos said.

Tuvallis nodded his head in approval. "How do we get him across the river?"

"We fly," the elf said with a smile.

And the Ekahal was true to his word. They made it to the river's edge and stood on a small bank that had been cut away slowly by the steady stream of water that constantly flowed from the headwaters high in the Tundren peaks. Hagar looked at the water apprehensively, clearly not a fan of deep rushing rivers.

"How do we *fly* across that?" Seli asked skeptically.

"You need not do a thing. Just trust me and don't move," Sargathos said as he began to chant. Seli looked at Tuvallis nervously but he just raised his eyebrows nonchalantly.

"Should be fun," was all he said.

Sar-gathos had already visually tried to show Hagar what he was about to do but he could not confirm if he understood it. He did comprehend that the ogrillion was not fond of water and that the idea of flying over it made his big heart pound in his chest.

The tip of his staff lit up with a green light and after a few seconds all five of them lifted off the ground. It felt as if they were standing on an invisible platform. It was solid and felt safe, but the feeling of looking down and seeing the ground below them gave them all an uneasy feeling of vertigo, especially Hagar who shuffled nervously as he was lifted off the ground.

"Don't move," Sar-gathos warned, "the platform is only so big. It will carry us across easily enough as long as you don't step off of it."

"Hagar, it is okay," Tuvallis said as he reached up and put his hand on the ogrillion's hand. Tuvallis's hand, which was big by human standards, looked like that of an infant as it gripped the beast's thick fingers. But the gesture was calming and Hagar stopped moving and looked at Tuvallis. Hagar was unaccustomed to being touched but the sensation calmed him, and was welcomed with a broad smile.

Sar-gathos sped the invisible platform across the river keeping them just above the water's surface. It took them a few moments before they were standing safely on the muddy river bank on the far side.

Tuvallis looked at the ogrillion. "You ready to meet some soldiers?"

Hagar simply looked at Tuvallis and continued to smile.

"Maybe we would have more success if we could tone down that smile. It looks like he wants to eat you," Hadrick said.

They all chuckled together as they headed for the hundreds of cook fires that were flickering nearby in the darkness.

As soon as they returned Captain Hadrick lit a fire away from the main group and called a meeting. Sar-gathos left and rejoined the commanders for further planning and to report his thoughts on the ogrillion. Hadrick sent word out through his officers and the fifty remaining Free Legion warriors arrived soon after. They had all eaten by now, but they were still weary from the forced march. But the Free Legion was accustomed to hard marching, and fighting, and a full day of strenuous work was not enough to cause any grumbling.

Hadrick had built his fire by another stand of trees and Hagar was hidden there with Tuvallis. Hadrick had planned on preparing his men about the presence of the ogrillion, and then simply bringing him out so they could see and meet him. So that is what he did.

"Men, I brought you here to share with you the truth about what happened last night. As you know Stephy was severely injured and they almost didn't make it. According to Bositch," Hadrick said indicating the scout who was standing near him, "they would not have if it hadn't been for Tuvallis." The men murmured their praise and it was clear to Hadrick that Tuvallis had already won over his men, which he knew was no easy feat. "But that is not the whole story," he continued. "Tuvallis alone could not have saved them all. Stephy, Bositch, and Tuvallis were aided by something else, something we have kept from you out of necessity. But I am here now to tell you the truth, and once you understand you will see the reason for the deception. Stephy was unconscious while Tuvallis and Bositch faced three dire wolves and their orc riders. But something came out of the darkness and killed two of them. They would have been killed if it had not been for this savior."

"Come on, Captain, who was it?" a voice came from the back. A general murmur of agreement erupted and the captain put his hands up to silence them.

"Not *who* but *what*," Hadrick said. "It was a half-ogre, half-orc. I guess they are called ogrillions and they are very rare."

"You must be joking," Torum said with a snort. Some others laughed but once everyone realized that neither Bositch nor Hadrick were joining in, they stopped. Stephy was not present as his wounds, even after consuming the healing draught, still needed attention from the healers.

"Bositch," Hadrick said, "perhaps you can elaborate."

197

"The captain's right. The beast is twice as tall as a man and looks just as you would imagine a cross between an orc and an ogre would look. He cannot speak but he seems to understand hand gestures all right." Some of the men were talking softly as they processed what they were being told. "I know it sounds impossible. But it's true, I was there. Stephy would have died for sure if it hadn't been for Hagar, and I doubt Tuvallus or I would have made it either."

"And that's not all," Hadrick continued, "the ogrillion wears armor and carries a weapon blessed by Shyann herself." The soldiers had stopped talking and were now just staring at them. "Furthermore, Sargathos, an elven Ekahal here at the garrison, magically evaluated the beast and detected no evil within him."

"Sir, with all due respect, this seems to defy common logic," a soldier commented.

"I understand your apprehension, which is why I brought you here so you can meet him for yourselves. Despite his size, he is very gentle and seems more afraid of us. Tuvallis!" Hadrick shouted. "Bring him out!"

The stand of trees was hidden by the night's shadows, so at first the men couldn't see much. But as Tuvallis and Hagar moved closer to the firelight the men around the fire began to shift nervously while some instinctively reached for their swords. As Hagar approached, his armor gave off an orange glow as it reflected the firelight.

"Don't worry, he is harmless...at least to us," Hadrick said with a chuckle. His laughter seemed to relax the men a bit. They had complete trust in their captain and if he wasn't worried, then they shouldn't be either.

Hagar shifted farther behind Tuvallis the closer he got to the men, the sheer numbers of warriors obviously making him as nervous as the men had been. His eyes lowered and his pace slowed as he unsuccessfully tried to hide his huge form in the shadows.

Tuvallis gripped his finger and gently nudged him forward to stand in front of the fire. "It's okay, they mean you no harm. Friends," Tuvallis said as he indicated the men. Nobody said a word as they stared at Hagar slack jawed. "This is Hagar. He has showed us only good will. He wants to fight with us."

"Hagar," the ogrillion said softly, gently tapping his huge fist on his chest.

"Ulren's blade, I have never seen anything like it," Torum said. "And look at that mace, it's magnificent."

"I would enjoy seeing what that could do to Malbeck's forces," another soldier said.

"Hagar, why don't you drop to a knee," Tuvallis said, using his hands to get the beast to kneel. Hagar laid the mace out before him and released the handle. "I think it would be good if you all greeted him."

"How in Ulren's name do we do that?" Morgan, a Free Legion veteran asked.

"Just come up and touch his hand. He actually likes it. But we will do it one at a time so as not to frighten him," Tuvallis said.

"Scare *him*, I think I already soiled my pants," Morgan said. Everyone laughed and it was infectious. Even Hagar chuckled. It was clear that he didn't know why they were laughing, but he thought he should join in.

***

Malbeck effortlessly squeezed his hand, snapping the officer's neck and silencing his screams. He was surrounded by five hundred Gould-Irin Orcs, and even more of his vermin swarmed around them like flies, trying to get a closer look. Gullanin, his Lich, stood next to him, red eyes glowing as he gazed upon the scene.

Malbeck held the dead warrior with one hand while he took a sharp claw from the other and punctured two holes into the arteries that snaked up the sides of his neck, releasing a stream of blood as he held the corpse upside down above the pulsing black egg. Lines of red and orange flashed across it like lightning, and as soon as the blood hit its shell it steamed and disappeared into the hungry egg.

Finally, Malbeck thought, the last of the sacrifices he would need to bring his new fiend to life. He had exhausted all the young fertile women and strong warriors, both of which who's bodies stored the most energy. This man would be last he would need. He could now start his march to Finarth and destroy the last vestige of humanity standing in his way east of the Tundrens. There would always be remnants of survivors and small outlying towns and cities foolish enough to stand up against him, but they would never have a chance against his army. Finarth was the prize, the last of the hold-outs that offered any possible defense against him. And that cursed sword was again becoming an obstacle. But Malbeck was not worried. Even if they did manage to free the weapon from its thousand year old prison, he did not think it could stand up to him now. He had become more powerful, and he held the power of the Shan Cemar, the book of elven magic that he did not have the last time he faced that sword.

Malbeck laughed and licked the tips of his sharp teeth as he plopped the dead man on top of the egg. The egg pulsed more rapidly as it drained the remaining blood from the soldier's body. Malbeck stepped his muscled body back from the egg and held the staff of Gould in one hand and the Shan Cemar in the other. He didn't have long to wait.

Several powerful followers of the Forsworn stood behind the Dark One, eager to see the product of his creation. One wore a black robe, edged in crimson, with a large hood covering his head and casting a dark shadow over his pallid face. Naz-reen's spider symbol was intricately woven across the priest's chest in expertly crafted patterns of red with strands of silver. If one could ignore the sinister theme of his robe, one would have found it quite beautiful. Next to this priest stood two clerics of Gould, outfitted in dark armor and helms, Gould's white eyes etched into each cuirass. One cleric carried a two handed sword strapped to his back while the other held a battle axe in one hand and a shield in the other. And to the warriors' left was a dark wizard to Dykreel. The wizard's head was shaved and gruesome scars covered his face. It looked as if a clawed hand had ripped the flesh on his face from his scalp to his chin. The man may have been handsome at one time, but the wound had damaged his face so badly, creating a network of raised and jagged scars, that one would have been hard pressed to imagine that he had been anything other than a hideous monster. Dykreel's barbed symbol was tattooed on both hands, one of which held a long dark wood staff while the other casually rested on the hilt of a short sword at his waist. Followers of the Forsworn did not always peacefully coexist; in fact there was sometimes as much fighting amongst themselves as there was against their enemies. The desire for power was strong, and the servants of the Forsworn were constantly jockeying to obtain more of it, hoping to show who of the three gods was the strongest. But the pecking order had been established long ago, and so far Gould had maintained the top position, while Naz-reen and Dykreel worked their evil intrigues in the shadows. But the balance of power was often precarious, and only a powerful leader could unite the followers of the Forsworn in a common goal, a role that Malbeck eagerly played.

The egg began to make a crackling sound and pulsed even more, growing to twice its original size. Malbeck stepped back further still, as did the Gould-Irin that were near. They were a fearsome bunch, almost as tall as he, their massive bodies and powerfully muscular limbs encased in heavy black and charcoal grey armor, with yellow eyes that reflected more intelligence than that of their cousins. They were warriors bred by Gullanin, now a Lich, Malbeck's right hand and most trusted servant.

As they all watched, steam began to burst from the egg and the cracking increased until finally it split open, spilling forth a series of shrill howls followed by a gust of red and black mist that shot up into the air. The howling soon became a thunderous roar and the Gould-Irin shuffled backwards away from the egg. The swirling mist gradually began to coalesce into a more defined shape and Malbeck smiled as the shape grew ever larger, hovering twenty paces above the ground.

Soon giant black wings began to appear, flapping rhythmically, and creating great gusts of wind that churned up clouds of dust. The Gould-Irin scattered and moved even further away. The mist slowly solidified, exposing long curved talons and a chest covered with scales. Hovering before them was a Blood Dragon, sometimes called a Demon Dragon. Either way, the name fit the beast perfectly. Its entire body was black with translucent veins of red and orange visible beneath the skin. The veins, periodically crackling with energy, were visible on all parts of its body except for its armored chest. Black spikes covered the beast's head, and blood red eyes scanned the monsters beneath it, finally resting on Malbeck. The creature swung its spiked tail left and right, creating the sound of swords slicing through the air. The dragon roared and the sound was deafening. Slowly it lowered itself and landed on the ground before Malbeck, stretching its wings wide, displaying its magnificent form in all its glory.

Malbeck stepped closer and marveled at his creation. It was fifty paces long from head to tail and its head was the size of a Gould-Irin Orc, with black teeth as long as short swords. The thing brought its head closer to Malbeck and made a deep rumbling sound in its chest. "Welcome Kil-Kannon...that is the name I give you. I have given life to you so you can serve me here on the material plane," Malbeck said as he touched the beast's scaled jaw. It was hard like iron, yet warm to the touch. "Together we will crush our enemies and you shall drink their blood."

The dragon rumbled again and steam poured from its nostrils. A Blood Dragon is born hungry and ready to feed. It was obviously hungry for more blood, and Malbeck would provide it with plenty in the months to come.

"Gullanin," Malbeck said, addressing his undead general. "Has the party retrieved the sword yet?"

"No, my Lord, they are still fighting for their lives. But they are near. They are powerful indeed and the Ekahal will be able to access the blade where we could not."

"They must not have it. What of the Banthras?"

"They are dead, my Lord."

"Send Korthanos," Malbeck hissed.

Korthanos was the Banthra king. He was the most powerful warrior in life and thus in death.

"It will be done," Gullanin said as he backed away from his master and moved to make the preparations.

Malbeck stroked Kil-Kannon's armored head and streaks of orange and red flared across its black flesh. "I have a mission for you. Are you thirsty?"

***

The orc army arrived at the garrison the next morning. The defenders were ready and the ramparts were lined with armed archers while the rest of the men readied weapons, saddled horses, and prepared for battle. The plan was a defensive one. Let the enemy come to them while they defend their walls and give the dwarven engineers enough time to fall the bridge. They would then retreat to Finarth and join the main army there.

There were easily five thousand orcs and over a dozen ogres, in addition to various other creatures scattered throughout the enemy army. There were no siege engines to be seen, thus it looked as if Captain Hadrick's mission had indeed been successful.

With luck they could keep the gate from being breached. That was their main goal. If the gate broke then the enemy would pour into the massive courtyard and the fighting would concentrate there. The plan was to slowly funnel the enemy down the causeway towards the bridge all the while being attacked by cavalry reinforced with footman. They also had men stationed along the rooftops above the courtyard and the avenue that led to the bridge. They would pepper the enemy with flaming jugs of oil, spears, and arrows.

Graggis had another plan that he had presented to the commanders earlier that morning. It would be risky for those involved, but if it worked it could prove useful indeed. But they would wait to execute the plan when the enemy was feeling at ease and confident that they would take the garrison.

The first day of battle went well considering the fact that they were outnumbered. Thousands of orcs stormed the walls trying to access the heavy gate while testing the garrison defenses. They were met, however, by waves of arrows descending on them, killing hundreds at a time. It was a tsunami of destruction as orcs fell one after another to the Finarthian archers. It went on like that for half the day, leaving hundreds of orcs dead, covering the grassy ground in great heaps.

Then they got smarter. The assault halted and garrison lookouts began to see a number of creatures scurrying about, gathering tools and felling trees. Scouts reported back that they were constructing ladders as well as several battering rams. There were plenty of trees available for that, and they would not take so long to construct. The rest of the first day melted away with no further attacks as the orcs prepared for the following morning.

As night began to fall, Graggis walked around the ramparts inspecting the condition of the men and trying to relieve his boredom. A warrior through and through, he hated the monotony of siege work. He wanted to engage in actual battle, to sweat and bloody his axe. The time would come soon enough though, and his spine shivered thinking about it. Most men, even warriors, did not look forward to battle. But Graggis did. It was the only thing that made him feel totally alive, that caused his heart to race with anticipation. The thrill of battle was his drug, and he was definitely addicted.

He did have one current mission, however, and that was to determine how many arrows remained in their arsenal. They knew that if the enemy continued their onslaught that they would soon run out. Graggis continued making his rounds along the ramparts, which had been illuminated by torches placed at twenty foot intervals. As he tallied the remaining arrows he spoke casually to the men stationed there. No one seemed to think an attack would come tonight, but one could never be too careful. By the time he had completed his rounds he had concluded that there were a little over a thousand shafts with the men and maybe a thousand more in storage. It would not be enough.

"We need more!" General Ruthalis slammed his hand on the table. "Those numbers will run out in less than two days."

"I have an idea," Lord Dynure said. He was the only other person in the room, going over plans with General Ruthalis when Graggis entered. They both looked expectantly at the prince from Annure. "They are not removing the bodies," the prince continued. "Why don't we send scouts out tonight and retrieve as many arrows as we can. The orcs are camped well away from their dead and they should be safe."

Ruthalis nodded thoughtfully. "A sound idea," he said, turning towards Graggis. "See to it."

"Yes, sir," Graggis said as he turned and left the room.

Day two started off the same, with thousands of orcs storming the wall. Horns blew and hundreds again fell to Finarthian arrows. They were able to retrieve several hundred arrows the night before, and they would continue their arrow retrieval tactic as needed.

But after an hour a new attacking group emerged within the mass of orcs. It was hard at first for the men at the garrison to see who they were since their vision was blocked by massive shields that many were carrying. But as they came closer it appeared to be seven or eight ogres, surrounded by hundreds of orcs, carrying a long battering ram constructed from a fallen tree. The orcs that surrounded them carried immense heavy shields to protect the ogre's legs from Finarthian arrows. Three other ogres, each carrying huge shields, marched in defensive formation around the heavily armored ogres that carried the ram, further blocking them from the flying missiles. The system worked, and it wasn't long before the ram crashed into the thick timber gate.

Spears and arrows rained down upon them. Some hit their mark while others crashed into metal shields and bounced harmlessly aside. Several orcs fell, along with one of the ogres that had been carrying one of the giant shields. But as they fell more scurried in to take their place. The ram crashed into the gate three times, but still it held.

Sar-gathos was on the far side of the wall when the ram had
arrived. The nimble elf ran with all haste as the heavy log crashed into
the gate. "Look out!" he roared as he skidded to a halt above the gate.
The ram hammered the gate again and everyone heard the timbers
crack. Archers and spearman obeyed instantly and moved away from
the wizard.

As the Ekahal whispered his words of power, blue flames leaped
from his right hand, coalescing into a ball of fire. He then leaned over
the battlement and hurled it at the enemy. The fiery missile crashed into
the shield of one of the ogres, exploding on impact and sending a wave
of fiery blue heat rushing upwards towards the defenders above.
Everyone dove back away from the battlements as blue flames shot
fifteen paces up into the air. The flames disappeared as quickly as they
had come and everyone ran to the battlements to look below. The ram
lay on the ground burning to a blackened husk. The blackened bodies
of orcs and ogres lay scattered across the ground. The few unlucky
enough to survive growled weak moans of pain as they attempted to
crawl away, some with missing limbs, their burnt and smoking bodies
encased in their armor, now a prison of glowing hot metal. The ground
was blackened in a circle that was easily fifteen paces in diameter.

The men cheered and yelled, raising their spears and bows into
the air. Several even had the courage to pat the Ekahal on the shoulder,
congratulating him, but most stayed well clear of the elf, leery of the
kind of magic they had just witnessed.

Yet their initial celebratory exclamations were cut short by the
frantic shout of a man farther down the wall. "Here they come!" he
yelled. Everyone looked along the line below and saw six massive
ladders being carried towards various points along the wall. Orcs and
scores of goblins were storming the wall again, shooting arrows up at
the defenders, trying to distract the warriors as the heavy ladders struck
the stone battlement. Orcs and goblins began ascending the ladders as
their brethren fired missiles at any who tried to topple the ladder or
attack those that manned it.

Graggis had seen them coming and ordered men to reinforce the
locations where the ladders had been mounted. "Take out their
archers!" he yelled. His job was to lead the men on the northern section
of the wall while General Ruthalis was on the southern side. Lord
Dynure was on the wall as well but his orders were to ready his men
below in case the vermin broke through the gate. Durgen and most of

the dwarves were steadily working on the bridge, hoping to have it down in three days.

Men rushed to the walls with bows and spears. Some were hit immediately and fell back as others took their spots. Healers ran back and forth along the wall seeing to the men that were wounded. Some were carried down to the medical rooms below and others, whose wounds weren't too serious, were treated on the spot.

Graggis had not only seen the creatures coming with the giant ladders, he had also noticed several ogres moving through the mass of orcs and goblins, carrying enormous ceramic jugs with a flaming cloth stuck into the open necks.

"Get back!" he yelled. But it was too late. Thrown by the powerful ogres, the jugs soared through the air and crashed into the battlements on both sides of the ladder. Flames spread across the stones in great waves of orange heat. Some men, engulfed in flames, tumbled over the backside of the wall to the courtyard below. Warriors screamed as they leaped away from the scorching fire.

No defenders could get to the ladder now, and orcs ran up it quickly, jumping over the wall with roars of rage. The flames impeded the defenders, but it also kept the creatures bottled up until it died down, which it did quickly as the oil burned out. Once the flames dissipated to a flicker, orcs and goblins jumped over them and attacked the defenders.

The walls were only three paces wide and that meant that only two men could fight side by side. Graggis pushed through several men to get to the attackers first. "Stay behind me!" he roared. He wore his Finarthian plate armor and carried his famous axe. He sometimes fought with a shield in formation as his prodigal strength allowed him to wield the massive axe with one hand if need be. But that was not his favorite style. He preferred fighting with only his axe, two handed style, and that was how he faced the orcs now.

One orc jumped over the flames and smoke, his howl cut short by Graggis's axe meeting it directly in the face, cutting the creature's head in two. No sooner had he flung the dead orc over the battlements than an orc and a goblin rushed at him, roaring in defiance. The goblin thrust a spear towards his belly while the orc swung a serrated sword down toward his left arm. Graggis pivoted slightly and caught the spear with his right hand while he flicked his axe blade to the left, blocking the strike of the orc. The orc had swung so hard that it stumbled forward to its knee. Graggis yanked the spear from the goblin and jabbed the blunt end into its face, forcing it backwards. Then he brought the blunt end of his axe down on the back of the orc's head slamming the beast to the stone pavers. Several axe swings later both of the creatures lay in heaps near the battle crazed warrior, blood spilling from their bodies.

Graggis felt intensely alive, his massive muscles energized by fury and the adrenaline of battle. He roared with defiance as orcs and goblins fell to his silver axe. None could get through him, and after a few short minutes he had worked his way to the ladder. Several men on the other side had cut their way through as well. "Push that ladder off!" he yelled over the din of battle as more monsters scrambled up the ladder.

Two men reached down to heave the ladder off the battlements, but they couldn't budge it. The weight of the orcs pressed the ladder firmly to the wall. "Sir!" one man yelled. "There is too much weight, we cannot move it!"

"Take that rung!" Graggis yelled indicating the one on the left. Both man grabbed it while Graggis put his hands on the right side of the rung. "Now!" he yelled. His muscles tensed and bulged as he strained, the veins on his arms resembling ropes, and slowly they lifted the ladder off the stones. The orcs howled and climbed faster. They were almost upon them. "Throw it to the right!" Graggis yelled just as an orc jabbed a short sword at his face.

The jerk of the ladder caused the orc's blow to miss and the creature stumbled and fell backwards, taking several goblins with it. The bottom end of the ladder teetered on the ground, and then slowly slid sideways off the battlements, crashing onto the ground below.

As Graggis looked left and right along the wall he noticed the attackers had tried similar tactics in several other locations along the wall where flames and black smoke filled the air. He could see fighting all along the walls as defenders fought desperately to keep the creatures from breaching the wall. He was about to jump into the fray again when he saw a great jet of blue flame again flash from the battlements, showering the orcs below. Graggis's eyes pinpointed Sar-gathos, the elven mage, standing on the edge of the wall, the tip of his staff lit as he shot flames at an incoming ladder, completely engulfing it and its carriers with fire. "Glad he's on our side," Graggis muttered.

The day went on as more ladders were repeatedly carried to the wall. And though the orcs and goblins nearly overran the defenders with sheer numbers, Graggis and Ruthalis were able to rally their men

and fight off the enemy, eventually killing their attackers on the wall.
They were not able to breach the wall and open the gate. By the time
the sun had set, the battlements were slick with blood and bodies littered
the stones. Healers moved with practiced speed attending the wounded
and tossing the dead beasts over the wall. Their own dead were carried
down and over the bridge to be cremated later, with honor, in a great
fiery pyre. Graggis, splattered with blood and drenched in sweat, had
several minor cuts and scrapes, but most of the blood he wore came
from his enemies

Chunks of bread, cheese, and dried meat were carried up to the
hungry and exhausted defenders. They sat along the torch lit battlements
eating their food and thinking about the many friends and comrades
they had lost. Their victory had come at a cost. Graggis knew that
General Ruthalis would want body counts, so he spent the majority of
an hour inspecting his men and counting the dead. A messenger soon
came, as expected, to inform Graggis that a war council was meeting
and his presence was required.

"How much more time do you need?" Ruthalis asked Durgen.
The rest of the men, including Lord Dynure, General Ruthalis, Captain
Graggis, Sar-gathos, and Captain Hadrick, sat at the table eating quick
rations and drinking cold water. Hadrick was asked, out of respect, to
join the meeting even though he had yet to have an opportunity to join
the fighting.

"We have cut through two of the foundations and unwound the
magic holdin' 'em," Master Trader Durgen replied, "and we will be
positioning the pins tomorrow and workin' on the last foundation. We
still need a day and a half I reckon," he ended somberly, knowing full
well the loss of life their army had suffered, and would continue to
suffer while they finished the bridge preparations. He had watched the
bodies being carried over the bridge and added to the huge pyre that had
been lit.

"Master Durgen, I am not familiar with stonework. When you
say 'pins' and 'unwound' can you explain that?" Hadrick asked.

"Aye, I will try. We dwarves can speak to the stone; it is an
ability we call *Daz-rothos*. We do not need magic to nullify the magic that
was embedded in the stone. We simply ask the stone to cast off the
magical weaves that were placed in the rock. But the degree to which
the process must be applied to this bridge takes time, and it is a difficult

thing to do. Only a few Daz-athros, or stone speakers, have the skill to do it. To speed up the process a handful of dwarves can link their minds and the Daz-athros will guide the chant into the rock."

"Is it magic?" Hadrick asked.

"Not exactly, it is hard to explain. We are on a level with the stone, we understand it," Durgen said, knowing his response was inadequate.

Sar-gathos then tried to explain, "Imagine energy vibrating in everything around you. It begins to take on certain characteristics, but yet it is all the same. Elves have the same affinity as dwarves, but with elements closely linked to us. We *understand* the forests and creatures that inhabit them just as dwarves *understand* stone and the minerals that lie deep within it."

"Aye, better words then me own," Durgen added. "As far as the pins go, the plan is to embed them in such a way that all we need to do to drop the support is to knock the pins out. It is a difficult task and requires precise skill."

"I see," Hadrick said, even though he really didn't.

"Graggis, how many men did you lose today?" Ruthalis asked.

"Two hundred and seventy five men, Sir."

Ruthalis let out a weary sigh. "We counted near that number on our side. That leaves us with five hundred men, while the enemy still numbers several thousand."

"Don't forget the fifty Free Legion soldiers that are at your disposal," Hadrick added quickly.

"Most of the physical labor on the bridge is done. I can free up fifty of me dwarves as well," Durgen said.

General Ruthalis stroked his stubbly chin as he thought for a moment. Then he looked at Graggis seriously. "I think it's time for your plan. Can it be done tonight? We need to lessen their numbers and put some doubt in their stupid orc brains."

"I can be done tonight. I've been preparing since yesterday," Graggis said.

"See to it," General Ruthalis ordered.

Graggis turned to Captain Hadrick. "You ready to stain your blades?" he asked. "I could use your help."

"When and where?" Hadrick replied.

Hadrick liked the plan. It was simple and held the element of surprise. But they only had the night to prepare and get into position and that meant no sleep and hard fighting at the end. There were six long boats that the garrison warriors used on occasion. Each boat could hold ten men. The boats, using several trips, would be used to carry a hundred men around the garrison wall to the far bank in the middle of the night. Sar-gathos would then use his magic to transport another hundred men, a combined force of Durgen's dwarves and Hadrick's warriors, around the other wall to the northern bank. Then, just before sunrise, the men would flank the army as they slept and attack. They would use hit and run tactics and then slip away and enter through the gate before the enemy could prepare a defense. If everything went well they would kill hundreds and lose very few.

It was half way through the night and Sar-gathos was becoming visibly tired. His skin was pale and his eyes were dark and sunken. He still had a quarter of the men to transport across the water and around the stone tower that emerged from the slow moving river.

"Are you okay?" Hadrick asked the Ekahal.

"Just tired. Holding this spell for this duration is taxing. I will need to rest a few hours after," he whispered wearily. Seli stood next to Hadrick and where she went, Tuvallis went. His massive form followed her like a shadow. Hadrick tried to get her to stay, worried that her wounds were not yet healed, but after Sar-gathos had healed her she felt perfectly fit.

Hagar was nearby, hiding in the shadows by the water's edge. Sar-gathos shared their plan with the ogrillion and using mental images with the wizard had requested to accompany them. Word had spread of the ogrillion and he had become sort of a celebrity. Most of the men stayed clear of the beast, but their eyes watched him with curiosity, fascination, and often fear. But word had come down from the top that Hagar was welcome and not dangerous. Those who had vouched for the beast were well respected among the men. If they said the beast was not dangerous, then the beast must be safe. These warriors spent their entire lives trusting in their comrades and commanders and their lives often depended on that trust. So when they saw Graggis standing next to the beast unafraid, they reasoned the ogrillion was not a threat. When the order came directly from General Ruthalis that the ogrillion be treated like any other soldier, they followed that order like any other. When they saw the Free Legion warriors casually interacting with the giant beast, they were again reassured that there was nothing to fear from the creature.

Finally, an hour later, Sar-gathos had transported everyone to the opposite shore. When Graggis was in place on the other side they would shoot a flaming arrow into the sky and that would be the signal to attack. It wouldn't matter at that point if the enemy were alerted as the attack would come moments after the signal. A horn would signal the retreat, and if the plan worked they would disappear into the darkness, reaching the gate before the enemy could organize a counter.

Everyone had stripped themselves of heavy armor and wore only dark clothes or light protection like leather armor if they had it. The mission required stealth and speed, which would be hindered by heavy plate armor and bulky weapons. Durgen and Hadrick led their men silently through the grass towards the enemy army. Bright fires roared in the distance and the orange glow could easily be seen in the darkness. But they all knew that orcs and goblins could see in the dark and they would probably have perimeter guards. That is where Tuvallis came in.

When the mission was explained to Hadrick, Graggis asked if he had someone in mind that could infiltrate the perimeter and take out their guards. The first person that came to mind was Tuvallis, who he actually knew very little about. There was something about the man though, and from what Stephy and Bositch had told him he would be just the man for the job. They had praised him incessantly during their retelling of the events that night several days ago and had referred to him as a ghost several times. And a ghost is just what they needed. When Hadrick had asked Tuvallis if wanted the task, he didn't hesitate.

As they neared the fires Hadrick motioned for everyone to stop and hunker down in the grass. The order was passed silently down the line and in moments everyone lay still hiding in the shadows of the night. Luckily the clouds were thick, creating shadows everywhere. Hadrick glanced at Tuvallis giving him the signal to go. Tuvallis turned to Seli who silently gripped his hand. Then he rose to a crouch and vanished into the night.

It didn't take him long to find the first guards. The enemy army was asleep, and based on their lack of defensive preparations it was obvious that they did not expect a night attack from a garrison with inferior numbers. Two orcs sat together in a grass clearing playing bones. They were talking loudly in orcish and it was easy for Tuvallis to hone in on them even in the darkness. He crept slowly towards them making sure to hide his bulk in the tall grass. The orcs had trampled a clearing so they could play and they were so focused on their game that they had no clue that he was near. He needed to take them out without raising an alarm and he had come prepared to do so. Instead of his long bow, which would be hard to conceal and use in these conditions, he brought a crossbow. It was already loaded and his plan was to take out one quickly with that weapon and use his knife on the second. He crept closer and made it to the edge of the small clearing. He was only five paces away and he could actually smell them. He had made sure he was upwind of them and luckily for him that put him facing their backs.

He stood up from the grass and moved slowly forward like the morning mist. For someone his size, Tuvallis could move incredibly silently. He had honed his ability to move silently during the fifteen years he spent hunting and tracking. When he was only four paces away from the orcs he leveled the crossbow and fired into the broad back of the beast on the right. He knew at this range that the powerful bolt would pierce any armor the orc wore. The crossbow made a subtle click followed by a thud as the bolt hammered into the creature, slamming it forward face first into the ground. The beast on the left stood up trying to figure out why his friend had fallen over, not fully registering the sound he heard from the crossbow. The orc didn't even turn around and Tuvallis capitalized on that. He dropped the crossbow and in one great leap he landed upon the lone orc, ramming his blade into the side of its neck, severing its artery. The orc gurgled incoherently and Tuvallis tripped it, slamming it face first into the ground. He then rammed his razor sharp knife into the base of the orc's skull and into its brain, instantly stopping its frantic spasms.

Tuvallis found only one other guard on the northern side of the perimeter and he dispatched him easily. They only needed a small gap in the perimeter and he had just created that. Within moments Tuvallis had rejoined the group. "It's done," he said. Seli smiled back at him obviously reassured that he had succeeded without incident.

Hadrick nodded. "Well done," he whispered, "see if you can get Hagar to stay back. He is too big and as we near them he could be seen. Tell him to join us once the fighting begins."

Tuvallis scooted five paces to the left and crouched down next to Hagar's giant form. He inhaled the pungent odor of the ogrillion, that of a wild animal, not so unpleasant to one who had lived years in the wilderness, but nevertheless wafting the hint of danger. Hagar had removed his beautiful cuirass and he now wore nothing but his furs. Most of his torso was bare but he did not seem to be affected in the least by the chilly morning air. Tuvallis put his finger to his lip, signaling for Hagar to be silent. He spoke, using his hands as well, in order to make sure the ogrillion understood. He wasn't sure if he was just good at it, or if Hagar was beginning to understand some of the words, but it seemed as if the beast was beginning to more quickly understand what people were saying to him. "Stay here," Tuvallis whispered, tapping the ground. "No crawl," he continued as he used his fingers to try to mimic a person crawling while he was negatively shaking his head. Then he used two of his knives and crossed them silently like a mini swordfight. "When fighting starts, get up and charge and kill as many as you can," Tuvallis whispered, pantomiming the action with his knives. The ogrillion's response was his brutish smile. Tuvallis smiled back and tapped the big beast's giant hand. "Be careful," he added as he scooted away from the ogrillion.

The hundred warriors crept slowly forward. Tuvallis cringed every time one of the dwarves stepped on a twig or stumbled against a stone, compromising the silence of their approach. They were not as suitable to this type of mission, but he knew that once the fighting began they would be invaluable. Dwarves did not live as long as elves, but compared to a human lifespan theirs was long indeed. A dwarf, if blessed with old age, could live to be three or four hundred years old. And the primary activities of a dwarf were eating, drinking, mining precious stones and metals, making weapons, and fighting. A lifetime of hard work and combat, combined with their natural constitution and physical strength, made them some of the deadliest warriors one could face.

They stopped within fifty paces of the enemy camp. Hundreds of fires were scattered over the grassy land, some smoldering and others burning brightly with fresh logs. Most of the enemy lay in the open near the fires but there were some crudely erected tents near the center of the camp, probably the home of the war leaders. Few of the creatures were still up, but they could spot a few of them wandering about, probably to relieve themselves in the woods or grab some left-over food from the night's dinner.

Everyone was tense, sweaty hands gripping swords, axes, and war hammers. They waited patiently for the signal, eager to quell the nervous fluttering's in their stomachs that always seemed to precede battle. They had only moments to wait before a streak of orange fire flashed into the night sky.

There would be no battle cries or screaming during this charge. Everyone stood up and ran silently, hunched over, towards the enemy camp, in an approach eerie in its silence. Within moments they had arrived at the perimeter of the camp, their silver weapons descending ruthlessly upon their sleeping victims. Then the screaming began. Hundreds died in the first few moments of the attack. Hundreds more perished as the enemy awoke, struggling to stand, while futilely trying to figure out what was happening before they came face to face with Free Legion steel and dwarven metal.

Twenty seconds into the attack fifty or more of the enemy warriors from the interior of the camp had managed to arm themselves and came at their attackers with no semblance of control or organization. It was a free for all as hastily armed orcs and goblins attacked them from the darkness.

By this time Hagar had leaped over the bodies of the orcs that had fallen during the first few seconds of the attack. He landed near one of their campfires and kicked his massive foot into the center of it, throwing burning logs and embers into the faces of four attacking orcs. The beasts howled and covered their eyes, opening them just in time to see the terrifying image of the giant ogrillion's spiked mace flying through the air. It struck the first orc in the side, and the force of Hagar's swing along with the weight of the mace propelled the weapon through all four orcs, shattering bone, ripping flesh, and scattering their bodies into the air. Roaring in defiance, he strode forward, swinging the mace in great arcs of destruction. The scene was awesome and horrific at the same time. Orcs and goblins alike had little chance of avoiding the tree-size weapon that tossed their crushed bodies left and right, throwing them into their comrades.

Seli and Tuvallis had remained next to each other, their steel swords flashing as they parried the clumsy orc weapons and sliced through enemy flesh. Tuvallis yanked his sword from the chest of a dying orc and scanned his surroundings. The darkness was slowly giving way to the morning light and what was black was now gray. He could now see hundreds of enemy warriors coming at them from the interior of the camp. More importantly he could see the massive heads and shoulders of five ogres lumbering towards them. "Sound the horn,

Graggis," Tuvallis muttered to himself. It was time to retreat as the enemy's numbers would soon overwhelm them. Besides that, they needed time to retreat back to the gate. The pounding of the ogres' huge feet grew louder, shaking the ground as the beasts drew near.

Durgen appeared next to him with ten grim looking dwarves. "Finally, something worth fightin'!" he growled, winking at Tuvallis. The ogres, attired in a motley combination of leather, furs, and mismatched metal armor, carried crudely made war hammers and long thick swords as big as a man.

"We need to be retreatin' or they will catch us out in the open!" Tuvallis yelled over the din of battle. As if Graggis heard him, the horn to retreat sounded in the distance. "Let's go!" Tuvallis yelled as he gripped Seli's arm and pushed her back toward the garrison. But the ogres had picked up speed and would be upon them in moments. He quickly decided to remain with the dwarves to halt their advance and give the others a head start back to the safety of the high stone wall.

Seconds later the ogres' giant weapons were sweeping towards them threatening to swat them away as if they were flies. But dwarves were experts at fighting giants, and their diminutive size enabled them to duck and dodge the deadly attacks from above.

Tuvallis narrowly dodged the swing of a huge war hammer; the head of it was the size of his torso. He jumped backwards just in time, feeling the displaced air from the swinging weapon swoosh by him. Then Hagar was there, his great mace glowing in the morning grayness as its wicked head slammed into the ogre's thigh, crushing it and puncturing the flesh in five different spots. The ogre roared in pain and fell to one knee. Hagar roared back, yanked his weapon free, and swung the mace like a logger splitting logs straight down on its head. Tuvallis looked away as blood and brains splattered everyone within five paces.

"Go!" Hagar roared, his legs spread wide protectively, both hands gripping the huge mace. Tuvallis needed no further urging as waves of enemy warriors poured towards them.

One unfortunate dwarf was not quick enough, and an ogre's broad blade sliced through his hip, nearly cutting him in half. Yet two of the massive beasts were down, their legs broken and shattered, while the five remaining dwarves, including Durgen, were slowly backing up, trying to disengage from the fight.

Hagar charged forward, crashing into an ogre who was busy trying to deflect the dangerous blows of the dwarves. The force of

Hagar's charge sent the beast tumbling into the ogre near him, freeing up the dwarves.

Durgen took advantage of the reprieve and yelled for them to retreat. "Run!" he screamed, just as he slammed his glittering axe into the knee of a beast that had been momentarily distracted by its falling comrades. The magical blade bit deep and the ogre hopped backwards on one leg, roaring in agony. Hagar's glowing mace flashed over Durgen's head, crashing into the chest of another ogre, and sending four spikes into its lungs. Durgen pivoted and grabbed a nearby comrade, forcing them both backwards away from the deadly ogrillion. Hagar's mace swung left and right, nearly as fast as a man could swing a short sword. Ogre weapons and bones alike shattered, and within moments there was no one else nearby to fight, except, that is, for the hundreds of orcs and goblins that were almost upon them. Hagar growled, turned away from the enemy, and retreated with the others back to the garrison.

Durgen and the five remaining dwarves were running as fast as their little legs would carry them towards the open gate of the garrison. Two hundred bowmen lined the battlements with arrows nocked ready to cover their retreat. Graggis and Hadrick's men sprinted across the grasslands as several thousand enemy warriors pursued them. Hagar was the last of them, but his great strides quickly widened the gap between himself and the enemy. The ogrillion easily caught up with Durgen and the other dwarves.

They began funneling through the thick gate but their increasing numbers soon created a bottleneck at the opening. As the enemy came within range, the archers sent a barrage of deadly missiles towards the enemy. Orcs and goblins fell as the arrows slammed into them. But their superior numbers allowed them to keep coming and it was obvious to any onlooker that they would overtake the men before they had all made it through the gate.

Hagar caught up with the mass of men as they frantically pushed their way into the opening. Graggis was in the back and he saw their predicament as clear as day, and instinctively screamed over the din of the chaos. "Men, form up with me! We need a sword wall!" Instantly Finarthian soldiers and Free Legion warriors that were stuck in the back turned and linked up with Graggis. Hagar, as well, turned in front of Graggis and planted his thick legs in a wide stance. Gripping the long handled mace with both hands he raised it above his head, roaring a thunderous battle cry while Graggis and twenty other men fanned out from him, protecting the entrance so the rest of the men could get through.

Arrows continued to slam into the enemy but still they came. "We have to shut the gate!" Sar-gathos yelled to General Ruthalis. "We can't risk letting the orcs through!" If they made it through the gate, it would be over. Sar-gathos had several spells in mind to destroy the enemy, but he was afraid of hurting the men as well.

"Not yet," Ruthalis said tensely as he looked down upon the scene.

As the army of orcs crashed into the wall of men, Hagar began swinging his glowing mace back and forth, hurling any creatures unlucky enough to be caught in its path, into the air, their broken corpses crashing to the ground in a bloody heap. The men did not have shields so they relied on each other to guard their flanks. But the sheer weight of the enemy's numbers forced them inexorably backwards towards the gate. Though several men in the shield wall had fallen, each second they held off the enemy allowed more men to rush through the open gate to safety.

But now the enemy was so close that Ruthalis could not hold the gate open any longer. "Shut the gate!" he screamed. Instantly the reinforced metal and wood gate began to close as the men at the rear frantically pushed forward.

"Go!" Hagar yelled as he glanced back at the closing gate. "I hold!"

Arrows continued to rain down from above, killing scores of orcs, but failing to halt the strength of their assault. Graggis, momentarily free from fighting, saw the gate slowly closing behind him. "Retreat!" he screamed. "The gate is closing!" Hagar's great mace swung back and forth like a farmer's scythe giving the men just enough time to turn and jump through the narrowing gap of the closing gate. Graggis glanced once more at Hagar who was pivoting back and forth with incredible speed for someone his size, blocking the gap in the gatehouse with his massive size and the powerful arcs of his mace. With just seconds to spare, Graggis then jumped through the gate as it slammed shut behind him. The massive wood and steel beam fell heavily into place, shutting the gate to the enemy, and to Hagar.

"Where is Hagar?" Tuvallis yelled amidst the chaos. He saw the gate shut with no sign of the ogrillion. Seli, standing nearby, also frantically searched for the beast's towering form.

"I don't see him," she said fearfully.

Tuvallis pushed through the throng of men to the gate and found Graggis. "Where is Hagar?" Tuvallis asked the burly warrior.

Graggis's face was a mask of despair. "Out there," he replied grimly. "He stayed to cover our retreat."

Tuvallis growled and ran for the stairs that led to the battlements on top of the gatehouse. He took the stairs three at a time and within seconds he was looking down from the garrison wall. Archers continued to fire arrow after arrow into the enemy as they stormed the wall and fought to break through the ogrillion's defenses. Whenever an orc raised his sword or readied his bow, archers from above targeted him, turning the beast into a pin cushion. But the archers could not target them all and some of their weapons found their mark on Hagar's flesh.

As he stood alone, blocking the entrance to the gate, his weapon flared with bright white light, crushing any who came too near. As bodies piled up around him, still he fought on. Tuvallis noticed several arrows protruding from Hagar's flesh and red streaks lined his arms and legs where he had been wounded. But nothing seemed to slow the indomitable ogrillion who showed no signs of tiring. If anything, the strength and speed with which he swung his mace seemed to actually increase, as countless orcs literally flew through the air, many of them crashing into their comrades.

"I've never seen anything like it," General Ruthalis said as he and Tuvallis stood watching in fascinated horror.

"We must do something!" Tuvallis said frantically.

"What?" the general asked helplessly. "We cannot open that gate."

Just then, a deafening roar shattered the cacophony of battle. Everyone looked up into the receding darkness towards the sound. It was dawn and soon the morning sun would bathe the horizon with light. Already its amber glow was pushing back the darkness of night. They heard the roar again, this time closer, very close. But they still could see nothing in the night sky.

Then they heard a great rhythmic rush of air followed by a third roar, so incredibly loud that everyone froze, even the orcs below, and stared up at the shadowy form descending upon them.

"Dragon!" Sar-gathos yelled.

But it was too late. Kil-Kannon, the Demon Dragon, streaked from the darkness and let loose a massive cloud of scalding hot steam.

"Stay behind me!" Sar-gathos bellowed as the stone in his staff flared a bright green. Everyone near the wizard, including Tuvallis and General Ruthalis, jumped behind the Ekahal just as the beast's hot breath covered them in a blanket of death. Agonizing screams and the odor of sizzling flesh assaulted Tuvallis's senses, but no heat penetrated the translucent shield created by the wizard.

As the giant beast flew across the entire length of the wall unleashing its deadly attack, its black skin flashed with crackling streaks of red and orange energy. Searing steam poured over the defenders all along the wall, a white cloud so hot that men cooked inside their armor. Hundreds died instantly while still more perished as they plunged off the wall frantically trying to evade its lethal breath.

After one sweep from Kil-Kannon the garrison wall lay deserted by the living. All that remained were the smoking bodies of the dead and the poor tortured souls who wished they were dead, crawling and moaning in pain as their skin bubbled and flaked off under their armor. The dragon's breath had created a strange sort of heat. There were no flames because it wasn't fire. It was super-heated steam capable of instantly cooking flesh without burning clothes or lighting anything on fire. Hundreds had perished in that one attack.

Luckily for Hagar, great clouds of the steam rolled off the wall hitting those below, though the impact of the vapor was much less than the poor souls on the wall had suffered. But it was enough to cause panic among the orcs as the scalding heat forced them back from the gate.

The cloud of steam had also slammed into Hagar, singing his exposed skin. But it was not enough to severely damage his thick leather-like hide. He could barely see as the hot mist drifted around him. All he knew for certain was that for the moment he was not being attacked. He looked back at the gate and saw no way through it. So he did the only thing he could do, run down the length of the wall, away from the attackers, towards the river's edge.

"In Ulren's name, what was that?" Ruthalis asked, bewildered, as the hot steam dissipated. Sar-gathos's light had disappeared along with the magical shield, and as they gazed down the length of the wall, their hearts sunk with despair at the destruction before them. The burned bodies of their comrades' lay everywhere. Not a living soul remained on the wall except for them. At least a hundred men had died in that one pass.

"A dragon, although I have never seen the likes of that beast. We must leave the wall!" Sar-gathos shouted. But no one needed his urging as they heard the great gusts of the beast's wings swoop around for another attack.

The courtyard was in chaos as hundreds of the defenders frantically raced for cover. Captain Hadrick ran down the causeway towards the front of the bridge. "Free Legion, follow me!" he yelled. In the ensuing chaos his men managed to hear their captain and sprinted after him. They had left their shields and armor at the entrance of the bridge and it was there that they headed. They would not have time to don their armor but their shields would be invaluable when fighting in close quarters.

The dragon swooped down and landed with a resounding crash on top of the gatehouse, its immense claws gripping the edge of the battlement, talons as strong as iron gouging holes in the stone surface. Again it roared, sending a shockwave of sound into the courtyard, scattering men and horses alike. It then drew in a deep breath of air before spewing forth another searing burst of steam. Those in its path died horribly, their skin literally melting off their bodies. Agonizing screams of the wounded and dying filled the courtyard, while the survivors added terrified screams of their own as they scrambled to get away from the giant creature.

Tuvallis had lost sight of Seli as she ran to join her brothers in the Free Legion. He had to remember that she was not a defenseless woman and that she had been a warrior for most of her adult life. In the chaos he ran and took shelter through an open door in the gatehouse. As he ducked through the door he heard a loud crash that shook the timbers of the gatehouse as the dragon landed above him. In seconds the courtyard in front of him was filled with the beast's scorching breath and for the second time he again recoiled at the sickening odor of burning flesh. Suddenly another deafening crash shook the very walls around him, followed by another, this one accompanied by the sound of splintering wood. "The gate," he whispered to himself.

With that knowledge he ran through the door and headed for the edge of the courtyard, taking shelter as he moved. The crashing sound came again. Tuvallis stopped behind a stack of water barrels and glanced back at the dragon. The black beast's wings were spread wide and its long neck reared high into the air. Tuvallis could see the muscles in its back suddenly twitch and contract and was just able to catch a glimpse of its huge tail before it disappeared behind the wall to crash into the gate, which cracked and caved inward. Another couple hits, Tuvallis reasoned, and the gate would shatter.

Lord Dynure and General Ruthalis were finally able to bring some control to the chaos. Their men were hardened warriors who had faced many dangers, but the thought of being cooked inside their armor was something for which they were not prepared. Nonetheless, the two war leaders hastily formed a line of men across the causeway that led to the bridge. The dragon had frightened most of the horses away but some of the Finarthian Knights had been able to regain control of their mounts. There were probably twenty mounted knights and twice that number of footmen lining up behind them.

It was then that the gate crashed open and everyone froze. The dragon lowered his horned head and glared at the defenders with blazing eyes. The dragon then raised its head and roared into the early morning sky, as if to announce the hundreds of orcs, goblins, and ogres who now rushed through the open gateway, screaming and howling as they stormed the causeway, like hoards of hungry cockroaches.

Durgen wanted to stay and fight but he knew he would be needed at the bridge. It was too soon. There was no way they could drop the entire bridge. But it might be possible to collapse the first and last span. That would create two gaps, over thirty paces wide, in the bridge. It would only stop Malbeck for a week or so as they could build temporary ramps over the gaps, but it was better than leaving the bridge entirely intact.

Several dwarves joined him and they ran down the causeway, past the Free Legion soldiers who were strapping on shields and forming up. Durgen led the dwarves a quarter of the way across the bridge and looked down at the support structures holding up the first span. Ropes and scaffolding had been built so the engineers could be lowered down to the supports underneath. "Lower me!" Durgen ordered. He jumped onto the narrow wooden platform and the dwarves lowered him to the network of hastily built scaffolding below. Five dwarves were there, scurrying around one of the huge supports like worker ants. A giant wedge had been cut out of the stone support and two iron rods as thick as a man's arm had been placed into the gap. Each pin narrowed to a point which fit into a hole on a metal plate. The plate was engineered so that a section of it could be hammered out which would cause the pins to slip and slide out. The support would crack and that end of the span would fall into the water. More than likely it would be enough to cause the other end to crack, bringing the entire span down. Durgen ran to a portly dust covered dwarf who was securing the plate into place with giant swings of a heavy hammer. "Gormly!" he yelled over the pounding.

The dwarven engineer stopped his hammering at Durgen's urgent voice. "What is it?"

"We be needin' this support down!" Durgen said.

"I be knowin' that, why do ya think I'm here?!"

"I mean now! They are almost upon us!" As if on cue they suddenly heard the clash of battle.

"We are not ready," Gormly retorted.

"What can ya do now?" Durgen asked.

Gormly looked around at the support and the other columns up and down the river as he thought about the situation. "We can take this support out and another on the far span. But we don't have the plates in place on the opposite support."

"Will the two spans fall with only those two supports gone?"

"They may, hard to say though, I didn't build this bridge," Gormly replied.

Durgen grimaced. "Send word to the engineers at the other support. We need to get as many people across the bridge as we can. Then, on my order, knock out the pins and may Moradin be with us. And Gormly, don't forget to jump into the boat."

It was a major risk for the dwarf who was picked to knock out the pins. The plan was for the engineer to leap into the boat that was tied to the base of the support and hopefully float down river before the structure fell. Timing was everything, and they were counting on the current moving fast enough to carry the dwarf to safety.

Gormly just smiled. "That be the fun part," he said.

"See to it, and good luck," Durgen said as he ran back to the platform and hailed his men to haul him back up.

Everything was in chaos near the bridge. The hundreds of orcs and goblins had forced the defenders backwards and they now fought on the bridge itself. Durgen found General Ruthalis on horseback behind four thick walls of soldiers. Most of the knights on horseback had fallen. The remaining soldiers on the bridge were now mostly from the Free Legion.

"We have to get everyone across the bridge! We're going to try and drop the first and last sections!" Durgen yelled up at the general.

"Do it!" the general said. "Retreat across the bridge!" General Ruthalis bellowed to the warriors in front of him.

Hadrick blocked blow after blow on his shield, slowly stepping backwards as the enemy pressed them harder and harder. He parried and thrust, blocking attacks aimed at his shield brother to his right while cutting into the enemy with precision. The Free Legion soldiers had worked together for countless campaigns and their skill in formation fighting was obvious as they held off the hoard of orcs, whose swords and axes smashed into their shields as they tried to cut through their defenses.

General Ruthalis's words sounded behind him. "Free Legion, retreat across the bridge! But stay in formation!" They had to hope that they could get across the bridge before it fell, then, if any orcs or goblins made it across with them, they could dispatch them easily enough as most would have fallen with the bridge or been caught on the other side. By now the morning sun had risen higher overhead, bringing a red orange glow to the sky and illuminating the strange black dragon swooping towards them from above. "Dragon!" was all the captain had time to yell before the scalding steam roared toward them. Without thinking Hadrick dropped his sword and shield and jumped off the edge of the bridge to the cold water below. A handful of others did the same, but the ones that didn't died upon the bridge.

Durgen, seeing the dragon descend upon them, ran to the side of the bridge, and grabbed one of the ropes used to lower the platform, and then leaped over the edge. Luckily he wore leather fighting gloves layered with bands of steel, protecting his hands from the burning friction as he slid down the rope to the scaffolding below. "Now Gormly! Drop the bridge!" he screamed as he raced to the boat tied to the edge of the support. Gormly grabbed a huge metal hammer, ran to the support pins, and slammed the heavy hammer head into the mechanism on the metal plate. Four powerful swings sent the plate flying into the water and the two support pins slid across the metal trough created for just that purpose. "Hurry!" Durgen yelled as he readied his axe near the rope that held the boat in place.

The weight of the stone bridge caused the pins to slide out forcefully, shooting them like missiles far into the water. Immediately the stone began to crack along the support. Gormly dropped the hammer and ran the five paces to the boat, leaping as far as his little legs could launch him. He hit the wood bench in the boat and tumbled to the bow just as Durgen brought his axe down on the rope freeing it from its hold. The span above them began to crack and give way as their little boat grabbed the current which carried it quickly away.

The dragon's scorching breath had killed most of the Free Legion defenders along with dozens of the attacking orcs. But as soon as the hot mist disappeared the army of monsters ran forward over the bridge. The weight of their numbers pressed down on the damaged support and within moments the support gave way, cracking in half and causing the span to shift and drop to one side. Gravity then took over and the other support broke under the pressure, bringing the entire span into the water with a tremendous splash.

Durgen and Gormly had drifted fifty paces down river when the first span crashed into the water. Several moments later the last span joined it, leaving a lone section of bridge still standing directly in the middle of the river. Gormly did not have time to pass word to the other engineer on the far span, but they must have seen what happened and once the first span fell they dropped their own. Another boat drifted down river on the far side and the four dwarves inside it sat gazing dazedly at the destruction they caused. "That ought to give us a few weeks," Gormly said

"Aye, but at what cost?" Durgen said somberly as he looked upon the destruction. Almost all of the defenders at the garrison were dead and the few that had survived struggled as they splashed through the water trying to get to shore. The poor souls wearing armor had either perished in the dragon's burning breath, or had sunk to their doom when they hit the water. Just under a thousand men had died trying to protect the bridge. Durgen wondered, was a few weeks of time worth those lives? That was a question that wouldn't be answered until Malbeck and his forces arrived at Finarth's gate.

Nine
The Sword of Ela

A few moments after Tolvar drank the healing draught he was standing and firmly gripping his axe. The burns on his face were still visible, the skin red and lightly blistered. He looked as if a fire had literally been lit in his beard.

"Impressive," Lor-telliam said as the Dakeen warrior stretched his arms wide, testing the movement of his muscles and assessing his residual pain. "He should be dead." Tolvar growled in response as if it would lessen his pain as he continued to stretch his stiff limbs.

"Well?" Cade asked.

"Hurts it does, like me skin has peeled off," Tolvar replied through clenched teeth.

"It has," Lor-telliam said, "you were severely burned and the potion is only strong enough to get you on your feet and lessen the pain somewhat. I'm afraid there will be serious scarring and the wounds will be painful for sometime.

"Can ya fight, Brother?" Cade asked the important question. Tolvar didn't even bother to answer; he just spit on the ground and hefted his axe.

Jonas had sat down on a nearby bench while everyone else was peering into the hazy grayness, nervously gripping their weapons as they waited for Tolvar to ready himself.

"Wizard, see to Jonas so we can get off these stairs," Kromm said. The king no longer had his shield as it had become a contorted mass of melted metal. His left arm was seared badly and blisters could already be seen on his forearm.

Lor-telliam walked over to Jonas and placed both hands on his shoulders. As he began to chant Jonas immediately felt the familiar warmth flood through his body. The pain began to ease as the elf did his work, and the pressure he felt in his bowels began to subside until he felt normal again.

"It is done," Lor-telliam said as he lifted his arms from Jonas's shoulders.

"Thank you. I am in your debt," Jonas replied.

Lor-telliam just nodded in acknowledgement and turned towards the stairs that led further up the hill. "Before we go, everyone eat some of this bread," the Ekahal said as he brought forth a small bundle of white paper from the small pack he wore on his back. Inside the paper were various small lumps of bread, each about the size of an egg.

"Elven bread," Allindrian said with a smile as she reached for a piece. "Eat it," she advised. "It tastes plain but it will revive your exhausted bodies."

Everyone eagerly complied, hoping to find any relief from their exhaustion. They knew that they probably weren't safe yet.

"Follow me, we are almost there," Lor-telliam ordered as he put his pack back on and began their ascent.

Jonas and Fil followed from the rear. He was worried about Tulari as she had not reappeared. The night wolf and been struck by the Banthra's fire and had jumped over the wall to escape the flames. He hoped she was okay but there was nothing he could do about that now. He couldn't even heal her if she needed it and the knowledge that he also couldn't heal his friends continued to anger him.

They made it to the top landing that led to the monument without further incident. And although there was still a layer of mist surrounding them, they could now see the subtle outline of the massive pillars surrounding the statue of King Ullis Gavinsteal.

"Where is the secret entrance?" King Baylin asked the Ekahal.

"At the base of the statue. Stay alert, there are sure to be more enemies," the elf cautioned as he moved up the last set of stairs towards the monument.

The landing at the top was deserted, and before them was a circle of ten huge stone pillars that were each thirty paces high. They rested on a raised stone platform that was flat except for the huge statue that sat directly in the center. The circle within the pillars was at least forty paces in diameter. The white marble statue itself was over fifteen paces high, and stood on a raised dais as tall as a man.

"There," Lor-telliam indicated as he walked across the expansive platform to the statue. "The dais hides the entrance to a set of stairs that lead to a room underneath. The armor and sword will be there."

"Let's get on with this," Allindrian said nervously as she turned from the statue and looked out into the shadows that surrounded them. But nothing was there, at least not that she could see.

"This spell will take a few moments and it requires my entire concentration," Lor-telliam announced as everyone surrounded the elf with weapons drawn. Then he began the incantation, slowly chanting as the elven words, hypnotically melodious, drifted from his mouth. He continued to softly chant as he faced the dais, and after a few moments he began to raise his voice.

Jonas looked back and noticed that the wizard now had one hand resting on the base of the dais while the other still gripped his staff. The incantation grew louder still, but Jonas could not understand the words, nor could he retain any of them in his memory. They resonated momentarily in his mind, then disappeared like a leaf in a gust of wind.

Then something began to happen. Words began to appear on the base of the statue, slowly taking on a moon-like glow, the graceful lines of the text emerging character by character as if someone were writing them. They were elvish, but of a dialect so ancient that no one in the group could read except for Lor-telliam.

Lor-telliam suddenly stopped chanting and the silence was followed by a grating sound. Everyone turned towards the statue and saw the giant structure actually moving. It was sliding backward, slowly revealing a dark passageway underneath. As the entrance was exposed, the glowing writing slowly faded until the white stone was clear again.

"All this time," King Baylin muttered in awe as he looked into the dark hole. "It was here all this time."

"Follow me," Lor-telliam said.

As the elf placed his foot on the first dust covered step, a series of sconces suddenly lit up, shedding a magical orange light along the stairway. Everyone moved quickly down the steps and emerged into a square room that was about the same size as the platform above them. It was simply built, using the same stone blocks that had been used to construct the monument. Like the stairway, everything was covered in dust. Sconces lined the entire room and they too emanated a soft magical light.

Everyone stopped at the bottom of the stairs and stared in awe at the artifacts that had been placed in the center of the room. There was a suit of stunning white and silver plate armor magnificently displayed on a human bust, the same type that a tailor might use to fit a king's clothes. The armor was a dazzling white lined with silver and the Finarthian symbol shone with brilliance on the spectacular cuirass. The helm covered the entire head of the bust, leaving slits for the nose, mouth, and eyes. Expertly carved eagle wings flared from both sides of the helmet. Everything a warrior needed was there, gauntlets, boots, greaves, shoulder guards and metal plates that protected the arms and legs. A white shield with the Finarthian symbol leaned casually against the bust. And there, resting in an ornate sheath strapped around the bust's waist was Tihr-Alliam, King Ullis's sword, the sword that had been created by the elves to combat Malbeck. Its two handed pommel was wrapped in white leather and the butt and cross piece was polished silver that looked very similar to the replica that King Baylin held in his hand. But it wasn't exactly the same, since the dwarven smith who had created the replica had based his design on stories and paintings, neither of which were truly accurate descriptions of the blade.

"What now?" King Baylin asked, gazing in awe at the treasures before him.

"No one can take them but you," Lor-telliam replied.

"Should I draw the blade?" the king asked.

"Yes, you may as well use the true power of the blade until you give it to Prince Riker, which you must," Lor-telliam said sharply as he noticed the pained expression on King Baylin's face. "Put the armor in here," he said as he handed a large cloth bag to the king. The bag was big and made of a strong canvas material.

King Baylin slowly moved towards the armor and when he was close enough he reached out and gripped the pommel of the sword. Immediately everyone felt a slight pressure in the room and then, when the king drew the blade there was a bright flash, causing everyone to momentarily shield their eyes. The light, however, quickly dissipated, and they looked back at the king holding the glowing blade before him, his wide eyes reflected in its brilliance.

"You are witnessing the Light of Ela," Lor-telliam explained. "Tihr-Allian is made from a metal that came from the stars, and within it its power resides. In your hands, King Baylin, the sword's true power can be found. Even I who helped create the blade cannot access its full Power. Only someone of Finarthian blood can unlock it."

"I feel so energized, and more alive," the king whispered as he gazed upon the glowing blade. No one had ever seen a light quite like it.

The magic of their own weapons paled in comparison to the brilliance that emanated from Tihr-Alliam. Within moments the light disappeared and the king now held a magnificent sword with a blade as brilliant as a polished mirror.

"Put the armor in the bag and let us leave this place," Kromm said, glancing back nervously up the stairs.

King Baylin reluctantly sheathed the sword and buckled on the belt. He then carefully placed the armor in the bag, strapped his own sword to his back, and grabbed the white shield. "Should I use the shield?"

"Yes, now let's go," Lor-telliam said as he hurried back up the steps.

"Kromm, take my own shield," King Baylin said, handing his shield to the Tarsinian king as he buckled the new one to his left arm. They all hurriedly followed the elf up the stairs. King Baylin and Kromm were the last to leave the darkness of the stairwell.

Lor-telliam began to chant again, and as the rhythmic magic of his words filled the air, the statue started its slow grinding movement to cover the opening once again.

"Elf!" Allindrian yelled, "We are not alone!"

Everyone jumped into action, spreading out around Lor-telliam as he completed the spell. The elf then turned to join the Blade Singer. "What is it?" he asked.

As he spoke, a dark form cloaked in black armor stepped out from behind a pillar. It carried a black shield and a long wicked sword with a serrated edge. Crackling blue energy danced around the blade. "I am Korthanos!" the creature growled, its voice deep and grating.

As it spoke, dozens of orcs jumped upon the platform from the darkness below. They were giant beasts with massive muscular limbs, yet their heads were more human than orc. They were armed with various combinations of shields, spears, swords, maces, and war hammers. These were the Gould-Irin, the same orcs that Kromm had faced in the mountains and at Cuthaine.

Jonas looked around nervously, realizing that the orcs had completely surrounded them. The entire perimeter of the monument was lined with the powerful creatures, and they looked hungry for blood. There was at least fifty of the Gould-Irin, maybe more, as he could not see into the shadows beyond.

"Korthanos," Lor-telliam whispered. The name would mean nothing to anyone but him. Long ago when Malbeck created the Banthras from the fallen cavaliers, Korthanos was a famous first rank warrior for Ulren. His powers and fame were renowned and he had never been bested until Malbeck captured him. He had been lured into a trap, one set by the Forsworn that even the mighty Korthanos could not evade. It was believed that it had taken Malbeck many years to crush the spirits of the imprisoned cavaliers, eventually turning them into the dark creatures known as Banthras. Every ounce of who they were had been wiped out and replaced with a core of blackness. Jonas, of all people, could empathize as he had nearly met the same fate when he was captured by Dykreel clerics. No one ever knew what had become of Korthanos…until now.

"Kill them," the Banthra hissed, his command instantly unleashing the hoard of orcs who swarmed at them from all directions.

"Back up against the statue!" Kromm yelled. Just behind them was the giant statue. The stone dais on which it rested would offer some protection from rear attacks. It would force the orcs to attack them from three, rather than four sides.

A few handfuls of the Gould-Irin Orcs were armed with spears, which they hurled with tremendous power into their midst as the group shrank around the dais, trying desperately to form a protective perimeter, a tactic that proved virtually useless against spears as thick as child's wrist and tipped with long barbed points.

Jonas had less than a second to respond, and he did the only thing he could think of that might save them. He used his cognivant powers to grab the particles around him, quickly forming a swirling shield of bluish energy. He didn't have time to create a larger shield so it only covered those nearest him, which included Fil and Lor-telliam. The others were at the mercy of their skill and luck in order to avoid the deadly missiles.

Allindrian pivoted in the tiny space she had between Tolvar and Kromm, snapping her sword forward and down upon one of the flying spears, cutting the weapon in two, the pieces clattering harmlessly to the ground. Both Kromm and Baylin had lifted their shields as several heavy spears crashed into them. One spear tip punched through Kromm's shield, narrowly missing his shoulder. The spear that struck Baylin's magical shield dropped harmlessly to the ground. But the force of the throw hammered his arm, throwing him back a full pace.

Cade and Tolvar did their best to avoid several of the dangerous projectiles, but unfortunately they were not as lucky as their comrades. And although the Dakeen warriors had miraculously deflected several spears by expertly using the flat part of their blades, a fourth slammed into Tolvar's chest, punching through steel, flesh and bone and vaulting the dwarf backward to crash into the dais. Normally, dwarven made Dakeen armor would stop most weapons, including spears and arrows. But this spear was twice as heavy as a normal one, and it had been thrown by a Gould-Irin Orc who was two times as strong as a man. Tolvar didn't have a chance.

"No!" Cade screamed. But he had no time to check on his brother as the orcs were upon them in seconds, their weapons coming at them from every direction. The sheer force and strength of their numbers pressed in on them like an iron vise.

Orc bodies began to pile up as the defenders of Tihr-Allian fought with all the skill they could muster, which was a considerable amount. One could live ten lifetimes and never see the culmination of skill that these warriors exhibited as they fought together against a common enemy.

Jonas's black blades lit up along their razor edges, their blue light tracing mesmerizing arcs of color as he fought with the skill of a master swordsman. The whistling of Allindrian's sword floated around the monument, its beautiful music interrupted only when she paused to plunge the blade into the flesh of an orc, after which the cadence of her swordplay would start again, so quickly that the human ear could barely perceive the pause before her silver blade resumed its deadly dance. Kromm and Baylin, meanwhile, were fighting side by side. Orc blades crashed into their shields, and yet they managed to hold their positions against the onslaught, their magical blades humming as they sliced easily through armor, flesh, and bone.

Fil had slipped on the blood drenched pavers and would have taken a blade to the head if Lor-telliam's sword hadn't been there to deflect it. The elf fought with a thousand years of experience, and his long sword and blade tipped staff seemed to be an extension of his arms. Fil scrambled to his feet, regaining his footing and jabbing his blade into the kneecap of the attacking orc, striking the beast's bone and slicing through flesh and tendons. Lor-telliam's magical blue blade sliced through the beast's throat while his silver sword parried another blade while thrusting into a second orc nearly simultaneously. But still the enemy came, and there seemed to be no end to the roaring creatures.

Cade had lost track of time. He fought on, energized by pure rage, the image of the orc spear hitting his brother flashing in his mind and fueling every swing of his mighty axe. His arms bulged with the effort of his powerful swings as he sliced through limbs and necks. He roared savagely as orc blood splashed across his body. Several orc blades had struck him when two or three had attacked at once. But the weapons had only grazed him and the wounds were minor compared to the hole that had been torn in his heart.

Baylin, wielding Tihr-Alliam, had never looked so magnificent. The sword, lit with the Light of Ela, the very essence of the energy that made the world, lit up the area like the brightest cavalier light. Each swing of the blade cut through anything that it met; swords fell in pieces, chests were cleaved in two. Nothing stood in his way and the total destruction that the sword caused left the ground and the king drenched in orc blood. A spear had managed to strike him from behind, its long point slicing across his bicep. He felt an instant flush of heat and then the pain was gone. The wound closed as the sword infused the king with its healing energy. Baylin roared almost ecstatically, lashing out at the enemy and fighting with what seemed to be boundless energy. Never had he imagined a weapon could be so magnificent. Never had he felt so utterly alive.

But the little group, despite their skill and momentary victories, were fighting a losing battle. They had fought all day against impossible odds, and the physical exertion and stress were taking a toll on their bodies. They were operating on little sleep and insufficient food. Even the mighty Kromm was beginning to feel the effects of the constant strain. Yet still the orcs came and the Banthra had yet to enter its sword in the fight. It was not looking good.

"We cannot keep this up!" Kromm yelled over the battle.

Then Fil went down. One orc had grabbed his shield while a second brought a wicked war hammer down on his exposed arm. Bones shattered and Fil nearly passed out from the pain. The power of the strike had sent him sprawling backwards, while everyone shuffled to fill the gap so they would not be separated and overrun.

"Fil!" Jonas screamed as he fought frantically to evade attack after attack.

"I'm okay!" Fil said through gritted teeth. The pain was obvious in his voice but it sounded like he would live.

It was then that they heard a loud roaring howl penetrate the din of battle, and there, directly in front of Jonas, appeared Tulari's huge form as it came crashing into the orcs from behind, scattering them with teeth and claw. She was so large and so powerful that she was able to literally toss the huge creatures left and right as her massive claws slashed back and forth. Before the orcs knew what had hit them she had fought her way through the enemy, and skidded next to Jonas, powerful jaws snapping into any orc who got too close. She was so quick and her claws so deadly that she could flick her paw, snag an orc, and yank the poor creature towards her in a mere instant, then rip it apart with tooth and claw. Jonas noticed that some of her thick coat had been badly burnt, exposing her bare skin, blackened and red from the Banthra's magic, but she moved as if the wounds didn't bother her.

"I have a plan!" the Ekahal shouted over the fighting. "We need to get back below!"

"But we'll be trapped!" Jonas yelled.

"Trust me," he responded.

"See to it!" Kromm yelled as he smashed his shield into the face of an orc who had tried to jump in and grab it. The beast's face snapped back and the beast collapsed into the throng of enemies.

"Go ahead, Elf, I'll fill the gap!" Cade yelled.

Lor-telliam jumped back and the Dakeen warrior expertly leaped into the gap created by his quick departure. The others shifted, purposefully trying to create space to fight but also not to leave any weak points for the enemy to penetrate.

Jonas heard the Ekahal chanting behind him, followed by the familiar scraping of stone on stone as the statue slid sideways. There was some shuffling behind them and he assumed that Lor-telliam had taken Fil, who was injured and incapable of fighting, and maybe even Tolvar's body, but he could not say for sure as he didn't dare take his eyes off his attackers.

A sword flew down towards him and he knew he couldn't get his left blade back into position in time. So he threw up a small cognivant wall and the sword crashed into it harmlessly. Jonas, suddenly overcome with anger, growled and used his power like a battering ram, mentally expanding the wall and hurling it forward, slamming into four orcs with the power of a dragon's breath. They flew backwards into their comrades and fell to the stones in a tangle of steel and limbs. The rhythmic pounding of his head reminded him that he had to use that power sparingly.

As more rushed at him he wearily brought his swords up to the ready with arms beginning to burn with fatigue. *I don't know how much longer I can do this*, he thought as he clumsily parried several strikes.

"Retreat back down the stairs! One at a time!" Lor-telliam yelled from the bottom of the stairs behind them.

"Jonas, go!" Kromm yelled.

Go, I cover, Tulari spoke in his mind when she saw Jonas glance at her. He cringed, not wanting to leave her by herself, but he reasoned that she could run if she had to. There was no way any of the orcs could catch her. So Jonas dispatched a huge orc in front of him, spun on his heal, and raced backwards down the dusty stairs. With a violent growl Tulari shuffled into the space, one powerful claw flashing out and catching an orc in the shoulder as it tried to follow Jonas. The orc's flesh ripped like paper and the beast flew backwards, crashing into several more orcs.

"Baylin, your turn!" Kromm yelled as he swung his massive sword in increasingly wider arcs, covering more space and killing anything that got near.

Baylin knew that it would be futile to argue with the king. He didn't want to stop fighting but he also knew the importance of the blade and he would not see it fall into enemy hands, not after what they had all gone through to get it. The Finarthian king swung the magical blade in a great arc at a near enemy and then jumped backwards and down the stairs.

Suddenly, great walls of orange fire erupted on both sides of the remaining fighters. Tulari, Allindrian, Kromm, and Cade were pushed closer together as the walls of flame covered their flanks. The flames, reaching twice the height of King Kromm, looked to be impenetrable. At least ten orcs were instantly consumed by the magical flames that erupted from the ground near where they stood, leaving nothing but smoldering piles of ash.

Kromm laughed maniacally as more orcs fell to his sword. Yet still they came at them, futilely trying to break through the wall of steel and determination that the defenders had created. "I'm beginning to like wizards!" Kromm roared over the fighting. Bodies were stacking up left and right and the attacking orcs were forced to drag some of their comrades away so they wouldn't stumble over the bodies as they moved forward. The defenders were slowly being pushed backwards almost to the opening of the steps, but the fire walls had created a smaller gap, so now only four or five orcs could attack at a time. The Ekahal had bought them more time by creating a funnel that had only one opening through which they could attack, an opening that was guarded by the greatest warriors in Kraawn.

"Allindrian, move!" Kromm yelled.

The nimble ranger was so fast that she was down the stairs before he had finished speaking. Cade and Kromm spread their legs wider, now blocking half of the opening. Tulari's huge bulk covered the rest. Kromm glanced at the blood drenched dwarf. The Dakeen warrior spit blood from his mouth and smiled back. Each warrior planted their powerful legs and stood their ground, and as the orcs pressed forward they encountered their steel. Nothing and no one could move them. It was as if their legs had been rooted to the ground. Each had suffered a half dozen wounds, cuts from which their blood flowed freely, mixing with that of their enemies. But still they fought on.

"Your turn, Dwarf!" Kromm growled as a hammer smashed into his shield.

"Stayin here, King! You go!" Cade answered back. He now fought with a hand axe in his right hand and his huge doubled bladed battle axe in his left. It was amazing that someone who had been fighting as long as he had with no rest could even wield a weapon that size with one hand, but he single handedly swung it back and forth with practiced ease.

Kromm glanced again at the dwarf and knew that he would not win this argument. The dwarf was determined to keep fighting. His brother was probably dead and maybe he figured he'd join him at Moredin's Hall. But the burning in his eyes and his determined stance canceled any rebuttal from the Tarsinian king.

Kromm blocked a sword swing on his shield and kicked his metal shod boot into the chest of an advancing orc. As the beast flew backward, Kromm turned and ran for the opening of the stairs.

Just as he did so there was a sizzling sound and the flaming fire walls crackled and disappeared in great billows of hot steam. Something, probably the Banthra, had dispelled the magic walls of fire. When the walls vanished orcs caved in on Tulari and Cade like an avalanche.

"No!" Kromm screamed from the opening as the black clad orcs surrounded the duo. He attempted to join them but a firm hand grabbed his arm. It was Allindrian. She was covered in sweat and blood and her eyes reflected a mixture of sad resignation, anger, and determination. Her hand was small on his muscled arm, but her grip was like iron.

"You will die. Your son needs you," she said. That was all that was needed. Kromm growled with frustration and despair, then turned away from the Blade Singer and moved off the stairs into the chamber. "Can they enter this place?" Kromm asked Lor-telliam who was busy drawing a symbol with white chalk on the stone ground.

He looked up quickly. "I don't think so. But guard the entrance nonetheless. I need a few more moments."

Jonas looked at Tolvar's body lying on the stones near the entrance. He was clearly dead and his eyes were open and vacant. He sighed heavily and went to Fil who was sitting against the stone wall. His face was pale and he looked even worse than everyone else. He held his left arm close to his body. "Where are you hurt?" Jonas asked as he knelt next to his friend.

"My arm, it is broken," he said, obviously in great pain. Jonas looked at his arm and cringed at what he saw. His forearm was clearly shattered and a sharp blood soaked piece of bone protruded from his flesh. "I can't move it, Jonas. I can't fight. You're going to have to leave me here."

"Not an option, Fil," Jonas said firmly.

Cade frantically continued to battle the relentless onslaught of orcs, spinning his battle axe in great circles and cutting down several more of the beasts. Tulari, growling in fury, twisted and turned, snapping her jaws and clawing at the countless number of orcs attacking her. Cade began to chant a dwarven war song and despite the cuts he suffered he continued to swing his axe with deadly efficiency, killing the creatures as they came at him from all sides.

"Enough!" a gravelly voice echoed behind the throng of orcs, shattering the sounds of battle and Cade's war song. The orcs surrounding Tulari and Cade immediately shuffled backwards to make room for the Banthra. Cade gripped his axe firmly and stood solidly before the entrance to the stairs. He glanced backwards thinking to make a dive for it. "You can try it, Dwarf," the Banthra said as he floated closer, his long black sword crackling with blue lightening.

At the bottom of the stairs, the group noticed the sudden silence.

"He stopped singing," Allindrian whispered. Beside her Kromm gripped his sword handle with evident apprehension and frustration.

"They fight no more. Whatever you're doing, Elf, hurry up," Kromm said as he fought to restrain the urge to run up the stairs to Cade's defense.

Cade knew he wouldn't get another chance. To stay there was to eventually die by orc steel or at the hands of the abomination before him. So he simply smiled, turned quickly, and jumped for the opening.

Tulari, seeing Cade's move, spun, and with lightening quick speed leaped far into the air and over the edge of the monument. She disappeared into the darkness before anyone had a chance to blink.

But Cade was not so quick. The Banthra was expecting the move and sent a sizzling bolt of lightning from its sword towards the Dakeen warrior. In a flash the bolt struck Cade in the back, the force of the strike lifting him off the ground, slamming him into the stone face of the dais just above the opening of the stairs. Then he fell through the opening, tumbling down the stairs to land at Kromm and Allindrian's feet in a smoking heap.

"I'm done!" Lor-telliam said. "Everyone, come stand in the center of this drawing." Jonas helped Fil up and they stumbled over to stand with the rest of the group. Kromm had picked up the smoking form of Cade and he and Allindrian ran and joined them.

Then they heard loud chanting from above the stairs and the opening of the chamber flashed with crackling energy. "We must hurry! The Banthra is trying to unravel the spell that is keeping them out," Lor-telliam yelled as he checked to make sure everyone was inside the symbol he had drawn.

The symbol was round with an outer circle surrounding it. Inside the space between the inner and outer circle was a series of intricate runes that looked to be some sort of writing. It appeared similar to elven script, though it was not exactly the same, perhaps a different dialect or an ancient form. The strange writing encircled them completely.

As Kromm set Cade down, the dwarf groaned in pain, his eyes fluttering open. "Where is my brother?" he asked weakly.

Allindrian knelt next to the injured warrior as Lor-telliam went through the last of his preparations. "He is there," she said, pointing to his body in the corner. "He did not make it."

"Leave me. I want to be with him," he whispered.

Allindrian looked closely at his wounds, shocked at the severity of the damage. He was bleeding from dozens of cuts, but most damaging was the lightning bolt that had struck him directly in the back at less than ten paces. The Blade Singer didn't know it at the time, but the Banthra that delivered that attack was twice as powerful as the Banthras that they had fought on the stairs. The skin on Cade's face had peeled away, revealing the red and blackened flesh underneath. His hair and beard were almost completely gone and his left hand was burnt so severely that it had fused around the shaft of his axe. His armor had been burnt so badly that in some places it had melted into his flesh. She glanced up at Lor-telliam. He sadly shook his head, verifying what she already surmised. "Kromm, carry him to his brother."

Kromm looked at the Ekahal and back at Allindrian. Then he looked at the dwarf at his feet and for the first time saw the extent of his injuries. He gritted his teeth, the muscles of his jaw flexing in frustration. But he reached under the dwarf and carried him quickly to his brother.

"Hurry, the weave is almost broken!" Lor-telliam yelled as Kromm made sure that Cade was next to Tolvar.

"It was an honor to fight with you," Kromm said, his voice cracking with emotion.

"Aye, same fur us," Cade replied as he closed his eyes and put his right hand on Tolvar's body.

"Now!" Lor-telliam yelled again.

Kromm raced to the symbol and the Ekahal took the stone from the tip of his staff and put it on the ground by his feet.

Allindrian saw what he was doing and her eyes went wide. "No, Ekahal, you can't!"

"I must, it is the only way. The sword must leave this place," Lor-telliam said with gentle fierceness.

"But at this cost?" Allindrian pleaded.

Suddenly there was a loud pop and a bright flash followed as the ground shook all around him. The magical weave blocking the entrance

238

had disintegrated and orcs now raced down the stairs, their heavy iron clad boots pounding on the stone steps.

In a flash the Ekahal glanced at the Dakeen brothers. "A cost that others have paid!" he yelled as he brought his foot down upon the stone. There was a flash of bright light that caused the orcs to stumble backwards and cover their eyes. When the light disappeared the white symbol in the middle of the room was empty. They had all vanished.

Ten
Out of Time

Tuvallis struggled to pull himself onto the muddy river bank. He was soaked and exhausted but his concern for Seli's whereabouts and the others gave him the strength to climb the brushy river bank to the flat grassland above. The current had washed him far down river but he was still close enough to see the destruction of the bridge and the fire and smoke from the garrison as the orc army destroyed and plundered it. He shivered as he saw the colossal black dragon raise its head over the smoking battlements, roaring loudly as it flicked a body into the air and swallow it with one great gulp. So that was why the dragon wasn't hunting down any stragglers, it was feeding on the dead and wounded that lay about the garrison.

He had fought his way to join the Free Legion and help guard the bridge, knowing that Seli, if she still lived, would be there. But the dragon had swooped in, unleashing its devastating breath before he could find her. Dozens of the Free Legion had leaped over the edge with him to escape its searing breath, choosing the possibility of drowning over being cooked alive in their armor. Indeed, it was likely that many of the men had drowned, exhausted by their struggle with the current and the weight of their armor. He had to hope that Seli was not among them.

He also worried for Hagar. The last he had seen of the ogrillion he was fighting for his life in front of the garrison gate. Things had not looked good for the courageous beast, but he also knew that Hagar would be a difficult opponent to bring down.

Tuvallis had dropped his sword when he hit the water and now he stood alone and unarmed. It was still early in the morning and the air was bitter cold on his wet body. He couldn't see any of the refugees that had been camped along the river bank. They had most likely fled when the fighting started, and terrified by the appearance of the dragon, they had hastily grabbed their belongings and headed west to Finarth. They would only be an hour or two along the road by now.

He only had a few options at this point. He needed to warm himself, arm himself, feed himself, and find any survivors. All of these things he hoped he would be able to find safely along the river bank where the refugees had camped. He was betting on the fact that the group had left fast, leaving behind various things as they hurried to flee from the dragon. So he crouched low, moving from bushes to tree clumps, scanning the open ground as he went.

It didn't take him long to find a small group of men that had already found each other amongst the survivors. They were huddled close together behind a screen of low lying bushes near the river's edge. They looked just as Tuvallis felt, cold, wet, tired, and hungry. But he was grateful to see that Captain Hadrick was one of the men.

"Captain, I be glad knowin' you're alive. But what of Seli?" he asked as he crouched down beside the four other men.

"Likewise, Tuvallis. Seli was near me when the dragon hit us, but I know not if she survived," Hadrick replied sadly. "Damn it!" Hadrick swore. "If it weren't for that dragon our little tactic would've worked and we'd be warm and ready to defend those walls another day. Now nearly all of my men are dead," Hadrick growled.

Bositch was one of the survivors and he asked what everyone else was wondering. "What do we do now, sir? We need to warm up and we will need food. And we have no weapons." Their clothes were drenched and they looked like drowned rats. It was not yet spring and the air was still cold. Everyone was visibly shaking in the morning air.

Hadrick looked at the men. Groban, the grey haired veteran, was among them, along with Jons, the brown haired youth who was a new recruit. Torum had made it as well, and despite the bleak situation the warrior tried to lighten the mood. "The bridge is down, that is good. They won't be able to follow us or the refugees for at least a few weeks."

"I think we should try to catch up with the refugees. They will have some food and perhaps some weapons to arm ourselves," Hadrick said.

"Agreed," Groban affirmed the suggestion. "We should check the camp as well. They left so quickly when the dragon arrived that they may have left something useful."

Groben suggested exactly what Tuvallis had been thinking. The five of them scooted along the river bank and made it to the deserted camp. They didn't run into any other survivors. They cringed hearing the howls and roars from across the river, though they knew they were relatively safe since the bridge had been broken in two different spots. Their only immediate concern was the dragon, though the beast was no longer visible.

"Perhaps the demon beast left, sir," Jons said as he stood above the undergrowth along the river and scanned the garrison on the far side.

"With luck," was Hadrick's response.

It was obvious that the refugees had cleared camp quickly, panicked by the terrifying apparition of the dragon. There were several smoking fires still burning, some with cook pots containing the morning breakfast of boiled oats and salt, still steaming. Several canvas tents had been abandoned, and various odds and ends of supplies were lying about.

They quickly stuffed their bellies with what food they could find, grabbed some old cloaks and other clothing items that had been left behind, and prepared to move out on foot to try and catch up with the refugees.

"I'm stayin'," Tuvallis announced to Hadrick as he took off his wet tunic and replaced it with a dry but dirty overshirt. They had built a fire behind a stand of trees, taking enough time to warm their bodies, eat, and dry their clothes before they moved out. They were all fit and well trained men and they had no doubt that they could catch up to the refugees in short time.

"You think she is alive?" Hadrick asked.

"I know not, which is why I'm stayin'. Hagar may be alive too. I'll catch up to ya with or without them," Tuvallis said as he used his hand to shovel another bite of warm oats into his mouth.

"Good luck, Tuvallis," Hadrick said as they shook hands in the warrior's grip. They all said their good byes and then the four men ran down the western road toward Finarth without a glance back.

"You too," Tuvallis whispered as the poorly equipped remainders of the Free Legion disappeared in the morning fog.

"Now, where would ya be if ya survived?" Tuvallis asked, addressing only ghosts, as he looked back down the long meandering river.

Hagar couldn't believe that he had escaped the orcs. He had expected to die defending the gate. There were so many of the beasts that even his great strength and powerful mace would eventually succumb to their relentless attack and sheer numbers. But ironically the dragon had saved him. Its deadly breath had forced the orcs back just long enough for Hagar to sneak away along the wall. By the time the steaming vapor had dissipated Hagar was fifty paces north and far from the focus of the enemy whose goal was the destruction of the gate.

He found the six long boats that had been beached that night on a sandy embankment. That was when he again heard the roar of the dragon in the near distance behind him. It wasn't long before the bridge collapsed and great waves of water rushed downriver, crashing into the bank and rocking the boats.

He had left his armor there since Tuvallis had instructed him to take it off when they were preparing for their night attack. That night everyone had removed their heavy armor in place of leather armor or no armor at all, hoping to lessen their load and reduce the noise they made as they stealthily approached the unaware enemy army. Hagar was reluctant to leave his armor behind, but he trusted the human, and none of the others had worn their armor so he thought it would be okay. He was now glad to put the familiar armor back on, and as soon as he did he felt renewed strength flow through his tired body. *Now what*, he thought. He knew he had to get across the river, but he wasn't sure if one of the long boats could hold his weight. The current was strong and the river was wide and deep. And swimming was not his strong point. In fact he'd never really swam in anything larger than small ponds and creeks that he had come across deep in the mountains. Besides, he was sure he would sink to the bottom with his armor on while carrying the giant mace.

He sat down on the sandy ground near the boats to think, which was not high up on his list of strengths. He heard screaming and fighting, followed shortly by orc howls and roars from that terrible dragon, and yet he had no idea how he could help his new friends. He couldn't go back the way he had come. He needed to get across the river. He looked again at the boats and wondered if he should try it. He knew he couldn't stay where he was forever.

"Hagar," a soft voice came from behind him. The ogrillion jumped to his feet, spinning quickly towards the sound and holding his long mace before him defensively. Seli crept from the undergrowth near the river bank and slowly moved towards him. She was soaked through and her dirty clothes were wet and stuck to her cold body. She had no weapons and her skin was pale and bluish in color. "It's me, Seli. I'm your friend."

Hagar recognized her as Tuvallis's friend. He smiled broadly and tapped his armored chest with his meaty hand. "Friend," he confirmed.

"I'm glad you're alive," she said, not sure if he understood her. He just kept smiling at her. "Have you seen anyone else?" she asked.

It was obvious that the ogrillion didn't understand her but he looked at the boats and pointed towards them. "Boat...go," he said in choppy common. "I...go," he said.

It took her a second to realize that he was asking her a question. Seli looked at his massive body and back at the boat. He was huge, but the long boats easily carried six men, and they could probably carry ten if need be. She figured a boat would carry them both. "Yes, we cross river," she said.

That had been her plan all along. She had been near the edge of the bridge when the dragon had attacked. Sar-gathos was nearby and they were frantically fighting off the enemy hoard that was relentlessly pushing the smaller force farther onto the bridge. The elf had been struggling with three orcs when the dragon had swooped down upon them. She had slain her opponent and looked up just as the breath came at them like a storm of death. The attack came so fast that no one, not even the enemy, had time to react. Its scalding breath scorched her back as she flew over the railing to the water below. She had no doubt that Sar-gathos and most of the others had died instantly. Her heart ached for her friends and comrades that made up the last of the Free Legion.

She had floated down river and when she finally struggled to shore, she hiked back up river hoping that the boats were where they had left them. Images of Tuvallis and her other friends haunted her the entire way. She kept hoping to see their faces emerge from the river or the low undergrowth growing along its edge. But no one came out to greet her. She was alone, cold, hungry, and weaponless, and her back felt like it was on fire, the pain intensifying as the burn began to blister. She felt defeated. That was until she saw the ogrillion sitting on the ground near the river bank. She was never so happy to see an eleven foot monster.

Seli maneuvered one of the boats so that Hagar could step his heavy body into it without tipping it over. As soon as he put a foot in and settled his weight on it, the boat sunk dangerously low. Then Hagar stepped all the way in and the boat dropped even further, the water coming up to less than a foot from its edge. It didn't look very seaworthy and she worried that with her added weight, the current, and their movement as they rowed, that it would surely capsize. She stepped back for a moment to analyze the problem. Hagar looked at her skeptically, realizing that his weight was too much. Then she had an idea.

"Hagar, step out," she said as she indicated for him to get out of the boat. He did so and then she grabbed another skiff and put them side by side. She looked at Hagar and then back at the boats. "Just might work," she said to herself. "Hagar, take off your armor and put it and your mace in the boat." It took her a second to show him what she meant but he caught on quickly. The sounds of the orc army plundering the garrison nearby made her sick and she wanted to get away from this place. Plus there was always a danger that they would be spotted. Once the armor was off she indicated what she wanted him to do. It took her a moment but finally she was able to get Hagar to walk out into the water up to his knees and then lower his body into the water so he was resting on his knees on the muddy bottom. She directed him to put his arms out wide and hold the boats under his big arms like flotation devices. Then she climbed into one of the boats. "Okay, now push off and kick hard until we get to the other side. Whatever you do don't let go."

Hagar looked at her nervously. His eyes were wide with fright, a strange look on such a fearsome beast. But she realized that Hagar probably couldn't swim and the thought of kicking into the current with two boats on either side holding him up frightened him more than an army of orcs.

She used her fingers to show kicking and indicated the length of the river. "It's okay," she said softly. "You can do it." Then she got down in the boat and mimed him kicking off, holding the boats, and paddling his feet. "Go, Hagar."

Finally the courageous beast took a deep breath and used his big legs to push away from the muddy bottom. Immediately the current caught them and Hagar kicked up great splashes of water as he frantically moved his legs. He looked like a puppy that had been thrown into the water for the first time. He kicked his legs desperately, never stopping as they moved further out into the current. They were rapidly floating down river, but the ogrillion's strong legs propelled them forward in hard jerky movements. Hagar's eyes were wide with terror but he kept kicking and kicking. They were now halfway across and Seli continued to urge the beast forward. It wasn't long before the shoreline was near. The river's edge was overgrown with thick brush and it would be messy trying to climb through it to the bank above. When they made it to the shore, she reached out and grabbed some brush just as Hagar's feet touched bottom. Immediately he let go of the empty boat, scrambling to the shore where he grabbed some thick branches and held the other boat in place in the current.

Seli leaped into the brush and crawled up through the thicket and mud to the bank above. She was scratched up a bit by the rough undergrowth, but it wasn't as difficult as she had expected. Hagar reached into the boat and with one arm heaved his cuirass up and over the low brush to the bank above. He did the same with the mace, the heavy weapon landing with a thud next to Seli. Then he released the boat, the current ripping it downriver, while he pushed his way through the brush and reached the embankment to join Seli.

"Well done, Hagar," she said as she touched the huge creature on the shoulder. His skin was hard like stone but he smiled warmly at her, clearly understanding her tone. Then his smile disappeared and he stood up quickly looking up river. Seli followed his gaze and saw three men running towards her. Well, one at least was a man. The other two looked to be dwarves.

Hagar quickly donned his cuirass and grabbed his shining mace. "They must be friends," Seli whispered as she stood near the beast for protection, just in case. As the newcomers got closer she heard Hagar chuckle. At least it sort of sounded like a chuckle, or a laugh; it was hard to tell. But then she realized why. He must have caught the scent of him before she recognized the man. It was Tuvallis, followed by Durgen and another round bellied dwarf that was struggling to keep up.

"Seli, you are okay!" Tuvallis shouted as he ran to her and hugged her fiercely. They had never showed each other any semblance of affection other than what would by typical between two soldiers. But both knew there was something more between them. And now, the relief of seeing each other safe and alive allowed those feelings to surface. Tuvallis actually kissed her and then held her at arm's length. "I thought you had died. How did you make it? And Hagar, I am happy that you made it too!" Tuvallis released the stunned Seli and reached up to grip Hagar's giant hand. They couldn't really shake hands because of the size difference, but Tuvallis held onto the beast's hand with both of his and smiled widely at the ogrillion.

"I jumped off the bridge when the dragon came," Seli said. "I was just lucky that I was near the edge or I'd be dead with the rest. I think my back is burnt pretty badly though. Hurt like hell when you hugged me."

A look of sudden concern came over his face, "I'm sorry," he said quickly. "Let me see." Tuvallis lifted up the back of her drenched and dirty tunic. The skin was red and blistering, but nothing was black, which meant they would probably heal, though they would definitely be painful. Infection was always a concern, but luckily it looked as if most of the blisters had not yet burst, which was good as that would lessen the risk of infection. "Looks bad but I think you will be okay, other than the pain of course," he added. "This is Durgen and Gormly. They were responsible for dropping the bridge, and as far as we know the only dwarven survivors."

"Well met," Seli said shaking both of their hands in the warrior style. "I'm sorry about your men."

Durgen simply grunted in acknowledgement. "I saw another boat get away from the far span so I should have some brethren out there somewhere." Then his narrow eyes looked up at the ogrillion. "So this be, Hagar."

"Aye, it is," Tuvallis said.

Hagar thumped his armored chest in his usual manner. "Hagar," he confirmed.

"Any other survivors?" Seli asked.

"Aye, Captain Hadrick made it as well as three others, Groban, Jons, and Torum," Tuvallis replied.

Seli smiled. "That is good news. Where are they?"

"They are on the heels of the refugees. We have little food and no weapons so they are hoping to catch up with them before night comes," Tuvallis said.

"We joining them?" Seli asked.

"Yes. Let's get you warmed up first and some food. We have some oats left."

Seli smiled. "That would be good. What of Hagar?"

"We be needin' something bigger to feed him," Durgen said.

"Let us see what we can find," Tuvallis said. With that they ran towards the deserted camp.

***

Jonas had no idea what had happened. The last thing he remembered was the Banthra and orcs struggling to get into the secret room underneath the monument on Ullis Hill. The magical weave blocking the entrance had been broken and the enemy had stormed down the stairs. Then Allindrian and Lor-telliam had argued briefly before the Ekahal smashed the stone that had been embedded in the tip of his staff. There had been a bright flash and a crack like thunder, and then everything went eerily silent, and dark as night.

Then he smelled the forest, an almost overwhelming fragrance of trees, grass, woodland flowers, and damp earth. It was that rich clean smell that you take for granted while you're there, but when you have been away from it, and are then suddenly exposed to it, becomes almost intoxicating. That is what Jonas was experiencing now. Then the darkness began to subside and he began to hear the sounds of the forest, the subtle sound of a breeze rustling through leaves, the songs of birds as they flitted among the branches searching for food. The darkness gave way to a soft light and Jonas began to orient himself to his surroundings. He was sitting on a mossy patch of ground, leaning against the trunk of a large tree. Once his vision was fully restored, he noticed that everyone else was sprawled around the ground, looking as mystified as he. The only one that seemed at ease was Lor-telliam, who stood before him looking up at something.

Allindrian was the first one up and she walked over to stand next to the elf, while the rest of the group slowly regained consciousness. Each one stood up cautiously, gazing at their new surroundings in awe.

They were in a forest glade, the warm rays of the morning sun breaking through the canopy of giant trees and dappling the woodland floor with soft light. The ground was covered in patches of soft green moss, various outcroppings of stone, delicate woodland flowers, and a thick undergrowth of shrubs, some laden with berries, as far as they could see. It was breathtaking, the most beautiful forest any of them had ever seen.

Jonas got up slowly and gazed up in the direction that was occupying the Ekahal's attention. Before them stood a massive tree, larger than any he had ever seen, larger even than the tree where Shyann was buried, one, that by her grace, he was able to visit many years ago. Its gray brown trunk, ancient and twisted, was larger around than all their arms linked together. Twisting and curving it rose hundreds of paces into the sky, breaking into more branches than the eye could follow, extending well beyond the canopy of the trees that surrounded it.

"It is magnificent," Jonas said as he stood next to Allindrian. The tree had caught everyone's attention and they now stood silently taking in the beauty of it.

Finally, after several minutes, Fil came to his senses. Instantly his good hand went to his injured arm, his expression one of shock. "My arm is healed," he said, surprise in his voice.

Jonas turned to his friend and felt bad that he had forgotten he was injured. It was as if the forest had put a calming spell on them all. Their recent battles, hardships, and the loss of the Dakeen warriors seemed a faded memory. "I'm sorry, my friend, I forgot you were hurt," he said.

"It's okay, I'm hurt no longer," he said as he showed Jonas his arm. It was completely healed, no evidence of any wound, no bone jutting from torn and bloody flesh.

"How can that be? How can *this* be?" Jonas asked as he indicated their surroundings.

"It was the Elf Tree," Lor-telliam said, still gazing at the tree.

"So that is an Elf Tree?" Kromm asked.

"It is," the Ekahal replied. "Few humans have seen one."

"What is it?" King Baylin asked.

The Ekahal turned to look at the Finarthian king. "I cannot tell you exactly as it is forbidden. But know this; there are few Elf Trees in existence. They are sentient forms of power and magic older than anything on Kraawn. Think of them as direct lines to the Light of Ela. The stone that was in my staff was no stone. It was a seed from an Elf Tree, this Elf Tree. Her name is Filisstaranthros."

"This tree is a *person?*" Fil asked.

"No, not as you think of the word. She is the energy of the forest. She was here during the forging of the world and her energy will be here long after our races are gone. She has seen more than we can understand," Lor-telliam explained.

"Is the Light of Ela the same thing as the Ru Ach?" Jonas asked.

"Yes, it is the energy of all things," he said. "It is what made the sky, stars, you, and even your gods. It is simply, *everything*."

"Was it the stone that brought us here?" Fil asked.

This time Allindrian spoke. "It was. The seed is linked to the tree from which it came. When it was crushed within the symbolic sphere the energy was transformed, bringing us all back to its source, back to the tree that dropped it. Only an Ekahal can break an Elf Stone and it is very rarely done. Filisstaranthros healed Fil and brought us all to safety. Only an Ekahal can use that power, and only an Ekahal will pay the price."

"What do you mean?" Kromm demanded.

"Elf Stones are only given to Ekahals and they may only be used in this way once in a lifetime," Lor-telliam replied softly, still staring up at the magnificent tree. "Filisstaranthros gave me this seed many hundreds of years ago when I took the title of Ekahal. She has loaned me this power for generations of human lifetimes, freely given as protector of her and the forests. But when I shattered it, the magic was used to bring us here, and heal us all. You will find that none of you have any cuts or wounds," Lor-telliam said. "But the seed's magic is no longer, so now Filisstaranthros will use my own energy to create another seed. That seed will be given to another Ekahal. It is a symbiotic relationship that all Ekahals have with their Elf Stone."

"So what are you saying?" Fil asked.

"Lor-telliam is dying, Fil," Allindrian said softly. "He will rapidly age as the Elf Tree takes his light. Then, like a mortal, he will die."

"You did that for us?" Fil asked incredulously.

"Not just for you, young man, for everyone. If Malbeck is not stopped at Finarth, then I believe that he will eventually bring his evil hordes here and destroy all that you see. I cannot let that happen. We must defeat him now, and if I can do that with my own life then it will be a small price to pay. It is a price that many have already paid, and still more will pay when the Dark One brings his army to Finarth," Lor-telliam said softly. "Besides, I may not look it, but I have lived a long and full life. Do not feel sad for me, young warrior."

"How long do you have?" Jonas asked softly, fully feeling the weight of the Ekahal's words.

Lor-telliam shrugged uncertainly. "Several months I would think."

Everyone stood in silence, taking in all that the Ekahal had said, and trying to come to terms with his sacrifice.

"Shouldn't we be going? They will be here soon," Allindrian said gently to Lor-telliam.

"Yes, you're quite right," Lor-telliam replied, finally peeling his eyes away from Filisstaranthros.

"Who will be coming?" King Baylin asked.

"The guardians of the forest, the Silvarious, elven rangers who protect our borders," Allindrian said.

"But what do you have to fear from them?" Jonas asked.

"Not us, you. You are not allowed here, my friends. I'm sorry, but we had no other choice. We need to leave now before they arrive. It will save us some explaining and we don't have time to be bogged down with politics. Let us depart," Lor-telliam said as he moved forward towards the tree.

"How do we leave?" Kromm asked.

"You are standing on a gate. The circle of stones around this clearing is one of many in these forests. Lor-telliam will ask Filisstaranthros to send us away, to another gate close to Finarth," Allindrian said.

Lor-telliam then placed both his hands on the tree and began to whisper softly. No one could hear the words but again it sounded like a soft chant. After a few moments the Ekahal stopped and moved back with the group who were all standing close together in the middle of the moss covered clearing.

"You will feel a pulse and then there will be a flash. Everything will go dark for a few seconds but do not worry. When you arrive at the other gate the light will quickly return. You will feel a little dizzy at first, but it will go away. Here it comes," the wizard announced.

Just as he spoke there was a gentle pulse, then a bright flash momentarily blinded them, followed by complete darkness.

Then, as Lor-telliam had told them, the light suddenly returned, causing Jonas to blink and momentarily stumble forward as his equilibrium shifted. He quickly regained his balance, however, and his vision rapidly cleared. He looked about and saw that everyone else was there and doing as he was doing, gazing around at their new environment while regaining their balance.

They were standing in the midst of a forest of tall pine trees interspersed with large rocks. The ground was covered with a thick layer of pine needles and clumps of dense undergrowth. Everything was wet, and based on the cloud cover it had obviously just rained. It was cold, but it was clear that winter was over and the spring rains were upon them. The forest was beautiful, but it lacked the lush magnificence of the elven woods they had just left. In fact Jonas couldn't help but feel a bit let down as he looked upon their surroundings. He was afraid that every forest he now gazed upon would bring him a subtle sense of disappointment now that he had gazed upon an Elf Tree and its surroundings.

"Where are we?" Kromm asked.

"We are near the mountain passes west of Finarth," Lor-telliam said.

"We are not too high, we must be close to Finarth," King Baylin reasoned.

"We are, a half day's travel at best," Lor-telliam said.

"Let us go then, I long to see my son," Kromm said, urging them forward.

***

"Come on, son, you have to keep your shield up!" Kromm admonished as he delivered a powerful blow to Prince Riker's shield.

Both missions had been successful, at least in the sense that they had achieved what they set out to do. But the cost was terribly high, especially for the defenders of the garrison. They had lost nearly everyone, man and dwarf alike. Word had spread quickly about a devil dragon that had killed everyone and destroyed the gate. The people of Finarth had learned that there had been few survivors; several came from the Free Legion, a few dwarves, a traveler from the Tundrens, and something that Kromm still could hardly believe, Hagar the ogrillion.

After seeing the wounds Hagar had suffered from the claws and teeth of the demon hound, he thought the strange beast had perished. When they had left him in the mountains he was unconscious and barely breathing. Jonas had done his best to heal him but the ogrillion's wounds were terrible, and Jonas had been exhausted. He could do no more than seal the lacerations so he would not bleed to death. But Hagar had made it and somehow found his way to Finarth with the Free Legion. The ogrillion had not been allowed into the city and even Tuvallis and Jonas understood that precaution. His heritage and immense size, in close proximity with thousands of nervous people, was a recipe for disaster. So Hagar had been forced to set up camp in the forest near the city, while his friends, who were some of the most powerful warriors in Finarth, would bring him food and walk with him along the outer wall's edge. The idea was to get as many citizens and soldiers accustomed to seeing the ogrillion, for when the time came to bring him inside, which was sure to come soon, they hoped it would not create panic. The people of Finarth had thus grown more accustomed to seeing the beast, and he was becoming less of a worry, and more of an ordinary figure who was ready to face the enemy with them.

When the survivors of the garrison battle arrived with the ogrillion they had come in with just under two thousand refugees. They had lost General Ruthallis, Sar-gathos, the elven Ekahal, Lord Dynure of Annure, and a thousand men and dwarves. Their severe losses were mostly the result of the deadly breath and claws of the mysterious demonic dragon. But, despite their terrible losses, they had given the Finarthians several more weeks to prepare the city, and everyone was working hard on their preparations so their deaths would not be in vain.

"Father, I am trying," Riker gasped, equally frustrated, as sweat poured off his brow. "The strength of your attack makes it difficult to keep the shield up."

"Do you think Malbeck will hit with any less power?" the king retorted.

"No, sir," Riker replied softly.

Kromm relaxed subtly, realizing how hard he had been pushing his son. Riker was actually an excellent fighter, trained since he could walk by the best warriors in Tarsis, including himself. But he was young and lacked the experience and confidence needed for what was to come. It would do no good to berate him. "I'm sorry, son. Look, when the strike comes, try to angle your shield to deflect some of the power. You may even throw your opponent off balance. But you have to be constantly shifting your weight. Sword and shield work is a dance. Never get caught flat footed. The warrior is constantly shifting and adjusting his weight to better capitalize on movement and speed. It's all balance, stay on the balls of your feet and be ready to adjust quickly."

Riker fought with his own armor, shield, and sword. Tihr-Alliam, the sword of light, was resting in its sheath under constant guard in his private chamber, along with the magical armor and shield. Riker had been allowed to draw the blade and he could still remember the feeling. He had heard a hum as he felt a pulse of energy shoot through him. He had never felt so alive, so confident, and so powerful. The sword had flared with a bright light that briefly blinded him before it receded into the mirror like finish of the blade. Kromm and King Baylin agreed it would not be wise to train with the blade in the open, but he could work with it in the evening inside and under guard. They could not risk a thief or assassin taking the blade, not after what they had gone through to get it. They had lost two Dakeen warriors, and soon they would lose Lor-telliam, the highest ranking Ekahal in their midst.

They exchanged a few more blows and then Kromm came at Riker hard. He swung his blade in a powerful upward stroke before smashing it down with all his strength onto his son's shield. Riker lifted the shield, taking the blow dead center, then quickly stepping to the right, angling the shield down and swinging his blade in a sideways arc towards his father. Kromm went with Riker's momentum, spinning away at the last moment, away from his son's blade.

"Well done, boy!"

"But I did not make contact," Riker said, shaking his head in frustration.

"No, and you're not going to easily make contact with me, nor with Malbeck. But you threw me off balance. I had to spin away too narrowly avoid your blade. Well done indeed," Kromm repeated as he gave his son an affectionate slap to the back.

Riker was almost as tall as his father, though with a slightly less imposing frame. Kromm was heavy with solid muscle, while Prince Riker had longer limbs, like his mother. He had long strong arms with sinewy muscle, while Kromm's resembled pythons, bulging and powerful. But their faces were spitting images, with long blonde hair that cascaded over fine narrow features and an angular jaw. Their eyes were ice blue splattered with gray, and they were so piercing that many found it difficult to look at them for too long.

They were training in a small courtyard inside King Baylin's inner castle. Stone walls rose up four stories from all sides, boxing in the duo as they fought across the cobblestones. Two guards stood at the west entrance, while another two watched the east entrance.

Jonas walked through the west entrance, and the guards, recognizing him, quickly stepped aside. Kromm, seeing Jonas enter, stopped fighting and lowered his sword. Tulari was with him and the night wolf lay down quietly at his feet. But now she looked more like a large dog than a night wolf. Jonas had learned that she could indeed change her form to better match her surroundings. Her fur had been black and gray, but now it was more white and gray, reflecting the color of the various stones that made the giant city.

"I heard the sounds of a swordfight, thought I could join in," Jonas said with a smile. Prince Riker wiped the sweat from his brow and joined his father, smiling back at Jonas. Kromm had asked Jonas to come and help train his son. The Tarsinian king respected the young warrior and knew that he had spent over two years training with Kiln. That kind of experience was invaluable. But Kromm had not told Riker that he had invited Jonas to train with him. The young prince idolized Jonas, and if he had told him that he'd be crossing blades with the ex-cavalier he would have never heard the end of it. It would have distracted him from his own work with him. "You have some energy left in those muscles?" Jonas grinned.

Riker stood up tall and looked at his father, then back at Jonas. "Yes, sir," he said.

"First, don't call me sir, I'm only four years older than you and I was born a common village farmer," Jonas said. "King Kromm, may I?" Jonas asked.

"Of course. Listen well, son. Many noblemen would pay dearly to have a private lesson from a cavalier," Kromm said, cutting Jonas's retort off with a wave of his hand. "Jonas, you will always be a cavalier to me."

Jonas nodded appreciatively and tossed Riker a warm roll fresh from the baker's oven. "Prince Riker, eat this and take water, then follow me. Let us take a walk."

"Yes, sir…I mean, Jonas," Riker said, stumbling over his words.

Riker followed Jonas out of the inner castle to the main city below. The two guards followed them and several more guards were ordered to do the same. By the time they left the inner castle and entered the city, there were five Finarthian knights following close by.

The hungry prince quickly consumed the bread as they talked briefly about the cities fortifications, meandering through the packed city streets. The city was overflowing with people. Every spare space was now occupied. Every person was doing their part in preparing the city for Malbeck's army. People were gathering water, food, and firewood, while others helped blacksmiths and engineers prepare the city's defenses. All able bodied men and boys continued to train outside the walls in basic formation fighting.

All people of Finarth, including the new refugees from Cuthaine, who were camped outside the gates, were now being brought inside. Some had set up temporary tents and sleeping areas on the ground between the first and second walls. This was the killing ground, designed to force any invaders who broke through the first wall to bunch up before the moat and come under archer fire from the defenders on the main inner wall. But for now the space had to be occupied as every available space inside the city was already filled. People were sleeping in courtyards, alleys, and even the king's rooms in his inner castle were occupied.

The two young men were readily recognized by many of the people as they walked down the main road of the city. Jonas, even without his cavalier armor, had become quite a celebrity, and although the prince was a relative newcomer, his father, the legendary battle king, was well known. Many of the Finarthians could not help but gaze with admiration and hope at the duo, as they made their way through the city streets.

"Where are we going?" the prince asked.

"Right now we are just walking. What do you see?" Jonas asked the young prince.

"Just a bunch of people," Riker said as he scanned his surroundings.

Jonas stopped and looked the prince in the eyes. "They are more than just a bunch of people. They are the reason why we are here, the reason we are defending this city. They are the reason that you must don ancient armor and take on the mantle of hero. These people are who Malbeck wants to destroy. They are the obstacle to his desires and they must be protected. Without them, the world as we know it will end."

Riker looked about more seriously, taking in the facial expressions of the men, women, and children that scurried about performing their tasks with practiced efficiency. "Do you think we can win?" Riker asked the young warrior.

Jonas sighed. "It will be a…*challenge*," Jonas said, picking the last word carefully. "But if situations were never bleak, then we would never need heroes. I am not much older than you, but I have seen things that no twenty one year old should have witnessed. I have been in situations that seemed hopeless, but the courage of the men and women who stood with me brought us through them. We will prevail. We have to prevail."

They continued their walk, crossing through the main gate and onto the massive bridge that spanned the moat, joining the countless refugees, soldiers, and merchants who continuously crossed the expanse as they went about their daily tasks.

"Are you afraid to die?" Riker asked, surprising Jonas with the question.

"I have been, but I am no longer. I have felt the cold grip of death several times, and from those experiences I was eventually able to accept the reality of my mortality, and to be at peace with the constant possibility of death associated with what I do. We are warriors, Prince, and you are of royal blood, both Finarthian and Tarsinian, and men such as we will frequently face death. But no less so than the farmer who scrapes his existence from the soil, barely surviving the harsh winters and roaming marauders while attempting to protect his family with little or no martial skill. Disease, famine, and brigands can kill just as easily as the claw of a demon or the spear of an enemy. A good friend once shared some wisdom with me, and now I will share it with you. You have more weapons than most to face the spectre of death. You are strong and from a line of great warriors. You are wise for your age and courage boils in your veins. You will face Malbeck, and you will live or die in the struggle. Only fate knows which. Do no fret over that which you have no control. Face your enemies with an iron will and courage in your heart. You will not be alone. The blades of Shyann," Jonas said as he tapped the black handled swords that hung from his hip, "will be with you."

The prince was silent for a while as he took in Jonas's words. By now they had moved outside the outer gate. Refugees were everywhere, hurriedly attempting the impossible task of taking down the tent city that had been erected over the last six months and moving everything inside the inner wall. Jonas stopped amidst the crowd and looked around intently.

"What are you looking for?" Riker asked, wondering why they had walked here.

"There they are," Jonas said as he looked down the long outer wall that protected the city. Two men were sparring and Jonas immediately started walking towards them. One was Graggis, wearing his Finarthian armor and carrying his huge battle axe. The other was Fil who was holding an infantry shield and spear. Riker quickly caught up with Jonas and soon they were all standing together.

"Prince Riker, you know Fil, but I'm not sure if you have met Captain Graggis, Third Lance of the Finarthian knights," Jonas said.

"Uh, yes, good to see you again, Fil," Riker said as they gripped hands warrior style. "Graggis, sir, it is an honor to meet you," Riker continued, gripping Graggis's hand in the same manner. "I have heard much about you."

Graggis was famous in Finarth. Not just for his fighting prowess and sheer size, but also for his unorthodox behavior and the crazy sparkle in his eyes. Everyone in Finarth loved him, and all his enemies feared him.

"Well met, Prince Riker," Graggis growled. "So ya ready to feel my axe?" the burley warrior asked, hefting the impressive weapon.

Riker glanced at Jonas uncertainly. "I thought I was training with you."

"You are, after you train with Fil and Graggis. It is rumored that Malbeck fights with a huge battle axe and a long magical spear. I have seen no better than Fil with a spear, and Graggis, well, by the look in your eyes you have already heard about his axe. You need to be prepared for what you will face. They will help you do so. And so will I. But you and I will start tomorrow, as I believe you will not be fit to train further today," Jonas said over Graggis's chuckle. "I will train with you daily. And we will try to find some time in the busy schedules of these two warriors to work with you as well," Jonas said. "You ready?"

Riker nodded his head and turned determinedly towards Fil and Graggis. He drew his long sword and held his shield up high. "I'm ready."

"Now! Position one!" Allindrian yelled. One hundred bows came up and held their arrows nocked at full draw while the Blade Singer inspected the line of women. She had recruited these women from over five hundred volunteers. Most were young, in their twenties, but some were well beyond that. There were several that were in their fifties but they were strong and fit from working long hours on their farms while bearing and raising children along the way. Hard work and lack of resources had not allowed them the luxury of vanity, so most were not much to look at, but that mattered not when it came to combat. They could draw the training bow, and they had shown courage just by volunteering. "Janniss, a bit higher," Allindrian encouraged as she quickly inspected the line.

A small diminutive girl, maybe eighteen years of age, lifted her shaking arms to the correct position. She was struggling to hold the position, as were many others, but they more or less got the position correct this time. Allindrian had been working with them for a week now and she figured she had two, maybe three more weeks to prepare them. In one more week each volunteer would take fifty more women and train them. Hopefully they could eventually end up with several thousand decent archers.

After she had walked down the entire line she gave the order to fire. One hundred arrows flew from the bows and arced into the air towards their targets. She had painted handfuls of rocks and placed them intermittently along lines all the way across the expansive grass clearing outside the outer wall. It had taken a group of several hundred women to perform the task. The white rocks marked one hundred paces while the red rocks beyond were placed an additional hundred paces further. The idea was that each position of the bow and arrow marked a specific angle, one that would carry the arrows the correct distance to one of the colors. Position one would propel the arrows to the white rocks, position two would carry them to the red rocks, while position three would take them a hundred yards further.

The arrows flew true, most landing along the line of white rocks. "Nock and draw! Position three!" Tired arms set their arrows and brought their bows up to a higher position. Fatigue had begun to make them clumsy and Allindrian had to wait a few seconds to allow everyone to reach the correct position. Several of the women had dropped their arrows and had to hastily grab another. She walked quickly down the line and helped a few of the women adjust their bows. And although most of their arms shook from the strain of the intense training, they gritted their teeth and doggedly struggled to follow Allindrian's instructions, not wanting to disappoint the Blade Singer. They looked up to her with the utmost respect and admiration, and were very grateful that she had given them the opportunity to take part in the battle to come. When she reached Janniss again she saw that the poor girl was trembling so badly that she had lowered her bow and was shaking out her right arm.

"I'm sorry, Blade Singer. I'm not very strong," the young girl said.

"Fire!" Allindrian yelled, not wanting to hold up the others any longer. They released the shafts and the black arrows shot into the sky in a long arc, pounding into the ground all around the marking stones. "Take rest," she said as she turned back toward the young girl. She was plain, but not unpleasant to look at. Her strawberry blond hair was pulled back and tightly secured with a leather thong. Her round face made her appear even younger than she was. She had sky blue eyes and a dusting of freckles across her cheeks. Her nose was small, though a bit pudgy, and her lips were thin. But when she smiled she exposed two rows of beautiful straight white teeth. "It's okay, Janniss, you've only been training for a week. What did you do before these troubled times?"

"I was apprenticed to my father who was a tailor at Gromsweld, a small town just south of the Gildren Garrison."

"Can you make clothes of silk?" Allindrian asked.

"Oh no, not yet anyway. Silk is very expensive and difficult to work with. Only a master tailor can work with it well."

"And how long have you been an apprentice?"

"Ever since I can remember."

"Mastering the bow is the same. It will take you many months just to gain the strength in your arms and shoulders to wield a bow comfortably, then years to fully master speed and accuracy. Do not fret about your skill, Janniss, you have just begun," Allindrian said reassuringly.

"I just want to do my part," she said.

"And you are. There are many women who are stronger than you but lacked the courage to volunteer. You have something they do not, and it will carry you through life. Just keep working at it," Allindrian said smiling. "Now everyone, let's go again!" she yelled, bringing all the women scurrying from their resting spots back to the line.

Tuvallis sat with Seli at a thick oak table in one of the mess halls located on the eastern side of the city. They were both enjoying a steaming bowl of stew accompanied by a thick hunk of bread and a savory round of goat cheese. They had been given an unofficial medal of honor for their service at the Gildren Garrison. It was this medallion, stamped with the king's signet, which allowed them access to the mess hall and other military locations that would normally have been off limits.

It was here that Jonas found him. Jonas had talked briefly with Tuvallis when he came in with Hagar, but his busy schedule hadn't allowed for much conversation. He was now glad to have a chance to talk with him. Jonas slid into one of the heavy oak chairs next to the mountain man as Tulari curled up beside him. Even in her dog form she still looked intimidating, and most stayed clear of her. There was something wild about her that made her appear not only unapproachable, but very possibly dangerous.

"Nice mutt," Tuvallis grunted, looking down at the dog. Tulari lifted her huge head and growled.

"Evening Tuvallis, I'm glad I found you," Jonas said with a smile. "I see you are still the same well-mannered gentleman."

Tuvallis swallowed some stew soaked bread and looked at Jonas. He shook his head in bewilderment. "I still can't believe 'tis you. You are not de same boy I met in de mountains. You've done well. Your ma would be proud of ya."

Jonas nodded his head in thought as his mind drifted briefly to his mother. Then he smiled quickly and looked at Seli. "I'm Jonas Kanrene, it's a pleasure to meet a friend of Tuvallis as I didn't think he had any."

"Well met, Jonas. I'm Seli of the Free Legion," she said, laughing.

Tuvallis dropped a chunk of bread into his stew and looked at Jonas menacingly. "And I didn't know we be good enough friends to jest so." Jonas's smile momentarily disappeared as he feared he may have offended the mountain man. Then Tuvallis grinned back at him. "I'm jokin' as well, son."

They laughed briefly together and it seemed to relax them all.

"If you don't mind me saying you look different without your beard, almost human in fact," Jonas said.

"Now they won't mistake him for an orc," Seli added, laughing. Tuvallis glared at them both as Seli winked at Jonas.

Tuvallis ignored them. "Jonas, I don't mean to pry, but I had heard that you were a cavalier. And now I see you are not. What happened?"

"It is a long story, Tuvallis, a story that I will gladly tell if we make it out of this fight alive. But yes I was a cavalier and I am no more. But know that I am still in Shyann's service."

"So you did not fall from her grace?" Seli asked.

"No, Seli. I was captured by Dykreel agents," Jonas said softly.

"I'm sorry," Seli whispered, clearly embarrassed she had brought it up.

"Do not worry. I survived, but I came out of the situation tainted in a way that made it impossible for Shyann to find me, to link her magic directly to me," Jonas said.

There was an uncomfortable moment of silence as they tried to imagine what it must have been like for Jonas. They could not imagine what a cavalier would have to endure in the chains of the Master of Torments. They had both heard terrifying stories of what could happen to someone at the hands of Dykreel clerics, and neither of them would wish any of it even on their enemies.

"I'm sorry, son. Seems a lot has happened since I saw ya last and not much of it good. What happened to your friend, Fil?"

"Finarthian soldier, he is training to be a knight," Jonas replied.

Tuvallis grunted and downed the last of his water.

"So what brought you here, Tuvallis?" Jonas asked. In their brief encounter several days ago Tuvallis had learned that Hagar and Jonas had met before, but they did not have time to discuss it further. Jonas was curious to know how two people who Jonas had connected with earlier in life had found each other and made it to Finarth together. He had seen the incredible armor that Hagar wore and he hoped that Tuvallis could shed some light as to how he came to own it.

"Durin' de winter I began to get a feeling, a feeling to leave the mountains and come here," Tuvallis said.

"A feeling?" Jonas queried.

"Hard to explain really, but it was very strong, like I was needed here. It felt like there was something inside of me driving me here. I didn't think much of it. Just thought it was me conscience tellin' me to do something different. So I listened and made me way down the mountains and that be when I found Seli."

Seli then spoke up, "Fifty of us had been picked to lead the refugees from Cuthaine before Malbeck's army arrived. I was one of those chosen. Late one evening, while we were all sleeping, an orc patrol attacked us, taking me as hostage. I was knocked unconscious and I woke to find myself tied to a post and surrounded by ten orcs." Seli swallowed in disgust as she thought again about what had almost happened to her. "Tuvallis found me and killed the beasts. It was very impressive," she said as she reached across the table and touched his hand.

Jonas didn't miss the gesture and it caused him to smile. It felt good seeing that people were still enjoying some pleasures in life while the world was in chaos around them. "I know...I have seen him fight. Years ago he too saved my life. Did he tell you about that?"

"He did," she said with a grin, gently tapping his hand before withdrawing it. She could tell that he was embarrassed by the praise and her touch. They had only talked briefly about his earlier show of affection by the river. It seemed that act had fractured the dam of emotions that they felt for each other, but the wall was still up. Seli promised herself that she would work on chipping away at it. After all, who knew how much longer they would be alive. It was a precarious time and it made you think about your life in a different way.

"Then you found the Free Legion column again I assume. What about Hagar, how did you connect with him?"

"On da way to de garrison our scouts found an orc army with siege engines. They were an advance group hopin' to take de garrison," Tuvallis said as he poured some more water.

"So it is true? You and several others snuck into their camp and destroyed the engines? You are quite a hero among the Finarthian army you know. They say you warned the garrison and burned every engine, allowing the defenses to hold out."

"I was not alone. We almost died that night and probably would have if not for Hagar. He just appeared from de darkness and killed three orcs and their dire wolves. One of de soldiers was badly injured and Hagar carried him the last few miles to de camp."

"And the armor and weapon he carries?"

"The Ekahal said Hagar had found de armor and weapon and he was led to it by a giant stag," Tuvallis said focusing his eyes on Jonas. "Sar-gathos had cast some spell that enabled him to talk with Hagar."

"A stag? You mean a huge deer led him to his armor?" Jonas asked incredulously.

"Yup," Tuvallis grunted.

Jonas's mind was whirling as he thought about what Tuvallis had just said. "But you had been led to us by a stag many years ago, do you remember?"

"Of course I do. It was de biggest deer I had ever seen."

"Sar-gathos thinks that Tuvallis and Hagar have been guided by Shyann, that her hand has been pulling strings for many years with the result being the culmination of you all here, at Finarth," Seli continued.

Jonas nodded his head in agreement. "I think he is right. She has had a plan for us all. I thought it strange that you had been tracking a massive stag before you met us those many years back. And then it just disappeared and you happened to arrive to save us from those two boargs. And now, years later, you are here and Hagar wears armor with her God Mark. She also used a stag to guide me to her tomb where she gave me my cavalier armor and weapons. Obviously all of this cannot be a coincidence."

"Nope, I reckon not," Tuvallis said.

"What now?" Seli asked.

"We do our duty and hope that fate keeps us alive," Jonas said seriously.

"I don't believe in fate," Tuvallis growled as he leaned back and gripped the pommel of his sword.

Jonas just smiled. "Sharp steel works too."

Tuvallis finally ran into King Kromm one day while training with Seli in the practice yard outside the king's inner castle. The courtyard there was reserved for the knights that guarded the king, and Tuvallis and Seli, being honored guests and living in the inner castle, had free reign of the area. Kromm had come down with his wife, Queen Sorana, and their son, Prince Riker, followed by a small contingent of guards, four Finarthian knights. They were there for the same reason; all armed with blunted practice swords.

Kromm looked over casually as Tuvallis and Seli sparred with similar weapons, his gaze stopping momentarily before looking back at his son, who was also preparing to spar. The queen, wearing casual light breeches and tunic, also carried a small short sword, and she too looked over at the two combatants, smiling warmly at them both. She kept her gaze on Seli, watching her intently as she went through various sword positions with Tuvallis. It was rare to see a female warrior in these parts, especially one as skilled as Seli, and Sorana enjoyed watching her skillful moves and powerful strokes.

Kromm lifted his sword towards his son, but was distracted by something familiar about the swordsman. The man looked familiar, and he searched his memories from long ago.

"What is it?" Sorana asked as she moved next to her husband.

"I don't know, there's something familiar about that man."

"Actually, I thought the same thing," the queen said, looking again at the stockily built man. He was strong and quick, his movements reflecting those of a skilled swordsman, one who had been trained in an elite military unit, and yet he did not wear the uniform of a soldier.

Tuvallis had seen the king and his family enter the training ground and his heart began to beat faster. He had known that he would face them at some point, but now the reality of it began to overwhelm him, releasing twenty years of pent up anxiety. The events that had happened long ago as a Tarsinian warrior had scarred him for life, forcing him to leave Tarsis and go into exile. He had not seen his liege since then, and even though he had traveled to Finarth knowing that the confrontation was sure to happen, he was nonetheless unprepared for it.

Seli saw him falter and glanced over her shoulder to see the king and his family. She slowly backed away from Tuvallis. "It's okay, you knew this would happen sooner or later," she said softly. "Everything will be okay. You should go talk to him."

Tuvallis lowered his sword and gazed at Seli, his eyes filled with emotion. "Me heart says I should, but me brain is tellin' me otherwise."

"Men," Seli mumbled, "so brave in battle, but so timid when emotions are involved!" Then she turned and marched right towards the king and his family. Tuvallis had no choice but to follow.

"Your Highness," Seli announced calmly as she neared the monarch, "I am Seli, one of the few members left of the Free Legion and I wanted to introduce myself. You've always been a friend of Cuthaine and I didn't think it fitting to fight next to you without introductions."

Kromm turned to face them both, lowering his sword and smiling in greeting. "Well met, Seli of the Free Legion; this is my wife, Sorana, and my son, Riker." As Seli greeted them Kromm looked directly at Tuvallis. "I know you, don't I?" he asked.

"Indeed, my Lord," Tuvallis replied. The emphasis on the word *my* did not go unnoticed by Kromm, and his eyes narrowed with interest as he looked more intently at the burly warrior. "I am Tuvallis."

Kromm's eyes widened as his memories, sorting through images long past, recognized that name. "I remember you," he said softly. "You are Tarsinian, and you were one of my soldiers."

"I was," he said.

Kromm's eyes softened. "I have often wondered what happened to you, and the others," he said.

"Really?"

"Yes, that decision was very difficult for me," Kromm replied. "You were trained by Kernan, right?"

"Yes, sir. I would have had me mark if ya hadn't kicked me out," Tuvallis said matter-of-factly.

Queen Sorana stiffened at his words, stepping forward and touching her husband's arm. "I saw you only once, Tuvallis, at your trial, but I want you to know that he was troubled for months about that incident long ago. The king in him knew he must punish you for your actions, but the husband and father in him understood what you did."

Tuvallis shook his head. "It was wrong, I know that now. I was so angry at me loss that I welcomed de order from me captain, even though I knew it be wrong to kill those whom had nothing to do with our losses. I was even angry at you for what ya did to me, but I know now that ya did what ya had to do. I do not place blame on ya, not anymore," he said with a weak smile.

"I am very grateful to hear that, Tuvallis. Kings are frequently forced to make difficult decisions, and that one, for me, has haunted me all these years. It is good to see you. Where have you been over the years?" Kromm asked, genuinely interested.

"Been away, mostly livin' in de mountains. I trapped most of da last twenty years near the town Jonas Kanrene be from. I knew da boy when he was a cripple," Tuvallis added.

"Small world," Kromm said. "You know, when this is all over, I plan on rebuilding. I'll be needing some good men. You interested?" Kromm asked.

Tuvallis turned to Seli, her face lit up with a wide smile. He looked back at the king, "I might be," he paused briefly, "You have room for two?"

Kromm, smiling in return, nodded his head. "Of course, and I hope you are referring to Seli, as I could use another strong sword arm. We're certainly going to need more good soldiers. Care to spar with us? My son needs to learn from the best."

"I would be honored, sir."

Eleven
Siege of Finarth

Word had spread like wildfire when the scouts had arrived with the news that Malbeck's army was on the move, and that the Dark One would arrive at their gate within the week. If things were chaotic before, they now paled in comparison to the atmosphere of anxiety permeating the city. The time was upon them, and no one knew if they could withstand the might of the Forsworn and their most powerful general, but those questions would be answered soon, and that thought alone added to the tension that seemed to be everywhere.

Everyone had moved inside the outer wall, including Hagar, who by now had become tolerated if not accepted by most people. Some still feared the beast and they tried to avoid him if possible, but for most people the anxiety of the impending battle seemed to erase any doubts about who this giant creature was. They saw him as a valuable ally that would surely help in their struggles. Alerion, the Finarthian court wizard, had been negotiating with Shyval to send battle wizards as reinforcements, and the reclusive school of magic readily agreed to send several wizards to aid them against Malbeck

Thus, Finarth gained a few more assets in their fight against the Forsworn. Shyval was far to the west, over the Tundren Mountains and all the way to the Algard coast. It was a school for wizards, providing a place of solitude away from the politics of the world. To become a wizard you had few choices by which to learn your trade. The cost of schooling and the time that was required to learn the intricate art was beyond most people's reach. Kings employed court wizards, but those positions were usually hereditary and those wizards passed their skills down the line to their heirs. If you weren't lucky enough to be the son or daughter of a court wizard, you had to find a school or another wizard to teach you. Since wizards were rare outside of a king's castle, you were usually stuck with a school, which was very expensive and that few could afford.

Shyval was ruled by a council that did their best to maintain their neutrality. Neutrality was difficult to maintain, however, since kings and other rulers were continuously vying for control of the power that could be found at Shyval. But this time the needs of the land were impossible to ignore. This battle would require the help of wizards to fight Malbeck, and if the defenders of Finarth didn't stop him, then who would? This was not a Finarthian problem, or a Tarsinian problem, it was a problem that was affecting everyone, and because of that three battle wizards were sent to Finarth to help. All three had volunteered for the job.

One of them was an elderly wizard who had taught most of the offensive spells at Shyval. His name was Boranthos and his sharp piercing eyes did not reflect the hunched-over gray haired man behind them. He was quick of wit and sharp of tongue, and many an enemy had mistakenly took his aged physique for weakness, a mistake they only made once. The second wizard was a heavy set middle aged woman from Onith, south of Shyval. Lizarcus was steady under pressure and sat on the council at Shyval. Her calm demeanor and superior skill was well respected there. The third wizard was a young but precocious man from Osrigard, a town located several weeks travel southwest of Shyval on the Ronith River. Talic was a handsome young man who exuded an arrogance that by all accounts was mostly justified.

As soon as the wizards arrived they took turns, along with Alerion and the two remaining Ekahals, patrolling the battlements day and night. Kromm had informed them of how Malbeck had breached the walls of Tarsis, and they did not want to repeat that scenario. According to the Tarsinian king, in the middle of the night Malbeck had cast a powerful spell that had created a deadly fog that killed any who breathed it. The mist had quietly drifted into the city, instantly killing all the guards and leaving the gate unmanned. After that it was a simple matter of getting the gate open and overrunning the surprised defenders. The power of the Shan Cemar, the elven book of magic, surely had played a part in creating such a powerful spell. The wizards from Shyval would hopefully provide a magical presence and keep a constant eye out for Malbeck and any other tricks that he might employ.

But Malbeck did not attack in the middle of the night. Scouts saw the advancing army early one morning and within hours the entire city was alert and ready. It was eerie to see that many soldiers on the battlements of the inner and outer wall, silently gazing across the Finarthian plains waiting for the largest and most formidable army they had ever encountered.

They heard it before they saw it. The slow rumble of pounding drums sounded in the distance, echoing the pounding hearts of all those who nervously waited. The cadence of the war drums was soon followed by the rhythmic pounding of marching boots. Then came the roars and howls of sixty thousand monsters all eager for Finarthian blood. A wave of blackness slowly and inexorably crept forward across the grasslands, the green of the meadow disappearing as the mass of black clad warriors, as wide and deep as the eye could see, trampled it under dark muddy boots.

No one on the walls said anything as they took in the sheer size of the advancing army. They easily outnumbered them three to one, and on top of that they had giant siege engines, catapults, ballista, and other machines of war, looming in the distance like beasts of prey.

Then, the loud and unmistakable sound of enormous flapping wings sounded in the distance, followed by the earsplitting roar of a dragon. The great black beast swooped down from the sky, slowing its descent with great heaves of its wings, and landing softly on the ground before the army. This time the dragon carried a rider, perched in a black saddle on its massive back, but they were too far away to make out much detail. Nonetheless, the dragon's presence had a terrifying effect on the defenders, and the archers on the walls nocked arrows while officers began shouting orders to the men working the catapults and ballista. Large ballista had been placed along the inner and outer wall for defense against the dragon, and rows of catapults lined the killing ground between the first and second wall.

King Baylin stood upon the battlements above the gate on the outer wall looking out at the enemy. Alerion, his court wizard, stood near him holding a wood staff capped with a pearlescent stone the size of a fist. Kromm was also there, along with Commander Kiln, Jonas, Allindrian, and Lor-telliam. Prince Riker, wearing King Ullis's magnificent armor and carrying Tihr-Allian at his hip, stood next to his father. Addalis, Kromm's court wizard, had argued to be there with him, but Kromm had ordered him to stay with his queen, Sorana, and he would not budge on the matter.

They were all well outfitted for war and even Lor-telliam had donned a beautifully crafted cuirass of elven scale mail, but their armor and weaponry all paled in comparison to the prince's. His glowing white armor, perfectly polished, was lined with silver that sparkled in the early morning sun. The Finarthian symbol on his cuirass, etched in silver, seemed to glow with some inner light. The young prince looked about as magnificent as a warrior could.

"Do you think that is Malbeck?" King Baylin asked.

"I imagine so," Kiln replied. "What kind of dragon is that? It looks similar to a black, but it's not. I've never seen the likes."

"It's no black. You see the pulsing colors of red and orange along its skin? Blacks don't have those. I've read about dragons that have those features, and that breathe a deadly mist, but I was not sure they actually existed. They do not live on this plane and I doubt one has ever been here until now. They are called Demon Dragons or Blood Dragons. They live in the Abyss and they feed on flesh, but it is mainly the blood of their victims that they crave.

"Can it be killed?" Jonas asked softly.

"Anything can be killed, but *how* is the question," Lor-telliam answered.

Jonas turned to the Ekahal, dismayed that he could already see the elf beginning to age. His face was losing its characteristic vitality, as dark circles framed his eyes, and wrinkles began to etch their way across his once smooth and flawless skin. It saddened Jonas, but what saddened him even more as he looked upon the massive army advancing before him was that he knew the days to come would be filled with more death and destruction than anyone could possibly imagine. Countless numbers would die, not just the warriors defending the city, but women, children, the old, and the infirm, with no regard to age, gender, or status. Those who managed to survive would not only witness unspeakable atrocities, but would have to live with the knowledge that their own friends and loved ones had suffered and perished, all because of an evil that lusted for power and destruction. It saddened him, but it angered him more.

"Still sticking with the plan?" Kromm asked, looking more at Kiln than anyone.

Kiln nodded. "We need to see what we're dealing with. Let them exhaust themselves on our walls and face our arrows before we commit to real battle."

"I agreed with you when you presented the plan and I agree with you now. I'm just concerned about my son. The longer we wait for the confrontation the more stressful it is for him," Kromm said, repeating what he had said the night before when all the war leaders had met one last time.

"It is necessary," King Baylin added.

"Father, I am fine," Riker interjected, "the confrontation will come. Be it today or a week from now, it matters not." He placed his gauntlet covered hand on his father's huge shoulder. "This is my destiny."

The plan that Kiln had devised was to let Malbeck's army throw everything it had at their walls. They would take advantage of their defensive position to kill as many enemies as they could. Then, when the enemy morale dropped from the horrendous death toll, they would lead an advancing army through the gate and confront Malbeck's army with various offensive maneuvers followed by organized retreats. Kiln didn't think that Malbeck would want to wait out a long siege; he was far too arrogant for that. He would attack with full force in an attempt to quickly bring the city to its knees. The hope was to gradually pick off their warriors and to draw Malbeck himself into the fight. Then they would do their best to set up a confrontation that would lead to his destruction. That attempt would, of course, be led by Prince Riker, though no one doubted that the Tarsinian battle king would fight, and die if need be, next to his son.

A loud horn bellowed a warning but no one on the wall needed it. Malbeck's army was clearly advancing. They could hear the ominous rumble of boots and the low creaking sound of massive siege machines being pulled by rows of giant fur clad ogres.

"Here they come," Allindrian said, nocking an arrow.

"Ready the oil," Kiln ordered.

One of the warriors standing behind him lifted a tall pole with a red flag attached to it. The signal was relayed down the wall as more poles and flags were lifted informing the men the entire distance of the wall to ready the oil and prepare the fire arrows. When the army was within striking distance they would be bombarded with a deluge of oil, followed by a barrage of fire arrows shot into their midst. The focus would then be to destroy the siege engines.

"They are readying their catapults," Jonas said, noticing them scurrying around the big machines. Ogres were loading huge stones onto the baskets and within moments the air was filled with stone projectiles nearly as large as a man.

"And we shall ready ours. Catapults, fire on my order!" Kiln yelled.

This time another flag was raised to signal the loading of the catapults. The battle had begun. The flying stones struck the wall with alarming force, shattering great chunks of it and sending fragments flying through the air. Some stones landed short, thudding harmlessly into the grassy ground in front of the wall. A few, however, flew over the wall landing in the killing ground beyond. Most of the soldiers who were readying the catapults managed to frantically jump out of the way but some were not so lucky. A handful of men were crushed as the projectiles crashed into the ground, bouncing erratically across the field and shattering their bodies as if they were dry twigs.

As Malbeck's army marched slowly but inexorably closer, it wasn't long before the defenders could make out the howling creatures themselves. They could see that most were orcs and goblins. Soon, the sound grew from a low rumble to the deafening sound of a thousand monsters marching, roaring, and rhythmically smashing their weapons against their shields.

"Archers, prepare to fire!" Kiln yelled. A third flag was hoisted and the signal raced down the wall like a wave, thousands of bows lifting, arrows pulled back at full draw. "Fire!"

The signal to fire was then transferred down the line and officers shouted the order. The sound of thousands of bow strings twanging reverberated in the air as the arrows were released, sending their deadly shafts arching toward the enemy.

"Catapults, fire!" Kiln screamed over the din of battle.

Within seconds, not stones, but hundreds of burning balls of fire, shot over the walls following the trail of descending arrows. These projectiles were thick canvas spheres stuffed with hundreds of iron balls as big around as a child's fist. The dense canvas had been soaked in oil and made to burn apart in mid-air, freeing the missiles within to fall in a deadly hailstorm upon the enemy. Within seconds, halfway through the air, the flaming canvas broke apart, filling the air with thousands of iron projectiles.

First the arrows slammed into the advancing army. Then, moments later, the iron balls crashed into the enemy, the destructive force of their impact launching orcs and goblins off their feet as the projectiles pulverized flesh and shattered bones, at the same time creating a deafening noise as the balls hammered into their armored bodies. But though hundreds of orcs and goblins fell instantly, still they kept coming.

Both sides continued to sling catapult missiles with deadly effects. As the stones found their marks, sections of the outer wall cracked and pieces of it began to crumble away. Fortunately, not many of the projectiles found human flesh, though the same couldn't be said for Malbeck's army as hundreds of creatures fell to the deadly assault of arrows and metal projectiles that continued to rain down on them. But despite their losses the massive army continued marching relentlessly forward, trampling over their fallen comrades as if they were nothing more than stones in their path. It wasn't long before they were too close to the wall for the catapults to be effective, and the defenders had to rely solely on the archers and more powerful ballista.

At this point the officers had ordered the archers to fire at will as the horde of orcs and goblins picked up speed, running towards the wall with frenzied abandon. Most of the defenders concentrated aiming around the siege engines as the huge ogres continued to pull the heavy machines closer to the wall. It would take many arrows to bring down an ogre, and most of the iron balls that had been fired from the catapults were too small as well, so the defenders then turned their ballista towards the lumbering beasts, launching giant spear-like projectiles into the hoard. Many found their marks, punching gruesome holes through the beasts and sending them spinning away to their deaths. But for every one killed, another joined the fray, and the colossal machines moved steadily closer.

Kiln was scanning the enemy along the wall when he saw the Blood Dragon lift off from behind a screen of orcs. The great beast rose slowly, then came at them with increased acceleration.

"Dragon! Ballista at the ready!" Kiln yelled, running towards the closest ballista. The machine was only twenty paces away and by the time he got there the two operators had already loaded the spear sized bolt.

The dragon swooped down at them as the soldier behind the ballista aimed the deadly bolt up at the creature.

"Stay behind me!" Lor-telliam yelled to the warriors near him. No one needed further encouragement. They had heard what this dragon could do.

Kiln nudged the soldier out of the way and grabbed the handles of the ballista. The dragon was almost upon them when he zeroed in on the creature. The angle was good and all he had to do was lead the dragon a few paces. The beast spewed forth its deadly steam just as Kiln released the shaft.

The bolt flew true, striking the dragon directly in the chest and cutting off its breath attack, causing the beast to jerk hard to the right and well clear of the wall. Everyone along the wall cheered as they saw the great dragon dive quickly to the ground below.

"Load it again!" Kiln yelled, running to the wall to look for the beast. The dragon had not fallen to the ground as Kiln had hoped. In fact it had merely landed gracefully, casually gripping the spear with one claw and pulling the shaft from its chest.

"Not good," Kiln whispered to himself, as he ran back towards the group.

The dragon had flung the spear to the ground and if anyone had been close enough they would have witnessed the gruesome wound close immediately.

"I was afraid of that," Lor-telliam addressed everyone. "The beast is not of this plane, I'm afraid only magical weapons can harm it."

"How do we fight that thing with swords and axes?" King Baylin asked.

"My magic may be able to kill it," the Ekahal replied.

"Well here is your chance," Kromm said as the dragon took flight again. This time the great beast flapped its wings hard, accelerating rapidly and swooping directly towards them. The ballista fired again but this time the dragon was ready for it, dodging the missile easily.

Lor-telliam began to chant and everyone moved behind the Ekahal as the dragon neared. Handfuls of soldiers panicked, frantically running down the length of the wall as they tried to put as much distance between themselves and the dragon as they could. Within seconds, however, they were engulfed and consumed by a hot white cloud that roared all around them. Jonas heard the men's anguished screams, yet he himself did not feel the heat of the beast's attack. Within seconds the mist cleared and Jonas watched as Lor-telliam pivoted, striking his hand forward and sending a crackling bolt of blue lightening towards the dragon as it streaked by.

The bolt struck the dragon in the tail, rocking it sideways as it roared in anger. The blow, however, only seemed to slow the creature down a bit, and it soon regained control of its flight, gaining altitude and preparing for another attack.

The dragon turned and dove down again, this time hitting another section of the wall. It flew in at a steeper angle, which made it difficult for the ballista closest to it to have a clear shot. The bolt flew wide and the dragon released its scalding breath along the wall. It was terrible to hear the men's screams as they cooked inside their armor. Many had leaped off the wall in both directions, frantically trying to avoid its breath, only to meet their doom on the hard ground below.

It was then that four siege machines rolled up against the wall, giant towers that extended several paces above the top of the wall. Inside the walled towers were crude stairs that allowed the invaders to reach the top of the wall. The stairs were protected by hinged panels of wood and steel that blocked any arrows or missiles fired at them as they climbed to the top, but could be quickly lifted up to allow the creatures to scramble out and over the wall.

Defenders along the wall were already preparing the hot oil. Big cauldrons of scalding oil had been placed in large carts that the men could roll over to any spot along the wall. As some of the soldiers readied the carts of oil, the Finarthian archers continued firing arrows down at the monsters below. Thousands of the beasts were milling at the base of the wall, some preparing to enter the siege towers, while others attempted to use smaller scaling ladders or defend the massive towers by firing arrows up at the archers above them. Most of the arrows deflected off the stone battlements but several struck men as they leaned over the edge to release their shafts. The defenders then began pouring the hot oil down upon the siege towers and the enemy warriors below, drenching them with thick splashes of the volatile material, followed shortly by a barrage of flaming arrows. Patches of flames erupted along the line as orcs and goblins were literally roasted alive.

One of the siege towers had managed to crash against the wall and two soldiers rushed to the scene with a cart of hot oil. They gripped the handles on the edge of the cauldron, lifted with all their strength, and dumped the scalding oil onto it, the black substance covering the wall of the tower, as dozens of orcs ran with all haste up the stairs inside, the pounding of their boots getting louder as they neared the top.

Lizarcus, the female wizard from Shyval, had been moving about along the wall, looking for where she would be most needed. The crashing sound of the nearby siege tower banging up against the wall quickly directed her attention to the new threat. She ran closer to help the men, clearly seeing that they would be hard pressed once the hinged door flung open on the tower unleashing the orcs onto the wall. "Look out!" she yelled as she heard the howling beasts climb to the top of the tower. She knew it would only be moments before the door swung open and the enemy descended upon the tired and struggling defenders. She pushed through the fighting men as the top panel of the tower flung open revealing four roaring orcs. She quickly lifted her hand to summon her magic. Instantly a ball of fire flared in her palm and she flung the flaming sphere up at the orcs just as they were about to jump out. Their roars were cut short as the ball exploded inside the confines of the tower, the force of the blast hurling the beasts violently backwards and down the tower's stairs, accompanied by their howls of pain. The soldiers on the wall felt the heat from the blast, the concussion from it throwing them backwards away from the tower. By the time they regained their balance the fire had found the oil and the tower had become a furnace of red hot flames.

Then the Blood Dragon was again hovering above them, its giant wings flapping powerfully, sending great gusts of wind into the defenders. As it ominously lifted its head, the wizard knew what was coming. She could try an offensive spell but she had no idea if it would do any damage to the dragon. She had seen the Ekahal hit the beast with a powerful lightning bolt which seemed to have done little damage. If the Ekahal's power couldn't harm the dragon then it was unlikely that anything she threw at the beast would be effective. Her only viable option was a defensive spell.

The dragon spewed forth a huge gust of hot steam just as the wizard lifted her ringed finger, calling upon its magic. Since the spells were already imbued in the ring, it only took a word to activate its power, allowing her to bring forth the magic before she was cooked alive. A bluish translucent shield had shot out from the ring, instantly creating a human sized barrier that wrapped protectively around her. As the hot steam roared past her she could feel the skin on her back begin to burn, but her pain was nothing compared to what the men around her were experiencing. And although she could not yet see anything she could hear their screams and smell their sizzling flesh.

Then the mist was gone and so was the dragon. There were easily twenty men around her when the dragon attacked and every one of them was now dead, their burnt bodies encased in seared and melted armor, and contorted into the unnatural positions characteristic of agonizing death. The stench of burnt hair and roasted flesh accompanied the terrible scene around her, and she felt the bile rise up in her throat.

That was when she noticed that the tower was no longer on fire. The steam, although it was searing, had managed to put out the flames. The roaring mist must have smothered it, which may have been the intent of the dragon's attack to begin with.

More howling monsters arrived at the open door on top of the smoking tower, leaping down onto the wall as Lizarcus scurried backwards away from them. She was no warrior. She didn't even carry a sword and she only had seconds before they would cut her down with their thick heavy blades. She heard soldiers behind her but they could not get to her in time. If she was going to live then it would be up to her.

She quickly recited a spell, bringing forth six magical bolts that instantly appeared beside her. As two big orcs came at her with their broad swords raised, she screamed in fright, simultaneously directing two of the bolts at them; the first magic missile struck one of the orcs in the throat while the second bolt slammed into the other creature's forehead, dropping it like a sack of bricks. Meanwhile, the other creature had stumbled to the side, gagging on its own blood. Before she could blink, two more orcs were upon her, and as she scuttled away from them her foot struck a body behind her, tripping her to the ground. Ironically that saved her life as she inadvertently fell beneath an orc's blade that whistled by her head. Still screaming and on the ground she shot two more bolts into the beast, gouging bloody holes in its chest, and tossing it backwards into another orc.

Lizarcus scrambled to her feet, dismayed to see even more orcs pouring from the tower and onto the wall. She was relieved to hear the sound of booted feet close behind her and knew that armed soldiers would arrive within moments. But she still had two bolts left so she shot each one into another attacker. Two more orcs fell and in an instant she found herself surrounded by charging Finarthian warriors. She scrambled to the rear of the group as steel met steel and the defenders frantically worked to stem the tide of attackers entering through the tower. Her heart was still pounding in her chest. She could hardly believe she was alive. The burns on her back were a painful but welcome reminder that she was not yet dead.

Graggis, who had arrived with the other soldiers, swung his mighty axe in great arcs as he cut down the enemy while blocking any attacks that came his way. His thick muscular arms spun and flipped the axe with deadly speed and precision. The soldiers flanking him knew better than to get in his way. Together they powered past the wizard, pushing the orcs back towards the tower. They had made it to the wizard just in time. Graggis and the Finarthian soldiers fought furiously, effectively boxing the orcs in a deadly prison of stone walls and sharp steel. They soon made it to the mouth of the tower where the parapet was now littered with the bodies of orcs and goblins.

"Now!" Graggis yelled, as he kicked an orc in the chest, dislodging the dead beast from the blade of his axe. Several men behind him had prepared clay jugs of oil that they had set afire, then tossed into the opening of the tower. One shattered against an emerging orc, flaming liquid drenching it and splattering against the wooden structure. The orc immediately became a giant living torch, orange flames covering its body. The doomed creature howled in pain, falling backwards into more monsters. The second jug of oil hit something structural inside the tower, causing a fiery explosion which instantly engulfed the entire top of the tower in bright flames. Needless to say no more enemy warriors emerged from the tower opening. "Throw this scum off the wall," Graggis ordered, turning to look for Lizarcus. He found her leaning against the wall vainly trying to gather her wits and calm her breathing. "Good work, Wizard. Thought we weren't goin' to get to ya."

"Just in time it would seem. Thanks for your aid, Captain," she said, digging into a pouch on her side for a small brown bottle filled with healing elixir. Her back was in severe pain and she hoped the potion would be enough to alleviate the discomfort.

"The thanks belong to you. We appreciate your help. Can I get you anything?"

"I'll be fine once I drink this," she replied.

"Very well. Be safe," Graggis said, departing to see to his men and make sure that the tower was fully destroyed. They also had to keep a constant eye out for that dragon, which appeared more rapidly than seemed possible for a creature of its size.

The walls continued to be bombarded by huge missiles that crashed against the outer wall, shaking its foundations. But still it held as each side traded projectile for projectile. Most of the enemy army was now close to the wall, and attempting to use the array of siege towers that now lined the defensive structure. Several had succumbed to the flames but six still remained. The enemy army continued to fling stone projectiles, but they soon began to switch to huge jugs of flaming oil, launching them over the walls toward the city buildings beyond. Crashing beyond the outer wall they splattered flames across men and catapults. For now the distance was too great for them to clear the inner fortification and land within the city, but they were slowly advancing, the great machines inching forward, and it would not be long before they would be in range to do just that.

"Fire the catapults again!" Kiln ordered, observing the enemy in the distance roll their great machines closer to the wall. The order was transmitted to the men below and soon they too were flinging great jugs of burning oil over the wall across the battlefield to land in the enemy ranks. Some missed, but several found monsters and machines alike, killing and destroying in great splashes of deadly flame.

"Kiln, below!" Jonas yelled, looking over the side of the inner wall. A magical door had opened on the ground near the gate and giant orcs were rushing from the opening like a swarm of angry hornets. It was the same dimension door that they had seen at Cuthaine when the orcs had attacked the gaming house. It seemed the Shan Cemar was being used again.

Most of the soldiers located along the killing ground between the inner and outer wall were working the catapults, but there were reserves armed and ready inside the main gate ready for just such a contingency. General Gandarin, who was in charge of the defenses of the inner wall and who stood above its gate, watched in horror as the creatures poured from the magical door. He quickly gave the order to open the inner gate and send in the mounted knights. The big gates opened and Captain Lathrin and five hundred Finarthian knights shot through the opening with lances angled down and shields held at the ready.

Jonas was already running down the stairs on the inner wall to the ground below. Allindrian was close on his heels, both leaping down six steps at a time. They looked like mountain goats easily navigating the most difficult terrain. Jonas's magical boots allowed him to move much faster and with more agility than even the most skilled human thief.

Allindrian was something to behold, firing three arrows from her bow as she quickly descended the stairs. Three orcs were already dead by the time she landed on the ground, her sword seeming to magically appear in her other hand.

Jonas leaped the last ten feet off the wall landing with a practiced roll to cushion the hard landing. He was standing about twenty paces in front of the door that opened into the gatehouse mechanics room. About fifty Gould-Irin orcs had managed to enter through the magic door, and now they were nearly upon him. They could not allow the orcs to get into the gatehouse and breach the outer gate, opening it up to the full force of Malbeck's army. He could see the glitter of the Finarthian knight's lances and hear the thundering hooves of their horses as they raced toward the monsters. He surmised that the cavalry had been ordered to attack from the inner wall. He was confident that they would eventually crush the relatively small number of Gould-Irin that were pouring through the magical gate, but he was worried they would not arrive in time to prevent the creatures from opening the gate. Would he and Allindrian be able to keep them at bay until the cavalry arrived?

But he didn't have time to ponder the question as Allindrian jumped down beside him. They had only enough time to share a brief smile before the orcs were upon them. Jonas quickly concentrated on calling forth his cognivant abilities. Almost immediately he was able to draw in the energy around him, then hurl it forward like a battering ram. The invisible wall slammed into the mass of orcs, and they were thrown backwards, momentarily stunned. He then withdrew his cognivant power, saving energy he knew he might need later.

Allindrian and Jonas then tore into the stunned creatures, creating a tornado of spinning razor sharp steel. Even the mighty Gould-Irin could not withstand the quick and deadly precise movements of their expert swordplay. The orc bodies began to pile up around them, but it wasn't long before their sheer numbers began to push the two warriors back...and they didn't have far to go before they would be pushed up against the door leading to the gate mechanisms. It mattered not how skilled they were when faced by such large numbers in a confined space.

Back on the wall Lor-telliam was scanning the enemy near the outer gate, dismayed by his sudden realization. Using his power to raise his voice, he yelled above the deafening sounds of battle, "There is a wizard nearby, and a powerful one at that! No mere conjurer could create and sustain such a dimension door! We must find him and kill him to close that opening!"

Prince Riker was looking over the outer edge when he saw a cloaked form surrounded by several giant ogres. "There!" he said, pointing to the right.

Lor-telliam ran to the prince, his eyes quickly following the direction of the prince's finger. The elf swore under his breath, "Ethereen," he whispered, already preparing a powerful spell. Ethereen was the elven name given to Gullanin, the most powerful evil wizard known on Kraawn and Malbeck's faithful servant. According to Kromm the wizard was supposed to be dead, but it looked as if that information was not accurate. It was too far away for anyone to see into the blackness of the cloaked hood but the Ekahal had a feeling that it was he, and the one who had found the Shan Cemar. But what he didn't know was that Gullanin the wizard was now a Lich, an undead wizard, even more powerful than he was before.

The Ekahal had begun chanting and everyone backed away to give him room. He slowly raised both hands, one gripping his staff, up towards the sky. The sky darkened as blue energy crackled above them. Then, without warning, a bolt of white lightning shot from the cloaked wizard below coming straight towards Lor-telliam. Everything happened so fast. Blue energy crackled from the sky, hitting Lor-telliam's staff. The energy was channeled from the staff and it instantly shot from his raised hand towards Gullanin just as the dark wizard's bolt streaked towards him.

Riker, without thinking, jumped in front of the wizard.

Screaming, Kromm reached out for his son as the bolt struck Riker in the chest. Lor-telliam's bolt struck true and crackling fingers of intense energy hit Gullanin and any creature that stood near him. There was a violent explosion and everyone within a ten pace perimeter of the blast was blown from their feet, fried to a blackened mass of melted armor and skin.

Riker was blasted into the Ekahal, throwing both of them backwards onto the stone path that lined the top of the wall.

Kromm raced to his son who was sprawled out near the back wall. "Riker!" he yelled, as he kneeled beside him. Lor-telliam was slowly getting to his feet. Everyone else ran over to the prince, hoping for the best but fearing the worst.

To everyone's amazement, the prince showed no signs of the attack. His white armor was perfect, shining with the same brilliance. Nothing was burning or smoking. In fact his eyes were wide and bright and a smile graced his face.

"Father, I feel so alive," he said.

"Thank Ulren, but how can this be?" Kromm whispered, helping his son to his feet.

"He is Ishmian," Lor-telliam said. "What he feels now is an awakening of his power. He absorbed the power of that spell, and that energy is racing through him, giving him new strength."

"I can't explain it. I feel as if I could fight anything," Riker said.

"You mean that any magical attacks will actually give him more power?" King Baylin asked.

"Yes. I suspected that may be the case. Now I am sure. And Prince, that was a foolish thing to do, but I thank you nonetheless," Lor-telliam said as he gripped Riker's shoulder. "Your courage honors us all."

No one was looking, however, as Gullanin the Lich lifted his skeletal body off the ground and walked away, the burnt edges of his cloak fluttering behind him, apparently unharmed by the Ekahal's powerful spell.

Just as Jonas and Allindrian were about to be pushed into the wall housing the gate mechanisms, they were relieved to hear the cavalry crash into the orcs. Then Jonas heard another sound that cheered him even more, a great roar that came from his left, and quickly followed by the massive form of Tulari leaping from the stairs and crashing into the orcs below. He had left her below the wall, along with Hagar, Tuvallis, and Seli, who were helping the men at the catapults. The ogrillion's great strength was invaluable when loading the heavy projectiles onto the throwing arms of the large weapons.

Jonas was amazed at her agility. To get to the stairs she would have had to leap over the mass of orcs surrounding him, both dead and alive, land on the stairs above, then pivot and launch herself back towards him. Each leap must have been at least fifteen paces.

He had no time to marvel at her skills, however, as the Gould-Irin continued their onslaught. Jonas and Allindrian had managed to slow the orcs' advance, but they were steadily losing ground, even with Tulari's presence. They had managed to hold their own so far, but they were severely outnumbered and were beginning to tire. Jonas struggled to react in time as two pitted and bloody swords came at him simultaneously. It was all he could do to block the powerful strikes. At the same time, the heavy boot of one of the creatures shot forward and struck him in the hip, pushing him backwards even further. Stumbling, he spun in a circle leading with a blade, and took the charging orc in the throat. Tulari, rushing to his defense, wrapped her huge jaws around its torso, and flung the massive creature into its comrades as if it were no more than a mouse she was playing with. It was a testament to her incredible strength that she was able to toss around a creature as large as a Gould-Irin orc, who easily weighed twice as much as a man.

Jonas had a brief reprieve as its body crashed into the front line of the advancing monsters. He glanced back and saw they were only five paces from the gatehouse door. When he turned back to face the orcs they were already charging. Then, out of the corner of his eye, he saw something strange, several orcs flying into the air, hurled from their feet like rocks from a catapult. Landing amongst their comrades they caused momentary confusion.

"Hagar!" Allindrian yelled with new vigor.

And she was right. Jonas saw the beast's upper torso pushing through the crowd of orcs, carving a bloody path with great swings of his huge mace. Crumpled enemy forms flew left and right as he smashed his way toward them, the rays of the morning sun sparkling off his mirror-like armor. Nothing could stand in the ogrillion's way. And though several orc blades had struck his legs, his skin was as tough as leather armor, and the blades' strikes were merely glancing blows, creating only minor wounds that did not slow him in the least. One orc hurled a giant spear at him, as thick as a man's wrist, striking the ogrillion in the chest. But it was deflected by his armor and dropped harmlessly to the ground, leaving not a single mark.

Within moments the eleven foot creature was standing next to Jonas and they were fighting side by side. Jonas risked a glance Hagar's way and was relieved to see that Tuvallis and Seli had joined the fight. The mountain man must have followed in Hagar's wake, and where Tuvallis went, Seli would not be far away. The trio seldom left each other's side. Tuvallis was one of the few humans that the ogrillion trusted and he had taken it upon himself to protect the beast from the fear and prejudice that were often directed toward the soft hearted monster. Most of the soldiers tolerated the beast, some even respected him, but many still looked upon the ogrillion with fear and disdain. It was hard for them to see past the reputation of his ancestors, and his giant form, fierce eyes, and the yellow fangs that were made for tearing flesh did little to alleviate their fears.

The magical dimension door had disappeared when Lor-telliam had attacked and injured Gullanin, the wizard who had conjured it, shutting off the steady flow of orcs. It wasn't long before the mounted knights had cut their way through the beasts to meet up with the defenders at the gatehouse door. The ground was littered everywhere with orc bodies, but they had piled up in greater numbers near the five warriors.

Lathrin dismounted, stepping over enemy corpses as Jonas wiped the blood from his blades on the dirty tunic of a fallen orc. "Well met. Impressive," was all he said as he looked around at the bodies. "If not for you they may have opened that gate." Lathrin looked up at the ogrillion with a mixture of surprise, gratitude, and uncertainty. "I have never seen a creature fight like that. He is…amazing, and…puzzling at the same time."

"I learned from a friend a while back that things are never as black and white as we think," Jonas said, momentarily melancholy as he thought of Taleen, wishing she could be with him, fighting side by side.

"You may be right," was all he said as he looked up at Hagar. "Thank you, Hagar, for being here."

Hagar smiled, revealing his fearsome teeth as he knelt on one knee. Reaching out he put a big hand upon Lathrin's armored shoulder. Hagar's hand was twice as big as Lathrin's head, making the gesture look rather awkward. Lathrin tensed instinctively. A giant monster reaching toward one's head with hands capable of snapping one's neck like a twig was a bit unsettling, to say the least. "Friend," was all he said before withdrawing his hand and standing up proudly.

Regaining his composure, Lathrin shook his head in bewilderment, and turned to give orders to his men. "Burn these beasts! And we will remain here to protect the gate in case the vile scum tries this again."

Jonas turned to Tuvallis, Seli, and Hagar, smiling warmly. "Thank you for coming to our aid. I fear it would have ended badly without your help."

Hagar, beginning to feel more comfortable with Jonas, tapped him on the shoulder and repeated his new favorite word, "Friend."

Jonas stumbled backward from the power of the *tap* and they all laughed, releasing some of the tension that comes from battle and confronting death.

The fighting continued throughout the day. Orcs and goblins attempted to storm the city. They continued to mass around the siege towers that rolled against the outer wall. Some machines were burned before they reached the wall, while others were destroyed by the spells of Alerion, Addalis, and the wizards from Shyval. Others were destroyed by oil and fire after frantic fighting along the battlements. So far, the defenders had been able to keep the monsters from breaching or destroying the wall, and by the time the sun had set the wall was still standing and the gate remained sealed.

The wizards from Shyval had been instrumental in destroying several of the towers, and on several occasions from keeping the monsters from overwhelming them. Boranthos, the old wizard, had sent a stinking wall of fog towards the opening of a tower as the creatures emerged with killing glee in their eyes. The stench of it was so vile and permeating that it caused them to fall back, stumbling down the stairs and clogging the tower stairs long enough to give the defenders time to regroup. Talic, the younger battle wizard burned one tower with a powerful fire ball killing at least thirty orcs. In one instance a group of orcs had nearly overrun several hands of defenders along the north wall when Lizarcus jumped to the top of the battlements, at the risk of exposing herself to archers below, and shot a magical cone of ice into the throng of attacking orcs. The only way to hit the orcs was to shoot the cone above the heads of the Finarthian warriors, and the only way she could do that was from an elevated position along the battlements. Her attack just missed the defenders, the front line of the orcs froze instantly, covered with a sheet of ice that extended outward and along the stone pavers causing the beasts behind them to slip and fall. This gave the defenders time to regroup and attack, massacring the orcs before they could recover. Unfortunately the brave attack did not go unnoticed below. Before Lizarcus could jump down from the wall, the orcs on the ground had riddled her with arrows, killing her instantly, her body falling to the ground where it was hacked to pieces.

The great black Demon Dragon continued its attacks throughout the day, killing thousands of defenders. They had no real defense against the beast and the spells of the two Ekahals barely seemed to slow the thing. At one point Alerion had managed to strike the dragon in the chest with a powerful fireball, but the explosion merely rocked the thing backwards, causing no more damage than a few singed patches of skin. Since the beast came from the lower planes of fire, it remained relatively unfazed by such an attack.

They had to find a way to destroy the dragon and that topic occupied most of the discussion at the council that night. General Gandarin was stationed on the outer wall and was in charge of the city's defenses while everyone else met in the king's council room to discuss the day's battles and what to do about the dragon.

"The thing seems to be resistant to spells, even my magic barely harms it," Lor-telliam said.

"What are our options?" King Baylin asked everyone at the table. The wizards from Shyval were in attendance along with Alerion, Addalis, King Kromm, King Baylin, Durgen, Jonas, Allindrian, and both Ekahals.

"Magical weapons," Lor-telliam said. "For some reason magical spells don't seem to harm it much, but I think magical weapons may be able to cut through whatever protective barrier has thus far thwarted our magic."

"But how do we get close enough to fight something like that with sword and spear?" Jonas asked.

"We need to knock it from de air," Durgen interjected. Everyone turned to look at the dwarf as he continued. "If I told ya that I had a great spear, a bolt made from mithril silver that could fit into a ballista, would ya be able to imbue it with proper spells to kill the dragon?" the dwarf asked the Ekahal.

The elf thought for a moment. "Yes, I believe so, but it would take several days and that means I would be off the wall while I worked on it." Everyone could now clearly see the Ekahal age, his once perfect skin etched in new wrinkles and his golden hair was now almost all silver.

"I think it may be worth that risk," Kiln said slowly. "That dragon is killing thousands and it may get bolder and try to break open the outer gate. We can't let that happen."

"Do you have such a bolt?" Kromm asked.

"Aye...me weaponsmith's been workin' on such a spear as soon as word about de beast arrived from da Garrison. It will be done tomorrow."

"We need to bring the beast down on our side of the wall where we can finish it off," Allindrian added.

"Will our weapons harm it?" Jonas asked.

"I believe some will," Lor-telliam said. "Jonas, yours would surely, as well as any sword made by Tsillerian Cho Andoran, which includes Allindrian's as well as Tihr-Alliam." Tsillerian Cho Andoran was the ancient weaponsmith from the elven kingdom of Mel'un-riam. She made Tihr-Alliam over a thousand years ago and she created the weapons for every Blade Singer for as long as any elf could remember, and that is a long time. No one really knew how old she was, but there was no maker of weapons that could compare, even the dwarf masters praised her skill, and a dwarf praising anyone, especially an elf, was a rare thing. "Allindrian, your bow may harm it as well," Lor-telliam added.

"I made this axe with me own sweat and blood," Durgen said, patting the blade that was leaning against the table. "It was imbued with spells by de greatest dwarven clerics. It will hurt dis beast," Durgen said matter-of-factly.

"Very well," King Baylin said. "We bring the dragon to the ground and if Durgen's spear doesn't kill it, then we will."

"We cannot risk the prince's life with this dragon," Alerion said. "He is too important."

"I can wield Tihr-Alliam," King Baylin said.

Everyone looked at the king, including Prince Riker who wore the blade at his hip.

"This is my city, and I should protect it," the king continued.

"What of Hagar?" Jonas asked. "His weapon is blessed by Shyann as well."

"Yes, and his power will be helpful for such a task," Lor-telliam responded.

"Then it is settled. Lor-telliam, please inform us when the spear is ready. Now, get some rest while you can," King Baylin added, standing up from the table. Everyone followed the king's lead and prepared to do just that, for they knew that they would need all the rest they could get for the battles to come.

It was late into the night when something awoke Durgen from his sleep. His men had been given quarters in the catacombs below the king's palace. The halls were narrow and the rooms' small, but it was perfect for a dwarf. Most of the musty rooms were used for storage and they had to rearrange quite a few supplies to make room for the nine hundred dwarven warriors. The king's secret escape passage was located deep within these tunnels and Durgen had been shown its whereabouts. A long tunnel led well beyond the walls and emerged in the forest beyond the city. The opening was blocked by a solid door of iron over which a concealment spell had been placed. There was no key hole or lock on the outside; it could only be opened from the inside, and only the king, Alerion, Kiln, and the generals had that key.

A low deep booming had stirred him from his slumber. At first he thought he was hearing things but then it came again, this time a little louder. Some dust shook loose from the wood rafters above and rained down upon him. Something wasn't right.

He was curled up on a cot in a small room. Ballick, his second in command, was sleeping on a wool blanket to his right. To his left lay Olandar Rockfist, a powerful cleric of Moredin and third in command after Ballick. Durgen woke them both and grabbed his mithril axe. The sturdy dwarf slept in his armor and boots so he needed nothing else. "Get up, I sense something is wrong."

Without a word Ballick and Olandar grabbed their weapons, slipped on their iron shod boots, and followed Durgen out the small door. The dark haired cleric wore silver armor etched with magical symbols and wards. His long beard was braided on both sides and there were streaks of grey in his long unruly hair. An intricate symbol was tattooed on the dwarf's left cheek and he carried a short war hammer and a small round shield called a buckler. Durgen hesitated in the hallway a moment, listening, but nothing broke the silence.

"What did ya hear?" Ballick asked.

"A low booming sound; it was not loud, I felt it more den anything." The tunnel they were in split to the left and the right. The tunnel to the right led to the storerooms and hundreds of sleeping dwarves, eventually leading to the inner castle. The left tunnel went further down into the ground and led to more storerooms that were temporary quarters for more dwarves. The tunnel then continued on to a magically sealed door that led to a final door that was magically concealed and opened to the forests located around the city. This was the king's secret escape route. Durgen remained in the hall, continuing to listen intently for anything out of the ordinary.

Leaning his axe against the stone wall he put both hands on the cold rock. The tunnel had been crudely carved with picks and every mark could be seen on the dull grey rock. Durgen was a Daz-rothos, which meant that he was able to speak to the stone; all master traders had that ability. As he touched the stone he began to chant. Anyone listening would have heard only gibberish, but to a dwarf who was Daz-rothos, the garbled sound that came from Durgen was a chant that connected him to the stone, conveying feelings through a sharing of energy transformed into images.

Durgen's chanting abruptly stopped as he pulled his hands away from the stone as if it were red hot. "Call the alarm, the enemy is near!" he yelled.

Ballick wore a ram's horn around his neck that was used for various signals in battle. He brought it to his lips and blew a series of notes. It was deafening in the tight confines of the passage and immediately they heard the commotion of dwarves jumping from their beds as the cry of alarm carried down the passageway.

They also heard distant howls come from somewhere deep to the left. Whatever was coming towards them had found the secret entrance and were already in the tunnels.

"Where do we make a stand?" Ballick asked.

"We have men down there," Durgen said as he advanced to the left, toward the approaching sound. "Let us make a stand there, where our numbers are greatest."

"Wait!" Olandar said. "Somethin's not right." The cleric thumbed an amulet around his neck, whispering words of prayer to Moredin, god of the dwarves. The silver amulet was a circle embossed with an anvil and hammer, Moredin's symbol of power. It began to glow, shedding a powerful light down the dark tunnel. Dwarfs can see in the dark, but they could not see the mist slowly creeping up the tunnel, a vile green cloud that was almost upon them. "Back up!" Olandar shouted. Both dwarfs quickly jumped behind the cleric. He began to chant louder, the light from the symbol flaring even brighter, this time hitting the noxious mist and repelling it backward. "It's poisonous and thick with evil," Olandar said, holding his ground, the magic light creating a barrier between them.

"What of my men?" Durgen yelled behind him.

"Killed in their sleep," was all Olandar said. Durgen swore, growling furiously.

Armed dwarves from the opposite tunnel emerged from various side rooms filling the tunnel quickly. Only two dwarfs at a time could fight side by side in the tight space, but this was the kind of fighting fit for a dwarf. This was what they were good at.

"Send a messenger to de castle in case they did not hear de horn," Durgen ordered. Ballick passed the message to a runner who pushed his way through the milling warriors.

Durgen turned to face his men. "Dwarves!" he yelled. "Something has found a way in and comes at us now! Whatever we face here must not make it past us!"

The war cries of hundreds of dwarves filled the tunnel.

A chorus of screeching sounds began to emerge from the dark hallway. Whatever was coming was getting closer. Dwarves could see in the dark and they gripped their weapons tightly as they gazed into the blackness. The mist was now retreating and in moments it had completely dissipated. The light from Olandar's amulet had also dissipated back into the silver symbol around his neck.

There were probably only two hundred dwarves filling the halls behind them, all that were left of the original thousand. Most of the men had been sleeping deeper in the tunnels where the strange mist had found them in their sleep.

The shrill howls suddenly got louder, erupting in a cacophony of screeches down the hallway. Whatever had gotten in was almost upon them. "Olandar, bring up your cleric light!" Durgen yelled over the din of eerie screams. The perceptive dwarf always trusted his instincts and something was telling him that the type of creature attacking them was not of their world, something dark and evil, which meant that the cleric's light, similar to a cavalier's, might aid them greatly

Olandar said not a word but this time lifted his hammer while he prayed to Moredin. Within moments the hammer lit up like a white star, the bright light bathing the dark tunnel.

What they saw coming at them was unlike anything they had ever seen before, creatures resembling scurrying cockroaches, human in form, but smaller, much thinner, and with longer limbs. Their skin was an opaque white, and large bulging eyes, the color of churned cream, with no pupils, peered out from their bony heads. Bat-like ears protruded from their skulls and their mouths, filled with razor sharp teeth resembling crystals, glittered in the magical light. The long digits of their hands and feet were tipped with sharp white claws that allowed them to grip the stone of the tunnel like lizards. Some scurried along the ground while others climbed along the walls and ceiling.

When they hit the light they screeched even louder, hesitating, using their hands to cover their large translucent eyes.

"Crossbows, aim for the ones on the ceiling!" Durgen yelled. The advantage of being short was that the dwarves could actually maneuver in the tight confines of the tunnel. Several dwarves with crossbows came forward and even with the low ceiling they could still fire the weapons above the heads of their comrades. Several bolts hit their marks and the creatures fell to the ground. But they did not die. They tore the bolts from their flesh and resumed their charge, despite the light.

"They are demons!" Olandar shouted as the creatures were almost upon them.

"None get by us!" Durgen shouted, swinging his axe, taking one in the skull, and splitting its head like a melon.

One leaped from the wall towards Olandar who lifted his buckler to protect himself, while swinging his glowing hammer at the same time. The creature hit the shield and the hammer struck it in the side. There was a bright pulse of light as the cleric's enchanted weapon crushed its torso, caving in bones and flesh.

Olandar and Durgen fought side by side, not giving up a foot of ground. Hammer and axe worked in unison, crushing and slicing the strange creatures as they came near. As bodies began to pile up they were forced to back up to keep from stumbling over the grotesque corpses.

The creatures were not only hideous to look at, but they also exuded a putrid stench as well, filling the narrow tunnels with the smell of rotting flesh and garbage.

Several of them managed to get past the two warriors by scurrying across the ceiling, but the crossbowmen easily dispatched them and they fell into the mass of dwarves where they met a barrage of axes and hammers, most of which were not magical, but nonetheless the sheer numbers of them pounded the creatures to a bloody pulp. Not all dwarves came away unscathed however. The crossbowmen couldn't load their weapons fast enough to keep up with the attacking demons. As more demons made it over the top of Olandar and Durgen, they began dropping onto the dwarves, oblivious of the danger, sharp claws and teeth finding their targets and killing handfuls before the demons could be dispatched by their comrades.

Olandar, seeing the creatures scuttle across the ceiling, switched tactics. "Give me a moment!" the dwarf shouted to Durgen, stepping back behind the axe wielding fighter. Durgen, understanding the move, blocked the narrow tunnel on his own, his glittering axe flashing left and right as he cut the creatures into pieces.

Durgen heard Olandar chanting behind him. Within moments the cleric yelled for Durgen to move. Durgen dodged to the side as Olandar shot his left hand forward, sending a devastating cone of fire down the narrow hallway. He could only use the spell one time a day, and he was hoping to save it, but their present need made the decision for him.

The searing flames filled the entire hall transforming the creatures into sizzling husks of burnt flesh. Thuds could be heard as the creatures fell from the ceiling to die with their brethren on the ground. The screeching sound of agonized howling reverberated down the tunnel as dozens of demons perished.

"Move back!" Durgen yelled as the vile smoke from the burning corpses filled the tunnel. Their retreat was slowed by the large number of warriors in the narrow tunnel, but eventually they were able to shuffle back, past storerooms, and into the main antechamber that housed the stairs leading to the inner castle. "Well done, Olandar," Durgen said to the cleric.

Olandar, grunting in acknowledgement, looked at the fighters around them. The antechamber held five grim faced warriors, all officers, and all carrying magical weapons. The rest of the dwarves retreated to the inner castle where by now the rest of the castle guard was surely preparing their defense. The stairs behind them were choked with axe wielding dwarves.

Their reprieve was brief, however, as they heard the screeching resume again. Within moments, waves of the pale creatures had emerged from the tunnel opening, moving so incredibly fast that the room was filled with them almost instantly.

"Block the stairs!" Durgen yelled as seven dwarves fought to do just that. Handfuls of the demons dropped on them from above as others attacked from all sides. "Form up!" Durgen ordered, realizing the impending danger.

But two of the dwarves were blocked by angry demons before they could backtrack to the line forming at the base of the stairs. They frantically swung their axes into the hoard of demons, but in moments they were overwhelmed and literally torn to pieces. Blood splattered the stone walls and the coppery smell seemed to drive the demons mad, the sound of their howls reaching a higher pitch as the blood stirred them into a frenzy. They wanted more, and with blood drenched teeth and claws, they leaped at the five defenders.

"Moredin!" Olandar screamed, lifting his hammer. Bright light pulsed from the weapon as he sent a shock wave crashing into the attacking demons, launching them backwards against the stone wall. Some crashed into their comrades, while others were crushed by the force of the strike as they hit the wall, their crumpled bodies falling to the ground like overripe fruit.

Prince Riker could not sleep. His mind was a whirlwind of thoughts and images, scenes of the fighting he had witnessed from the walls, anxiety about the coming days, and the frustration of facing the unknown. The enormity of his task, that of which was to confront and defeat Malbeck, was a heavy burden and it consumed his thoughts to the point where nothing else filled his head. He needed to walk, to try and calm his mind.

Climbing from his bed he slipped on his breeches and tunic. The stones were cold on his bare feet. He found his boots at the foot of the bed and put them on. King Ullis's armor was draped over a bust near the bed and Tihr-Alliam leaned against it. Riker sighed, grabbing the sword and leaving his chambers.

There were always two guards outside his door. They were surprised to see him at such a late hour. "I can't sleep," the prince said. "I need to take a walk."

One guard looked at the other uncertainly. "My Lord, we have been ordered to watch over you," the knight said.

"Are your orders to keep me locked in my room?" Riker asked, slightly annoyed.

"Uh.... no, my Lord," the knight stammered.

"Well then, why don't we take a walk together? That way I get what I want and you are still following orders."

The other knight looked at his partner and shrugged. "As you wish, my Lord."

A horn suddenly shattered the silence of the night. The sound was slightly muffled and reverberated from the stone floor and up through the walls. The guards looked at each other and quickly drew their swords. "Sounds like it's below us," one knight said, unsure of what to do.

"The dwarves, they are in the catacombs," Riker said as he unsheathed his own blade. Immediately Tihr-Alliam flared white, chasing away the shadows of the dark hallway. The knights, shocked by the sudden light, instinctively stepped back. Even in his night clothes and boots the prince looked like a king of legend while holding that enchanted blade. "Sound the alarm!" Riker shouted as he sprinted down the hallway. All guards wore horns for just such a purpose and soon the bellowing of warning alarms sounded throughout the inner castle. After sounding the alarm both guards hastily ran after the prince.

Riker's room was next to his father's and mother's quarters, and he knew that Jonas, Allindrian, and the other esteemed guests were also quartered in this wing of the castle, but his exuberant youth took over and he ran past them, following the steps to the lower sections of the castle. He knew they had heard the alarm and would be just behind him. An unfamiliar anteroom loomed before him and he hesitated in front of its two doors. Both guards skidded to a halt behind him.

"Prince, what are you doing?" a guard asked, sucking in deep breaths.

They were interrupted by the familiar sounds of fighting coming from somewhere below them. Piercing screeches punctuated the sound of clashing weapons, the rumble of boots on stone, and the screams and battle cries of the chaos of war. "We are under attack. I am going to their aid. Which way to the catacombs?"

"We can't allow you to go down there. We don't know what is happening, it is too dangerous," the other guard stammered as the entire castle came awake. The sounds of fighting below grew even louder and they also heard the sound of approaching boots on stone above them.

"I'm going through one of these doors whether you like it or not. You can stay with me as my guards or stay here, the choice is yours, now which way?" Riker asked again.

One knight looked at the other, sighing in acquiescence. "Take the right, but we go first."

Riker nodded and stepped aside.

A few of the creatures managed to get past the five warriors but dozens fell to their dwarven steel. Bodies began to fill the anteroom and the defenders on the stairs and beyond engaged many of the lizard-like creatures that scurried across the ceiling. But still they came, in countless numbers pressing in on the five warriors who were valiantly attempting to guard the entrance to the stairs. One dwarf, a veteran warrior, finally succumbed to the demons. As he was trying to yank his axe from the bony chest of one of the fallen creatures, he was left vulnerable for a split second, just enough time for the long arms of one of the beasts to snake out with lightning speed and, like a hunting cat, sink its sharp claws into the unfortunate dwarf, pulling him into their midst. The warrior's screams died in seconds, his blood streaking the floor below them.

One of the demons raced above Olandar, dropping straight down on him as he struggled with two others. Sharp claws found his flesh between the seams of his armor and the sharp pain shooting through his body added strength to the swing of his hammer as he crushed one demon while blocking the attack of another with his small shield. Luckily for the cleric there were other dwarves behind them and one of them instinctively snapped his axe forward, burying it into the spine of the creature attacking the cleric. It was a dangerous move. If he had missed he may have hit the cleric. But he didn't miss, and the demon convulsed briefly, then fell to the side. The weapon, however, was not magical and the temporarily stunned creature quickly revived, reaching up with long curved talons and raking deep cuts down Olandar's inner thighs. Screaming from the pain he stomped his metal shod boot on the creature's chest, following up with a powerful strike of his war hammer. The demon's head burst like a putrid bubble, its bile green contents splattering those around it. It was then that the cleric felt himself being yanked backwards by strong arms.

"Up the stairs!" Durgen yelled, slowly retreating up the stone steps, fighting all the while, as the endless wave of monsters continued to emerge from the tunnels below.

Olandar was faintly aware of being carried up the stairs by his courageous comrades, though he was slowly losing consciousness. The last thing he remembered was the feeling of pulsing liquid running down his right leg.

Durgen made it to the top of the stairs knowing they would be in a bigger anteroom than the one before. No more demons emerged from the dark hole marking the opening to the stairs they just ascended. This room was used as a guardroom to the storage rooms below and it was now filled with fighting dwarves and the dozen demons that had made it past them. It was a relatively spacious room with walls lined with bunks and a big oak table sat in the middle. Durgen knew that six guards were stationed there, and was grateful to know they would be able to join in the fight.

Less than a dozen demons had made it past Durgen and his comrades, and within moments they had all been slain. The room was eerily silent as forty dwarves and six Finarthian knights stared into the dark opening with weapons drawn. The prone body of Olandar caught his eye and Durgen noticed that the unconscious dwarf had a tourniquet tied around his right leg. He had obviously lost consciousness and that worried him. Durgen knew that he had at least a hundred more dwarves behind them blocking all entrances into the king's palace and that the palace guards would now likely be joining his men in a defensive position.

"Form up," Durgen growled. Immediately twenty dwarves ran forward and formed a perimeter against anything that might come up those stairs. The other dwarves formed a second line and the few palace guards stood behind them. "Get the wounded out of here," Durgen ordered and the palace guards made themselves useful, following his orders, several grabbing Olandar and carrying him from the room.

As the wounded were carried away, they heard something come up the stairs. It was a slow scraping sound as if something were being dragged up the stone steps. As they stared into the darkness of the opening, two glowing red orbs appeared, followed by a black cloaked spectre that stepped through the darkness and into the room. A skeletal arm reached forward from the darkness, holding a black staff in its hand, an appendage which appeared to be nothing more than bones covered with flakes of decomposed skin. It carried no other weapons.

A wave of fear buffeted the defenders, and every man and dwarf stepped backward, a little less sure of themselves in the presence of this creature. One bony hand pulled back the dark hood revealing the face of a corpse, dried and rotting skin drawn tight around a skull covered with patches of matted gray hair. Decayed yellow teeth and rotting gums were fully exposed as it had no lips with which to cover them.

Gullanin, the Lich, laughed, the sound coming out like a gurgling hiss. "Well done, I had not expected the catacombs guarded, and by dwarves no less."

"You killed hundreds of my men," Durgen said, his voice a low rumble, infused with anger.

"More will die, as will you," the Lich said. Then he began a low hoarse chant.

"Shoot him!" Durgen yelled. Several dozen dwarven crossbows twanged but the bolts fell harmlessly to the ground as if they had hit an invisible wall.

Gullanin then casually flicked his hand and every dwarf and man in the room began to choke, except Durgen, who looked about frantically as his men, including Ballick, his longtime friend, dropped their weapons, and grabbed at their throats. The sounds of them gasping for breath filled the room, and almost immediately they began to fall to their knees, desperately attempting to inhale air that was no longer there.

"You can watch your men die," the Lich hissed.

"No!" Durgen roared, charging the undead creature. He came in low, swinging his axe in a wide arc trying to cut the thing's legs out from underneath it. Gullanin flicked his staff to the right and Durgen was hurled forcefully against the wall by some invisible force. The impact was great but Durgen was a dwarf, an enraged one at that, and he righted himself quickly, coming at the Lich again.

This time Gullanin whispered a few words releasing a bolt of lightning which shot from its staff, striking Durgen. But the undead wizard had forgotten about Durgen's axe. Not so long ago, when Gullanin was human, he had attacked Kromm in the Tundren Mountains. The magical attack meant for Kromm hit Durgen's axe and was absorbed by the magical weapon. The same thing happened again, the burning energy of the bolt was absorbed by his axe. But just as before, the power of the strike knocked Durgen from his feet, and this time he didn't land on the soft ground but was smashed up against the stone wall a second time. This time he wasn't so fast in getting up.

The rest of the dwarves had stopped struggling, lying still in death, but more raced into the room to take their comrades' places. They looked around in horror as the last of their friends died, the sturdy warriors gagging on their own tongues.

"Ah, you're *that* dwarf?" Gullanin said. "I owe you," he hissed, and he began chanting again, just as fifteen dwarves charged him, eager to help their struggling leader. This time a vortex appeared in front of the Lich, and from it emerged a huge swarm of hornet-like insects, each as large as a man's thumb, which descended on them like flies on garbage. Within seconds every dwarf in the room was covered by hundreds of the stinging creatures. The warriors screamed in pain, futilely swinging their axes and hammers in the air. But this was an enemy they could not fight with steel, and as more warriors rushed into the room, more began to die.

"Now it's your turn," the Lich whispered, turning towards Durgen. He raised his arm, releasing an invisible force that lifted the dwarf off the ground and slammed him against the wall with such incredible force that Durgen nearly lost consciousness. Then Gullanin did it again, and again, until Durgen was a limp hunk of flesh. Finally the lich dropped him to the ground with a thud.

"Stop!" someone bellowed from the opening that led to the upper castle. A dazzling bright light filled the room as Riker emerged carrying Tihr-Alliam. The two palace guards flanking him stared in horror at the scene before them, their eyes wide with terror. Dwarf bodies filled the room in piles; their lifeless forms swollen beyond recognition from thousands of lethal stings. The hornets had quickly retreated from the light, disappearing back into the swirling vortex where it snapped out of sight.

Gullanin moved forward slowly, his bony feet scraping on the stone floor. "What do we have here?" he said, but he was tired of playing games. "Remember me? I will have to rectify the mistake I made when I faced you and your father at Cuthaine." And with just a few words lightning crackled from his staff, striking all three of them. The palace guards were hurled into the wall, dying on impact, their bodies burnt and smoking. The bolt aimed at Riker struck the sword and evaporated into his body.

Gullanin's red eyes flared wide in confusion. It wasn't just that his magic had been negated; it was as if it had been wiped away, as if it had never existed. It didn't even stun the warrior who wasted no time in charging him.

Riker, roared in fury, his Ishmian energy ignited, giving him the strength and courage of ten men. He charged the undead wizard, who lifted his staff with both hands to block the attack. His sword met the

Lich's staff and a blinding light flared as the staff split in two. The explosion that followed launched the evil wizard off its feet.

Gullanin slid across the ground, immediately raising his arms to bring forth more magic. His hands erupted in flames and two large flaming cones of fire shot forward, striking Riker directly in the chest.

The prince felt something, a force of some sort, rise up in him. It was as if his skin was covered with a thin layer of shimmering light, and if anyone witnessed it they would have been amazed to see his form briefly encased in the orange flames. The protective energy that surrounded him fed on the magic of the fire and soon the flames dissipated into smoke and steam, but Riker stood their unharmed, his eyes bright, and energized with new power.

As he stood facing a bewildered Gullanin, the room flooded with more defenders from the castle above. Jonas, Allindrian, Kromm, and over thirty elite palace guards had hastily armed themselves and rushed down the stairs to defend against this new threat. They stopped momentarily as they quickly took in the scene before them.

"Son," Kromm said in bewilderment, unaware that Riker had already left his room before the others.

Meanwhile Gullanin had regained his feet. This time he quickly conjured a giant disembodied hand which materialized next to him, forming a fist which instantly hurled itself forward in a powerful punch toward Riker. Riker, swinging his sword defensively, sliced through the magical hand easily, causing the magic to falter and flutter, consequently doing no damage to the prince. Unfazed by the wizard's attack he continued his momentum, stepping forward into the Lich, reversing his swing and slicing into the wizard from hip to shoulder. Gullanin stumbled backwards as the tip of Tihr-Alliam cut through his flesh. Riker wasted no time and brought the enchanted blade across Gullanin's throat, separating the wizard's head from his body for a second time. There was a flash of light as Gullanin fell to the floor, his head landing a few seconds later. His body burst into flames, the magical energy used to create him dissipating, leaving behind nothing but ash.

"Riker, in Ulren's name what has happened!?" Kromm yelled, rushing forward to join his son. Riker turned to face his father, his eyes glowing. Kromm stepped back slightly, having never before seen his son in such a state. "Are you okay?" he asked as the others joined him and the palace guards went about their duty of checking for wounded among the many bodies strewn throughout the room.

"I'm fine, Father," he said. "I've never felt better. That thing's magic could not harm me, did you see that?"

"I did. You did well," Kromm said, gripping his son's shoulder. "But next time wait for us."

Before Riker could reply they heard a low groan from the corner of the room. Turning, they saw Durgen stir slightly, his body crumpled against the wall, blood dripping from his ears, mouth, and nose. But his eyes were open.

They ran to him and Allindrian was the first to arrive at his side. "Durgen, can you hear me?" she asked, cradling his head in her lap.

"Not feelin'…good," he mumbled weakly.

Kromm turned to the palace guards. "Get a healer in here now!" he ordered.

King Baylin then rushed through the door with his sword held low, surrounded by a dozen guards. Kiln was with him. They rushed over to the group in the corner, eyes wide with shock at the destruction around them.

"What happened?" the king asked.

"We know not," Jonas answered. "When we arrived the prince had just killed a black cloaked wizard. Everyone had already been killed. The only one alive is Master Durgen."

"It was Gullanin the wizard. He was some type of undead demon," Riker said.

"A Lich," Allindrian spat.

"You killed it?" Kiln asked the young warrior.

"Yes," Riker replied.

"Impressive," Kiln said, tapping the young warrior on the shoulder.

"I can do a healing spell," the Blade Singer said, "but my power is limited and I'm afraid that without further aid he will die. It looks like he has suffered severe internal damage." She immediately began to chant, and her hands began to glow with a soft blue light. She placed them on both sides of his head as she sent her limited healing power into the mortally wounded dwarf. Durgen shuddered once before losing consciousness.

"What matter of creature is this?" Kiln asked, kicking at one of the beasts lying on the ground.

"It appears to be some sort of demon," Jonas said.

"When I came into the room I saw the wizard fling Durgen against the wall. He was the only one left. I think all our answers will come from the dwarf," Riker suggested.

"Then we need him healed. Where is that healer!?" King Baylin demanded.

Twelve
The Final Fight

Durgen lay quietly in his room covered with blankets, his eyes open, feeling nothing but pain and anger. There was a knock at his door and King Baylin entered wearing battle armor, his face covered with sweat and grime.

"How are your injuries?" the king asked, pulling up a chair next to the tired dwarf.

"I'll live thanks to your healers," he grumbled.

"They say you'll be up tomorrow. That's amazing considering how many bones were broken. You're lucky we got to you when we did."

"Luckier than me men it would seem."

"Aye, that is why I came here. I want to thank you for your courage and sacrifice. If you and your men had not been in the catacombs those creatures would have entered the castle and slaughtered everyone in their beds. This war would be over."

Durgen looked at the king. "It's not the deaths that anger me so. We dwarfs are miners, but also warriors, and death looms over all warriors. It is how they died, their axes and weapons useless in their hands. That wizard killed them dishonorably with black magic and me heart aches to avenge them."

"You must have a big heart to hold all that revenge," the king said. "Be careful or it will consume you as it is consuming me. I have known no joy for over a year. There seems to be no room in my heart for anything but thoughts of revenge. It is poisoning my soul. I fear the only way to escape it is by death."

"If death eases my pain then so be it," Durgen muttered, "I will be with me brothers in Moredin's great hall."

"You haven't lost everyone, good dwarf. You had men working on the bridge and they are alive still," the king said as he stood to leave. He placed his hand on the dwarf's shoulder. "Thank you again, Master

Trader. By the way, the spear is ready for tomorrow. Will you be joining us in that fight?"

"Aye, I'll be with ya."

***

Malbeck slammed his fist onto the table, splitting it in half and scattering maps and parchments everywhere. "Thrice now that wizard has failed me!" Malbeck stormed. The Dark One wore charcoal gray plate armor and Gould's eye was etched in red on his breastplate. His armor was the antithesis of what a cavalier would wear, dark, foreboding, smothering anything of light.

Years ago, when Jonas's mother was pregnant with him, Malbeck had taken on the image of Jonas's father, though much larger, with features altered by magic that gave him a demonic appearance. The followers of the Forsworn had made it their duty to seek out those with pure souls and destroy them. When Jonas's mother had become pregnant they had discovered that her unborn child was one of the rare souls with a pure heart. So Malbeck's servants secretly poisoned her, hoping to kill her and her child. They then took his father as a slave, and the clerics of Dykreel had brutally broken him, allowing Malbeck's energy to possess his body when the Dark One was retrieved from the Ru'Ach. Somehow Jonas's mother survived, but the poison affected her child who was born a cripple, and the story of Jonas's life began. The followers of the Forsworn had failed, and now that failure had come back to haunt Malbeck.

Korthanos, the last of the Banthras, and their most powerful leader, stood passively next to the Dark One. They were in a large tent with sconces around its perimeter, subtly lighting the interior with their flickering orange and yellow flames.

"He paid for it with his life force," Korthanos whispered. The great Banthra was covered from head to toe in black spiked armor, red eyes glaring through narrow slits in his helm.

"Who killed him?" Malbeck demanded.

"Our spies reported that the young prince killed Gullanin," Koranthos replied.

"Tihr-Alliam," Malbeck whispered to himself, knowing that the only weapon capable of killing the Lich was that sword. "Why does the prince have the sword?" Malbeck asked, pondering momentarily before looking back at Korthanos. "Prepare the army. I will wait no longer. We breach that wall today!"

***

"Here it comes!" Jonas yelled over the sounds of fighting surrounding them. It was day three and the morning had started off like the mornings before it. Before the sun was even up orcs and goblins again rushed the wall while large stones flung from catapults continued to pound them. The wall was beginning to show signs of the relentless onslaught of stones and missiles. Portions of it were cracked like an eggshell, while great chunks of it were missing in other sections. Parts of the wall were coming dangerously close to caving in. But still it held, and Finarthian archers and soldiers continued to pummel the enemy below with hot oil, spears, and arrows. The sounds of catapult arms releasing their projectiles filled the killing ground between the walls as huge missiles were flung over the outer wall towards the enemy machines in the distance.

Malbeck still had not shown his face, but it was not him they were looking for on this morning...it was the dragon.

They didn't have to wait long, as Kil-Kannon the dragon swooped down towards the gatehouse where Jonas, Allindrian, and Lor-telliam were standing. Kiln was positioned behind the ballista twenty paces away, and loaded in that great machine was a long spear, tipped with a barbed mithril point half the length of a grown man. The glittering silver tip sparkled like fish scales in the sun and embedded in the shaft at the base of the spear point was a series of diamonds. Diamonds were the most effective precious stone for containing magic, and they were often added to magical weapons to maintain and stabilize the magical properties imbued in the weapon. Lor-telliam had spent the last forty eight hours adding spell after spell to the spear. It would not break, and the razor sharp edge could cut through any substance; stone, metal, and dragon scale. The magical properties of the weapon should be able to cut through the dragon's natural defenses and hopefully kill the beast, or at least injure it and bring it down to the ground, but there was only one way to find out for sure.

King Baylin, now wearing King Ullis's armor and carrying Tihr-Alliam, was waiting down in the killing ground with Hagar, Kromm, Tel-andorsis, the other remaining Ekahal, and Durgen. Several priests, among them the king's best healers, had worked on Durgen, sharing the difficult task of getting the dwarf's broken body ready for battle. His injuries were so severe that it had taken a full day to heal him. But the tough dwarf was not yet ready to die, and now he was standing next to the king, his silver axe held at the ready.

The plan was to knock the dragon out of the sky with the spear, hopefully dropping it on their side of the outer wall, somewhere between the two walls. Then they would attack it from the ground while Tel-andorsis shielded them from its breath. It was a dangerous plan and many things could go wrong, but it was a necessary risk as the great beast was killing their men by the hundreds each day.

The dragon was flying their way. Lor-telliam, who was standing on the parapet above the outer gate, began to chant, and within moments the air around him turned bitter cold. He lifted his right hand and a sphere of swirling white mist began to coalesce in his palm. It grew to the size of a human head just as the dragon, sensing the magic of the Ekahal, tucked its wings and dove down at him.

"Wait!" Allindrian yelled. The timing had to be just right for the plan to work.

The dragon was almost upon them when the Ekahal threw the white sphere towards the beast. The magical ball of ice grew larger as it closed the distance, tripling in size, before striking the dragon in the center of its chest.

There was a loud explosion as ice enveloped the creature, forcing it to slow its descent with great flaps of its wings. It shook its head, shattering the frosty white layer of ice that covered it. The beast roared in fury as it frantically hovered just before the gatehouse wall, the weight of the ice making it difficult to fly. As it continued to scream in fury, its body pulsed red and orange, and almost immediately the air around it was filled with scalding steam, completely melting the ice that had covered it.

"Now!" Lor-telliam yelled.

The hovering beast was now an easy target for Kiln. The spell had done little damage but had served its purpose by temporarily halting its dive and providing Kiln with the best opportunity to hit it. They had only one bolt and one chance to destroy it.

Kiln pulled the trigger and released the bolt. Everyone on the wall intently followed its trajectory, knowing full well that this was their only opportunity to use the magical spear. The dragon, sensing the danger, veered to the right and Jonas looked on with horror thinking that the bolt had missed. But then they heard the beast roar in pain, a sound they had not yet heard, and suddenly it was falling directly at them.

"Look out!" Jonas screamed as he ran from the dragon's path. Everyone cleared the top of the gatehouse just as the creature crashed where they had been standing. It was as large as the gatehouse and its immense weight cracked stone and ripped the battlements off the wall. Rocks and dust flew into the air as the beast tumbled from the wall, smashing into the ground and stirring up a cloud of dust and debris.

Jonas, Allindrian, and Lor-telliam quickly regained their footing and raced down the stairs to the killing ground below.

Kil-Kannon roared in pain, stumbling as it attempted to right itself, the long spear jutting from the joint of its left wing. Finarthian soldiers scattered away from the beast knowing full well that they would not be able to harm it. Besides, that was not the plan.

The dragon had literally landed directly in front of King Baylin and the others, and despite the fact that they were prepared for such an event, the incredible size and power of the creature set them on their heels.

Jonas and Allindrian landed gracefully behind the dragon, pausing momentarily to take in the scene. The dragon was frantically beating its right wing, but the left hung uselessly at its side, black blood gushing from the terrible wound. Dust and dirt flew everywhere as the beast's single wing beat back and forth. But more dangerous, even than the wings, was its tail which was swinging side to side and crashing into the ground with enough force to shake the wall behind it.

Tel-andorsis had already prepared a defensive shield in front of the king and their comrades, but the dust was so great that no one could advance because they could not see through the haze.

Then suddenly the dragon stopped struggling, finally realizing that it could no longer fly. It reared up on its hind legs glaring down at the king with malevolent feline eyes. Within seconds the area around the group was filled with blistering hot steam.

Allindrian shot several arrows into the dragon's flank as the hot breath surrounded the Finarthian king. The arrows flashed momentarily as they penetrated its tough hide, but it paid no more attention to them than if they had been mere pinpricks.

Instinctively, even though he knew the Ekahal's shield wall would protect him, the king lifted his magical shield as the hot steam surrounded him. The mist roared around them but none could feel the killing heat, and within moments the steam was gone. Then they attacked.

Hagar bellowed a war cry and with long powerful strides he raced to the right of the dragon while King Baylin and Durgen charged to the left. The plan was to attack the beast from every angle, breaking up the dragon's ability to use its dangerous breath on all of them. But the danger now was they were not protected by the Ekahal's shield.

Kil-Kannon snapped its deadly jaws toward Hagar simultaneously swinging its powerful tail around its body at the king. Hagar swung his mace and managed to connect solidly with the beast's snout, smashing teeth, scales, and flesh, but he was unable to withstand the strength of the dragon's attack, and its head struck the ogrillion's armored chest, sending him flying backwards fifteen paces and skidding half that distance across the ground.

The tail of the dragon came at the king so quickly that he did the only thing he had time for, lift his shield and swing his sword. The glowing blade cut into the beast's scaled tail but only briefly before it struck the shield, lifting Baylin from his feet and launching him even further away than Hagar. The king landed hard, rolling several times across the ground.

Durgen fared better, his diminutive size enabling him to duck under its tail, where he pivoted and managed to slam his wicked blade into the beast's appendage before it could pull away from the deadly weapon.

The dragon then scuttled forward on its four legs faster than anyone thought possible. One claw shot out to grab the still dazed king when Tel-andorsis acted, shooting a bolt of lightning into its limb. The beast roared in fury and jerked its claw away, pivoting angrily towards the elf. The dragon leaped forward like a frog, both clawed hands landing on top of the elf and pinning the Ekahal to the ground with crushing force. Everything happened so quickly that the unfortunate elf didn't have time to raise another spell. With two quick jerks of its claws the dragon tore the elf in two, then lifted both bloody parts into the air, letting the gushing blood drain into its open mouth.

Kromm, who had been standing ten paces from the elf, was so stunned and horrified as he watched the terrible scene before him that he nearly gagged before his repulsion was replaced with insurmountable anger. He had seen many men suffer violent deaths on the battlefield, but never before anything as brutal as this. It was incomprehensible, and it filled him with rage. The battle king did not stop to ponder whether his sword, Cormathian, could harm the dragon, but the blade had never let him down before. In fact, the sentient weapon was begging Kromm to attack, and that is exactly what he did.

The dragon was so sure of its own power that it ignored anyone who was not directly in its line of vision, and at the moment the beast was still focused on its grisly meal. The dragon was sitting on its hind legs with its body extended, arms raised as he held the bloody feast above its mouth.

Kromm did not hesitate; he ran forward as silently as he could, using the momentum of his charge to ram his blade into the dragon's belly. There was a flash of light as Cormathian penetrated the beast's thick scales, sinking halfway into its abdomen. Kromm could sense the blade purring with delight as it hummed with magical energy.

Kromm knew it was not a killing blow, not by any means. He also knew that he couldn't stay there or he would die. So with one powerful pull he yanked the blade clear and jumped with all his strength to the side, narrowly avoiding the bulk of the dragon's weight as it dropped the elf's corpse, falling back onto all fours to protect its wounded belly from further attacks.

However, Kromm was still far from safe. He had landed and rolled to his feet only several paces away from the powerful dragon. And as quick as the strike of a snake, Kil-Kannon's claws shot out, grabbing the king and lifting him completely into the air. Kromm's sword arm was trapped and he screamed in pain as he felt his armor start to give way to the power of the dragon's grip. In seconds he would be crushed like a bug.

Riker was on the inner wall watching the battle before him. He stared in horror, fear gripping his heart, as his father was lifted from the ground. "No!" he screamed, leaning over the edge of the battlement, his fingers turning white as he gripped the stone in panic.

Jonas saw Kromm lifted from the ground, but he didn't know what to do. Fighting a creature this size was nearly impossible, but he had to do something and he guessed he only had seconds before the battle king was crushed.

Allindrian saw it too and in a flash sent three arrows into the dragon's wrist. Each arrow sank in deeply since the scales there were not as thick. Roaring in pain the dragon dropped Kromm like a hot coal.

Jonas, silently thanking Allindrian's quick bow arm, then summoned his cognivant energy, wrapping it around one of his blades and sending it streaking towards the base of the dragon's head just behind its ear. It struck true and buried itself deeply in its neck. The very next moment, however, the dragon's powerful tail snapped out and struck Jonas solidly, launching him into the air. The force of the blow had knocked him unconscious even before he hit the ground, where he tumbled over repeatedly as if he were no more than a rag doll.

By this time both Hagar and King Baylin were up, but Hagar was the faster of the two. Running forward, he slammed his huge mace onto the dragon's left foot, crushing bone and flesh and splattering the ground with black blood. Hagar had learned the hard way just how quick the beast was, so he didn't linger to relish his attack; he jumped away as quickly as he could in order to distance himself from the dangerous beast.

Kil-Kannon roared again in pain and fury, shaking his bloody claw like someone who had stubbed their toe. The dragon had never before experienced such a powerful blow. He turned his deadly eyes on the big ogre-like creature who had dealt it. Just as he was about to roast Hagar alive with his breath, he felt a fiery pain in his side and a gush of warm liquid pour across his flank. Instinctively Kil-Kannon kicked out with its hind foot like a horse, its leg connecting with something solid. The great beast turned its head to look at the wound. There was a gash the length of a sword and Kil-Kannon could see bone and flesh underneath. Black blood poured like a waterfall from the gruesome cut. Then the pain came, and for the first time the dragon felt fear.

The dragon turned in fury to face the warrior that had so grievously wounded him. The beast knew that no human could deliver such a mortal blow, but then its eyes found the glowing blade held in his hand as the warrior struggled to get up, knowing that his sword was the source of its pain. The demon dragon sucked in its breath as King Baylin regained his footing, turning around to face the dragon. The great beast kicked him and violently tossed him to the ground and forcefully knocked the wind from his lungs.

The king blinked once, and the next instant he was engulfed in the dragon's scalding steam. The magical armor protected the skin underneath, but there were plenty of areas not covered, and the deadly vapor found them all. Skin under his helm bubbled and melted away, and the searing steam found every gap in the armor, burning the king all over his body. The flesh around his stomach, hands, armpits, and thighs was instantly seared. Excruciating fiery pain consumed him and he dropped to his knees, screaming in agony before falling face forward to the ground. Fortunately the hot steam burnt through his pain receptors so quickly that the intense agony vanished almost as quickly as it had appeared, and he was dead before his face hit the ground.

Allindrian looked on with horror, grinding her teeth in anger. Dropping her bow she raced forward, leaping into the air impossibly high and landing directly on the base of the dragon's tail.

"No!" Kromm screamed as he ran at the dragon, hoping to distract the beast from Allindrian's presence. Durgen too raced in, his short legs pumping quickly, carrying him to the dragon's side with surprising speed for one so small.

Kil-Kannon shook its hide like a wet dog, but the agile elf would not be dislodged. Allindrian was jumping from spine to spine, her silver sword held at her side.

Everyone on the main wall watched the scene below them, mesmerized and bewildered at the same time. The Blade Singer was literally running up the dragon's back.

In desperation the dragon snapped its huge tail up and over its back aiming for Allindrian. Incredibly she dodged it, leaping forward and gripping a sharp spike with one hand while the tail cracked against its own back. She then swung herself up, landing like a cat on both feet. Those watching could hardly believe their eyes, never before had they seen such a combination of agility, strength, and speed.

Kromm charged in swinging his blade as hard as his prodigal strength allowed into the dragon's right leg. At the same time Durgen brought his sharp axe down on the back foot of the dragon, severing two of its toes.

Kil-Kannon momentarily returned his attention to the wound in his side hoping to get a better look at the damage, simultaneously flicking its good wing out and slamming it into Kromm, knocking him to the ground again. The beast then flicked its broad tail towards the small attacker at its back leg hoping to crush the pest between the flesh of its tail and hind quarters. But Durgen saw it coming and jumped into the crevice behind its leg and tail, barely dodging the crushing force of the dragon's attack. Then, raising his axe high over his head, he brought it down, like a lumber jack splitting wood, at the base of the dragon's tail. The magical mithril axe blade cut a quarter ways through its tail and again the dragon roared in pain. The dragon was being attacked from all sides, and every time it went to use its breath, someone else cut into his flesh, causing it great pain and distracting the beast from using its breath attack.

"She's going for its head," Riker murmured under his breath. General Gandarin stood beside him, both men watching the scene play out with a mixture of fear, amazement, and hope. Everyone watching the battle was feeling a tumultuous ride of emotions as the heroes fought, and died, for all of them. Many had just witnessed their king make the ultimate sacrifice for their safety and some were openly crying while others stood stock still, rigid with anger. Thousands on the outer wall had no time to watch the fight as they continued to battle the enemy who relentlessly continued their attack. But the battle with Kil-Kannon the dragon would be a tale told and retold a thousand times in the years to come, a battle that made heroes and inspired young boys, and even girls to lift up a sword.

"Amazing," was all the general could say as Allindrian made one last leap, landing directly on the base of the dragon's head.

Kil-Kannon had been wounded in many places and the pain was distracting, but it could still feel the little elf on its neck. The beast shook its head violently and Allindrian was nearly thrown from the dragon. Falling to the side she glimpsed Jonas's blade imbedded in its neck. Reaching out she snagged it with her free hand, and as the dragon shook its head up and down, she timed it perfectly and used its momentum to swing her body, releasing her grip on the handle she flew forward with her silver sword held in both hands. The Blade Singer landed on the dragon's head, and with one smooth motion she rammed the blade deep between its eyes. If you blinked you would have missed her jump from its head, somersaulting through the air and landing gracefully on both feet.

Everyone on the inner wall cheered with hope as the dragon roared the loudest yet. This time it was a piercing howl, a terrible cry they had not heard before.

The great beast was stomping its legs and flapping its good wing, shaking its head in an attempt to dislodge the painful weapon. Finally it fell forward and laid its head on the ground, desperately trying to grip the weapon with its damaged claws to yank it free.

In all its pain and suffering it did not see Hagar bound towards it. Lifting his magnificent weapon, Hagar brought it down with all his strength on the dragon's skull. The beast's head was angled away from him and one claw was pawing at Allindrian's sword when the mace struck. The blow was so powerful that even people on the inner wall could hear the skull crack. It sounded like a thunder clap as bone and flesh were crushed under the strike.

A normal mace, even a magical one, in the hands of a trained warrior would inflict little damage to the dragon's thick skull. But Hagar stood at eleven feet and he towered over the dragon's head, giving him the leverage needed for such a powerful blow. And with his incredible strength and the might of his weapon, the beast didn't stand a chance. The metal ball of the mace was as big around as a man's torso, with each protruding spike as long as a short sword, an incredibly deadly weapon, especially when wielded by an ogrillion. Four of those spikes were now buried deep in the dragon's brain.

The dragon was already convulsing as Hagar, roaring with battle fury, yanked the weapon from the grisly wound, and then brought it down for a second time on its skull, this time splattering brains and blood in a wide circumference around its crushed skull. The dragon gave a final violent jerk before it lay still.

Hagar, lifting his bloody mace into the air, roared in victory. Everyone on the wall cheered exuberantly with him, and soon the cries of victory were echoing across the killing ground, bouncing back and forth between both walls.

The sound of horns blowing from both walls, however, interrupted their victory celebration, reminding them the war was not yet over. For some reason the enemy was retreating, signaling something new might be amiss.

The survivors of the battle surrounded the burnt body of the king, bowing their heads in silence. "You're free now," Durgen said, reflecting back on the conversation he had had with King Baylin. The monarch had done his duty protecting his kingdom. He had sacrificed more than most, and now he was free of the anger that was poisoning

313

him, feeding the fire of revenge. Warriors nearby moved forward to honor their king, and within moments there were closer to fifty soldiers surrounding him.

Allindrian had run to check on Jonas who was slowly regaining consciousness. Kiln, surrounded by several of his personal guard, ran from the wall to join the heroes of the fight.

"Remove his body," Kiln ordered. "We will honor him when this is over!" Kiln yelled to the men. "His sacrifice was for us, and we will not let his death be in vain! We still have a war to win! For Finarth!" Kiln drew his sword, lifting it in the air. Every soldier around them followed his lead, drawing their blades and shouting "Finarth!" Then several of the men gently and respectfully carried the king's body from the field.

"Send for healers immediately," the commander ordered one of his men. Allindrian slowly lifted Jonas off the ground and with her help Jonas limped toward them. "Well done," Kiln said to everyone. "Songs will be sung of your victory. Who is hurt?"

"I may have broken some ribs," Kromm said casually, showing no sign of the pain.

"Father!" Riker yelled as he ran to them, skidding to a halt. "Are you hurt?"

"Aye, but I'll be fine," Kromm said, reassuring the young warrior.

"Jonas, you don't look so good," Kiln said with concern as the two joined them.

"I look like I feel," he said through painful breaths, "I know my ribs are broken and I think I fractured my left arm."

"Healers will be here momentarily," Kiln reassured him. Then he addressed the group, "I need all of you with us. Riker, get the armor and sword. Malbeck may be showing his face soon," he said grimly.

Riker looked questioningly at his father who nodded encouragement. "Yes, Commander," he said. Then he raced away toward the main gate to the city.

"Your boy has great courage. I believe he can do this," Kiln said, hoping to reassure the worried king. Kromm looked up from the ground and nodded. "See to your wounds and meet me on the wall."

It wasn't long before everyone except Allindrian had joined Kiln on the outer wall. The gatehouse was badly damaged and the battlements above it had been destroyed, so the small group stood on the wall to the left of the gatehouse. They needed the protection of the battlement as the gatehouse no longer provided that.

Allindrian had stayed back to assemble her female archers. She had trained over a thousand women and they were hastily forming lines along the killing ground behind the gate. Most were nervous, gripping their bows with trembling hands. None wore armor and few carried swords, both items being in short supply, and therefore reserved for the men who were trained to use them. Nonetheless they stood in perfect rows, their eyes on Allindrian waiting for her command and hoping to find some reassurance in her steady gaze.

"Me engineer says the gate's damaged," Durgen said as he stood against the battlements, his head barely reaching over the top of the stone wall. "The dragon's weight hittin' the wall fractured de stone and one of the hinges be loose."

"Hopefully the integrity of the gate still exists, but we can't do anything about it now," Kiln said, looking intently at the enemy army. "I think they are going to come at us with everything."

"What do you suggest?" Jonas asked.

"Stick with the plan. We take the fight to them, which makes even more sense now if the gate is truly that damaged," Kiln announced, lifting a horn to his lips.

"I finally get to spill some orc blood," Durgen growled.

Kiln blew a series of notes and immediately the defenders went into action. Both gates began to slowly open and thousands of infantry and cavalry moved from the inner castle over the bridge and through the outer gate.

Everyone ran from the wall to take their positions with the army. Within moments ten thousand Finarthian infantry had formed massive squares, the squares themselves positioned in a giant V formation outside the gate. These men were an elite group of warriors who had trained tirelessly to quickly assemble in this formation. Some of these men had already been killed, but the remaining adjusted to the smaller numbers by forming smaller squares. Armed with long stabbing spears, infantry swords and shields, and armored with chainmail and hardened leather cuirasses, these men could inflict heavy damage on a larger army of ill-trained soldiers. Each square held around two hundred soldiers all facing outward, and the square formations were placed far enough apart to leave gaps for the enemy. Behind the infantry were two thousand Finarthian and Annurien cavalry led by King Olegaurd. So far the

Annurien king and most of the infantry had been waiting inside the inner wall for their turn to fight. They were eager to do their part and shed enemy blood, especially the king, who had lost his brother at the Gildren Garrison.

The idea behind Kiln's formation was to allow the enemy to break through the gaps where they would be sandwiched between the squares of cavalry and infantry, and since the fighters in the formations were all facing outward it would be impossible to surround them. Then, after killing the enemy that had been pushed through the gaps, they would break formation, forming solid lines and slowly retreating back through the gate.

The squares were packed tight with three reserve lines so when one soldier fell, others could fill the gap and maintain the integrity of the square. Kiln had used this technique only once before many years ago and on a much smaller scale. He had been fighting against a small untrained Sithgarin tribe and it had worked extremely well, but now they were attempting it on a larger scale with a much bigger army. It was a calculated risk designed to do as much damage as possible while limiting the loss of life on their side.

Kiln positioned himself in the lead square while Jonas, Hagar, Tuvallis, Durgen, and Seli flanked him. Kromm, Riker, and Lor-telliam were on horseback positioned at the very back in case Malbeck showed himself. If so, they would attempt to find him, engage him, and hopefully kill him, ending the battle right then and there.

General Gandarin remained inside the killing ground with five thousand reserves in case things went wrong and the enemy broke through the gate. Two thousand of those men were refugees with little fighting experience. The dwarven engineers that remained had been working tirelessly for a way to bring down the bridge between the two walls if the need arose. They had informed Kiln that they could do it, and they were prepared to do just that if the situation became desperate. There were several thousand more men manning the inner wall, half of which were archers prepared to unleash their barrage of deadly arrows on any creatures that managed to breach the outer wall.

If things went as planned, Kiln's infantry would deal a heavy blow to the enemy before retreating safely behind the outer wall with minimal loss of life. If things didn't go as planned, they would be overrun, with thousands dead, and Malbeck would power his way through the outer wall, breaching the gate and gaining access to the killing ground.

Thousands of people inside the city had climbed to the rooftops to get a view of the battle, anxiety heavy in the air. Many had friends and relatives fighting for them, and they feared for their safety, nervous eyes scanning the milling enemy army and hoping that their warriors and loved ones would prevail. They knew that their own survival teetered back on forth on the skill and courage of the warriors and their commanders. Word had spread quickly about the king's death but it wasn't long before people were whispering about the destruction of the dragon and the heroes who killed it, including their own king. King Baylin's death pained them greatly, but his courage brought his people hope as well, and now Kiln, the best war commander in all of Kraawn, was leading them, and if anyone could beat this great and terrible army, it was him.

Malbeck sat astride a giant ebony horse, flanked by Korthanos and forty thousand warriors. It wasn't really a horse, however, it was a Nightmare, a demon steed similar to the horses the Banthras rode but even more powerful. This horse was much larger, and built like a big bull, and its hooves were covered in flames matching its fiery eyes. Fire and smoke shot from its cave-like nostrils as it kicked the ground eager to get into the fight.

Strapped to the side of the horse was a large black shield painted with Gould's eye in red, matching the cuirass of Malbeck's armor. He held the spear of Gould at his side, and strapped to the other side of his demon steed was a giant double sided battle axe. A thick black leather satchel was buckled to the belt around his waist and inside it was his most powerful possession, the book of power, the Shan Cemar. He had already used the magic of the book to further his cause, turning the corpse of Gullanin into a Lich, locating the secret tunnel into the king's castle, creating the deadly mist, and bringing forth the demons whose job was to kill the inhabitants of the castle. The book had been very useful and in Malbeck's hands it would continue to be an integral part of taking the city.

"I tire of this," Malbeck said to Korthanos. "Send in the worg riders and crush that formation. When I destroy the gate press them hard with infantry. Try to flank them with the ogres and cut off their retreat, then we close the noose and kill them all. I want to be within that outer wall before the sun sets. Don't fail me, Koranthos. I've had my fill of it."

The Banthra nodded its armored head in acknowledgement. "It will be as you say," the demon hissed.

Allindrian stood on the wall looking out at the enemy army as it began to move. Huge drums pounded somewhere in the distance and then the familiar sound of catapult arms filled the air. Great jugs of flaming oil shot into the air sailing over the advancing orcs and crashing into the Finarthian infantry. Some missed completely, exploding and sending great splashes of hot fire across the ground, while others scattered men, engulfing them in deadly fire.

Orders were given for their own catapults to join in the fight, sending projectiles of fire and stone flying over the wall into the enemy ranks. The destruction on both sides was devastating. The heavy bombardment nearly caused Kiln's carefully planned formations to fall apart. In one case a flaming projectile smashed into the center of one of the square formations, instantly crushing several men, but worse, throwing the burning oil over scores more, causing the square to disintegrate from the inside. Graggis, who was leading that formation, was able to adjust quickly, reforming the integrity of the group with a barrage of screaming orders. Fil, who had been marching in the formation near where the oil had struck, frantically worked to put out the flames and drag the wounded and dead men away. Everyone nearby worked together, following Graggis's orders and helping Fil, working to keep the formation together. Somehow, amid the shouts and screams and the constant barrage of catapult missiles, the formations remained intact and ready.

It was then that they heard the deafening howls of several thousand giant worgs and their riders as they burst forward from the enemy's line, surging across the field toward the defenders.

Allindrian turned to her archers below and raised a black flag. Immediately a thousand women lifted their bows to the highest position and pulled the nocked arrows back, the creaking of the bows audible between the two stone walls. The Blade Singer looked back, gauging the distance of the riders and their speed, dropping the flag when the timing was right. A thousand arrows shot into the air, quickly soaring over the wall, past the defenders, and slamming into the riders like a hailstorm. Hundreds of the worg wolves, along with their riders fell to the barrage of silver barbed arrows. The Blade Singer then lifted a red flag, and for a second time the female archers pulled their bows back, lifting the weapons to the pre-set position they had practiced hundreds of times. A drop of the flag sent thousands more arrows into the disorganized charge, killing hundreds more. But now the enemy was too close to their own men to risk another volley. And the worgs and their riders continued their charge, howling with frenzied fury.

Kiln and every other soldier angled long spears forward as the riders neared. He noticed that the enemy army beyond was splitting, and just before the worgs slammed into them he saw two groups slowly converge on their flanks. Their own V formation would offer protection all the way back to the wall; he had to hope that the squares that made that formation would hold. If the enemy breached the formation by breaking through the squares they would be doomed as the more numerous enemy would surround them and cut them to pieces.

But he had no time to ponder that possible outcome; besides, he had already spent restless nights going over every possibility, and he knew that continuing to dwell on every conceivable flaw would serve no purpose. He shut the thought away and lifted his shield and spear, angling the long weapon towards the chest of a charging worg. The big wolf-like beast tried to veer away from the weapon but the other riders were too close, giving it no room to maneuver. It roared as it leaped into the air to avoid the deadly point. Kiln quickly raised his spear, puncturing it in the neck as it flew overhead, ripping the weapon from his grasp. Then the sounds of battle echoed across the battlefield as orc ridden worgs crashed into the formations with deadly force.

Casualties were high on both sides as men and beasts alike were killed almost instantly in the violent attack. The skilled Finarthian soldiers fought valiantly to reform their formations as the force of the onslaught threatened to break them. The gaps between the square formations worked perfectly as countless worgs and their riders instinctively funneled through the openings only to find themselves face to face with a solid wall of Annurien and Finarthian cavalry. Most of those caught in the gaps were skewered by the long lances of the knights, while others turned to attack the infantry from the rear, thinking they would be an easier target. What they found instead was a wall of grim faced infantry and their deadly spears.

King Kromm and Prince Riker sat astride their large warhorses, surrounded by ten of the very best Finarthian knights, one of which was Captain Lathrin. Lor-telliam was mounted on a light footed chestnut mare, easily a hand or two smaller than the powerful steeds surrounding him. Riker stood up in his stirrups to get a better look at the battle before them.

"Easy, son, your time will come," Kromm said softly, sensing Riker's nervousness.

"Do you think he is out there?" Riker asked over the din of battle.

"He is, and most likely he will show himself this day," Kromm said.

"How do you know?"

"Because that is what I would do," Kromm stated simply.

"How do you remain so calm?" Riker asked.

"I have not always been so. I was sixteen when I first bloodied my blade. It made me physically ill, not just because I had taken a life, but from the anxiety and anticipation of the battle itself. It took many years of gaining experience and skill before my confidence transformed my pre-battle fears into an intense desire to fight. For your sake, I pray you will never yearn for battle as I do. It brings little peace."

Before Riker could respond, a horn bellowed a few notes from the wall behind them.

"They are flanking us!" Lathrin yelled over the din of battle, as he spurred his horse towards the king.

"Reinforce both flanks!" Kromm ordered. Immediately Lathrin carried out the command and within moments mounted knights rode in solid lines, moving quickly to reinforce the square formations on their flanks, the ones closest to the wall, the likely location where the enemy would hit hoping to surround Kiln's entire formation. Kromm and Riker remained in the center, eyes constantly scanning, as they searched for their target.

Hagar swung his mace so hard that the impact not only shattered the worg's skull, but it snapped its neck as well. The orc rider, unseated as his mount fell dead, struggled to regain his feet. He righted himself just in time to meet the reverse swing of the ogrillion's mace, which sent his crushed and broken body flying nearly ten paces away.

Everyone fought valiantly, side by side with the best infantry in the lands. Hundreds of men died in the struggle, but enemy bodies piled up at a much faster rate. It wasn't long before the worgs and their riders were dead. Kiln's plan had worked perfectly. Nearly a quarter of the worgs and their riders had been killed on the long spears when they struck the formations. Another half, thinking they were breaking through the formations by slipping into the gaps provided between the squares, met the steel of the mounted cavalry, dying quickly to the skill of the knights. The rest were cut down along the edges of the strong square formations. But there was no time for celebration as an awesome but terrifying sight appeared before them. There, a bow shot away, a massive wave of orcs, goblins, and other creatures were slowly marching towards them, with even more beasts branching wide to try and encircle them. It was hard to tell but it looked as if the enemy were easily ten beasts thick, with ogres dominating the enemy flanks, clearly hoping to use their massive size and strength to break through the rear of their formation and swarm around them, cutting the Finarthian defenders down under sheer numbers. They were trying to isolate the defenders and cut off their retreat, a plan that Kiln had anticipated, and soon they would be upon them.

"Drink from your skins!" Kiln yelled. "Remember your training. Hold the formation until the order to retreat is given, then have the reserve lines move back through the gate while the front holds the line!"

Everyone knew that the front line would suffer the most casualties; hence the front was occupied by their strongest warriors, men made of gristle and sweat, veterans of countless military campaigns, those most eager to defend their comrades, families, and homes, even if death met them on the field.

Allindrian stood on the wall, scanning the ongoing battle. At first things seemed to be going well and Kiln's plan was proving successful; but then the enemy began to flank them, a move that most expected. It was not the enemy tactic that forced Allindrian to second guess Kiln's plan, it was the sheer size of the enemy army. For as far as she could see, rows and rows of various beasts were closing the distance, slowly wrapping their deadly embrace around the Finarthian defenders. From her vantage point on the wall she had a clear picture of the enormity of Malbeck's army, and it was frightening to watch the situation unfold below her. It didn't seem possible that Kiln's men could maintain their formations under such an onslaught. Allindrian was more than nervous.

She ran to the back side of the wall and looked down at her archers. "Janniss!" she yelled, pointing to a small girl positioned on the end of the line. "Bring everyone to the wall! We need your bows up here!"

The young petite girl looked around to make sure Allindrian was speaking to her. Then she went into motion, yelling at the women to move up the stairs to the wall. Some hesitated, knowing that the plan had always been to stay away from the direct fighting, but one look at Allindrian yelling and frantically waving at them to join her changed their minds. A thousand women ran across the killing ground and up the stairs, lining up quickly along the battlements.

They were not soldiers and had no experience with warfare, so as soon as they saw the bloodshed of the battle below many began to lose their composure. Tensely gripping the hard stone of the battlements they looked down upon the death and destruction, eyes wide with fright.

"Nock your arrows!" Allindrian yelled. The thirty women closest to her obeyed, while the rest were so focused on the destruction below that they didn't even hear her.

"You heard her!" Janniss screamed, her shrill voice finally breaking through their fear. She ran along the line yelling and shaking them, urging them to listen. Eventually she and Allindrian managed to rouse them from their paralysis and they were able to pull themselves from the wall and bring arrow to string.

"The enemy is flanking our men on both sides! We can't do anything about the south side but we can inflict damage here! If they break through the formation we are finished! We cannot let that happen!" Allindrian shouted over the noise of the battle below. Anxious eyes darted from Allindrian back to the chaos below, bow arms trembling as they fought to control their fear. "There are no positions this time! When they get within range you will lean over the battlements and fire at will!" she yelled, leaping to the top of the battlement, her elven cloak fluttering in the breeze. No one said a word along the line; their eyes were glued to Allindrian as they waited for orders, hoping that some of her courage would find them.

Hundreds of other Finarthian archers lined the wall on the south side of the formation. With them were the two wizards from

Shyval. Anyone on the wall watching the scene play out, knew they had to do everything within their power to help the brave men below fight off the two arms of Malbeck's army that were closing in on them.

"We must not break!" Kiln yelled, facing his men as the enemy neared. "When it feels like all is lost, reach deeply within yourselves. For there you will find the strength and courage to do what we must to prevail!"

The bellowing of the enemy horn across the battlefield punctuated Kiln's admonition as thousands of monsters, howling in unison, charged the defenders. Jonas glanced left and right and saw friends and strangers plant their feet firmly in the soil, gripping their weapons tightly until their knuckles turned white, glaring at the ferocious enemy with iron determination.

"Spears to the front!" Kiln ordered. Immediately men from the interior of the square passed their weapons to the front, replacing those that were lost or broken during the worg wolf charge.

Jonas blinked and then they were upon them, crashing into shields and spears with tremendous force. He had no shield so he stood behind others until the charge ended. Then he pushed his way forward, both swords slicing and stabbing, spilling enemy blood. Hundreds of the enemy had perished as they charged into the myriad long spears of the defenders, but the sheer volume of Malbeck's army was gradually pushing the formation back. The men at the rear frantically dug their heels into the ground and leaned forward, pushing with all their might to keep the formation stable. But as each square was pushed slowly back, the gaps between them began to close, defeating the purpose of the original plan.

Spears were abandoned as the soldiers switched to swords in the tight confines of hand to hand combat, swinging them left and right, up and down, in deadly rhythm as they sliced into the enemy that continued to pound the formations. The defenders that fell to enemy javelins and hacking swords were replaced by the reserves behind them who stepped over their lifeless bodies to fill the gaps.

Hagar roared furiously as he swung his brilliant weapon in wide arcs, meting out death to countless beasts unlucky enough to come near him. Orcs and goblins literally disappeared as his mace swept back and forth, tossing their crushed bodies into the air. Durgen and Hagar fought well together. The dwarf's small form allowed him to easily avoid the giant ogrillion's dangerous swings, while his silver axe chopped and sliced through the hoard of creatures surrounding him. Kiln fought with shield and sword in a deadly dance, spilling enemy blood as he pushed relentlessly forward, urging the others on with constant screams of encouragement.

Eventually the center square, led by Kiln, began to push forward into the enemy and the gaps widened, allowing the howling untrained beasts to rush wildly into the open spaces where they were trapped between the inner sides of the squares and the defenders' cavalry. Several hundred were slaughtered as they had nowhere to go.

It was then that the enemy flanks struck the base of Kiln's V formation. This group, led by giant ogres swinging massive clubs, caused an immediate and devastating effect upon the square formations that, together, made up the massive V formation. The Finarthian defenders located at the base began to buckle under the ferocious attack of the powerful ogres, supported by thousands of orcs and goblins.

Allindrian watched the scene unfold before her. "Go for the ogres!" she shouted. "Fire at will!" Her bow hummed and a rapid blur of magical elven arrows slammed into one of the ogres, two of them penetrating its neck, while a third arrow pierced its eye, burying itself feather deep into the beast's brain as it fell lifelessly to the ground.

A thousand women pushed aside their fear, and fired their arrows at the enemy army below. Even with their poor aim their attack was effective. At such close range and with so many monsters confined in one space, they were able to inflict significant casualties. But their success also drew the attention of the enemy.

The orcs and goblins positioned behind the ogres turned their attention to the archers on the wall, throwing javelins and firing their bows and crossbows. Hundreds of bolts and arrows struck the stone wall but others found flesh. Fifty women were hit, their bodies jerking violently back from the battlements, and crumbling to the floor, where they lay moaning in pain or lying silent in death. Several dozen screamed, while twice that faltered and ran away. But at least half, however, found the courage they didn't know they possessed, and continued to fire their arrows into the enemy below.

Janniss fired her bow, screaming encouragement to the others all the while. She heard a sharp cry from the woman next to her, and turned to see the poor woman spin around, exposing the end of the black shaft of an arrow protruding from her eye. Stumbling, she dropped to the ground in spasms, blood quickly pooling around her head.

Things were worse on the ground. The ogres relentlessly stomped their way into the formations, swinging giant crudely made swords, clubs, and hammers into their midst, dispersing the men like dirt from a broom. The effect was disastrous as the formations near the wall began to crumble and hundreds, if not thousands, of orcs and other monsters broke through, howling with rage.

Kromm saw it all happen as if it were in slow motion. Lathrin had reinforced both flanks with mounted fighters, but Kromm was unsure if it would be enough. The ogres presented the most danger, and that was where Kromm turned his attention. Lor-telliam had moved towards the southern flank as that side began to buckle as well.

The battle king turned to his son, not knowing if the decision he was about to make was the right one, but realizing that it was all he could do. Prince Riker was a young man now, and a trained soldier, and he had to hope that it would be enough to carry him through this day. "Son, we go for the ogres. Stay by my side," he counseled, as he turned his horse toward the left flank and angled his lance downward.

Riker swallowed nervously, but his eyes shone with determination. "Yes, Father, I am eager to fight beside you," was he all said as he lowered the visor on his beautifully made helm.

"And I you," Kromm replied, doing the same

They spurred their steeds toward Lathrin's knights who were fighting like demons against the rush of enemy warriors bombarding them. The knights had long abandoned their lances and now fought with small shields and long cavalry swords.

Kromm saw several large ogres swat aside two knights, opening a gap in the line, so that was where he headed. Lowering his lance and angling it to the right, he urged his horse forward just at the beasts pushed through the opening. Riker was beside him and together they flew forward, aiming their lances at the two ogres, striking them with incredible force. The two warriors then released their shafts, their momentum carrying them past the ogres and into the throng of monsters behind them. Their warhorses crashed into the enemy and sent them scattering. Both men were mirror images of each other, drawing forth their swords, rising up in their stirrups, and swinging their deadly blades into the enemy.

The two ogres, futilely grasping the shafts that had pierced their chests, fell to the ground with a loud thud. Orcs and goblins alike cowered before the bright white light emanating from Riker's blade, just before its razor sharp edge ended their miserable lives. Other knights fought furiously to join them and push the enemy back, but they could not quickly cut through the enemy warriors between them. Kromm and Riker, surrounded by dozens of monsters, spun their steeds in circles, protecting each other while relentlessly cutting into the attackers, littering the ground with their corpses.

Riker's magical armor deflected most of the arrows aimed at him, but one managed to find its way through the tiny gap between his cuirass and his heavy leather belt, piercing his hip. But, in the midst of his battle lust, the young warrior's pain just enraged him further, spurring him on to more violently attack the enemy. Growling like the beasts he was battling, he tore into their ranks, cutting them down by the dozens. Kromm was equally effective, swinging his giant sword more rapidly than seemed possible, cleaving skulls and spraying orc and goblin blood in all directions.

Despite the death toll of the monsters around them, one ogre managed to push its way forward, coming directly at the prince, roaring maniacally and swinging a club as large as a sapling, striking Riker's steed and connecting so solidly with the animal's neck that it cracked like a dry twig. The horse spun around, crumbled, and fell to the ground, throwing the young prince from its back to land amidst the enemy hoard.

"No!" Kromm screamed, as he saw his son fall. Frantically he tried to get to him, but instead he came face to face with two ogres himself.

"Protect the prince!" Allindrian shouted, simultaneously sending three arrows toward the ogres. The Tarsinian king and prince were surrounded by the enemy, and Allindrian was worried that the knights, who were frantically trying to cut their way through to help them, would not make it before the enemy's superior numbers overwhelmed the warriors. "Watch your aim! Don't hit the king or the prince!" she screamed, worried that a stray arrow from the inexperienced archers might hit one of them.

More than a hundred of the female archers had been killed, with an almost equal number wounded. But, remarkably, they were proving their worth, grittily holding their positions on the wall, despite enemy fire from below. The remaining archers, nearly six hundred strong, fired their missiles into the monsters surrounding the king and his son, killing or wounding enough of them to keep them temporarily at bay. But then the prince was thrown from his horse and he disappeared into the midst of the enemy.

Allindrian swore under her breath and did the first thing that came to her mind. She had to get to the prince. Just to her left, ten paces from the wall, were the smoking remains of a siege tower. It had been badly damaged but was still standing, supported by charred and unsteady beams. The Blade Singer dropped her bow on the wall and raced along the narrow battlements, leaping gracefully off the edge toward the damaged tower. It was an incredible distance to jump, but the agile ranger cleared it, grasping a round support beam and flinging her body through a burnt hole in the structure. The structure on which she landed was so damaged that it would have never been able to support the weight of an orc, nor even an armored man. But it held Allindrian's weight as she ran, dexterously jumping and leaping from beam to platform until she descended the tall structure, landing lightly on the ground below. She quickly hid behind a pile of rubble and tried to ascertain her next move. She'd only thought as far as getting to the ground. "Now what?" she whispered to herself.

Janniss leaned over the edge in complete shock. What was Allindrian doing? She had just leaped off the wall, swinging like an acrobat onto the charred skeleton of a tower, only to land on a battleground swarming with monsters.

Riker tucked his shoulder and rolled across the ground, bouncing quickly to his feet, knowing that his life depended on it. He was surrounded by a myriad of beasts, their stench nearly overwhelming him as they attacked with maniacal glee reflected in their yellow eyes. The prince repeatedly blocked their strikes with his magical shield, while swinging his sword in great arcs, slicing through weaponry, armor, and flesh. Tihr-Alliam seemed to relish the blood, glowing increasingly brighter, literally blinding the enemy around him. The blade turned warm in his hand as it hissed through the air, cutting through everything like a warm knife through butter. The young prince actually felt himself become stronger as new energy coursed through him from the handle of the blade. The magical sword was somehow feeding off the darkness of the creatures it destroyed, creating new energy for Riker. He didn't know if the sword was taking the energy from the creatures, or if it was their blood feeding it, but there was an obvious transfusion of energy. He felt as if he could fight forever; and by the looks of it he would have to if he wanted to survive.

Suddenly, warning horns sounded from the battlements above, startling Kiln to action. He spun away from a recently dispatched orc and hurried back, leaving the formation and heading towards the rear where the cavalry was located. Several warriors immediately jumped in and took his place. The commander made his way through the formation, breaking free and running through the chaos behind it. Mounted knights were fighting furiously to destroy the enemy that had managed to break through the gaps, a strategy that seemed to be working just as Kiln had planned. However, it took him only moments to discern that they were in danger, hence the warning bugle from above. He was dismayed to see that groups of ogres had broken through the formations near the walls. The cavalry and infantry were dangerously close to caving in, which would allow the enemy to completely encircle them. They could not let that happen.

Kiln brought a horn to his lips and blew the retreat signal. They had practiced the maneuver many times but never while being pressed from all sides by hoards of murderous creatures. Instantly the square formations broke apart and hundreds of men filled the gaps creating a solid V formation two and three men deep. But the formation was not holding; the base of the V was buckling under the pressure from the enemy, and it wouldn't be long before they would close off their retreat.

Jonas, Tuvallis, and Seli were slowly moving backward, which was inevitable considering the large numbers of screeching orcs and goblins that were hammering into them. They had been fighting hard and their arms were beginning to tire, sweat was filling their eyes and their legs had begun to feel like lead weights.

A giant orc jabbed a serrated sword towards Jonas's belly. Jonas reacted by tucking in his stomach and turning the blade away with his sword, simultaneously drawing his other weapon across the orc's face, slicing through its open jaw to the base of its brain. Gurgling, the beast fell back into the hoard of his enemy comrades, while more immediately surged forward to take its place.

But as Jonas readied himself to take on the next foe, he heard Seli scream. He glanced sideways and saw her clutching at a short javelin stuck in her thigh, while frantically trying to fight off a sword wielding goblin. Jonas quickly drew forth his cognivant energy. Using his left sword, he directed the energy forward like a fist, crushing the two monsters attacking Seli, hurling them backwards so forcefully that they tripped up a score of beasts behind them.

Taking advantage of the reprieve, Seli yanked the barbed weapon from her thigh, releasing a flood of crimson. She immediately cried out in pain as she fell to her knees. Tuvallis, who had never left her side, caught her, dragging her backwards as infantry soldiers, seeing the gap, jumped in to seal it.

Hagar had heard Seli scream and instinctively bellowed a defiant roar, so loud that the ground around him shook. He quickly dispatched three more orcs before moving back through the ranks of men frantically looking for Tuvallis and Seli. Finarthian infantry parted around him, filling the substantial gap that he left behind. Durgen continued to fight, every swing of his axe enforced by the focus of a dwarf who had lost his son. Yet no matter how much enemy blood Durgen spilled, it failed to wash away the memory of his dead boy moaning in death, an orc arrow jutting from his flesh. Jonas, concerned about the warning horn, withdrew his blade from the chest of a dying orc and followed the large form of Hagar to the rear of the line.

The gate began to open, as planned, but Kiln looked around frantically at what was happening with the retreat. The problem was the base of the V, where the formation was the widest. This section was supposed to hold the enemy at bay, while the point, or wedge, would fold in on itself and retreat through the opening. As they filtered through the gate the men at the base would slowly close the gap they had created until they too could safely make it through the gate. It was expected that some of the enemy would make it through as well, but Kiln was confident that they could close the gate before a significant number of the creatures entered. But the base was now caving in, making that plan obsolete, and potentially spelling out their doom. He couldn't let that happen.

The officers had been ordered to move behind the formations when the retreat horn had been signaled, and that was where Kiln found Graggis. Though dirty, sweaty, and covered with blood, his fiery eyes reflected the intensity of the battle around him. "What are your orders?" he asked the commander.

"We need to reinforce these flanks or we are doomed!" Kiln yelled. "Pull the men from the reserve line."

"Sir, if we do that they may break through, trapping the tip of the wedge behind the enemy," Graggis countered.

"I know, just do it, Captain," Kiln said sternly.

"Yes, sir," Graggis replied, then turned and ran to find the subordinate officers to pass on the orders.

The commander, hearing loud screams and battle cries coming from the gate, turned to see the source of the commotion. Hundreds of men wearing miss-matched armor and carrying an odd assortment of weapons were storming from the interior of the gate and rushing forward to reinforce the flanks. They were the refugees. Kiln smiled, realizing that General Gandarin must have recognized the danger and sent them out. They lacked skill and were ill fitted for formation fighting, but their numbers alone would bolster the infantry who were fighting for their lives trying to keep the beasts from breaking through.

Kromm had finally cut his way through the enemy to his son's side. "Grab my hand!" he yelled. He reached down and pulled the blood splattered prince onto the saddle behind him. Seeing the large number of orc and goblin bodies piled high around the prince, Kromm couldn't help but feel pride for his son. By that time, a dozen knights had fought their way through, and fresh infantry soldiers were running from the front wedge to reinforce the back, giving the knights time to escort the king back to the safety of their own lines.

For now the lines were still holding, and men from the rear of the wedge began to veer away from the fighting, slowly making their way through the gate, all the while the tip of the formation was beginning to disappear. The flanks were holding but fighting there was furious. Men and beasts alike were falling by the hundreds and the ogres that remained were doing serious damage.

Hagar and Jonas found Kiln directing men and overseeing the retreat. Tuvallis had carried the injured Seli through the gate to the healers as she had already lost consciousness from loss of blood. An endless stream of wounded was pouring through the gate as healers and boys too young to fight carried stretchers back and forth.

Then the sky turned suddenly dark, and ominous black clouds rolled in, swirling and seeming to appear from nowhere.

"I don't like this," Jonas muttered as he looked up at the foreboding sky. Lor-telliam ran from the melee with sword drawn and his previously immaculate armor splattered with blood. He had obviously lost his horse in the fighting as had many other knights.

"It smells of magic!" Lor-telliam shouted. "Powerful magic! It must be Malbeck!"

Suddenly the air exploded with the boom of thunder, shaking the very ground they stood on, followed by crackling blue bolts of energy dancing across the sky. Then without warning, bolts of electric energy shot from the sky and peppered the formation, striking men and then exploding outward in smaller but equally dangerous bolts. The lightning struck in hundreds of places throughout the battle field, killing three times that number, the electrical currents arcing from man to man, attracted to the armor and steel everyone had on their person. The smell of burnt flesh filled the battlefield.

Jonas instinctively dove as a bolt smacked the ground between him and Hagar, hot burning energy searing his flesh. Everyone was flung from their feet, including Hagar who suffered severe burns on his leg despite his thick skin. Then, as quickly as it had appeared, it was gone, and the clouds drifted away.

Lor-telliam helped Jonas to his feet and they quickly surveyed the damage. The power of the spell had been devastating; thousands now lay dead, their smoking bodies scattered everywhere. But most of the damage had occurred behind the main wedge of men.

"The formation is breaking!" Kiln yelled as all eyes turned toward the tip of the wedge, seeing the truth of his words. The spell had been concentrated in certain spots, specifically near the tip of the wedge and the base of the formation, and the hundreds, if not thousands, of dead men, created weak points in those areas. Ogres, orcs, and goblins were now breaking through the weak points and surging towards them in waves of bloody steel. The men at the tip of the wedge, now totally isolated, would be massacred in minutes.

"In Ulren's name, Fil was fighting there!" Jonas screamed, terrified for his friend as he turned to face the enemy running towards them.

Durgen's axe hit an orc so hard in the chest that it creased the beast's breastplate, crushing its sternum and heart on impact. Fil fought beside the dwarf, working his shield and short sword as fast as he could, desperately trying to keep the enemy from overwhelming them. His arms were heavy with exhaustion and his mouth felt as dry as a cotton ball. The lightning had burst from the sky, striking the ground behind them in a blinding electrical explosion. The screams of the soldiers and the smell of burnt flesh assaulted their senses as they continued to fight, each strike becoming more difficult as the strength of their bodies was sapped. They were now fighting a losing battle with exhaustion.

At first Fil wondered why the lightning hadn't struck those in the front. But it soon became apparent. The men fighting near Fil were screaming and yelling that they had been cut off. And then Fil understood. The spell was designed to break their formation in two, isolating the tip of the wedge from the base, and then crushing the smaller groups individually. But he had no time to ponder his possible death as every ounce of remaining strength was being used to keep enemy steel from spilling his blood.

The howls, roars, and screeches of the monster hoard pressed in on them from all sides as Durgen and Fil fought side by side. Fil could feel their group shrink, as his comrades dropped to orc blades and goblin spears. The seriousness of their situation had already sunk in, but before he had time to dwell on it, a giant sword crashed into his shield, shaking him from head to toe. Instinctively, he ducked low, slicing his short sword across the thigh of an attacking orc, then reversing his swing while narrowly blocking the jab from a goblin spear.

There was nothing more to do. They would keep fighting, knowing they were cut off and would die to the last man. No one was coming to save them. Images of his family and friends flashed through his mind as he contemplated his last breaths.

But those ominous thoughts were fleeting as he was instinctively preoccupied with staying alive, desperately trying to keep the enemy from slicing into his flesh. An orc came at him, sword raised to strike, and he frantically blocked it with his sword, then, at the last moment, raised his shield in an attempt to block another attack from his flank. A large orc had swung a morning star and the heavy descending ball was nearly on him as he lifted his shield. But he wasn't fast enough; the edge of the shield caught the chain and acted as a fulcrum point, the spiked ball snapping over the shield onto the top of his head. Even his helm could not fully protect him. The impact was so great that all he remembered was a flash of pain and then nothing. Fil went limp and fell amongst the countless bodies that littered the ground.

If he had been conscious he would have seen Durgen leap over him and ram the spike of his axe into the chest of the orc as the beast prepared another strike. The enraged dwarf yelled to his god as he stood his ground, cutting into the enemy, every swing, parry, and attack fueled by his sheer will, as he had finally exhausted the energy of his physical body. He smiled, blood splattering his face as he swung his axe through the throat of an orc. He was not afraid of the end, he welcomed it. He knew that it wouldn't be long before he could sit with his son in Moredin's great hall.

Allindrian glanced out from her hiding place inside the tower trying to figure out her path of action. She had planned to get to the prince but luckily his father had reached him first, hauling him onto the back of his horse. She could see their torsos above the orcs as they retreated back to the center of their lines. What could she do now? At the weakest point of the enemy line in front of her, there were probably ten to fifteen monsters separating her from her own men. She had committed herself now. The only way to safety was through the gate and to get there she had to get past those beasts. The only good thing was they had their backs to her as they were concentrating on the Finarthian infantry in front of them.

Janniss leaned over the battlements looking for Allindrian. Orc arrows continued to zip by but the numbers were less now that they were concentrating on breaking through the infantry formation below. The young girl looked down the wall and saw that the stone pavers were covered with hundreds of bodies, women riddled with arrows or punctured by spears, sprawled awkwardly in death. There were probably only two hundred archers left, wearily firing the last of their arrows down into the enemy below.

Janniss looked back and saw Allindrian lift her head up from some smoking and blackened wood. She could see her looking at the orcs in front of her. She knew the Blade Singer enough to guess that she was likely planning on rushing those orcs and trying to break through them to reach their own men beyond. That would be crazy, but then again Allindrian had just leaped off a towering wall, swinging and jumping to the ground on a burnt and destroyed tower that looked as if it might fall down if you looked at it wrong. Janniss had an idea.

"Archers! Over here!" she yelled as she ran farther down the length of the wall to get a closer shot at the orcs below them. Thirty or so women that were near followed her, arms hanging tired beyond exhaustion, but newfound courage and blind determination carrying them beyond their limits. "Concentrate on those orcs there!" she yelled, pointing at the weakest section of the orc perimeter. "Kill as many as you can, we need to create a brief gap."

Janniss leaned over and drew forth an arrow. The others followed her lead, sending arrows flying down in a tight formation, the concentrated number of missiles slicing into orc flesh until they looked like pincushions.

Allindrian saw the arrows rain down on the orcs, which drew a quick smile from the ranger. She drew forth her silver sword and ran from her hiding place so quickly that her feet were a blur, and by the time the orcs knew she was there she was already in their midst, her sword flashing left and right, slicing across hamstrings and creating chaos as she flew by them. The archers had killed a handful of them which gave her some room, but there were still at least five orcs in front of her battling against the faltering Finarthian infantry.

Allindrian didn't slow her pace, however; in fact she sped up, leaping high and planting her right foot on the shoulder of an orc, continuing her momentum forward by using the backs and heads of the beasts as platforms, flying over the top of them like a breeze, then leaping free and landing amongst her own astonished infantry. Her appearance was so sudden that even they had no time to react to her as she practically materialized in front of them.

There was no time to think as the enemy surged forward. The well trained infantry had formed a quick perimeter giving the rest of the men time to retreat through the gate, but anyone watching from the wall above knew that they could not hold out long.

Jonas, Hagar, Kiln, Riker, Kromm, and everyone else who could, ran for the gate opening. Jonas's heart ached for his friend, knowing full well that if he was indeed in that front formation that he would not make it. But there was nothing he could do. There were probably a thousand enemy creatures between him and the others. There was nothing left to do but try and get as many survivors as they could through the gate before they were all overwhelmed. Archers on the wall continued to fire down at the enemy but it was like trying to stop a swarm of bees with a spoon.

As they ran through the gate Hagar stopped and turned back towards the brave men keeping the enemy at bay while the rest retreated to safety. Jonas stopped with him, looking up at the great beast. "Hagar, we must go, there is nothing we can do."

The ogrillion shook his head. "Hagar stay, protect gate," he rumbled. He turned back towards the enemy, planting his feet wide, and tightly gripping his giant mace. He looked back at Jonas. "You go, friend. My duty," he said, tapping his iron chest. The beast's language skills had improved over the weeks that Jonas and Tuvallis had been communicating with him.

Jonas knew he would not convince the ogrillion to change his mind, he could see it in his eyes. He reached up, touching Hagar's arm. "Friend," he said. The flood of men pouring through the gate finally pushed Jonas back, carrying him away like a leaf in a stream, and leaving Hagar facing out towards the enemy. If Jonas could have seen his face, he would have seen the ogrillion smile.

The great ogrillion ran forward toward the enemy, shielding more men as his magnificent mace swung back and forth forming a wall of deadly steel, crushing any monsters unfortunate enough to come within range. And despite their large numbers none were able to unhinge Hagar's tree stump legs from where they were rooted. Ten, fifteen, twenty more men ducked behind the beast and ran through the gate to safety.

Within minutes most of the men had made it through and Kiln couldn't wait any longer. If the gate were left open much longer, he was afraid enough of the enemy could breach it, and they would not be able to close it. Finally he had to give the order to shut the gate. Everyone knew it had to be done, but the anguish of watching the brave men struggle to get through was almost unbearable. The creaking of the gears was an ominous reminder that not all of their men would make it through, sealing their fate to that of Hagar's.

When the gate finally crashed shut, twenty men had been left behind. They turned and stood resolutely beside Hagar, and within seconds the enemy was upon them. There was no screaming or crying out in fear. The soldiers had already accepted their fate. They faced the enemy, planting their feet firmly in the ground, and flanked the giant ogrillion.

Hagar's mace flashed left and right, destroying orcs and goblins by the handfuls. The remaining Finarthian warriors formed a wall of shields and swords cutting into the enemy as they crashed into them. But it was as if they were ants trying to keep a boot from crushing them.

Within moments the brave soldiers had been cut down, leaving Hagar surrounded and alone.

Jonas and everyone else had run to the wall and were now looking down with horror. They watched as the ogrillion was repeatedly stabbed with long spears and pierced by countless arrows. And yet still he managed to wield his spiked steel, dealing death to those who came near. Nearly fifty monsters had fallen to his mace, when suddenly they all pulled back leaving Hagar alone by the gate. His body was riddled with arrows, and his thick skin was covered in blood from the numerous wounds that had been inflicted on him. Yet despite his grievous injuries, Hagar ground his feet into the ground, holding his mace firmly in front of him, growling defiantly before the enemy.

The army parted and a lone rider trotted forward on a huge steed, fiery flames fluttering around its hooves. Everyone knew without a doubt that it was Malbeck the Dark One who approached, his presence followed by a shadow of thick evil. Even from the wall they felt it; like a clinging stench that you couldn't shake.

Tuvallis ran forward to stand next to Jonas. His eyes were wide with fear. It was the first time Jonas had seen this much emotion on the typically stoic warrior. "What is he doing?"

Jonas shook his head sadly. "He blocked the entrance while the gate was shutting. He saved forty men."

"I need to get down there!" Tuvallis shouted, frightened but determined to go and find a way to help his friend.

Jonas grabbed his arm in an iron grip. "Do not; do not let his last act be diminished. Do you think he wants you to die next to him?" Jonas asked. "He chose this."

Tuvallis wilted in defeat and resignation. "He doesn't deserve this," he whispered as he turned dejectedly back to the wall.

"Of course he doesn't," was all Jonas could say as a lump formed in his throat.

Malbeck trotted his horse back and forth gazing in disdain at the injured ogrillion. It was deathly silent. "Interesting," he whispered, but somehow his voice easily carried to everyone. "I have heard of you, but seeing you in the flesh is another matter. What an anomaly you are. But you stink of Shyann's touch and I tire of this game we are playing. They," Malbeck indicated the city in front of him, "cannot stop me. Nor can you."

The Dark One lifted the Spear of Gould high into the air. As he began to chant the tip began to glow red with an intense heat. Everyone on the wall looked on with stunned expressions, morbidly waiting for what was to come and knowing that it could not be good. Within seconds a beam of red light burst from the tip of the staff and struck Hagar in the chest. The light flashed even brighter as it lifted Hagar off his feet, sending him catapulting backwards into the gate with such force that the weakened hinges cracked from the stone. The massive doors caved in, opening the entrance for the enemy. Hagar's still form broke through the gate and rolled for twenty paces across the ground of the killing field.

The defenders shot into motion, running from the wall, and taking the stairs two and three steps at a time to reach the men below. The outer wall had two ways to reach the ground. Some took the stairs flanking both sides of the gate, while others ran the length of the wall to the towers on each corner where other stairs were located.

There were probably two thousand men crammed into the killing ground and on the bridge, blocking access to the inner gate. They were the same men who had fought valiantly all day and had watched countless numbers of their brothers in arms die. But they knew that if the enemy managed to breach the inner gate it would be over. Thousands of beasts would enter the city, raping and pillaging, killing all and destroying their home. The wounded had already retreated across the bridge and through the gate, leaving only the best of the Finarthian infantry in the killing ground. There were an additional four thousand men inside the inner wall and many of them now lined the battlements with arrows nocked to string. Everyone knew that they could not allow Malbeck's army to breach the inner gate. They would all die trying to protect their families inside.

Fifteen men lifted Hagar's body and carried his still form across the bridge and through the gate to the safety of the inner wall. No one knew yet whether he was dead or alive, but his courage would never be forgotten. The soldiers blocking the inner gate gripped their weapons tighter, inspired by the ogrillion's courage and sacrifice, and more determined than ever to risk their lives to protect their home.

Riker had been able to find another horse and he was mounted again next to his father when the gate had crashed open and Hagar was flung through it like a limp doll. Kromm quickly ordered the men to form defensive lines. All their commanders were dead, but they willingly followed the king's orders. The men were well aware of Lord Kromm's reputation, Battle King of Tarsis, a legendary warrior with whom they were honored to fight. The men formed up quickly, bracing their feet in the dirt before the bridge, steel held firmly in their iron grips.

Kromm was impressed. "Good men to die with," he said. He looked at his son, and felt a rush of conflicting emotions, fear for his safety, eagerness to fight by his side, but most of all an overwhelming pride. "You could leave, boy." Though he knew in his heart what his son would say.

"I'm staying," Riker said firmly.

Kromm just nodded, looking back towards the gate just as a dark rider, mounted on a large black horse, emerged like a wraith's shadow. Another mounted warrior wearing similar black armor was just behind him, followed by a dozen huge ogres and hundreds of orcs and goblins. They began pouring through the opening but within moments they had come to a standstill, as the great number of large beasts had caused a choke point at the outer gate. There were thousands more enemy fighters milling about outside, but they could not get through the outer gate as their own brethren had virtually blocked the entrance. There were just too many of them.

Kiln, Jonas, Allindrian, and Tuvallis had joined the defensive formation before Malbeck had entered, and now Kromm and Prince Riker rode forward, joining them on the front line before the Dark One.

Lor-telliam had stayed behind on the wall, gazing down at the confrontation brewing on the killing ground. He was not alone. The remaining twenty or so archers, specifically the females trained by Allindrian, had remained, unsure of what to do. They converged on the Ekahal knowing that he would have a plan. They looked up at him expectantly, eyes wide with fear.

He began to assess the situation. Probably twenty thousand of the enemy remained outside the outer gate eager to get in and shed bled, while the defenders numbers were probably close to eight thousand. Malbeck and Koranthos were already within the gate. It was inevitable that unless they were stopped they would breach the inner gate by the end of the day and all would be lost. So, how to stop Malbeck? It all rested in the hands of Prince Riker. But for the courageous young prince to be able to kill Malbeck, he had to be given the opportunity to face him.

Then it came to him. It was simple actually, and Malbeck's arrogance had provided the opportunity. The Dark One didn't have to enter the conflict himself, he could have sent Koranthos, or have just waited for the superior numbers of his army to overwhelm them. But he thought he was invincible and his blind pride had led him to the front ranks. This could prove to be his downfall, the Ekahal thought, as he began to formulate a plan.

The outer gate was damaged and agape, but if Lor-telliam could somehow close the opening, Malbeck would be cut off from the rest of his army, giving the defenders and the prince a chance to kill him. He had an idea.

He addressed one of the female archers standing near him and he urged her to crouch with him behind a battlement. "What is your name," he asked. She had big bright eyes and was very young, maybe eighteen winters.

"I'm Janniss, sir."

"How many arrows do you have?"

Janniss looked in her quiver at her hip and saw only four arrows. "Not many, sir, just four."

By this time the other female archers had crowded around the Ekahal, each one looking over their remaining arrows. They didn't have many, but enough for a couple of barrages.

"Listen carefully," Lor-telliam addressed the group. "I'm going to use magic to shut the gate, trapping in Malbeck and his warriors. When I give the word I want you all to attack the back of Malbeck's army inside the gate with all that you have. Focus on the back lines so you don't hit any of our men. Do you understand?"

"Yes, sir," they said in unison.

Malbeck and Koranthos rode their dark steeds forward into the space between the two armies. "I have longed to face you on the field of battle," he whispered, facing the group of defenders, though no one was really sure who he was addressing.

Jonas felt a lump rise in his throat. The face they were looking at was the same face that he had seen while unconscious and struggling against the magic of Dykreel who was trying to take his soul. Could it be true? Had the apparition he had faced there told the truth? Was Malbeck's form that of his father, taken possession of, tortured and twisted over a period of twenty years to become the receptacle for Malbeck's spirit?

"Ah, Jonas, the fallen cavalier," Malbeck slowly whispered. "As prophesied you have been a thorn in my side for many years. Finally, I can now rid myself of your existence."

"Not fallen, but reborn. Surely you can feel the power of Shyann around me," Jonas countered. Everyone in the killing ground had become deathly silent, waiting and listening intently, primed and ready for action.

Malbeck's laugh sounded like the soft hiss of a snake. "You will die, just as your father did. His form has served me well these last few years," Malbeck continued, confirming Jonas's worst fears. "I have expended far too many resources trying to kill you. Everyone around you dies, yet you still live, a vexing situation indeed. I guess your weak goddess only has enough strength to protect you. She has allowed everyone else to die, your mother, your entire village, your father, Taleen, Myrell, and now your best friend, Fil, I think his name was. And there have been many others as well." Malbeck smiled, exposing needle sharp fangs. "Surely you must find it difficult to live, surrounded by the ghosts of those who perished because they knew you."

"You killed them, not Shyann. Their deaths rest on your shoulders and no one else's," Jonas said, his voice shaking as the impact of the Dark One's words slammed into him. He felt his heart pound as a wave of anger and pain washed over him. Was Fil really dead? Jonas knew it was a strong possibility, but it had not yet been confirmed. Or was Malbeck just baiting him?

"Well that is true, indirectly I guess, but you were my real target, you always have been, along with the king here," Malbeck said, turning to face Kromm. "I found spells, many spells in the Shan Cemar. The book has given me important secrets, riddles that have provided me with valuable information. Kromm must die, for he stands in the way of my plans. You should have died when I destroyed your city, another failure I will have to rectify today."

"You seem to have lots of failures," Kromm retorted. "I too have longed to kill you."

"Such confidence," Malbeck laughed again. Then the Dark One turned his milky white eyes on Riker. "You are wearing the armor of King Ullis Gavinsteal. Did I misread the riddles? Is the threat the king of Tarsis? Or is it the prince? Please tell me that the lives of everyone here do not ride on your shoulders, young prince. Surely this is a joke. Let your father wear the armor so killing him will at least be a challenge."

Riker immediately tensed, tightly gripping the Sword of Light and raising it higher, challenging the Forsworn's minion with a fierce glare. "You talk a lot, let's get on with it."

Malbeck laughed louder, his mocking confidence unnerving enough by itself, but amplified further by the dark aura that emanated from him, surrounding the defenders with a suffocating blanket of fear. "Tihr-Alliam will not be enough, young warrior. Although I applaud your impotent courage."

As the dialogue progressed, on the wall behind them Lor-telliam began to chant, a soft whisper slowly reciting the words of a powerful spell. Janniss and the others nervously waited behind the battlements with arrow to string waiting for the Ekahal's orders.

The spell soon unleashed a glowing wall of iron which burst from the ground, pushing upward and instantly solidifying between the gate's frame that was now empty, with the shattered gate laying in pieces across the killing ground. Some creatures had tried to push through the magical wall as it was forming, their efforts ending with limbs severed as the glowing green wall crystalized into solid iron over a hand's width in thickness. Malbeck was now cut off from his army and he had only a few thousand beasts surrounding him. Their odds had suddenly improved.

"Now!" Lor-telliam yelled. He then stood up from the wall and immediately began to chant another spell. Janniss and her archers stood up quickly, firing into the back row of monsters below them, starting a chain reaction of fighting on the ground below.

Kromm screamed "Finarth" and spurred his horse forward, attacking with a vengeance. The prince was right beside him, his sword held high, the bright light from the blade shining like a star. Their fearless charge broke the spell of fear that had temporarily paralyzed the Finarthian defenders. Emboldened by Kromm's courage, they screamed for Finarth and fearlessly charged the enemy.

Malbeck remained ominously still while the monsters around him poured forward to meet the defenders with steel. But they kept a path open for their master to fight. Koranthos, the king of the Banthras, moved next to Malbeck, drawing his great sword of fire from his back.

As the two charging Tarsinian warriors drew near, Malbeck lifted his spear again, and with only a few words sent a crackling blue bolt of lightning toward the king and the prince. The bolt split in two, striking them both. Kromm was flung from the saddle and thrown backwards, landing hard amidst the men that were charging forward. Riker, however, instinctively lifted his shield, but it was not needed as his cognivant power absorbed the bolt into his body. He tensed his muscles as Malbeck's power was redirected, spreading throughout his entire body.

Koranthos spurred his black horse forward and met the prince head-on, his sword of fire crashing into Riker's shield, sending sparks flying into the air. The vicious power of the attack nearly overwhelmed him and he felt an instinctive urge to flee, but something inside him pushed his fear away as Riker realized that his Ishmian powers were blocking the magical fear created by the Banthra, just as it had absorbed the energy of the lightning bolt. There were very few beings capable of taking on a Banthra. Normally only a cavalier would, or someone with an iron will and immune to fear, someone like Kiln, or his own father. But he too had his own tricks.

The power of the blow was incredible, but Riker's magical shield held, and he returned the strike with his own as he pivoted his horse and swung his blade towards the Banthra's hip. The Banthra's devil steed quickly turned, however, and the Sword of Light just scraped against Koranthos's armor, sending up a shower of white sparks. Just then a sizzling bolt of electricity slammed into Koranthos from above, the power of the magic throwing the demon from his horse and sending him crashing to the ground on his back.

For the prince, time had seemingly slowed down. Men and monsters surrounded him, screaming and howling as they fought. But no one came near him. His entire body was glowing as he held the Sword of Light low to his side. He now turned his horse towards Malbeck, spurring it forward and flying toward the Dark One, the Sword of Light urging him forward. Both warriors came at each other as fast as their steeds could carry them.

The Banthra was struggling to its feet. The Ekahal's lightning bolt had badly damaged the demon, but still it stood, and Allindrian and Kiln were there to meet it. Swords flashed, sparks flying as they cut into the demon's magical armor. But Koranthos was not finished yet. His sword flared brightly as he swung it across his body, the long blade erupting in hot flames that shot out several paces. Both Allindrian and

Kiln ducked away, but not quickly enough to prevent their exposed flesh from being singed. Koranthos took advantage of their retreat, stepping forward and slashing his blade towards Kiln's stomach. Kiln barely got his sword up in time to keep the blade from disemboweling him, but the power of the strike sent him sprawling several paces away. The Banthra called on his innate ability to paralyze his opponents with fear, sending out a chilling wave of terror in hopes of freezing the two warriors in its grip. Allindrian felt the dark magic grip her momentarily, but she shook it off just in time as Koranthos's blade came at her faster than she thought possible. The demon had put all of his strength in that blow and the Blade Singer took advantage of that. The Banthra was quick, but Allindrian was quicker. Ducking under the blade, she pivoted towards its sword arm while bringing her singing sword down and across it. Her sword, forged by the greatest elven sword smith, sliced through the demon's armored arm, sending up bright sparks as both the flaming sword and the arm fell to the ground.

Riker felt an incredibly thick presence of fear in the air as Malbeck neared, but again his cognivant power blocked it and the Dark One's power fell away from him harmlessly. Just before the moment of their impact, Riker lifted his shield as Malbeck, using his spear like a lance, struck him head-on. The shield held, but the power of the strike sent Riker flying from his horse. He landed hard on the ground, knocking the wind forcefully from his lungs. Miraculously he still held the sword in his hand. In fact it felt as if the weapon had been fused to it. Apparently Tihr-Alliam did not want to leave the prince's grip. Riker struggled to his feet as Malbeck turned his nightmare steed around and galloped towards him, again leveling the spear directly at him.

"I do not know how you are surviving my magic, *Prince*," he snarled, spitting out the last word. "But it matters not, you cannot beat me physically." Malbeck's horse snorted, shooting flames from its demonic nose, causing Riker to jump back from them. Malbeck then bolted forward in another attempt to skewer the prince with his spear. Riker had learned many lessons from his father, Jonas, and Graggis. One of them in particular was how to deal with an overconfident adversary, who would often expect their opponent to retreat when confronted with a strong offensive maneuver. He learned that advancing on the attacker could sometimes throw him off balance, giving you the advantage. So that was what Riker did.

As the spear shot towards him Riker shuffled forward on the balls of his toes, lifting his shield up and pivoting to the side, his sword arm already in full swing. The spear glanced off the shield and Riker's blade struck its shaft just behind the sharp point, splitting it in half and releasing a powerful explosion of magical energy. The Spear of Gould was an artifact of great power, with only one weapon on Kraawn that could break it. And that was Tihr-Alliam. The explosion threw Riker to his back for a second time, but it proved much more deadly for Malbeck's nightmare steed, whose head was literally blown off, causing the Dark One to tumble to the ground as well.

Malbeck regained his footing, grabbed his huge double bladed battle axe from the horse's side, and walked slowly towards Riker. The Dark One stood a full head taller than the young prince, and he easily held the cumbersome axe in one hand.

Koranthos had jumped back, and using his good hand he shot a burst of flames directly at Allindrian, hoping to avoid her deadly blade. But the flames hit an invisible wall, veering to the side and missing her completely. Then a black sword slammed into the Banthra's chest like an arrow, pushing the thing backwards as blue sparks erupted from the wound. Allindrian smiled as Jonas appeared by her side, holding a single sword edged in blue light.

Kiln was now engaged with one of the big ogres whose comrades were wreaking havoc on the soldiers. They were crushing as many as two at a time with powerful swings of their giant clubs. The battleground was a chaotic melee of hundreds of disorganized pitched battles being fought all over the killing ground. Several ogres had even fought their way through their defensive line and had run forward over the bridge to the inner gate. But they didn't make it far. Ballista bolts fired from the inner wall stopped them cold, fatally piercing their thick bodies and dropping them dead onto the bridge stones.

Meanwhile, Allindrian and Jonas had spread apart and flanked the Banthra. Suddenly a flying beast slammed into the demon from the side, its massive jaws clamping onto the demon's head. Tulari landed on all four feet, jerking her head left and right in an attempt to snap its neck. Normally the strength of her jaws alone would have ripped its head from its shoulders. But Koranthos was the most powerful of all the Banthras and he would not be killed so easily. The demon knight drew a black blade from its hip and rammed it hilt deep into Tulari's side. She howled in pain, releasing the Banthra's head from her jaw and leaping away from the cursed blade.

It was all Riker could do to keep the giant axe from splitting him in two. His shield arm had been badly battered and bruised since he had been taking most of the strikes dead center on his shield. Malbeck's axe swooped in left and right, down and up, coming at him impossibly fast from every direction, and he didn't seem to be tiring.

But *he* was. His arms felt heavy and his chest heaved, sucking in desperately needed air. Tihr-Alliam was glowing fiercely, the sentient sword feeling the presence of its ultimate enemy, the thing it was made to destroy, directly in front of it. The prince felt a cold fear embrace his body as he contemplated his own death. Suddenly, death became a reality, and he didn't want to die. He wanted to raise a family, and see his children grow up and rule an empire that he helped create, a kingdom free of Malbeck and his minions.

Again Malbeck brought his axe down on Riker's shield, easily wielding it with only one hand. Simultaneously he lifted his other hand, shooting a massive bolt of red electrical energy into Riker's sword arm. The fatal bolt, however, became an infusion of magic that was instantly absorbed by Riker's body, exploding within him in a surge of renewed vigor.

In a flash, and with more power and strength than he thought possible, Riker pivoted as he angled his shield down, causing Malbeck's axe, and body, to slide forward. Then, without stopping, he stepped forward and spun a full circle, Tihr-Alliam leading the way. It was the same move he had used against his father, but this time his body was fueled by the potent magic he had absorbed. His sword flared with a blinding light as the point sliced through Malbeck's stomach, dropping the Dark One to his knees. Malbeck dropped his axe. Clutching his abdomen, he looked up at the prince in complete shock.

Riker was equally shocked, and instead of finishing him, he stepped backwards, his sword arm shaking from adrenaline.

"Kill him!" Someone yelled nearby. The prince looked over and saw his father stumble towards them. His arms and legs had been badly burnt, his clothes and armor were charred and smoke drifted from his entire body. But still he lived. The battle king held his sword at his side, running as best he could towards his son. "Finish him!" he yelled again, lifting his sword to deliver the death blow himself.

Koranthos, a bit dazed from Tulari's attack, tried his magic one last time, releasing crackling bolts of energy towards the Blade Singer, but Jonas intercepted the move. Instead of creating a cognivant shield in front of Allindrian, he wrapped the Banthra itself, causing the magic to dissipate harmlessly against itself. Using his powers against the power of a Banthra was very dangerous. It took a tremendous amount of effort, severely straining his body and mind. He had already been forced to use it twice and this third time weakened him so badly he fell to his knees. The pain in his head exploded like a volcano, nearly immobilizing him. But he knew it would soon fade to a dull ache and he was confident that Allindrian would take advantage of the time he had given her.

And she did. Running forward like a gazelle she bounded into the air, sword swinging, the Banthra momentarily immobilized by Jonas's cognivant energy. Just as her sword struck, Jonas released the energy of the shield, and her magical blade sliced through its armored neck, sending the Banthra's head into the air in a shower of sparks.

Malbeck, turning his milky eyes on the battle king, lifted one hand, and again whispered his words of power, releasing another bolt of crackling red energy at the king. The power of the strike stopped him in mid-stride, throwing him violently backward. He fell to the ground, convulsing briefly before lying still.

"No!" Riker screamed, turning in fury toward Malbeck as he swung Tihr-Alliam toward the demon's body.

The Dark One turned, and instinctively relying on magic again, he lifted his other hand, bringing forth a wall of energy to block the young prince's attack.

Riker could sense the shimmering wall when he struck it, but his cognivant power pushed through the shield as if it were no more than a light mist as he continued his powerful swing.

Malbeck could not understand how this young boy was countering his most powerful magic, magic that had been bolstered by the Shan Cemar. But his thoughts were literally cut off as Tihr-Alliam struck his neck, severing his head in a massive explosion.

A powerful wave of searing energy blew outward from Malbeck's body, launching Riker fifteen paces into the air before he landed hard and tumbled across the ground. In the process he could feel his body virtually boiling with energy, almost as if he too would explode, incinerating himself in the process. But somehow his body was able to withstand the massive amounts of energy that he had inadvertently absorbed into his body. He was able to diffuse it, subduing its tremendous power as if it were no more than a flame in the wind. But the earth around the explosion was scorched black in a massive circle, the power of the explosion incinerating nearly a dozen of the enemy. Unfortunately, six Finarthian warriors had also perished from the intense energy released by Malbeck's death. But more would have died, however, had the prince not absorbed the tremendous energy released by the explosion

A chorus of cheers sounded from above as thousands of men and women along the inner wall screamed with joy over Malbeck's death. The inner gate opened as four thousand more men rushed forward shouting "Prince Riker!" and "Finarth!" eager to join in the fight now that the Dark One was dead. There was no longer a danger of Malbeck breaking down the gate and soon the defenders swarmed over the remaining and demoralized enemy, cutting down the invaders with new energy fueled by hope. Within the hour every monster in the killing ground was dead and three thousand men and women were lifting their bloody swords in victory.

Jonas and Allindrian ran towards the explosion to find the prince. Lying nearby was Kromm's body, still smoking and covered with burns. In his hand he still gripped Cormathian, his sentient sword. Allindrian swore softly as she knelt down and checked for a pulse. She listened for a moment, then her eyes lit up with joy. "He lives, but barely I'm afraid. Check on the prince."

Immediately Jonas ran towards the prince's body as Allindrian channeled her meager healing energy into Kromm. She did as much as she could for him, then shouted frantically for more healers to come.

The prince was lying face down on the ground. Jonas gently turned him over and was relieved to see his chest moving. The young warrior let out a low groan and slowly opened his eyes, causing Jonas to step back in surprise as they flared briefly with a glowing white light before quickly returning to normal. "Is he dead?" Riker asked.

Jonas smiled. "He is....well done." Jonas helped Riker to his feet.

"Is my father dead?" the prince asked, looking past Jonas towards his father's body.

Jonas's eyes grew serious. "He lives, but just barely."

"Help me to him," Riker said, limping forward on a damaged knee.

Riker put his arm around Jonas and together they walked over to the fallen king. The prince knelt next to his father and gripped his hand firmly. "Father, can you hear me?"

"I have done what I can, but he needs expert healing," Allindrian said. "I cannot believe he survived that magical attack, and twice," she whispered softly.

Kromm's eyes fluttered open, his pupils focusing on the Blade Singer. "It will take more than that to kill me," he said weakly, his voice a harsh whisper. Surprised, Allindrian looked down at the king's sword arm. Sure enough, his badly burnt hand was already turning a healthier shade of pink. She suddenly realized it was the sword, sending small waves of healing magic into its master, keeping him alive when he shouldn't be.

"I killed him, Father," Riker said.

Kromm smiled. "I'm proud of you, son. You have saved us all."

Sweaty men covered in blood, some wounded, all exhausted, began to surround them. Among them was Kiln. He lifted his bloody sword into the air. "Finarth!" he screamed. Thousands of voices exuberantly joined him, their cheers echoing loudly between the walls. Soon, they were shouting "Prince Riker!" over and over, and within moments, from within the city itself, the cheers were loudly echoed by the men, women, and children of Finarth, the sound of victory, and the sound of hope, resonating throughout the city.

Outside the gates, unsure of what to do and no longer held together by Malbeck's power, the enemy army began to disperse. Many pillaged the bodies that littered the battle field, while still others fought amongst themselves over weapons and other items of value. The chaos outside the gate lasted for hours, but finally thousands of orcs and goblins drifted away, dispersing into the forest and the approaching night in small clan groups, no longer unified under the yoke of the Forsworn. They moved in all directions, but most went east into the mountains, leaving behind a vast and bloody battlefield of churned and trampled soil littered with the dead and dying.

Epilogue

The funeral pyres burned brightly in the night, one built higher than the rest, the other two flanking it.

Thousands of people, civilians and soldiers alike, filled the walls and grounds surrounding the pyres, looking on in solemn silence. King Baylin's body burned in the flames and on either side of him, in positions of great honor, was the bodies of Durgen, and Hagar. Jonas, Allindrian, Kiln, Prince Riker, King Kromm and his wife, Sorana, along with Tuvallis and Seli, stood on the ground at the base of the fires looking on with a mixture of sadness and hope, knowing that the honored had sacrificed themselves for the greater good of Finarth, and so had thousands of others.

The day after their victory was perhaps tougher on everyone than the fighting itself. It was then that everyone had time to contemplate their losses, to think about what had happened over the last few days. Enemy bodies were dragged away and burned in massive fires, while their own dead were buried with honor across the plains near the city. Farm land was taken and thousands of graves dug, each body carefully wrapped and laid to rest deep in the earth. It would take several days, with thousands working, to bury all the dead, for they had lost nearly ten thousand men and women.

Much had to be done. The cities walls needed to be repaired, the gate replaced, but more importantly the wounds of the minds and hearts needed to be mended, and that would take much longer, for some even years, and for a few, never.

Jonas had frantically searched for Fil's body amongst the dead. When he found him, he had dropped to his knees in anguish, but moments later new hope surged through him as he head Fil moan when he rolled him over. He was alive.

"Fil, what happened? Where are you hurt? It took a moment for Fil's eyes to open, and even when they did he did not look right.

Then Jonas saw his helm. One side was caved in and blood coated that side all the way down his neck. Something big and heavy had struck him in the head. His eyes fluttered open briefly and he mumbled something incoherently. Then he was still again. "I need a healer! Now!" Jonas screamed. There were lots of men and healers about sorting through the dead, looking for survivors, identifying bodies, and it wasn't long before a priest of Ulren was at his side and he immediately went to work on Fil.

Durgen had been found nearby; bodies of enemy fighters were stacked up around him. He had fought bravely to the end, killing many, but eventually the numbers had overwhelmed him and all the other defenders. The dwarf's lifeless hand was still gripping his son's axe. The axe was given to the few remaining dwarves to be taken back to Dwarf Mount where it could be placed in a position of honor.

Jonas spent a long time on the battlefield, helping where he may, but much of the time was spent walking amongst the dead, thinking about all those who had died in the struggle. He didn't know what happened to you when you died, and he had come to realize that it was possible that maybe Ulren's silver palace was just a story made up to make people feel good about death, but it made him feel better thinking that at least the energy that made up the dead would rejoin the Ru'Ach and once again be a part of everything around them, the wind, trees, and stars. And then maybe there was a place you went to when you died. The fact is, he did not know. Jonas's heart hurt. It ached for all the losses…for all the deaths he had witnessed. But it had also begun to harden, to lose the naivety of youth. His heart had slowly been building a thin wall, like an egg growing in a dragon's womb, slowly hardening by each loss he had experienced. Taleen's death, along with everyone else, had felt like a dragon was squeezing his heart, and the only way to protect it was to build a wall around it. And that was what he did.

The following day Jonas was up early and he stood on the outer wall looking out at the battlefield below. Tulari, now the size of a big wolf, nestled her head into his thigh, feeling the pain he felt and wishing she could take it away.

He heard someone approach, turning he saw the Blade Singer move next to him. They were silent for a moment, and then she gently placed her hand on his shoulder. "How is Fil?"

"He is going to live. The healers said that he suffered severe head trauma and that it will be a while before he can walk. But they said that with time he should heal fully. I'm glad he will live. He was my first true friend."

"But he is not your only friend," she consoled, stepping in closer and leaning her head against his strong shoulder. Instinctively he reached out and put his arm around her, pulling her in tight. They had never really embraced like that, and it felt good. It felt nice just to feel someone near him, to feel her flesh and heat, to remind Jonas of why they fought, of why they risked their lives to do away with evil in the world.

"Did Lor-telliam leave?" Jonas asked. He knew that the courageous elf planned to return home where he would die within the next few weeks. His last act was to find another secure location for Tihr-Alliam and the armor, as well as the Shan Cemar that was recovered intact. There had been a heated debate about the sword, many thinking it should remain with Prince Riker, knowing that he was the only person alive who could use its true power, but in the end Lor-telliam won. Possessing the sword brought great risk to the owner, and he believed that it was better off in hiding, where someday it could be brought forth again if needed. Jonas had already said his goodbyes to the Ekahal, but knowing that the world was losing another champion brought more pain to Jonas's already heavy heart.

"He was gone before the sun rose," Allindrian answered. "I am happy he will get to spend his last days at home, with his own people."

"It is nice to have a home. I do remember that feeling, sitting in my chair before the hearth, smelling my mother's soup boiling. Is it strange that I miss the days when I was a cripple?"

"Each part of our life brings joy and pain. Fear not, Jonas, you have lost much, therefore I think happiness is searching for you as we speak," Allindrian reassured him.

Jonas squeezed her shoulder, taking comfort in her words. "What has the council decided?" Jonas asked her. The last couple of days the Council of Lords had been meeting trying to figure out who will be the next king. King Baylin had no heir, and some spoke of Kiln taking on that role, and yet others thought that Prince Riker, who shared Finarthian royal blood, should be the next king. Kromm of course was against that idea. He wanted to go home and rebuild his city with his son by his side.

"They have not decided and I have not yet heard what Prince Riker desires," Allindrian replied.

"Speaking of that, what are your desires now that this is all over?" Jonas asked.

Allindrian looked into Jonas's eyes. "I was hoping you were going to ask me to join you," she said with a smile.

Jonas couldn't help but smile back. "I thought you wanted to go home."

"No…not yet. Besides, if you are going to be this Shadow Knight, you need to learn to live in the shadows. That is something I can teach you."

"You will train me?" Jonas asked with a mixture of excitement and astonishment.

"I will," she said. "And I think I need your company as much as you need mine."

They had never really opened up to each other and it felt good for Jonas to hear her words. Jonas squeezed her tighter, leaning down he kissed her head. "You're right, I do need you," he confirmed. There was a long pause before Jonas spoke again. "We have lost so much, so many people; do you think it was worth it?"

Allindrian looked up at him. "Of course it was."

"But so many died."

"Say their names, Jonas. Let us honor their courage, and sacrifice, together."

"My mother…my father…our entire town, all dead because of greed and power," Jonas said as he choked back the lump forming in his throat. "Taleen, killed to save a king and his family. Myrell, Kilius, Durgen…King Gavinsteal and his son, King Baylin. Embry at the Oasis, all the guards and patrons there, plus the soldiers and people of Tarsis and Cuthaine, not to mention the thousands killed here. Lortelliam and the other Ekahals who gave up their lives to defend a far off land." Jonas paused to wipe the tears from his eyes. "And Hagar, a gentle heart who died to protect a people that would probably never have accepted him. Evryn, who died to save me in the Hallows. Cade and Tolvar, great warriors who will never again be able to serve their king." Jonas stopped to look at Allindrian. "And there were many others, too many to name here. So many, Allindrian."

"It is true, and my heart aches for each of them. But it also gives me hope, hope that we all, when the time comes, will come together to protect each other from the evil that wants these lands. Because rest assured Jonas, that this fight is not over…it has just been halted. It may not be us, or even our sons and daughters, but it will be someone who will have to face a similar threat again, as that is the nature of evil men. They will always want what they don't have, and as long as there are men and women like us, like the ones that died in this cause, then there is always hope. And that eases the pain, just a little."

Jonas smiled down at her. "You sound like Fil, although you are much more eloquent."

"I knew I liked him for more than just his charm." It was her turn to smile, and together they looked out at the horizon and thought about the adventures to come, feeling better about the unknown, knowing they would be side by side, a powerful force against any who brought darkness where there was light.

And Jonas couldn't help but wonder if maybe, just maybe, there was something deeper between them, a bond that was even more than friends, and he smiled as he thought about the possibilities.

Years later.....

Jonas stepped through the inn door and carefully looked around, as he always did when he entered an unknown place, especially an unknown establishment located at a town far from home. He had been travelling long and hard and finally he had come to his destination, a small town called Cer'une, located on the Ronith River that flows west of the Tundren Mountains. His dark grey cloak was pulled tight around his body and his hood kept his face in shadow. The patrons occupying the various chairs of the inn's tavern looked up momentarily, their eyes appraising him briefly before turning away, back to their own conversations. *That is good*, Jonas thought. The whole point was not to draw attention to himself. Little did they know that the two swords he wore around his waist were enchanted by Shyann herself, and literally everything he wore, including the bow presently nestled in the quiver on his back, was blessed by the goddess, Shyann. But to any observer they looked like your average weapons worn by a typical traveler. But Jonas was no mere traveler.

Jonas moved his way through the throng of men and women and found a small unoccupied table in the corner. He was famished and thirsty, and with any luck the inn would have a spare room for him. The room was open and spacious, dominated by a long pine bar on one side and a large river rock fire place on the other. Several deer and elk skulls with large racks adorned the wall above the bar while the rooms pine walls were covered with woven tapestries of wool expertly depicting various animals. Oil lanterns hung from the ceiling and each table was lit by a large candle. An impressive fire burned in the stone fireplace adding to the cozy feeling of the inn. A huge black bear fur lay on the floor in front of the fire place and a big tired looking mutt lay upon it, sleeping soundly. It's a good thing he left Tulari outside, Jonas thought. The big wolf would have drawn a lot of attention and the inn's dog might not have welcomed her, which would have ended poorly for the old mutt. But the night wolf was aptly named and she would be fine outside, in the shadows, waiting for Jonas.

A young serving lady made her way through the tables checking on her patrons, greeting each with a warm smile before finding Jonas at his table. She smiled at Jonas and despite her heavy set frame and straight simple hair; Jonas found her features quite beautiful. Her eyes sparkled with a warm light and her smile made Jonas feel at home. "What can I get for you traveler?"

Jonas reached up and removed his hood. His hair was long now, wavy and shoulder length, drawn back and tied with a leather thong. It had been five years since Malbeck had attacked Finarth and Jonas no longer looked like the youth of those long ago, but not forgotten, years. A week's growth of stubble covered his face and his skin was tanned from the many years on the road, traveling the lands, moving from one city to another, one kingdom to another kingdom, searching for areas of strife, for areas where darkness was trying to take root. Jonas was Shyann's Shadow Knight, her warrior, her champion whose purpose was to help those in need, to try and steer them onto the correct path, and if that turned out to be impossible, then he would be forced to use the blade so they would not be corrupted by evil.

"I was hoping for a warm bed and meal. Do you have any rooms available?"

"We do. I am Galeen and my parents own the inn. We have several rooms left and I'd be happy to give ya one for two silvers."

"Very good," Jonas said as he produced the coins from the pouch at his side. "And what do you have warm from the kitchen?"

"You are in luck stranger. Tonight my ma roasted several elk tenderloins with potatoes, mushrooms, and onions. And our fresh bread is the best in town. I'll be honest and tell you that the elk is a little expensive, but it's worth it. If you have the coin, you will not be disappointed."

"I trust you Galeen," Jonas said as he returned her smile. "I'll take a plate of the elk and a healthy chunk of bread."

"Very good. Would you like some ale?"

"No thank you. Water will be fine."

"So it will be another silver for the food, and that will include breakfast in the morning."

Jonas produced another coin and gave it to Galeen, along with several coppers. "Would you mind drizzling some honey and butter on the bread, I have a bit of a sweet tooth this evening."

She smiled as she saw the extra coins. "Of course, sir, we have lots of honey. And you came in just in time. My sister will be singing in just a moment and you will swear you've heard nothing so beautiful. I'll be right back with your food."

It didn't take her long to return with a heaping plate of steaming meat covered with onions, mushrooms, and potatoes. Two big pieces of thick bread flanked the meat and each piece was dripping with a mixture of butter and honey. And she was right, the food was worth the silver. It was one of the best meals Jonas had had for quite some time.

He wasn't half way through it when he noticed that the clamoring of voices suddenly died down. Jonas looked up from his plate and saw that everyone was intently looking in the direction of the big blazing fire, and then Jonas saw why. Standing with her back to the fire, a young beautiful girl looked out at the patrons. Everyone must have known who she was as they were whispering eagerly to each other, obviously excited for the upcoming entertainment. She was thinner than her sister, and maybe a few years older. But she had her sister's glowing eyes and dazzling smile, her dirty and well used apron doing nothing to damper the glow that surrounded her.

Then she suddenly began to sing…and Jonas stopped eating. Her melodic voice was soft and tantalizing, but with enough power and energy to snare everyone with her words. And she sang a ballad that Jonas recognized, a song that brought back many memories. Jonas set his spoon down, closed his eyes, and lost himself in her beautiful words and the many images that the ballad produced.

Against the battlements I stand, eyes on the horizon as a storm approaches,
The minions of Malbeck march, the gnash of teeth, the stomp of boot,

Glimmer in the Shadow

Like a dark relentless bruise staining the land, spilled blood,
Viscous, wet and cloying, petulance pushing against our gate.

Against this evil, oily and oppressive, the fair and righteous stand,
Heroes of Finarth all; dwarf, elf, beast and man,
Sentinels, strong, shielded by the sword and armor of kings,
Mace, axe, wielded with muscle and grit, stances forged from courage and faith.

As if in defiance, above the walls, dropping like a gale bursting from the clouds,
Blackness, veins of blood, an eclipse of wings, teeth, and dread,
Like a crimson clawed hand reaching, Kil-Kannon the demon dragon
Renders a rancid tear ripping across Kraawn's sky.

Off to the side a massive ballista swivels sharp, like a vicious smile,
A lance of mithral and diamond snaps into the air, cutting through the screams of war,
A wake of Ekahal blue light and might pierce the hell spawn wing,
A roar of pain, jets of steam stream from the beast's maw in a twisted fall.

Like an avalanche of scales and boney spines, the beast glances off the gatehouse walls,
Landing in the courtyard, ground trembling as taloned claws grip, gouging the granite,
Rearing up in a serpentine rage, veins of crimson and orange pulse with an inner fire
As the dragon releases a roar of heat and malice, fear radiating like a shockwave.

A step, shields raised, a squint of eyes, hands gripping weapons, another step, leaning forward
With determination and hope, fear beat back, ethereal like smoke
As battle kings, mages, and warriors; the defenders of Finarth
Answer back with a growl, a rush of feet, a twist and leap, an exclamation of sword slicing.

Against the battlements I stand, a wet heat beating against my face with each dragon breath,
Through the steam and blood tinged fog, the sound of rending flesh and bone,
I witness the fabled blades Cormathian and Tihr-Alliam, like diving shrikes
Of molten steel, glimmering talons, rising and falling, catching the rays of light.

Rising and falling, crushing tail, snapping jaws and cleaving claws,
Ebb and flow, arrows singing through the air, mace macerating,
The dragon speaking in turbulent tongues of jetted fog,
A terrible voice sizzling silence into the living.

Twin blades purr, piercing dragon hide, honed by Shyann's hand
And forged from the great roots of her majestic oak, the blacksmith of her faith,
The whistling keen of a blade singer's blade reverberates off the castle walls,
Lamenting the loss of a King, embraced by vapors of swirling searing death.

Like a boulder, tough skin and jagged edges, hewn from hardship, corded muscle bunching,
A ball of steel and spike hammer into the beast like a thunder clap,
Like an applause for a dance, dexterity dipping, a ranger rises high
Flowing up the articulated neck like a feather caught in an updraft,

A leap, deft duck and spin, elven blade singing sharp, leading the way
Landing perfectly, splitting scale and bone, punching a hole in hatred,
Knocking the beast to the ground, stunned, eyes clicking shut, and never opening again,
As a mithral mace arcs through the air and smashes the dragon back to darkness.

A mighty roar, his mace held aloft like a sun burst,
Metal reflecting, a composition of light dancing off black blood.
Against the battlements I stand, elation and hope fueling my voice, arm held high
Shouting with my people, screaming our defiance against the storm.

...and then the ballad was over. Jonas slowly opened his eyes as the patrons clapped and cheered. But Jonas heard none of it, his thoughts were somewhere else, searching for images of his friends, some lost on that day, and others now on new paths. He would never forget that day, when they faced the dragon, or when they met Malbeck's power with steel and courage. But more importantly, he would never forget the heroes that died in that struggle, that died so that others could craft songs about such deeds, and listen to beautiful ballads sung in their honor. Jonas smiled to himself as he finished the rest of the meal, happy in his role, happy to know that his actions, and those of others who live by the sword, do make a difference. And that sometimes, just sometimes, it is the light reflected off of polished steel that can keep the shadows at bay.

The End

About the author

Jason McWhirter has been a history teacher for eighteen years. He lives in Washington with his wife, Jodi, and dogs, Meadow and Macallan. And yes, their new puppy was named after one of his favorite scotches. He is a certifiable fantasy freak who, when he wasn't wrestling or playing soccer, spent his childhood days immersed in books and games of fantasy. He'd tumble into bed at night with visions of heroes, dragons, and creatures of other worlds, fueling his imagination and spurring his desire to create fantasies of his own. When he isn't fly fishing the lakes and streams of the Northwest, or wine tasting and entertaining with his wife and friends, he spends his spare time sitting in front of the computer writing his next novel or screenplay.

Glossary

Ru'Ach: An elven word used to describe the source of all life...thought of as a river of energy that created all things.

Kulam: Training facility for cavaliers.

Ekahal: An elvish wizard

IshMian: Elven name for a cognivant, a person gifted with mental powers. Little is known of this power but the gifts range from telekinesis, ESP, to mind control.

Ty'erm: Sharneen term used to describe a meditative state.

Akron: Military term that means a thousand men.
Modrig: Military term that means five hundred men.
Ludus: Military term that means two hundred and fifty men.
Pandar: Military term that means fifty men.

Nock, or Nocking: The *nock* is the end of the arrow that has a crevice for the string. To nock an arrow is to put an arrow to string.

Telsirium: A form of magic use where the wizard can use the energy of the things surrounding him/her. The energy can be accessed quickly but only in small amounts, contrary to accessing the Ru'Ach directly, which gives the wizard as much power as he or she can control.

Kufura: Training facility for Blade Singers located deep in the Aur'urien Forest.

The Silvarious: Elite group of elven rangers whose job is to patrol and protect the borders of the Aur'urien forest.

Togric: Dwarven rank which means Master Trader, second rank.

Al'dun-mera: Elven for stone of power. These stones are rare and are thought to have fallen from the sky. They hold energy and can be used to bind spells.

Dakeen: Dwarven elite guards to the king of Dwarf Mount.

Daz-rothos: Dwarven skill where one who is Daz-athros can speak to the stones.

Daz-athros: Dwarven stone speaker. A rare skill reserved for Master Traders.

The Cavalier Trilogy

Join Jonas in all his adventures!

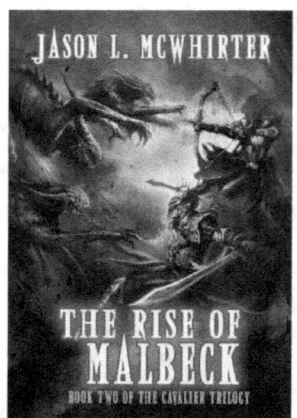

Follow Jason L. McWhirter at...

www.twiinentertainment.com

twiinentertainment.wordpress.com

www.facebook.com/twiinentertainment

www.ingramcontent.com/pod-product-compliance
Lightning Source LLC
Chambersburg PA
CBHW071213250626
47159CB00001B/299